USA TODAY Bestselling Author

Valerie Hansen

and

Sharon Dunn

To Protect from Harm

Previously published as *Tracking a Kidnapper*
and *Scene of the Crime*

LOVE INSPIRED

INSPIRATIONAL ROMANCE

Special thanks and acknowledgment are given
to Valerie Hansen and Sharon Dunn for their contributions
to the True Blue K-9 Unit: Brooklyn miniseries.

LOVE INSPIRED®

INSPIRATIONAL ROMANCE

Recycling program
for this product may
not exist in your area.

ISBN-13: 978-1-335-42461-7

To Protect from Harm

Copyright © 2021 by Harlequin Books S.A.

Tracking a Kidnapper
First published in 2020. This edition published in 2021.
Copyright © 2020 by Harlequin Books S.A.

Scene of the Crime
First published in 2020. This edition published in 2021.
Copyright © 2020 by Harlequin Books S.A.

This edition published by arrangement with Harlequin Books S.A.

For questions and comments about the quality of this book, please contact us
at CustomerService@Harlequin.com.

Love Inspired
22 Adelaide St. West, 41st Floor
Toronto, Ontario M5H 4E3, Canada
www.LoveInspired.com

Printed in U.S.A.

CONTENTS

Valerie Hansen was thirty when she awoke to the presence of the Lord in her life and turned to Jesus. She now lives in a renovated farmhouse on the breathtakingly beautiful Ozark Plateau of Arkansas and is privileged to share her personal faith by telling the stories of her heart for Love Inspired. Life doesn't get much better than that!

Books by Valerie Hansen

Love Inspired Suspense

Emergency Responders

Fatal Threat
Marked for Revenge
On the Run

True Blue K-9 Unit: Brooklyn

Tracking a Kidnapper

True Blue K-9 Unit

Trail of Danger

Visit the Author Profile page at LoveInspired.com for more titles.

TRACKING A
KIDNAPPER

Valerie Hansen

Blessed are they that have not seen,
and yet have believed.
—*John* 20:29

To my Joe,
who will always be missed more than I can say.

ONE

Traces of fog lingered along the East River despite the rapid warming of the August morning. Off-duty police officer Vivienne Armstrong paused at the fence bordering the Brooklyn Heights Promenade to gaze across the river at the majestic Manhattan skyline. Her city. Her home.

Slight pressure against her calf reminded her why she was there, and she smiled down at her K-9 partner. "Yes, Hank, I know. You want to run and burn off energy. What a good boy."

The soft brown eyes of the black-and-white border collie made it seem as though he understood every word, and given the extraordinary reputation of his breed, she imagined he might. She was wearing shorts and a sleeveless shirt for jogging, and her K-9 was also out of uniform. Put a regular collar and leash on him, and he behaved like any other dog. Show him his tracking harness, and he was more than eager to work instead of play. It was uncanny.

Vivienne adjusted the band of her sun visor to lift her short dark hair off her forehead, pivoted to check her surroundings and commanded, "Heel," as she started out. Hank kept perfect pace at her side. "Good boy. You know I love you, right?"

His tongue lolling, the canine met her gaze with the equivalent of a doggy smile.

Under working conditions, she wouldn't have distracted her dog with chatter, but their time off was different. Besides, she reasoned, Hank was family, her furry baby, particularly since she was beginning to despair of ever finding a good man and raising human children.

That was one of the drawbacks to exercising on the Brooklyn Heights Promenade. It was almost always crowded with other people's children, mothers and nannies enjoying an outing with their charges—darling little people who had their whole lives ahead of them and the wonders of the world yet to discover.

A piercing scream jarred her back to reality. Hank barked, circling at the end of the leash. Vivienne skidded to a halt and listened, looking for the source.

"Jake! My baby! Where's my baby?" a woman screeched.

Other passersby froze, making it easy for Vivienne to pick out the frantic young woman darting from person to person. "He has blond hair. Bright green pants. Have you seen him? Please!"

There was no need for Vivienne to give Hank orders. The dog followed her rapid response perfectly.

"I'm a police officer," Vivienne told the hysterical woman. "Calm down and tell me what happened. What's your name?"

The fair-haired mother was gasping for breath, her eyes wide and filling with tears. "My little boy was right here. Next to me. I just… I just stopped to look at the boats and when I turned to pick him up and show him, he was gone!"

"Okay, Mrs...."

"Potter. Susanna Potter."

"Where were you when you last saw your son?"

She pointed with a shaky hand. "Over there. By the fence. Jake's always been a good boy. He's never wandered away like this before. I didn't dream..."

Vivienne could tell the mother was about to lose control again, so she led her to a bench while she called in the report on her cell phone. "Sit here, Susanna."

"No! No, we have to go find Jake."

"I'm on the phone with the police," Vivienne explained, adding a description to her verbal report. "Jake Potter. Blond hair." She looked to the mother. "Is that right?"

Susanna nodded. "And bright green pants. There's a picture of a duck on his yellow T-shirt."

"Age?"

"Two—almost three. He's very precocious. Smart. Sweet. Wait! I have a picture on my phone." She was unable to hold her hands still so she handed the cell to Vivienne, then covered her face and began sobbing.

She repeated the description of the child's clothing. "Two years old, almost three. I'm with the missing child's mother at the promenade, close to Pierrepont Street. I'm sending you a photo from Mrs. Potter's cell phone."

She paused to listen, then said, "Copy. Hank is with me on scene. I'll see what we can do until backup arrives."

Seating herself next to the distraught mother, Vivienne gently touched her shoulder. "I'm a K-9 officer and my dog is trained for search and rescue. Do you have any item of your son's clothing that I can use for scent?"

"No. It was too warm for a jacket." Tears streaked Susanna's pale cheeks and she was choking back sobs.

"Anything. A hat, a toy, anything Jake touched."

The woman blinked rapidly. "Yes! In my bag."

Vivienne watched as Susanna pulled out a well-loved, yellow, stuffed toy rabbit. "Perfect."

When she stood, so did the frantic mother. Vivienne blocked her with an outstretched arm. "No, please, ma'am. You need to wait here in case Jake comes back looking for you. Other police officers will be here in a few minutes, too." Vivienne wanted to know where to find Susanna when she needed her again. If she did. The sooner she and Hank got moving, the better their chances of finding the lost child.

Assuming he's merely lost, she mused, feeling her stomach knot. New York was a big city, and Jake was a tiny little boy. Without Hank's training, the chances of locating him were very slim. Even with the skilled K-9 there were no guarantees. Children were kidnapped all the time, many never seen again.

Except in this instance a rapid rescue was a possibility. She bent to present the stuffed rabbit and watched her K-9 sniff it, clearly ready to go to work.

In full professional mode, she straightened, loosened her hold on the dog's leash to give him leeway and commanded, "Seek."

Hank circled, returned to the place at the river fence that Susanna had indicated earlier, then sniffed the air before making up his mind and beginning to run.

The leash tightened. Vivienne followed as hope leaped, then sank. The dog was following air scent.

Therefore, the missing child had not left footprints when he'd parted from his mother. Someone had lifted and carried him away. There was only one conclusion that made sense.

The little boy had been kidnapped!

FBI agent and profiler Caleb Black was in conversation with Sergeant Gavin Sutherland, head of the Brooklyn K-9 Unit, which had been formed just months ago, and the deputy police commissioner. They were inside a meeting room in the appellate courthouse in Brooklyn Heights to easily accommodate the commissioner, who'd had a press conference there earlier. The sergeant wrapped up what he knew about the department's ongoing efforts to locate a recently identified murder suspect, Randall Gage. A twenty-year-old investigation into the shooting deaths of the McGregors, a married couple with two children, had been revived after a very similar double homicide. The MO in the current case involving another couple, the Emerys, was almost identical, down to the killer sparing the life of the victims' young daughter, Lucy, just as he had left Penelope McGregor unharmed many years before. It was going to be up to Caleb Black to compare clues, a clown mask and a stuffed monkey toy, and decide if the same murderer was truly back in action, or if they had a copycat on their hands.

Gavin stood and offered his hand to each man in turn, concluding their meeting. "Thank you for joining us, Commissioner. We appreciate your assistance, Agent Black."

"Anything I can do, Sergeant," Caleb replied, shaking hands with him. "Before I write up a formal profile, I'd like to speak with the survivor you mentioned. Penelope McGregor?" The McGregors had a son, too, ten years older than Penelope, but he hadn't been home during the murders; in fact, for a while Bradley McGregor had been considered a suspect. Fully cleared, he was now a detective with the K-9 unit. "I know it's been twenty years since her parents were murdered but sometimes the smallest detail will give me a lead."

"Fine. Penny's our front-desk clerk. We can head over to the K-9 unit building now and you can also meet the team. I'm very proud of them."

"I've heard great things," Caleb said. "I hope they won't mind outside help on the case."

"We're all looking for the same result—justice for the McGregors and Emerys. So I think you'll find the K-9 unit accommodating. I take it that's not always the case?"

Caleb chuckled and raked his fingers through his short, dark blond hair. "Unfortunately, no, it isn't. I don't go out of my way to step on anybody's toes, but it can happen. Please keep that in mind as we work together."

"Noted." Gavin gestured toward the door of the conference room. "After you."

Caleb exited. He'd meant the compliment about this unit. It had been formed by bringing in K-9 officers from all around the city and seemed to be functioning cohesively despite its short history. That said a lot about its leadership.

As they were walking down the hallway, Caleb heard the sergeant's cell phone ping. Gavin paused to read the text, then hurried to Dispatch.

When Caleb caught up to him, he was being briefed. The news didn't sound good. An off-duty K-9 officer was reporting suspicions of a child kidnapping. Before he had a chance to volunteer his services, Gavin drafted him.

"You can ride with me," the sergeant said. "We're very close to the promenade and hopefully we'll meet up with my tracker there. She and her K-9 were already on scene and have picked up the boy's trail."

"Got it." Much of Caleb's work was done in an office or on a computer, so a chance to work in the field was a welcome change. That, and he was looking forward to assisting a special unit like this one. Their success was his success.

Besides, he reasoned as he climbed into the passenger seat of a patrol car while the sergeant slid behind the wheel and prepared to drive, anything that helped find an innocent child was always his first priority.

Sobering, he fought against the memories of losing his own family. No matter how many days, months and years passed, the ache—the emptiness—remained. So did the weight of guilt. He should have done more, should have protected his wife and baby. But he hadn't been vigilant enough. He'd been so focused on doing his job he'd lost sight of the danger to his loved ones.

Caleb's jaw clenched. His beloved wife was gone and so was his only son. That couldn't be changed. But he could do his best to protect other people's children. And he would. For the rest of his life. Regardless of personal cost.

Panting, Vivienne trailed her dog. Hank was straining so much that his collar was making him cough, but there was no time to go home for his tracking harness.

Keeping him out of trouble during his reckless dash along the promenade was the best she could do.

A flash of bright green and yellow in the crowd caught her eye. Then it was gone. Could she have imagined seeing the colors? Any error was possible for human senses. Hank, on the other hand, was positive they were on the right track. Vivienne trusted the intelligent, dedicated K-9 beyond her own eyes. If he believed Jake was ahead, then he was. The only question was how far.

They dodged a woman pushing a double stroller with twins then barely missed an oblivious jogger wearing earbuds. "Excuse me. Pardon me," Vivienne shouted. "Police officer in pursuit!"

Up ahead, someone in a dark gray hoodie pivoted and glanced back at her. That was all the confirmation it took. A little blond boy wearing bright green pants and a yellow T-shirt was crying and pushing at the tall, middle-aged woman carrying him off in her arms.

"Stop! Police," Vivienne shouted. She had to catch up. Once their quarry left the promenade it would be harder for Hank to track. Plus, the kidnapper might have a car waiting. Her K-9 partner was good, but no dog could follow a closed vehicle in Brooklyn traffic.

Sides heaving, laboring to breathe, Vivienne pressed on. Her legs ached. She had a stitch in her ribs. Adrenaline kept her going while her exhausted body screamed for her to stop. To give up.

"No way," she muttered, positive she was close enough to hear the wailing little boy in spite of the noisy chaos around her. Whoever the woman was, she was carrying the extra weight of the child. Surely a physically fit officer and her K-9 could overtake them in time.

Dear Lord, give me the strength to do this! she prayed silently.

Gathering herself, she shouted again. "Police officer. Stop! Let the boy go."

Did the abductor falter? It looked like it. "I said, freeze. Put down the child."

Over the cries of the boy, the shouts of passersby and Hank's barking, Vivienne thought she heard a siren. *Hurry, hurry, hurry*, she thought. *Block the street exit.*

Suddenly, the woman in the hoodie staggered. Almost fell. She regained her footing only to trip again. The strain of the foot pursuit was showing, and she had apparently realized she was not going to escape as long as she was weighed down by her victim.

Little Jake looked surprised when the kidnapper set him down none too gently. He plopped onto his bottom and raised a renewed cry.

Hank closed in. Vivienne was right behind him. She watched the hoodie disappear into the crowd as she approached Jake Potter in all his weepy, sweaty, red-faced glory. She quickly called 911 and identified herself, then relayed the description of the kidnapper. A BOLO would be sent out immediately.

Fighting to catch her breath, she pocketed her phone and bent over, hands resting on her knees, and grinned at the child. She'd never seen a lovelier sight.

"Hey, Jake, it's okay. You're safe now." Still panting, she reached for him. "I'm going to take you back to your mommy."

The child was too frightened to respond to her kindness and attempted to scramble away. Vivienne plunked down on the ground beside him, offered him his stuffed bunny to keep him close and used her cell phone to relay a full description of the abductor and news of Hank's success. Then she lavished the K-9 with praise instead of paying undue attention to the child. In moments she was able to ease Jake into her lap. The border collie provided comic relief by trying to lick her face. And Jake's.

This was why she was a cop. This was why she'd put off marriage and starting a family of her own. This kind of triumph made all those personal sacrifices worthwhile even though they had cut her off from normal opportunities to date. Circumstances had even driven her to explore online dating apps, which was more than a little embarrassing.

A yammering crowd was gathering. People were aiming cell phones and taking photos of the aftermath as Vivienne embraced the toddler and rejoiced. Uniformed officers soon got between them and the throng, insisting they be given breathing room.

"Thanks, guys. One of you loan me a radio, and I'll report."

"That won't be necessary," a voice from behind the closest officer announced. "Dispatch relayed your calls. We have a good description of the perp."

She recognized her commanding officer, Sgt. Gavin Sutherland, greeted him with a broad grin and got to her feet with the boy in her arms. "Hey, Sarge. Can you send one of the uniforms to go get Susanna Potter? A frantic blonde woman. Waiting on the promenade. Straight up that way. At least I hope she followed my orders because I promised this little man I'd reunite him with his mommy."

Sniffling, the child wrapped his chubby arms around her neck. Her heart swelled. She reached into her pocket, searching for a tissue as she gently patted the boy's back.

A tall man with a crew cut and wearing a dark suit and tie stepped forward to offer her his folded pocket square. Reluctant to accept anything from a stranger, particularly something silk and so elegant, Vivienne hesitated.

Gavin said, "This is Caleb Black, FBI."

The profiler. *What was he doing out here?* "Sarge mentioned you'd be coming to the station today." She noticed a woman pushing a stroller nearby and asked for a baby wipe, then concentrated on cleaning the boy's face. "If I'd been expecting to babysit this morning, I'd have come better prepared."

Caleb tucked the square back into his chest pocket. "No problem."

The rumble of his deep voice skittered along her nerves and nearly made her shiver despite the heat. His gaze was fascinating, and perhaps a little too intense. There was something about the green of his expressive eyes that reminded her of parks and trees…during a summer storm. His military-cut, light hair was on the blond side of brown, making it seem tipped with gold.

He glanced at her briefly before beginning to focus past her into the crowd. Vivienne realized what he was doing and appreciated the effort even if it did increase her nervousness. The FBI profiler was assessing the gaggle of observers, one by one, looking for anything out of the ordinary. Looking for threats.

She shivered. He was right. There was a strong possibility that Jake's kidnapper wasn't working alone, particularly if the attempted abduction was part of a child-trafficking ring like the one the NYC K-9 Command Unit had taken down in Brighton Beach last year.

Pulling Jake closer, she cupped the back of his curly blond head with her free hand and assumed a guarded posture.

Caleb Black gave a barely perceptible nod, clearly approving. He had only spoken two words to her, yet she felt as if they were already operating in sync. It was uncanny. And welcome.

TWO

Caleb picked out the boy's frazzled mother the instant she came into view. She was running, arms spread wide, weeping openly and calling to her son.

"Jake! Jake, baby!"

The child's tears returned, and he began to strain to escape Vivienne's protective embrace. Not only was she grinning at the frantic mother, but she also had misty eyes. It was not Caleb's place to judge the K-9 officer, but it worried him to see that much emotion on display. The best law-enforcement agents kept their feelings to themselves. Like he did. He had to, in order to function.

After observing the beginnings of the touching reunion, Caleb turned away. There was only so much emotional tenderness he could stand, and he wasn't about to watch when he didn't have to.

Gavin Sutherland left him to join a uniformed K-9 team that included an imposing-looking German shepherd.

Patrol officers had corralled the still semihysterical mother and were taking down her story while she clung to her son. The crowd began to disperse. Since the black-and-white dog and its handler were free at the moment, Caleb decided to bestow praise where it was due.

"Good tracking job," he told Vivienne. "That was a close call."

She nodded, balling up the soiled wipe. "Yes, it was. I don't see a trash can."

"Give it to me. I'll dispose of it for you," Caleb remarked, holding out a hand. The grin she immediately shot him was a little surprising under the circumstances. When she gave voice to her thoughts, however, it made perfect sense.

"Speaking as a member of an FBI Behavioral Analysis Unit, would you say that offer shows a tendency for chivalry, or is it an expression of obsessive cleanliness? Did you ever play in the mud as a child?"

He had to laugh. "Yes, I did. Let's call it both."

"Good to know."

Despite her light-hearted attitude, Caleb could tell the stress of the pursuit was starting to affect her so he gestured toward a nearby bench. "Sit a minute? I'd like to hear everything that happened this morning."

"I guess it won't hurt." He saw her eye her boss before joining him. "Sarge can find us if he wants to debrief me."

"It's hard to miss you with that black-and-bright-white dog in tow. Is he a border collie?"

"Yes." She removed her sun visor, then raked her fingers through her long bangs and tucked the ends behind her ear. "Hank is search-and-rescue trained. In this case I was able to put him on the trail immediately so tracking was easier, even after the woman picked the boy up."

"You're positive the kidnapper was a woman?"

"Positive. I saw her face," Vivienne said.

"What tipped you off to the crime?"

With a nod toward the child and his mother, Vivienne explained. "Screaming. Mrs. Potter was yelling that her son was missing. I know kids wander away all the time and that's what I expected when I put Hank on the trail." She shivered despite the heat while her K-9 sat obediently at her feet.

"As soon as the medics are through checking the boy you should let them look you over, too. The intense physical and mental stress of what you just went through—"

"I'm fine. Worn out, but fine."

He nodded. "Good thing you and Hank were right there," he said, loosening his tie. "Gotta love August in New York."

"Where are you from? DC?"

"Not presently. We have a field office in the federal building in Manhattan and a resident agency—a satellite office—right here in Brooklyn. Why?"

"I just wondered." She eyed him up and down. "You look more like a CEO or a politician than an FBI agent."

"Maybe I'm in disguise," he said as he slipped his suit coat back on, added reflective sunglasses and squared his shoulders.

That comment brought a light laugh that pleased him. He didn't have a reputation for carrying on humorous conversations, but this K-9 cop seemed to bring it out in him.

"Now you look like Secret Service," Vivienne teased.

"Thanks. That's the image I was going for." It felt odd to be grinning at her after the serious incident. At least this time the outcome had been good. "What else can you tell me about the person in the hoodie?"

She squinted up at the tree providing shade, recalling all she could. "She turned around for only a split second, so I didn't have a long look, but enough. Middle-aged. Tall and thin but not agile. She ran out of steam pretty quickly once we started chasing her. She wore shorts and I think she had varicose veins."

"Excellent. Hair color? Complexion?"

"Ruddy, although her face may have been flushed from exertion. I couldn't really see her hair under the hood. If it had been very dark or very light the contrast might have shown up. And I think there was an orange tattoo of a flower on her ankle. She was wearing flip-flops. They certainly hampered her running. That she didn't cover up an identifying detail and wore flip-flops makes me think the kidnapping was impulsive instead of the boy being a premeditated target."

"Either that or she couldn't afford better shoes. Besides, it is summer." He stared at her for a moment. "You told all that to Dispatch?"

"Of course. I may not be in uniform like Belle Montera over there with Justice, the German shepherd, but I assure you I didn't forget my training."

Caleb raised both hands, palms facing her. "Whoa. I wasn't being critical. Just wanted to be sure everything got done. I know you're exhausted and as soon as the rush of adrenaline wears off you'll be a zombie."

"Never," Vivienne snapped. "What you see now is what you always get."

Caleb muted a smile. This was a pretty, athletic, witty woman, and if his life hadn't been ruined by his past he might even have been interested in getting to know her better. That was not going to happen, of course. He'd learned his lesson the hard way. The most painful way possible. He'd been a devoted husband and father. Once. He wasn't about to risk that kind of pain again.

Without thinking, he used his thumb to touch the wedding band he still wore. Professional counselors and friends had urged him to take it off, but he wasn't ready. Perhaps he never would be.

Noting the K-9 officer's glance toward his left hand, he hoped she wouldn't ask about his marital status. An adequate explanation was still painful, yet few strangers were sensitive enough to keep from posing hurtful, personal questions once he revealed that he'd been widowed.

Caleb clenched his jaw. Might as well get it over with. He displayed his hand, fingers splayed. "Widower" was all he said.

Instead of having to fend off an inquisition he was relieved when Vivienne merely said, "Sorry," and turned away.

The last thing Vivienne wanted to do was admit the FBI agent was right about her physical stress. Unfortunately, as the minutes passed, her body agreed with him. The bottles of water the EMTs had given her and Hank had helped quench her thirst but hadn't done much to restore energy levels. This excessive fatigue wasn't unexpected, it was merely the aftereffect of intense physical exercise coupled with razor's-edge concentration.

Frustrated, she continued to picture the kidnapper's face, wondering if she'd be able to set aside preconceived notions well enough to work with a sketch artist. Maybe. Probably. The key would be visualizing the event, then stopping time in her mind to study the face in detail. That was difficult because the brain tended to fill in unknowns on its own.

"Ready to go?" Gavin Sutherland asked as he approached.

Vivienne wasn't sure whether he was speaking to her or to the FBI agent. "I walked over from my apartment,

Sarge," she said. "I'll be fine getting home on my own."
A stifled yawn punctuated the end of her sentence.

"Nonsense. You and Hank can hitch a ride with me.
I'll take Caleb back to his car, anyway, which is parked
near the courthouse, so I may as well swing by your
place on the way. If you won't do it for yourself, do it
for your partner."

Rising, she stretched. "Well, since you put it that way."

"I do."

"Oh, and Caleb," the sarge said, "if you'd like to
offer your assistance on Vivienne's case, too, we'd appreciate it. I'm sure as an FBI agent, you've dealt with
plenty of kidnappings."

Vivienne froze. Did her boss just actually assign the
guy to work with her?

"Happy to help," Caleb said, eyeing her.

Vivienne intended to follow the two men, but they
took up positions on either side of her as they left the
promenade. She didn't object. Something intangible and
indescribable kept sending little bolts of electricity zinging up her spine and tingling the nape of her neck. She
might have discounted those feelings if her K-9 hadn't
been acting as if he, too, was disturbed.

"Your dog," Gavin said. "See how he's acting?"

"Yes. I've been watching him."

Caleb slowed his pace and pivoted, his back to the
others. "I'm not used to working with K-9s but this one
is sure antsy. I take it that's not normal."

"No," Vivienne said. "Border collies can be high-
strung, but Hank should be pretty tired. Instead of relaxing he's on alert. See his posture? Tail position? The
way he's moving his ears? He's picked up on something
the rest of us haven't."

"You two wait here to minimize exposure," Gavin said. "I'll get my car and be back in a sec."

If the humans had been the only ones acting tense Vivienne might have argued. Since Hank was so restless she opted to take her sergeant's advice. Someone was either watching them or trailing them—someone who had Hank on alert. Vivienne glanced around but didn't see anyone suspicious.

Caleb looked around, too. "I don't see anybody, but that doesn't mean we're not being followed or watched." He sidled closer to her, placing his body as a shield. Vivienne knew what he was doing and took the action as a sign he didn't think she was a fully capable officer of the law.

"I am not helpless, you know," she said.

"Never said you were."

"Well, you're acting like it so back off. A bullet could just as easily pass through you and take me out." The instant she spoke he whirled around, staring at her. His color seemed paler, his green gaze more intense, and she could see the muscles in his square jaw clenching. If she'd been the profiler instead of him, she might guess he'd once been in that very situation.

"I'm not moving," he said, "so deal with it."

Recalling what he'd looked like without his jacket, she was positive he wasn't wearing a protective vest. Unfortunately, neither were she and Hank. It was the dog that concerned her the most. The stubborn man could look out for himself.

"Suit yourself," Vivienne told him in a pseudo sweet voice. "I'm going into that recessed doorway over there to protect my K-9 whether you like it or not."

"Why didn't you say so?"

She traded a chuckle for a huffing sound at the last second. Nobody liked to be laughed at, and agents who were the strong, silent type were the worst. Plus, this one was a man. Male egos bruised easily. They were going to have to work together, at least in theory, so the happier she could keep him, the better.

Not that she was going to bend over backward to please him. She simply didn't want to purposely make an enemy. Besides, unless her imagination was working overtime there had been something poignant, almost tender, about his expression when he'd first approached her. Of course, she'd been cuddling Jake and Hank when he'd arrived with her boss, so maybe he merely had a soft spot for kids or dogs, or both.

"Hank, heel," she commanded, pivoting in the narrow recess of the doorway and positioning herself to look out with the dog seated on her left side. It didn't surprise her when the FBI man reassumed his position in front of her like a sentinel.

"I do appreciate your concern," she said, hoping to make peace.

"But?"

"But this really is a peaceful, upscale neighborhood. You must know that the original houses bordering the promenade have been restored and sell at a premium if they're ever put on the market."

"Rich people are no different at heart than the disadvantaged," Caleb argued. "The same thing goes for criminals. Push someone too far and anything is possible."

He had a valid point. She smiled when he glanced back at her. "I grew up right here in Brooklyn."

"Family?"

"A much older brother who moved to the West Coast.

My parents are gone." *Which is another reason why I crave a family of my own*, she added silently. There was still time left on her biological clock, but that didn't mean she was willing to let those years slip away. "What about you? Do you have extended family close by?"

All he said was "No," but the undertone convinced her there was a lot more to his story than simply being a widower.

Vivienne squelched a strong urge to pat him on the arm. To offer comfort for his sadness. She knew better than to touch him and chance having her gesture of compassion misunderstood.

Caleb leaned forward to peer up the crowded street. "I think I see your boss's car coming."

"Good." Suddenly, he extended his arm and abruptly pushed her back. If he'd explained she wouldn't have had to ask the question. "What's wrong?"

"Across the street. You can't see her face right now because her phone is in front of it. I think somebody is taking your—our—picture."

Vivienne peered past him. "Where?"

"Right below that Open sign in the drugstore window. There. She's lowering her phone. Look."

"No hoodie, but…" Vivienne inhaled a gasp. "I think that *is* the kidnapper. How did you pick her out?"

"Instinct. Her intensity. And the fact that taking a lot of photos is typical of a fixation."

"But why now? Why me?"

"A guess? She's ticked off that you stopped her and wants to remember you and your K-9."

"Terrific. If I try to go after her, she'll run. Do you think you can get over there and grab her without being noticed?"

"I can try."

Vivienne figured it would have been an easier task if Caleb hadn't been so tall and well-built. There were enough businessmen on the street to keep his clothing from being different, but his height was a definite disadvantage.

He cupped a hand around his mouth, evidently meaning to speak to her privately. Vivienne leaned closer to hear. As he bent slightly she heard the singing crack of a gunshot. It echoed back and forth between the taller buildings, making it impossible to accurately pinpoint origin or direction of travel. Actions of passersby, however, told a clearer story.

Caleb instinctively ducked. So did she. Some people on the sidewalk screamed and dodged while others across the street, where the shot had apparently come from, ran for their lives, pushing each other aside and falling down in a wild effort to escape.

"Get down!" Caleb shouted, stepping out despite the danger and waving his arms. "Everybody down."

That was enough to spur more action with the majority taking cover.

"Inside," Vivienne yelled to him as she leaned hard against the glass of an exterior door leading to upstairs offices.

She and her K-9 partner made room for Caleb. When he joined them seconds later, he was swiping at his short, darkish blond hair and what looked like fine rubble was falling to the floor.

"The kidnapper took a shot at me?" she asked. "Why?" He brushed at the gray powder on his suit jacket.

Without thinking, Vivienne began to help him dust the back of his shoulders. "It could have been random."

Frowning, Caleb said, "You can't be serious. We just

spotted a probable criminal right across the street. She was looking straight at us and taking pictures. She must have been armed, too."

Vivienne sighed. "With all the police hanging around down here you'd expect any shooter to be more cautious."

"If he or she was sane to start with," Caleb replied, scowling as he went on to report the incident by cell phone and request backup.

The face in the hoodie flashed into Vivienne's mind. Those eyes. That flushed skin. The way the woman had been clutching the child. Now that she thought about it, no part of the woman's demeanor had struck Vivienne as even marginally normal.

Her sense of accomplishment over recovering the boy faded. She was now a kidnapper's target, likely for foiling the woman's crime.

She peered past Caleb. Gavin's patrol car was nosed into the curb less than twenty feet away. Half a dozen police officers were taking defensive positions while others held back curious onlookers. Everything was typical. Except—

Vivienne grabbed Caleb's forearm and pointed. "Look! Unbelievable. I think she's still over there!" It was hard to swallow past the dry-cotton feeling clogging her throat.

Gavin had left his car idling and he joined them. When Vivienne tried to point out the woman she and Caleb thought they had identified in the crowd, she had vanished.

THREE

Rather than pick up his black SUV and head back across the bridge to FBI headquarters in Manhattan, Caleb followed the Brooklyn group back to their station. He told himself he was merely there to make sure Vivienne didn't leave out any details in her report, but even he didn't fully buy that excuse. Nor was he willing to dive deep enough to analyze himself. He'd had his fill of his own and experts' questions about the tragic assault that had cost him both his wife and their baby son. Yes, it hurt. It still did and probably always would. But he'd learned to live with those memories. To function despite personal pain.

The secret was to compartmentalize the past, Caleb assured himself. The same went for the present and what was to come. There was nothing to be gained by letting himself brood or relive events that couldn't be altered. That part of his life was over. It had ended in the few agonizing seconds when his family had been obliterated. And with them, he realized sadly, had gone his joy, his faith and his hopes for the future. Settling into his job and focusing only on work had saved him, in a way, by keeping his mind from imagining what might have been and not making too many forays into his wounded psyche. It wasn't an ideal response, but it worked for him.

Entering the three-story limestone-faced building that housed the Brooklyn K-9 Unit, he smirked briefly. It took a pretty savvy agent to convince examiners that he'd healed when in reality the wound was still raw. Still painful. He'd known what they'd wanted to hear from him and had delivered pat answers on demand. He desperately needed to keep working, to feel useful. Necessary. Being sidelined might have literally killed his spirit.

The K-9 unit offices were surprisingly modern inside. Desks were arranged geometrically, and spare kennels had been stacked neatly against one wall.

Caleb hung back until Gavin addressed him. "Since you're assisting, I'd appreciate if you'd come into my office and listen to this debriefing, too, Agent Black. You may have noticed something the rest of us missed."

"Okay. Thanks." The dubious expression Vivienne displayed was not nearly as welcoming as that of her boss. Nevertheless, Caleb followed.

Vivienne took the chair the sergeant indicated. Hank circled twice and curled up at her feet. Caleb could tell she was nervous. Who wouldn't be? Being shot at would do that to a person, even one as seasoned as he was. For all he knew, this might be the first time this K-9 officer had been under fire.

"The second look I got at the kidnapper when we were waiting for you to pick us up may help even more than my first encounter," Vivienne volunteered. "Don't you think I should meet with a sketch artist ASAP?"

Gavin nodded soberly. "I do. I just want to make sure

I understand everything about the shooting. We can't be one-hundred-percent certain that it's connected to the attempted abduction, but it's probable."

Vivienne nodded.

Her smile was a little tremulous although she did seem to be recovering well, Caleb concluded. This was one resilient woman. That part of her character reminded him of his late wife. Too bad that being a cop hadn't saved her.

"As I said, the woman I saw was tall, wiry and thin, middle-aged," Vivienne said. "When I saw her wearing the gray hoodie I couldn't tell what her hair color was, but in the crowd across the street from where Agent Black and I were standing, it looked sandy gray. Short and curly. A tight perm, although now that I think about it, she could have been wearing a wig."

Gavin looked to Caleb. "Do you think she was your shooter?"

"I do. The bullet impacted the stone above our heads and thankfully didn't ricochet into us. It could have come from an upper window across the street, but judging by the way the crowd scattered I assume they heard or saw a gun go off right next to them. That would be hard to miss."

"All right." Gavin turned back to Vivienne. "Write up a full report. I want every tiny detail, not just bare bones. I'll read over what the patrol officers got out of the boy's mother on the promenade and we can compare notes later."

"Yes, sir." She stood.

"I don't want you out on assignment for any reason without clearing it personally with me," Gavin said.

"Yes, sir."

"Caleb, perhaps you and Vivienne could compare notes, too, see if there's anything either of you saw or heard but didn't think to mention." He turned to the K-9 officer. "Vivienne, I'll assign a patrol unit to drive you home when you're ready to leave for the day."

"I could take her and the dog," Caleb said, letting his feelings override common sense. Playing bodyguard was not in his job description.

Sergeant Sutherland's eyes narrowed as he studied them. "We'll see. Right now I want you to both wait in the outer office while I organize my thoughts. You go do the same."

That order didn't surprise Caleb, but Vivienne seemed unsettled. She made a face. "What was that all about? Sarge seems very comfortable with you. Are you two buddies or something?" she asked, wending her way between the desks and leading him into the break room.

Caleb shrugged. "Nope. But this is his domain so he's in charge."

Vivienne looked over the room with appreciation and sighed. "This old station and the building next door were recently remodeled to house our new unit. I love the beaux arts architecture, don't you? It was built in 1910. You don't see stonework like this on modern construction." After giving Hank a down-stay order, she crossed to the coffeepot. "Want a cup?"

"I don't know. Was it made this year?" Caleb deadpanned.

She eyed the glass pot. "Good chance. Maybe even this week."

"In that case I'll take a cup." He pulled out a chair from beside a small dinette table and sat.

"Cream? Sugar?"

"Black, thanks. With a name like mine I almost have to drink it plain."

To his relief he got her to smile. "Caleb Black. Right. So, Agent Black, what brought you into the FBI?"

"A search for justice and truth.'"

"Sounds heroic. Do you mean it?"

"Very much so. An unsolved murder in my hometown when I was a kid got me interested in law enforcement. I became a cop, then applied to the FBI and became a rookie all over again. Profiling came next. It was a natural fit."

"I've wanted to be a cop since I was a kid, too—just was always in awe of the uniform," Vivienne said. "I haven't been at it as long as you have."

"I'm not *that* old." He arched an eyebrow.

"I think it's the suit," she countered, smiling. "It makes you look so serious."

He took a sip of tepid coffee and tried to keep from grimacing. "I am serious. It goes with the job."

"Really? The people I work with do their best to lighten the mood around the station. Keeps us sane."

Caleb laughed as he watched her realize what she'd just intimated about him. "Hey, I'm the profiler here, remember?"

"Sorry. I didn't mean it personally."

"Sure you did. It's okay. No offense taken. None of us is completely normal the way we assume civilians are. If we were, we couldn't bear the tragedies we deal with on a daily basis."

"Think so?" She joined him at the table while Hank rested beneath it on the cool vinyl. "I don't know if I buy that."

"Careful. You could be profiled."

"It might be fun," Vivienne said thoughtfully. "I've often wondered what made specific people behave the way they do. I don't mean hardened criminals. I don't need to know if their parents were mean to them or they failed English class in school and that ruined their lives. What puzzles me is why one sibling turns to crime while another leads an upright life."

"Well, when you figure that out please let us all know." He paused, sipped, made a face and set aside his mug. "Take the woman you were chasing this morning, for instance. She may be part of a gang that steals children or somebody who craves a child and can't have one. Or she may want a little boy for some obscure reason that's not yet evident. Whatever her trigger is, she's apparently the kind who holds a grudge." Pausing in his analysis, he saw Vivienne shiver.

"I don't see why else she would shoot at me."

He nodded. "Her, or an accomplice we didn't notice when we spotted the kidnapper taking photos of you."

As they compared notes on all the details, as Sgt. Sutherland had asked, Vivienne wondered aloud if the shooter would try again.

After leaving Hank to nap in one of the kennel runs in the K-9 training center next door, Vivienne reported to the interview room. Instead of pencil and paper, the bejeweled, brightly clad woman waiting for her had brought a laptop and was seated at the table.

Vivienne offered her hand. "Hello. Vivienne Armstrong. Sorry if I looked surprised when I came in. I'd expected Eden Chang."

"I'm Danielle Abbott. Eden's busy and I was free so

they sent me over from the Command Unit." Danielle bestowed a joyful grin as she shook hands, her bracelets jingling. "Don't worry about doing this. Just trust me and your memory."

Mirroring the smile, Vivienne joined the tech-savvy forensic artist at the table, where she was opening her laptop. "You don't actually draw the face, right?"

"In a manner of speaking, I do. We use a computer program that creates the features. You and I will go through this program together, step by step, and you can decide when we're done."

"I'm not sure I remember enough."

"That's a typical fear. Don't sweat it."

"Okay, I…" She startled when someone knocked on the door.

Danielle called out for the person to come in, and Caleb entered.

"Caleb!" Danielle greeted him with a wide grin. "Good to see you again. It's been ages since I did a reconstruction picture for you."

He nodded. "Sorry to interrupt—I know you're about to start. I just wanted to let you know I'll be waiting outside to see the finished product. I wish I could be of more help, but I only got a look at the woman from a distance."

Vivienne knew he'd come for moral support. She gave him a smile and nod, then turned to Danielle. "Okay, I'm ready."

He smiled back with a you've-got-this expression and left.

Vivienne couldn't help being curious. "You know him well?"

"Well enough," the tech guru said with a sad smile. "He's had it pretty rough."

"He told me he was widowed."

Distinctly penciled eyebrows arched. "He did? He actually said it? Out loud?"

"Yes. Why?"

"Because he usually keeps everything about his past to himself. At least he used to. If he's talking about it these days, that's a very good sign."

Vivienne was slowly shaking her head. "I don't know. He acted awfully grumpy and only said one word. *Widowed.*"

"That's understandable, given how he lost his wife and baby to a killer who was after him, instead." She shook her head.

Vivienne inwardly gasped. She'd had no idea.

"Nevertheless," Danielle continued, "he mentioned it. Do you have any idea what triggered him to reveal that?"

"I think it was because I noticed him fiddling with his wedding ring. He still wears it."

"Yeah, I know. Sad, isn't it?"

"Not to me," Vivienne said. "I think it makes clear that he loves his late wife even though she's gone. Someday I'd like to find a guy who will love me forever and ever."

Danielle smiled. "They're definitely out there. I found one."

"When and if I ever find the right man and fall in love, I'm committing for the rest of my life…and beyond. Somewhere out there is the perfect husband, someone who was meant for only me."

"Then I hope you find him the same as I did,"

Danielle said, reaffirming with a new smile. "In the meantime, what do you say you and I get busy? We'll put together a likeness of the kidnapper that we can circulate to all patrol officers."

"Right. Since she didn't get away with the Potter boy she may focus on another child soon."

Although the woman nodded in agreement, Vivienne knew what else she was thinking. Then Danielle added, "Or take another shot at you and your dog."

"Yeah, there is that possibility. I hope it doesn't keep me from working in the field." She remembered feeling sorry for K-9 unit detective Henry Roarke and his beagle partner, Cody, when they were sidelined for a few months. Not to mention Noelle Orton and her yellow Lab partner, Liberty, who were currently having their duties curtailed because of a bounty being put on the K-9's head after a successful arms raid. "I'd hate to be stuck doing desk work all day."

"Better for you to stay off the streets than to be carted off in a body bag."

Vivienne scowled. "You do have a way with words."

"Just tellin' it like it is, or can be. I've been to too many cops' funerals in my career. None of them can count on going home at night and don't you forget it. So please be vigilant."

What Vivienne wanted to say was that she trusted God to look out for her. Unfortunately, she also realized that her faith wasn't meant to be used like a talisman. If she truly trusted Christ she also had to be ready to accept His will for her life. Even if she didn't live long enough to fall in love with the perfect man and raise the family of her dreams? she mused. She shivered again, battling nameless fear, and the answer was *yes*.

FOUR

Caleb stalled as long as he could before rejoining Vivienne and Danielle. He'd wanted to ask to stay, to see if he could help, but he'd been afraid his influence might hamper the efforts at identification, and he also wanted to get a look at the finished product, not just bits and pieces as the women put it together. Seeing the face morph into its final shapes could adversely affect a person's memory, distorting it until mistakes were made despite efforts to recall details accurately.

When he knocked on the door to the interview room and stuck his head in, he was prepared to back off. Vivienne's broad grin showed him it wasn't going to be necessary.

He smiled back at her. "Done?"

"Yes. At least I hope so." Vivienne pushed back her chair. "Come tell me what you think."

"What *you* think is what matters. You saw her up close. I just caught a glimpse across a busy street."

She nodded, got to her feet and urged him closer to the laptop displaying the face. "True. But I was anxious and you were calm. That has to make a difference."

"It can," Caleb said kindly. "Sometimes being on

edge will wipe out a person's memory completely. Other times, nerves can imprint on a mind so thoroughly that the image lingers for years. Maybe longer. Studies have shown uneven results."

Danielle nodded. "That's because it's practically impossible to scare somebody out of their wits when they know it's an experiment."

"Very true." He sidled past Vivienne and made his way to the table, where he could peer over Danielle's shoulder. The "drawing" was black and white, and looked as if it had been hand-drawn with a pencil or maybe charcoal. The kidnapper's skin looked wrinkled and droopy on a thin face and the eyes were narrowed, as if squinting. Her mouth turned down at the corners, completing a very unpleasant countenance.

"There is something familiar about her," Caleb said. "I only got a glimpse, mind you, but you've captured her menacing aura."

"I thought so, too," Vivienne said. "I suggested we picture her with short hair instead of wearing that gray hoodie because she didn't have it on when we saw her on the street."

"Good idea."

"Glad to hear it's a solid composite," Danielle said.

"Have we heard from any of the investigating officers on scene?" Vivienne asked. "Were they able to come up with witnesses who saw her shoot at us?"

"No." Caleb sobered and shook his head. "You know how it can be. Unless a family member or friend is the target, bystanders often plead ignorance."

"They may do that even if it's not a loved one. I've never understood making that choice. I mean, you'd think they'd stand in line to give evidence that would put the bad guys in jail."

"It depends on the situation," Caleb said. "Sometimes the criminals have stronger influence than family."

"Is that what happened in your case?"she asked gently.

Caught by surprise, he didn't know how to respond. First of all, he wasn't aware that she knew about his past. Second, he'd been asked plenty of questions before, but never one phrased quite like Vivienne's.

"In a way, yes," he finally said.

"No wonder you go about your job the way you do. I'm really sorry."

Caleb watched empathy fill her expression. She seemed to intuitively understand his deep-seated need to catch and punish the man who had ruined his life, stolen his joy and his future, yet it was hard for him to accept sympathy.

"The assailant was identified and arrested," Caleb said flatly.

"Sentenced?"

Latent anger began to rise as Caleb remembered the charges leveled at the trial. Attempted murder for trying to kill Caleb. Manslaughter for the deaths of his wife and baby. His jaw clenched. He struggled to keep control of his temper.

Vivienne seemed to see into his heart. "No punishment can be equal to what you've suffered. Even if their killer had received the death penalty in a state where it's still legal, that wouldn't have been enough to take away the pain. Not even close."

Touched, yet determined to keep from showing it,

Caleb stood very still, back ramrod-straight, chin lifted in defiance. If she kept talking about his loss, he wasn't sure how he'd respond. As a fellow law-enforcement officer, she was merely trying to be kind and offer moral support, he knew, but he had almost reached the limits of his tolerance. Men and women he worked with daily were well aware of his reluctance to discuss the worst day of his life, so they didn't prod. But Vivienne Armstrong had no knowledge of his unwillingness to talk.

The forensic tech had been quiet during the conversation, but clearly heard something in his voice that told her he'd had enough. "So what do you say we get this show on the road? I'll email this file to all precincts and see that we get printouts, as well."

Danielle was smiling with her mouth, but Caleb could tell by her eyes that it was forced. He whipped out his cell phone. "Send it to me, and I'll see that my unit is informed, too."

He gave her the number and waited until he'd received the drawing, then offered his hand with a simple "Thanks."

"Anytime." She laughed softly. "I'm like a kid. Sometimes it's hard to make myself go back to work after a field trip."

"How about lunch?" Vivienne asked her. "I know a place that permits K-9 partners if you don't mind pizza."

"Mind? Girlfriend, I was raised on the stuff and if you mean Sal's, you can definitely count me in." She paused and looked at Caleb. "How about you, FBI? Loosen your tie and you'll fit right in."

"I've been to Sal's. They don't have a dress code."

Chuckling, Vivienne said, "They will for my Hank. I'll go get him and his working harness, change into my spare uniform and meet you in the front office. We can walk over."

Caleb nodded. Danielle held up a hand to offer Vivienne a high five. "Gotcha. Can't wait."

As soon as Vivienne left, Caleb turned to Danielle. "Thanks."

"Nothing to it. You looked like you were getting ready to explode. All I did was change the subject."

He inhaled noisily. "Yeah. It's been seven years, but I still have trouble, particularly if I think I'm going to have to explain the details again. It's not like I forget. I'll never do that. But talking about the details can hurt like taking a bullet myself."

"I get it." He ran his index finger inside the front of his shirt collar and partway around his neck, then loosened his tie. "I'll open up more about it to Vivienne if it becomes necessary for some reason. I don't expect to be here long. I'm only on loan."

"Checked out like a popular library book?" Danielle laughed. "When are you going to get back into circulation, anyway? You can't brood forever."

He wanted to say "Yes, I can," but decided to treat her comment as the light-hearted observation she'd intended. "Too many dog-eared pages and a tattered cover on this book," he said with a slight smile. "There's a lot of mending yet to do." Opening the door, he held it for her.

"It's what's inside that counts," she insisted. "And don't you ever forget it."

The crowd at Sal's was thick, as usual, with a line out the door and down the sidewalk for those waiting to buy a slice to go. Those who chose to get a whole pizza or pasta order had filled all but one table in the rear and Caleb led the way to it with Danielle, Vivienne and Hank close behind.

Having the working dog along helped clear a path. So did Vivienne's blue uniform. He did, however, wish she'd also kept an extra belt and service weapon at the K-9 unit so that she'd be armed if need be between here and home. The station was certainly a more secure location to leave a duty weapon than any apartment in the city.

Caleb turned to her. "Dog on the outside?"

"Yes, please. He'll scoot under the table but it's easier for me if he has access to the open area." She gestured. "After you."

Danielle chose the right side of the table and loaded the fourth chair with her laptop and voluminous purse before sitting down. Caleb had little choice but to make room and welcome Vivienne on his side. It was crowded, to say the least.

"I should have ordered for us before we sat down," he said, starting to push back his chair.

"Not a problem. This was my idea, so I'll take care of it." Vivienne smiled at him and Danielle. "Instead of telling me what you like, how about keeping it simple? Just tell me what you hate."

"I'm good with the basics," Caleb said. "It smells so good in here I may die of hunger before we're served."

"I know." She chuckled. "How about the Sal's special and a pitcher of ice water? Or would you rather have soda?"

"Water's fine," Danielle said.

Caleb nodded in agreement. "Me, too."

He reached for his wallet, but Vivienne waved it

away. "This is on me. If you want dessert after we polish off an extra large special you can buy it. Personally, I doubt any of us will be hungry when we're done."

He watched her place Hank on a stay with the flat of her hand in front of his nose, then she jostled her way through the crowd. Caleb sighed. Unfortunately, Danielle noticed.

"Ah-ha. You like her, don't you?"

"I like everybody. You know that."

"Do not. I know for a fact that you're put off by that blonde receptionist at your Manhattan office."

He rolled his eyes. "'Put off' is right when it comes to her. I've never given that woman one reason to think I was interested in her and she won't give up."

Danielle's grin widened, her eyes sparkling. "That's because you're irresistible."

"Oh, please."

"I'm serious. It's your wounded heart that gets 'em every time. They want to hug you and make it all better. It's an instinctive female thing."

"So how do I put a stop to it?"

"Move on, I guess." She made room on the table as Vivienne returned carrying an icy cold pitcher and three glasses.

"They'll call *Armstrong* when the pie comes out of the oven. In the meantime, drink up. It's hot outside."

"What about Hank?" Caleb asked.

"He has his own dish and I gave him plenty to drink back at the station. We discourage our working dogs from eating or drinking anything that isn't offered properly and by the right person. Hank has me."

"Suppose something happened to you?" Caleb asked. "What would he do then? Starve?"

"Nothing is going to happen to me." Her smile waned. "At least I hope not."

"I've had my eye on you the whole time we've been out," he assured her.

Danielle giggled behind her hand. "That's the truth."

He blushed. "Don't pay any attention to her. She has a weird sense of humor."

"Don't we all?" Sliding in next to him, Vivienne bumped his shoulder and Caleb imagined the temperature in the already warm little restaurant had risen twenty degrees.

He busied himself pouring ice water into all the glasses and sliding them across the slick tabletop to his companions. More than one businessman in Sal's had already stared at their party as if he wished Caleb would share—and he didn't mean the water. Being in the company of two good-looking women would normally have been quite enjoyable. This time, however, it was making him decidedly uncomfortable. Danielle was laughing at everything and Vivienne was smiling, too, although she was also blushing. Therefore, his attitude had to be the problem.

As a profiler he didn't have to wonder what was wrong with him. He knew he turned moody whenever he was even slightly attracted to a woman and in this instance he found himself unable to keep from admiring Vivienne Armstrong. She was more than attractive—she was witty and smart and braver than many he'd met in law enforcement. Under normal circumstances that might be all. In this situation, however, he considered himself her guardian and protector. It didn't matter whether that was part of his official assignment or not. It simply was.

Again, he couldn't help making a comparison to his late wife. He'd been lax in his defense of Maggie and she had been taken from him. Was he being given a second chance? As far-fetched as that sounded, Caleb wondered if it might be true, at least in part.

So what if it was? That only meant he needed to be extra vigilant, not that Vivienne was destined to take Maggie's place. No one would ever do that. No one could measure up.

Plus, Vivienne was a cop, too, just like Maggie had been. A confident officer of the law whose job was to put herself out there and protect the citizens of Brooklyn and all of New York City. She may as well have had a bull's-eye painted on her uniform.

Caleb's stomach churned and not from hunger. The more he thought about it, the more he realized he was beginning to care too much. Any degree of personal interest was too much as far as he was concerned. So how in the world was he going to stop his feelings when his job and her job had brought them together and might keep them in close contact?

Answer: he wasn't. Sergeant Sutherland had specifically asked him to work with Vivienne on the kidnapping case. Meeting her that first time on the promenade had led to this moment and probably many to come so he may as well get used to it. Accept it. Deal with it as best he could, then put it all behind him as soon as he was free to leave Brooklyn.

Given that he was working with the K-9 unit to find Randall Gage, whose DNA had been found at the crime scene of the McGregor double homicide twenty years ago, *and* that he was helping Vivienne track down the kidnapper, he wasn't leaving Brooklyn anytime soon.

And granted, his headquarters was just across the river in Manhattan, but given the population of the city his chances of accidentally running into Vivienne afterward were slim.

That notion settled in his heart and gave him pause. They barely knew each other, yet he was already certain he was going to miss her.

"Armstrong" blared from the PA system and bounced off the walls.

Caleb pushed away from the table as soon as Vivienne stood and sidled past her with a brusque "I'll get it."

What a relief it was when she let him go. He blinked back the unwelcome moisture gathering in his eyes and lost himself in the crowd on the way to the counter. By the time he was ready to return, he was certain he'd have regained his self-control. That was crucial, both to his stalwart image as an agent and to his carefully crafted, unruffled persona.

It had been a long time since he'd grown this emotional in public. He supposed thinking about losses of all kinds had gotten to him. Hopefully, it would be a longer time before it caught him by surprise and happened again. If he hoped to convince others that he was fine, he was going to have to do a much better job of proving it to himself.

And that began here and now. He scanned the crowd as he passed through. A flash of movement near the exit caught his eye, then was gone. Caleb stared. Anything abnormal could signal a threat. He couldn't afford to overlook the slightest clue.

On high alert, he headed for the door. Peered out.

Saw a shadowy figure in a gray hoodie disappearing in the distance. Coincidence? He didn't think so.

Turning, Caleb headed for the pickup area at the counter only to see Vivienne carrying their meal to the table herself.

He caught up with her. "Hey. I said I'd get that."

"For a minute, it looked like you decided to leave." She stared up at him. "What were you doing?"

There was no choice but to tell her, regardless. "I spotted something suspicious, so I went to check it out."

"And?" Vivienne had paused at the table, still holding the tray with the pizza on it.

"And I saw somebody running away. He or she was wearing a gray hoodie."

Caleb caught the tray as Vivienne's hands began to tremble, settled it on the table and pushed her into the farthest seat so he'd be between her and the door.

"You—you didn't give chase?"

"Too far away. We could call the station right now and report the possible sighting."

Vivienne shook her head. "Forget it. It may not have been the kidnapper. And any identifiable threat is already long gone, as you said, plus we can check the security-camera footage."

"True." Caleb gestured at their steaming lunch. "We may as well dig in."

Danielle reached for a slice and dragged it onto her plate. "I love a sensible man," she quipped, "especially when I'm starving and he offers food."

Pretending to be amused, Caleb served Vivienne and himself, then began to eat. His concentration never wavered from the doorway for more than a few seconds. If the person he'd seen returned, he would be ready.

FIVE

Vivienne barely tasted her meal. Oh, she ate, of course, but the pizza might as well have been made of cardboard. While the company sharing her table kept her fascinated, like Caleb, she was constantly checking the people in the crowd.

Danielle kept up a lively banter. Caleb gave one-word answers or comments as they ate. Having conversed with him before in full sentences, Vivienne was concerned that she may have offended him by asking about his lost family. What she should have done was wait until she could speak to Danielle in private again and get more personal details from her. She knew the basics but perhaps it would help to know more.

Why do I need details at all? she asked herself. *Good question.* One with no pat answer.

"So," Danielle said as she blotted her lips and started to gather up her gear. "This has been fun but it's time for me to boogie. I have plenty of work waiting for me back at my regular post. Glad to be of help when you guys were in a bind, though."

Caleb stood. Vivienne got to her feet, too. "Okay. I guess it is getting late. We don't want to hog this table with so many hungry New Yorkers waiting for a place to eat."

"You two go first," Vivienne said. "I'll bring up the rear with Hank." She could tell by the stern look Caleb gave her that he didn't like her choice of being unprotected from any angle. Thankfully, he didn't argue… this time.

Out of habit she reached to hitch up her utility belt and check the position of her sidearm, then realized with chagrin that both were waiting at home. Hank heeled. As their party of three and a K-9 reached the exit she morphed into cop mode as easily as always and that gave her added confidence.

Caleb was holding the door open. Danielle passed through first, tossed off a quick wave and headed for the subway.

Vivienne looked around for the gray hoodie but didn't spot it. Caleb seemed to be surveilling the area, too. They'd just reached the center of the wide sidewalk when the dog froze in his tracks.

Frowning, Caleb was at her side. "Why did you stop?"

"I didn't. Hank did." She was scanning their surroundings again, as was the FBI agent. "I don't see any threats, but this dog is never wrong."

"Never?"

"The only thing that might throw him off is a flock of sheep coming down the middle of the street." Although she was tense, she managed a smile. "See any?"

"Nope. Your precinct is close by. Let's get going." He reached for her arm.

Vivienne evaded him. "Do you seriously think I'm

going to let you shepherd me around like one of Hank's imaginary lambs?"

"Sorry. Guess I'm too used to being in charge."

"You're forgiven." There was a time for asserting independence and a time for listening to wise advice. This was the latter, particularly since she was unarmed.

She rolled her eyes and headed back toward the station at a brisk walk. Hank reluctantly paced beside her, looking back from time to time until they were actually inside the building again.

"Conference room," she said flatly, gesturing to Caleb. He wasn't smiling. Neither was she. As soon as they were alone in the separate room she pulled out her cell and dialed.

"Who are you calling?" Caleb asked.

"Eden Chang. She's our usual tech guru but she had the morning off. She's likely in the station now." Vivienne held up her hand, signaling Caleb to wait. "Eden? Vivienne Armstrong. I need you to check any video cameras that show the streets near Sal's in the last half hour or so. That's right. The pizza place. And while you're at it, scan the ones covering our station, too. You're looking for a thin, middle-aged woman with a tattoo on her ankle. She may be wearing a gray hoodie. Okay? Thanks."

She ended the call and turned to Caleb. "Satisfied?"

"For the moment. Hank must have caught the scent of the kidnapper just before. Could anything else have set off your dog? And don't tell me he smelled a lamb's wool coat. It's August."

That comment brought a smile. "I can't get over how observant you are, Agent Black. You noticed right away that nobody was wearing a heavy coat."

"Or a hoodie, since we're comparing intellects," he countered.

She started for the door. "I do think she was hanging around nearby Sal's, waiting to catch me alone, perhaps." She glanced down at Hank. "I'm going to kennel Hank while I go home to get my gun. When I get back, I'll start whittling down the pile of paperwork that's accumulated since this morning."

He shrugged and followed. "Seems like a lot longer than that, doesn't it?"

"Oh, yeah. I think I've aged ten years."

"You look like a teenager when you're out of uniform. How old are you, anyway?"

"Old enough to have a degree in law enforcement and have completed specialized training as a K-9 handler. I'm twenty-eight. Come on. Let's put my K-9 to bed."

They left the station by a side door and were passing through a grassy open space between the K-9 unit and the training center next door. Police cars were parked in designated spaces on Bay Ridge Avenue, blocking her view of the street.

Suddenly, Hank dropped to the ground, flat on his stomach. Milliseconds later Vivienne heard a shot and feared he'd been hurt. She hit her knees, hunched over her K-9 partner and reached for her gun…that wasn't there.

Caleb covered for her. He took a shooter's stance over the pair lying on the grass, ready to fire.

"Do you see anybody?" Vivienne shouted.

"No." He sidestepped and passed her. "Stay down."

"As if you have to tell me!" A cursory examination was all it took her to realize Hank had reacted as trained and dropped at the threat of shooting. He was not only unharmed, but was also wagging his tail, as if proud of himself.

She, however, was breathless and her heart was pounding. Caleb had his back to her. He'd reached the front sidewalk and was scanning left and right, still ready to fire. That was fine as long as one of the other officers stationed there didn't take him for an assassin and drop him where he stood.

The leap to her feet was wobbly but quick. She held out her arms to block several men in uniform who had raced out the side door brandishing firearms at the sound of gunfire. "Stand down!" she yelled. "He's FBI. Shooter in the street."

Caleb must have heard her, too, because he raised both arms, his pistol pointing skyward, and started back toward her while her colleagues fanned out.

"Is the dog hit?"

"No." Embarrassed to be so emotional about it, she sniffled and fought tears of relief. "He's better trained than I am."

"He had a faster response time than either of us," Caleb said as he holstered his gun. Then he started shaking hands with the nearby officers and simply said, "Thanks."

"Did you see the shooter?" Vivienne asked him.

"No, unfortunately. But hopefully your colleagues will find her." Vivienne assumed a wide stance, fighting to balance without showing how unsteady she felt. "I'll go kennel him now."

At her feet, Hank circled and pranced, clearly eager to be taken to his kennel, where he could drink and rest.

Those antics were just what Vivienne needed. Smiling at the happy dog, she reached the door to the training building and punched in the access code, a little surprised when Caleb didn't rush ahead to open the door for her. Clearly he knew she'd be safe in the training center. And maybe she liked his chivalry more than she'd been willing to admit. As long as he respected her as a police officer, he could open all the doors he wanted for her when they were operating as civilians. That made sense.

Sense? Hah! The words echoed in her thoughts, making her focus on the irony of the situation. The only thing that actually made any sense lately was her rescue of the little Potter boy. Anything after that included Caleb Black and struck her as total guesswork.

They were guessing why the kidnapper was trying to kill Vivienne. As payback? They were guessing why the boy had been snatched in the first place. Plus…

Vivienne continued her line of thinking as she kenneled Hank and gave him fresh water. Plus, she finally added, she was guessing at why she seemed so drawn to an FBI agent she barely knew and why his personal losses had hit her so near the heart.

After talking to the K-9 unit officers who'd looked for the shooter—no sightings—Caleb had trailed Vivienne and Hank into the kennel area and waited while she'd tended to her valuable dog. Once again, although he'd been on his guard, someone had gotten off a shot without being detected. If the assailant had been a better marksman the outcome could have been tragic.

She patted Hank, told him goodbye and latched the gate behind her.

"How can you smile after what just happened?" Caleb asked her.

"Because of my dog. And these others," Vivienne said, sweeping her arm in a wide arc while a dozen nearby canines of various ages sounded off. "This is my happy place."

"How do you stand the noise?"

"They're just doing their jobs. You're a stranger, and we disturbed their afternoon naps."

He raked his fingers through his short hair and shook his head. "I could use one of those after the morning we had."

"Hey, I was the one who ran almost the length of the promenade."

"And we've been dodging bullets ever since. I forgot to ask. Did your sergeant say if they found any shell casings?"

"They didn't. If this was the same shooter a few minutes ago and he or she used the same gun, they probably won't this time, either."

"Right. So we can assume they have a revolver."

"Either that or somebody else picked up their ejected brass, which is pretty unlikely," Vivienne said. "I'm sure our guys are going over the street very carefully."

"Mmm-hmm." Caleb set his jaw. His assignment was to profile a murder suspect and perhaps tie him to a more recent homicide that had the same MO, not shadow a K-9 officer as if he was her stalker.

Following Vivienne back to the K-9 unit, they stopped to talk to the sergeant and gave a report, then he trailed Vivienne to her desk. She sat down and swiveled her chair to face a computer keyboard.

"I thought you were going home to get your duty gun."

"I was. I am. Sarge doesn't want me to go on my own

and none of the officers can drive me right now." She stared at him. "Don't you have something else to do?"

"Yes. And no. Are you trying to get rid of me?"

"I might be." She blushed. "I'm not used to being shadowed all the time. It's a little unsettling."

"So is taking a bullet because there's nobody there to watch your six."

With a telling sigh, she stood. "Tell you what. I'll go change back into my street clothes, sneak out the back door and take a cab home."

"No, Vivienne. It's not safe. Wait for me—*inside*. I'll check in with your sergeant and let him know I'll take you home and back."

The off-putting expression on Vivienne's face failed to make him feel reassured, but he proceeded, anyway, positive she would be sensible enough to follow his instructions. It wasn't that he considered the streets of Brooklyn particularly dangerous—it was simply the apparent bull's-eye on this particular officer that gave him pause. For some crazy reason—other than the obvious—he was beginning to feel responsible for her welfare.

Going straight to Sutherland's office, Caleb found it empty. He stopped at the first cubicle to ask where their boss had gone, then worked his way across the room with no success.

"All right, plan B," Caleb muttered. Unsure of the layout of the main floor, he left by the front door and circled the building to get his SUV and pick up Vivienne. Judging by prior experience waiting for his wife to dress to go out, he figured he still had plenty of time for Vivienne to change back into her street clothes.

Caleb's jaw clenched. *Maggie again.* Always Maggie. Whenever he showed interest in another woman his late wife made an appearance in his thoughts. He didn't mind. At least he hadn't until recently. Right now, this second, it was Vivienne Armstrong he need to focus on.

Pulling around the corner of the building, he drove past a dented green trash receptacle and scanned the perimeter. The station exit was clearly marked and was keypad protected, so he couldn't easily go inside. Therefore, he'd wait. Surely it wouldn't be long before the K-9 cop emerged.

His heart reopened to thoughts of his late wife. A casual glance around was instinctual…until he saw a familiar jogging outfit and a young, athletic woman climbing into a taxi in the distance. "Vivienne!"

She never faltered, didn't look back. Caleb was astonished, then angry. He grabbed the steering wheel and sped after the departing cab. If she thought she could ditch him, she was in for a surprise.

Seconds later an older model, tan sedan slipped into traffic directly behind the cab. Caleb whipped around it as soon as he had an opening. He was not going to lose sight of her no matter how erratically the cabbie drove.

SIX

Vivienne smiled as she climbed the interior stairs to her third-floor apartment. It seemed a bit strange to not have Hank at her side, but not worrying about him right now was a relief. She wasn't proud of ditching her tall, handsome shadow, but she wasn't going to let Caleb Black boss her around. She'd told him she'd take a cab and she had.

She let herself in, shedding her jogging clothes on the way to the shower. She turned on the water, and by the time enough hot water had reached her apartment she had a fresh uniform laid out and her duty equipment waiting. That made redressing a snap. So did her short, easy-to-care-for haircut. A couple swipes of the brush and a touch of lipstick and she was good to go.

The belt was heavy with the holster, flashlight, cuffs, radio and extras for her K-9. She had it buckled and was reaching for the doorknob to head back to work when someone hit the door so hard it shook.

Instant reflexes had her palm on the grip of her pistol. "Who is it?"

"Me!"

That was all the introduction she needed. Caleb

Black had somehow followed her and was less than thrilled with her leaving him behind.

As soon as she checked the peephole, she opened the door. His fist was raised, ready to pound again.

"Hi."

"Hi? That's all you have to say?"

"Um…hi, Agent Black?"

He pushed past her. "Very funny. Not. What did you think you were doing taking off like that? By the time I got here and found a parking place you could have been dead."

Extending both arms in a display of well-being, she smiled at him. "As you can see, I'm fine."

Clearly, he was fighting with himself to regain more self-control. Although he wasn't shouting at her she could tell he was still plenty upset. Well, too bad. She was a cop, not some damsel in distress who needed coddling. Nevertheless, it was nice to see concern even if it was misplaced.

"You drove?" she asked.

"Followed your cab."

"Great. Then you can drive me back." She strode past him to the door, opened it and walked through. "Coming?"

To his credit he followed, jerking the door closed behind them and giving the knob a twist to make sure the apartment was secure.

"Where did you park?" Vivienne asked lightly.

Caleb gestured. "Next block."

Gruffness in his tone remained and she didn't know why she felt the urge to placate him. After all, she was a well-trained officer of the law and she was now fully armed, including her smaller ankle gun. She didn't need a plainclothes bodyguard and it was high time he accepted that fact.

A brief pause at the outer door was enough to show her there was no danger, no stalker waiting to harm her, so she pushed it open and bounced down the stone steps onto the sidewalk. "Left or right?"

Caleb pointed with his key ring, keeping it in hand to unlock the car doors. Once they reached the SUV she was able to climb in before he circled and slid in to drive. His hands gripped the steering wheel so tightly his knuckles whitened. Strong hands. Capable hands. A good man. A good agent. And, in a way, she had let her sense of independence hurt him.

As soon as her seat belt was fastened Vivienne reached out to lightly touch the sleeve of his jacket. "I'm sorry. I shouldn't have ditched you. It wasn't nice."

"It wasn't safe," he snapped back.

"There were a lot of cops still out looking for the shooter. I knew I'd be okay so I called a taxi service to pick me up."

He sighed. "You should vary your habits. And the times you travel."

Vivienne wanted to make him feel needed so she agreed. "Under the circumstances, that may be a good idea until we catch the kidnapper, who's clearly trying to take me out."

"No. All the time."

"Really?"

"Yes. You need to be more wary, more cautious about everything you do."

"It's not good to act paranoid," she said, positive he would accept her conclusion.

Instead, Caleb glared over at her and said, "You're only paranoid if nobody is after you."

* * *

Once Vivienne had returned to her desk and got busy working, Caleb was able to relax. He was still mad at her but no longer furious, the way he had been. The intensity of emotion had been a shock at the time. It was one thing to be upset or disappointed about a coworker and quite another to invest so much of himself that it tied his gut in knots and made him act unprofessionally.

Thankfully, she didn't seem to be holding a grudge.

"So do you plan to stay right there and finish your paperwork?" he asked.

Considering the way she rolled her eyes and arched her eyebrows, she hadn't totally forgiven him. "Unless I'm dispatched to another incident. Why?"

"I thought I'd go talk to Penelope McGregor and see if she can recall anything new that might help my deductions. I know she's been interviewed many times the past several months and that she was very young when her parents were murdered, but she may have ideas that she didn't voice before."

"It's better than trying to interview Lucy Emery," Vivienne said, leaning back. "Poor little thing was really scared after the murder of her parents. She's only three. If her aunt Willow hadn't taken her in immediately afterward, I don't know what would have become of her."

Caleb was relieved to be back to discussing business. "Murders of two sets of parents twenty years apart and leaving a young daughter alive in both cases. Add the clown mask the killer wore and his gift to each child of a stuffed monkey toy, and you have enough similarities to suspect the same perpetrator."

"We only have a DNA match in the McGregor case," Vivienne reminded him. "What would make a guy like

Randall Gage wait twenty years between crimes? I mean, if he's really a heartless murderer I'd think he'd keep at it, wouldn't you?"

"That's one of the things I have to decide when I profile any criminal," Caleb told her. "They may have similar patterns of behavior or be totally different in all but a few critical areas. That's why every little detail matters."

"Have you talked to Lucy's adoptive parents? Willow Emery, her aunt, and Nate Slater, one of our K-9 cops, got married and are providing a safe home for her. They live right here in Bay Ridge."

"I saw that in the file. I'll get to them. I want to start with Penelope McGregor. Sergeant Sutherland says she works here in the station. Reception, right? I'd planned to talk to her yesterday but never got a chance."

"Want me to introduce you?"

"That won't be necessary. I'll stop by Gavin's office on my way. If he still isn't there, I'll wing it." Worry lines began to crease his forehead again. "You won't leave the building?"

To his relief Vivienne smiled. "Okay, okay. I promise I will sit right here until—" she glanced at the precise time posted on her computer screen "—until at least five. How's that? Will it suit you?"

"Well enough. Understand, I'm not trying to boss you around. I've been present during attempts on your life. That's not something to take lightly."

Nodding, Vivienne stopped laughing. "Yeah, I know. I'm just not fatalistic about it. I have faith that God has put me here for a purpose and He'll be with me until the job is done."

She paused, studying him so intently it made him

uncomfortable. When she continued, she definitely touched a raw nerve. "Are you a believer? A Christian?"

Caleb took a deep but shaky breath. "I used to be," he said. "Not anymore."

Sitting very still as Caleb walked away, Vivienne felt bereft. Crisis always brought a change, sometimes for the good, sometimes not. A person had the chance to choose an upward path, trust God and try to make the most of his or her own life. Or they could opt to give up. To reject spiritual help. To turn away from their faith, even to deny God. And then what? Then, they floundered just as Caleb Black was demonstrating.

Sadly, she had never felt right preaching to others. In Caleb's case there was no way she could reason away his sorrow or explain why good people died and evil ones lived on. The problem was not solvable that way, nor would it ever be. Some survivors nursed survivor's guilt for years while others grieved differently, thanking God for the blessings of the past and stepping forward into whatever life had in store for them.

"It's the difference between joy and happiness," she told herself quietly. "Happiness depends on circumstances. Joy is deeper and eternal."

A broad, cold nose poked her in the elbow as a friendly voice said, "That's right."

Vivienne jumped. "Oh, Belle! You startled me." She reached past the cold nose and scratched the huge German shepherd under his chin. "Good boy, Justice."

"Where's Hank?" the other K-9 officer asked.

Sighing and swiveling her chair to face Belle Montera and her protection-trained K-9, Vivienne gestured with a lift of her chin. "Next door in the training center, resting. We had a tiring morning."

"So I heard. Where's your good-looking bodyguard? Gavin said an FBI agent was watching your back and working with you on the kidnapping."

"Who says he's good-looking?"

"Every woman I've asked," Belle responded with a grin. "And judging by the way you're blushing, you think so, too."

"He's one of those brooding guys that bring out our motherly instincts, I guess. That's why I was thinking about happiness versus joy. He doesn't seem to have either and it's painful to watch him suffering like that."

Belle huffed. "Really? What does he do, go around with a long face all the time?"

"Not exactly. Most of the time he seems fine. The thing is, he's not okay deep down inside. I've only gotten a glimpse of his pain." She leaned close to whisper. "He lost his wife and baby to a shooter who was reportedly out to kill him, and I can't even imagine how he feels."

Belle leaned away, aghast, causing Justice to tense up and visually search the office for a threat. "Whoa. How awful." She laid a calming hand on her dog's head. "It's okay, boy. Take it easy."

Vivienne understood how in tune the K-9s were to their partners, so she didn't fear the big shepherd. It was actually a relief to see him ready to defend Belle and anyone else she sent him to. "Yeah. The thing is, he seems to be stuck in the angry stage of grief instead of moving on to healing. He has a short fuse."

"What makes you think he'll ever change?"

Shaking her head slowly, Vivienne tucked her hair

behind one ear and pressed her lips together, then said, "I pray he will. I know he'll never forget the terrible loss, but for his own sake he needs to come to terms with the fact that there is more to life than the past. Right now he's so wrapped up in the tragedy he doesn't realize that he can have a good, worthwhile future."

"How long has it been?"

"That's irrelevant," Vivienne answered. "No two people grieve the same way or at the same speed. As a profiler he surely knows that there is no chart, no perfect progression, for things like that."

"And that matters to you because…?"

Vivienne was reluctant to postulate. She shrugged. "Beats me. All I know is that he blames himself. That's who he needs to forgive."

"You plan to talk him into it?" Belle looked incredulous.

"No. No way. My job is to accept him as he is. Caleb believed in God once. He can embrace that again. And once he does, I truly believe his faith will bring him through."

"Sounds to me like he's mad at God, too."

"Probably. I imagine I would be if I'd placed all my trust in Him to protect my loved ones and they'd been killed. The thing is, we don't see the whole picture. It's like the murders of Penny and Bradley McGregor's parents twenty years ago. The aftermath brought Penny to work for us and Bradley became a great K-9 detective."

Belle began to smile. Her cheeks colored. "Carry that notion further and you can see that it also brought my Emmett to Brooklyn. We might not have met otherwise."

The other woman's obvious delight gave Vivienne a jolt of unearned jealousy. Belle Montera and US Marshal Emmett Gage had each other. Willow and Nate Slater were already married. Raymond Morrow and Karenna Pressley were madly in love. Even K-9 unit member Henry Roarke had found bliss with Internal Affairs officer Olivia Vance, yet here Vivienne sat, unattached, unmarried and running out of time to see her dreams of a family come true despite joining those dating apps as a last resort. It wasn't fair.

Then again, she reasoned, perhaps the recent attempts on her life indicated that her future was going to be short.

She struggled with that unwelcome concept. Granted, no Christian was promised a lack of trials, but they were assured that the Lord would be with them no matter what. It wasn't a matter of blindly accepting disaster. It was more the opportunity to do the right thing at the right time and then trust the Lord with the outcome.

Belle had to run, so Vivienne bid her colleague goodbye and turned back to the computer. *Trust* was the secret, the answer to temporal questions regarding infinity.

It was okay to not be omniscient, to not control the universe, to admit to being human and confused. Which was where Vivienne was at the moment. She didn't know why she cared so much about Caleb Black's faith and his future. She just did.

An internal shiver shot up her spine and made the roots of her hair tingle. Someone currently had her in his or her crosshairs and was trying to end her life. That was a fact.

And God had provided extra protection in the form of an FBI agent. For that she should be thankful. God would handle the rest. She just wished she had a hint about how.

SEVEN

Caleb's time in Gavin Sutherland's office should have been short and uncomplicated. It was not.

"I hate to disagree with you, Sergeant," Caleb said, "but you need to find somebody else to work with Officer Armstrong from now on and to keep her safe. My superiors did not send me over here to babysit."

"No, they sent you to help us figure out if Randall Gage killed both the McGregor parents and the Emerys or if we're dealing with two killers. But since you were right there with Vivienne when the kidnapper shot at her, I thought you'd want to work with her on finding the woman."

He did. But... Things were getting complicated. "I want the kidnapper caught and the threat against Vivienne gone. But I also need to focus on the profile. I want to interview Penelope McGregor as well as Willow Emery. I plan to do that separately, although I know they've been interviewed many times."

The sergeant nodded. "Detective Slater and Lucy's aunt, Willow, are caring for the girl and whenever Lucy comes up with some new remark pertaining to losing her parents we're immediately informed."

"I'll take the McGregor crime first. I've read the file and pulled up the old newspaper reports, but as I said yesterday, I'd still like to hear the story from Penelope herself."

"I'll buzz her and let her know to expect you. While you're talking to her I'll put in a call to your unit chief and get his okay to use your skills as I see fit."

Caleb didn't like the implication. Nevertheless, he kept his thoughts to himself. His position was as secure as he could make it, considering the mandatory time off he'd had to take after his family tragedy. Yes, he knew his superiors kept their eyes on him, just in case, but he'd passed all his evaluations and had been certified as emotionally stable. There was nothing anyone could do to prove otherwise.

Unless I make a mistake, he added, leaving the sergeant and weaving his way to the reception area, where the first person on his list waited.

A young, red-haired woman rose from behind the front desk, smiled and extended a hand. "You must be the FBI profiler."

Caleb shook her hand. "Yes, Caleb Black." He looked around the area. "Can you get somebody to sub for you so we can talk in private?"

"Sure." Still smiling slightly, the brown-eyed clerk circled her desk, spoke to a coworker, then joined him. "All set. I'll take my afternoon break now."

"We can use one of the interview rooms. Would you like to grab a coffee first?"

"I'll get a bottle of water later. Follow me."

As he did so, Caleb noted her tall, slim grace. Pictures of her older brother, Bradley, showed the same basic coloring, although his hair was more of a dark auburn. It would be interesting to see if little Lucy Emery had any freckles or red in her hair. Every possible connection had to be compared.

Penelope led the way to an empty cubicle at the rear of the large squad room. "Will this do? I really don't like to sit in those tiny spaces where we question suspects."

Glancing around, Caleb nodded. "Okay. We'll keep our voices down so we don't disturb anybody."

She sat in an armless chair, leaving the desk open for him, and Caleb took his place at it. He'd memorized enough of the files to know what to ask without referring to past answers. Part of his job was to put the subject at ease and explain what he would be trying to do.

Leaning forward, he assumed a relaxed pose. "The human mind is a funny thing, as you probably know. If it isn't sure about something it will often fill in the blanks with what it thinks fits. That's what happens when we see one of those scrambled sentences and are surprised to be able to read them. Our mind has sorted out the confusion."

Penelope was nodding, watching him intently, so he continued.

"That can also happen when someone witnesses a crime, which is how a dozen witnesses can come up with as many differing descriptions. They're all telling the truth as their brains have interpreted what they saw."

Sighing, she said, "So by this time, what I think I can recall about what happened twenty years ago has to be far from reality. Is that what you're saying?"

"Yes, and no. You were interviewed right away, and you were very young at the time. You wouldn't have had a lot of life experience to draw on. That helps, in a way."

"I still have nightmares about the clown mask. Not as often as I did at first but they do still occur."

"Does it always look the same to you in your dreams?"

"It had white and red paint on the face and blue hair. That's about all I remember."

"Okay. What about the toy monkey the killer gave you before he left?" Caleb saw her try to hide a shiver. "Have you ever seen another one like it?"

"No, and I hope I never do." She folded her arms across her chest and hugged herself. "It should be stored in evidence if you need to look at it."

"It is. It's not exactly the same as the one left with Lucy Emery, of course. I wouldn't expect it to be identical this many years later."

He paused to give Penelope time to calm herself. The trauma had obviously left scars on her psyche regardless of whatever counseling she'd received as a child. "Right now I'd like your impressions. Never mind searching your memory for details. Just talk. Tell me whatever pops into your head."

"Anger. And fear. You'd think I'd be over it by now, wouldn't you? There are days, weeks even, when I honestly don't think back to those terrible events. When there was a killing on the twentieth anniversary of losing my parents it all became fresh again, as if I were going through it with Lucy."

"I'll be speaking to the Emery girl soon. I wanted to start with you to keep the events chronological."

"How will that help Lucy?" Penelope asked. "We know Randall Gage's DNA matches the sample on a watchband found at my house all those years ago. I'm so thankful the police kept all the evidence safe in storage until it could be properly tested using newer forensic methods."

Caleb nodded. "Right." The team had gotten lucky with a hit from an ancestry site, leading to a relative of US Marshal Emmett Gage. As hard as it was for the marshal, he'd identified his cousin Randall Gage as the probable suspect, then had managed to get Randall's DNA to prove the match. But Randall had gotten away twice since and was still at large.

"But what about Lucy? Was he responsible for killing her parents, too? I mean, if he was, why wait so long between similar attacks?"

"That's one of the questions I hope to answer," Caleb said. "Close your eyes and let your mind drift back. We know what you remember seeing. How about hearing? Or smell? Was his voice familiar?"

"No. I don't think he said much of anything."

"How about strange odors? Odd or unpleasant?"

Penelope squeezed her eyes shut tight for several seconds. When she finally spoke, Caleb was disappointed to hear her response. "Sorry. Nothing."

"Okay. I hate to ask you to dwell on something so traumatic but I'd appreciate hearing about any little thing that pops into your head, even if you don't think it matters." Caleb handed her his business card for reference. "My cell is on here. Call anytime. Day or night."

"All right." She checked her watch. "I should be getting back to my desk."

He stood when she did and thanked her. Like it or not, asking victims to recall their traumas was often the only way to learn enough to put together a proper profile. Firsthand commentary plus police records formed a more complete picture. All he had to do was extrapolate on the facts without letting his imagination interfere.

His jaw clenched. Yeah, like when he involuntarily recalled the personal trauma that had cast a dense shadow over his life for the past seven years. It had morphed into a tolerable sense of loss, but it never went away. Never.

A sudden urge to check on Vivienne Armstrong stopped him in his tracks. This was the first time he had realized how connected he felt to her. Admitting it, even to himself, was decidedly unsettling.

Worried about her friend and coworker, Vivienne lingered in the reception area of the police station, waiting for Penny to return from being interviewed. One quick glance at the younger woman's face told her what a trial the session with Caleb had been.

Vivienne opened her arms and offered a consoling hug. Penny hugged her in return, then took her usual seat behind the counter, ostensibly looking over the waiting messages and other notes. Vivienne wasn't fooled by the diversion. "Bad time, huh?"

"I've had better."

"I'm sure you have. Which reminds me, have I told you about my latest blind date?" The lopsided smile she saw arising on her friend's face was exactly why she'd changed the subject and brought up the funny story.

"Another success?"

"Oh, yeah. Totally. I'm not sure whose picture he posted online but it sure wasn't his. Still, I figured it was only fair to give him a chance so I stuck with it. Until he excused himself to use the restroom and split."

"He stuck you with the bill?"

Vivienne chuckled. "Oh, yeah."

"What did you do?"

"Well, first I ate my dessert. Then I ate his. And then I paid the tab and waddled home." She rubbed her stomach dramatically. "Ate too much and learned another lesson."

"Which was?"

Vivienne was delighted to see the amusement in Penelope's expression, the sparkle in her eyes, so she embellished her answer.

"Well... I learned that people sometimes lie."

"Duh." The younger woman rolled her eyes. "You just figured that out?"

"Confirmed it," Vivienne said. "I've decided it's taking me too long to find Mr. Right. I may never realize my dreams of mothering a big, happy family."

Penelope was encouraging. "You have plenty of time. Your biological clock may be ticking, but you have time. Keep looking."

"And praying to be led to the perfect man," Vivienne added. "According to Danielle Abbott from the NYC K-9 command, they do exist."

"That's a relief," Penelope said. "Hey, what about considering my big brother, Bradley? He's single."

"He is sweet. And good-looking. Unfortunately there's no chemistry between us."

"Maybe you're going at this wrong. Maybe you should be thinking with your brain instead of your heart."

"Uh-uh. I don't want to get married only for the sake of making a family. I intend to marry for love and let the rest come as God blesses. I wouldn't even care if the guy had a few kids already. The more, the merrier."

"If you say so." She shuffled the stack of memos on her desk. "Maybe you've already met him and just haven't recognized the attraction yet."

Vivienne sobered. "I kind of hope not."

"Why?"

The truth stuck in her throat and she briefly considered keeping it to herself. "Well, it's this way. I'm not sure that what I've been feeling lately is for the right reasons and it's left me in limbo."

When Penny glanced back the way she'd come, Vivienne followed her lead and noticed Caleb Black standing across the room, watching. Was her interest that obvious? she wondered, hoping otherwise. Admittedly there was something about the FBI agent that drew her, yet those sensitivities might be skewed by pity, among other things. There was a certain pull to a man who was permanently out of reach the way Caleb Black was. Any woman who fell for an emotionally wounded guy like him was bound to be hurt in the long run.

Part of her—the sensible part—agreed. The part of her that understood loneliness and commiserated with him kept asking if it might not be worth taking a chance.

Internally laughing at herself, Vivienne shook her head. Why speculate about an opportunity that would never present itself? Wishful thinking couldn't take the place of prayer for discernment and trusting the Lord to lead her to the perfect partner. Her job—her only job—was to stay out of God's way and not try to run His universe for Him. Surprisingly, that was hard to do.

"Right now, my biggest problem is staying alive long enough to fall in love with the man of my dreams," she told her friend. "I'd better go pick up Hank and do some refresher training before I think too much and get depressed. See you later."

With a final quick glance in Caleb's direction, she turned and fled the station, expecting him to follow. The intensity of the stare he'd been leveling at her stuck with her all the way out the door and beyond.

She was crossing the grassy alley to the building next door when she heard a loud bang, like a gunshot, and realized with dismay that she'd been so lost in thoughts of Caleb she hadn't bothered to check the alley for threats.

Vivienne hit the ground, rolled and drew her gun. She bounced up into a shooter's stance, staying low, and swung her aim in a protective arc. Perspiration dotted her forehead and made her hands slippery. Her pulse pounded in her temples, her breathing rapid and ragged.

She'd almost let daydreaming bring her down. Worse, it had been errant thoughts of a certain man that had nearly cost her the very life Caleb had vowed to preserve.

Three men burst from the station's side door, Caleb in the lead.

"Where did the shot come from?" he demanded.

"I don't even know if it was a shot," Vivienne told him. "If there was a shooter, they fled when you three came out."

Other officers joined them and fanned out to cover the alley.

Turning away from him, she shouted to her fellow officers, "Anybody see anything?"

Negative replies did little to settle her nerves. Neither did the uncomfortable closeness and aura of power coming from the FBI agent beside her.

EIGHT

Caleb had been reading lips and trying to eavesdrop while Vivienne had talked to Penelope. It was his task to learn as much as he could about Penelope, so paying close attention hadn't bothered his conscience one bit…until he'd discerned bits and pieces of what Vivienne was talking about. He'd inched closer, unable to quell his interest.

The conversation about finding a mate had torn at his heart in a way he hadn't expected. Could she have been referring to him? Both women had looked his way so it was certainly possible. That would never do. He had to make Vivienne understand that he was not in the market for another wife, let alone a family. Love hurt too much when it ended. And the deeper it was felt, the worse the pain.

And yet… Caleb's brow furrowed. His sense of great loss lingered, yes, but it had become slightly hazy, as if softened and perhaps not quite as clearly defined. That realization did not sit well with him. He didn't want to forget, to adjust, to give up the strong connection with his missing loved ones that he'd been holding on to for so long.

Before he could muse further his cell phone rang. "Black." The caller was his immediate superior, not the unit chief, but that hardly mattered considering the message.

"We're making one of our safe houses available to you and the K-9 cop you've been assisting," the agent said. "I'll text you the address. Continue with your previous assignment but move her and the dog into the safe house with you for the time being."

"But—"

"No buts about it, Agent Black. The commander of the K-9 unit has requested it and we've gotten it cleared with the higher-ups."

Caleb pulled the phone away from his ear and stared at it. If he'd been a suspicious man, he might suspect that Vivienne's boss was playing matchmaker, which was way out of line. There was only one way to find out. He went straight to the sergeant's office, knocked once, then walked in.

Sutherland looked up. "What's wrong?"

Caleb shut the door. "I hear you made an official request that I look after one of your people."

"I told you I was going to ask for that option."

"I don't think it's in Officer Armstrong's best interests for us to spend extra time together. You need to choose somebody else."

"I disagree." Gavin picked up a piece of paper from his desk and held it out. "Take a look at this screen capture from outside the station. See the orange tattoo on the ankle?"

"Looks like a flower."

"Tech thinks it's a lotus, whatever that is. But that's not the kicker. Here."

Caleb hesitated.

The sergeant thrust another piece of paper at him.

"Take it. It's a record of a phone call Dispatch received for Officer Armstrong. It won't bite."

It might, Caleb thought, slowly reaching for the note. He blinked. Cleared his throat. Reread the cryptic words aloud. "'You can't get away and neither can your mutt.' When did you get this?"

"Date and time are recorded. It was hand-delivered to me a few minutes ago."

"Vivienne never said anything about it. Does she know?"

"Not yet. I've asked her to come see me. She should be here any minute."

Caleb was about to hand everything back to Gavin when the subject of their conversation arrived, knocked and eased open the door. Seeing him there, she seemed reluctant to enter.

"I'm sorry. I didn't mean to interrupt," she said.

"Come in," Gavin said, motioning to her. "And close the door. This concerns you both."

As Caleb stepped back to give her room and she joined the small group, Gavin gestured to him. "Let her see the picture and that threatening phone memo before we get to the other details."

Caleb watched as she read the transcript of the telephone call for the first time, then he said, "Now look at the photo."

"Umm. Not good." She passed the papers back to him and he handed them off to Gavin. The sergeant gestured at nearby chairs. "Have a seat. Please. I was just discussing something with Agent Black."

Vivienne sat but fidgeted. "It's been almost half an hour since this phone threat came in." Her words sounded like an accusation. "Why wasn't I informed immediately?"

The expression on her boss's face showed disapproval. "I'll let that go because you're under duress, Vivienne," Gavin said. "Bear in mind that whatever is done here is for your own good."

Because Caleb had been watching her, their gazes met and locked when she turned to him with a frown. "What's going on?"

Gavin explained. "You'll be staying in an FBI safe house here in Brooklyn for a few days. And don't look at Agent Black that way. It wasn't his idea, it was mine." He harrumphed. "He's no happier about it than you seem to be."

"Terrific. What about my K-9? Hank can't live just anywhere. He has needs. Requirements. Does this house have a fenced yard? If I have to walk him on the street it will negate any benefits of supposedly being kept hidden."

Caleb broke in. "I'll make sure there's everything Hank needs. It shouldn't be for long. If I can put up with it, you can." *Uh-oh. Bad choice of words*, he realized, seeing a flash of hurt in her demeanor.

She recovered rapidly, squared her shoulders and sat straighter in the armless chair. "Fine. I will have to go back to my apartment again to pack a bag. I can get K-9 equipment and dog food here, but I'll need clean uniforms and a couple other changes of clothes."

Looking to Gavin, Caleb wasn't sure he was going to permit the side trip, so he offered, "I'll go with her if you want."

Sergeant Sutherland nodded. "Okay. Go. Vivienne, I'll want you to report by phone as soon as you're settled in the FBI house."

"Yes, Sarge," she replied. "After I go off duty."

"No. Go now. Before I change my mind and ship you

off to New Jersey." Gavin shooed them out with one hand as he picked up the receiver of his phone with the other.

Caleb held the door for Vivienne, then followed her out. "Where to first?"

"My apartment. I have two roommates, but neither is home right now. One is a flight attendant and the other is on a trip to visit family."

"That's handy. Then you won't have to worry about them."

Vivienne gasped. "I hadn't thought of that. They'll need to be warned, too." She was slowly shaking her head. "What a mess."

"No worse than most cops face," Caleb reminded her. "You're just more identifiable because of your K-9 partner."

"I'm not leaving him behind, if that's what you're hinting at."

He held up both hands in mock surrender. "I wouldn't dream of suggesting such a thing."

"See that you don't," she replied, making a face. "Where I go, Hank goes. I told you. He's not supposed to even accept food from anybody else."

"I imagine that can get bothersome if you want to do anything personal for longer than a few hours."

"Hank is totally worth it," she countered.

"I don't doubt that." Caleb was trying to be more agreeable. He didn't blame her for the intense reaction to the safe house. His own had been less than stellar. Nevertheless, they were both law-enforcement officers and had responsibilities to their superiors and comrades in arms. In Vivienne's case, that also included her K-9. She and Hank were looked upon as a single unit—a functional human with superior senses provided by an intelligent dog.

Vivienne turned misty eyes to him and asked, "Truth?"

"Absolutely. What do you want to know?"

"Your opinion. Nobody can be sure if that phone threat is legitimate. I want to know what your training and instinct is telling you. Should I be worried about Hank?"

"Always," Caleb said quietly. He stepped closer to her and spoke softly to keep their conversation as private as possible. "Even if that particular threat isn't serious, I think your dog should be protected at all costs." He cleared his throat. "Except in a case where it's either him or you. I don't want to see either of you harmed."

"But you disagree on my using the safe house?"

"No, no." Shaking his head and moving both hands in an erasing motion, he met her steady gaze with one of his own. "I think it's a fine alternative for you. I just don't see why our bosses are insisting that I stay there, too."

"At least we agree on one thing," she said sharply. "Come on. I'll get Hank and his gear so we don't have to come back here after we pick up a few things from my apartment. While you're driving, I'll text both my roommates to make sure they don't come home unexpectedly and put themselves in danger."

He nodded and seemed lost in thought for a moment.

Leading the way through the grassy alley once more, Vivienne said, "Why can't criminals understand we're just doing our jobs? It's nothing personal."

"Now there's where you and I don't agree," Caleb said. "For me, it's very, very personal, particularly when I'm able to help an innocent child."

"Like Lucy Emery, you mean?"

Speaking past a lump in his throat, Caleb simply said, "Yes."

NINE

Vivienne's mind was working a mile a minute as she prepped Hank for their time away from home and perhaps from the station, as well. It had occurred to her that Caleb's warning was right on. Anybody who'd managed to follow her and Hank from Bay Ridge when her shift ended could figure out where she lived pretty easily.

Seated beside Caleb in his unmarked black SUV, she watched the sidewalk and sized up pedestrians they passed. To her dismay she discovered that she was so keyed up she'd begun imagining an enemy lurking in every group. Although she kept trying to hide her physical reactions to those pseudo sightings, she wasn't surprised when Caleb asked, "Why are you so jumpy?"

"Um…" Vivienne quirked a nervous smile. "Bullets whizzing past my head? They tend to put me on edge."

"Oh, really? You could have fooled me. I thought you were worried about being stuck with me."

"What gave you that silly idea? I'm not a bit scared of you." *At least not in the way you're probably thinking*, she added to herself.

"Good to know." He leaned to look out. "We're getting close to your building."

"Yes. You can let me off and circle around while I grab my go bag if you want."

To her chagrin, he was shaking his head. "I'll find a spot. Don't panic."

"I *never* panic," she snapped, surprised when her remark came out sounding antagonistic. "Sorry. I guess I am more uptight than I thought."

"Understandable."

His calm demeanor and even tone needled her something awful. Staying in control was the goal of all law-enforcement officers, of course. It was just that in her case the attacks had become personal and thus she couldn't help taking them as such.

Memory of Caleb's previous reactions brought her thoughts full circle. Every now and then, his guard lowered just enough for her to get a glimpse of the man beneath the unruffled exterior. That was the real Caleb Black. That was the man who appealed to her—the tenderhearted agent who could identify with frantic parents and minister to them with genuine empathy. That was the man she wanted to know better—the person who scared her...in a good way.

To get him to open up to her she was probably going to have to do the same and that was the frightening part. She would have to be so real that her heart would be vulnerable. And she was going to have to ask him to drop his guard, as well. *Could he handle doing that?* she wondered.

A better question was, could *she*?

"Is this spot close enough?" he asked, jolting her out of her poignant musings.

Vivienne leaned to peer out. "Yes. Grab it before somebody else squeezes past us."

"Not to worry. I drive in Manhattan, remember."

She had to smile at his parking expertise. "Smooth. If you ever lose your FBI job, you'll make a great cabbie."

"Good to know."

She was already unbuckling her seat belt and opening the door.

Hank joined her on the sidewalk, his tail high and waving with delight. "Sorry, boy, we're not staying," Vivienne told him. She led the way to the outer door and punched in a code to enter the lobby.

Caleb stayed with her. "Stairs or elevator?"

"Stairs. It's good exercise."

She started to climb. "It seems as though we packed a week's worth of trouble into one long day."

"One very, very long day," he agreed. "I think tomorrow, unless you have a specific assignment, we should plan to interview the Potter boy and his mother. I know local patrols are keeping an eye on them, but I think we should suggest they leave town for a while, too." He and Vivienne had wanted to interview both Potters right after the kidnapping, but word had come back that both mother and son needed time to decompress.

"Sounds logical."

"Thanks."

She chuckled. "How do you know that was a compliment?"

"If it wasn't it should have been."

"That's one of the things I like about you, Agent Black—your humility."

As they reached the third-floor landing, Hank faltered. Vivienne immediately picked up on this change of attitude and stopped in her tracks.

Caleb followed suit. "What's wrong?"

"Not sure. Look at my K-9. He's gone into a crouch as if he senses a wolf about to attack his personal flock. That's us, by the way."

"Okay. Now what?"

"We take it slow," Vivienne said in a near whisper.

"What's that on the floor by your door?"

Vivienne took a step forward and peered down the dimly lit hallway. "I'm not sure. Maybe one of my roommates ordered something online."

"You didn't?"

"Not me. Anything I'd ever want is available right here in Brooklyn."

"Okay." He held out his hand to block her. "Stay right there. I'll go take a better look."

"No way." She gave him her most stubborn stare.

Caleb shrugged without giving ground. "Suit yourself. I thought you and that dog were supposed to protect each other. Is he a bomb sniffer?"

"No, he's a tracker. Still…"

"That's what I thought." He held up his cell phone. "Compromise. I'll call it in and you can give the other cops orders—or try to—when they get here."

Trembling as the possible contents of the unexpected package registered fully, Vivienne eyed it with suspicion. If Caleb hadn't been with her and if Hank hadn't acted odd, she might have walked right up to the small, brown cardboard box and been blown to bits. Or not.

"It's not a bomb," she insisted. "It can't be. My enemies can't possibly know where I live."

"Suppose they followed your cab home earlier when you ditched me? Or maybe they followed me when I was chasing after you. Are you ready to stake your life on it? I can hold your dog while you go check the box."

"Oh, that's big of you. Thanks a heap. Protect the K-9 and let me go risk my life."

He huffed and grinned. "Hey, you're the one who insisted it was harmless. So go prove your point."

"I'll wait," Vivienne conceded, trying to keep from smiling and failing. "You win. This time."

Joking around helped her cope. Having the probably harmless package investigated and finding out she had been worried for nothing was going to help a lot more.

Surely that was what the outcome would be. Anything else was unthinkable.

Caleb noticed both K-9 and handler relaxing as the minutes ticked past while they waited for backup. He, on the other hand, stayed on high alert. Vivienne's apparent nonchalance bothered him enough to mention. "I'd feel better about all this if you looked a little more scared."

"Really? You want me terrified?"

"That's not what I meant. You just don't seem bothered much by another attempt to harm you."

She rolled her eyes. "A *possible* attempt, you mean. We don't know that there's anything suspicious about the box. And even if the kidnapper-shooter did follow me earlier, the list of tenants only has the leaseholder's name—one of my roommates. Knowing that it's best for cops to keep a low profile we did that on purpose. So the perp wouldn't know which apartment is mine."

"Hank alerted."

She frowned. "True."

"I'd be more impressed with your precautions if you hadn't gone running off solo."

"Tell me you wouldn't have been tempted to do the same thing if you were in my shoes."

"There's no comparison," he argued.

"Why? Because you're a big, strong man and I'm a woman?"

Caleb huffed. "I'm surprised you didn't say 'just a woman.' That's what you were thinking, isn't it?"

"Maybe."

Did he dare tell her what had been going through his mind and why? A bigger question was, would it help? He didn't want to appear vulnerable in her eyes, yet it might be worth taking the chance if his confession resulted in the preservation of life.

Nodding, he squared his shoulders and faced her. "You'd be right if that's what you thought, but it doesn't have anything to do with you personally."

"I beg to differ. I'm the one standing here."

"But you're not the person who died because she was so sure she was equal to any man alive. My late wife was like that. She came close to winning, but she was also a mother and that's what ended up causing her to make the choices she did. Fatal choices."

Thankful that his voice was remaining strong and his emotions were staying in check, Caleb went on. "She thought she could outsmart an assassin who had come after me. And she was wrong. He turned the tables on her."

"I'm so sorry. You don't have to say any more if you don't want to."

"I think you need to hear it. You and Maggie are far too much alike. Oh, you don't look like her, but the same spark of independence and intelligence is in there." He pointed to her head, intending only to make a point, and wound up tucking back a lock of her hair before he could stop himself.

Vivienne looked shocked but accepted the gesture without protest. He withdrew and stuffed both hands into his pockets, then gazed up at the ceiling, seeing the past instead of dingy acoustic tile.

"We knew a hitman was coming. My wife argued that staying with me was best because that way the killer would figure I was unaware and make his move while a task force was in place to capture him."

"That sounds logical."

"I thought so, too, at the time. I thought I could protect her, and she intended to protect me."

If Caleb had seen pity in Vivienne's expression he might have stopped his story right there. Because she was listening, wide-eyed and still, he kept talking.

"My wife decided, all on her own, to make a realistic dummy of me and stand it behind a shade so it threw a shadow. It was actually a brilliant idea. When she got it fixed the way she wanted, she went to get our son from his crib to feed him. On the way to the kitchen she insisted I go look at the dummy. She wanted my approval, that's all."

He paused to clear his throat, to try to squelch his emotional reaction to the telling of his story. "I was just coming into the room when I heard the first shot. A bullet hit the dummy and the force knocked it over." Despite tears welling he went on. "Maggie had our baby in her arms and I guess the natural reaction was to turn and shield him with her own body instead of hitting the floor the way we're trained."

Astonishment on Vivienne's face and shared pain

in her eyes told him she already understood where his story was going.

"Yes," Caleb said. "The assassin had time to fire again. That rifle bullet went through Maggie's back and killed our son, as well. She died instantly. The baby died in my arms. He was so little, so innocent." He coughed to cover a sob and give himself a moment to recover. "Now do you understand why I lost my faith?"

She was nodding. "Yes, and no."

"It's not open to debate," Caleb said flatly. "God, if there is a God, failed me. Failed my family. I'm not telling you this to get sympathy or a lecture in theology. I'm telling you so you will understand why I need to make up for my mistakes. To protect other people and their children."

"I'm a cop, Caleb. I can protect myself and others, too."

"I know. I saw you save a child. What you and your K-9 do is vitally important and should be protected at all costs. That has become my job and I intend to do it to the best of my ability."

"So you feel you were lax in the past?"

"No."

The sparkle in Vivienne's eyes may have begun as unshed tears but it now resembled sparks of fire. Caleb tried to read her thoughts and failed. When she spoke it was with calm assurance. "Then stop blaming yourself. Evil exists. We see it every day. Some things defy explanation but that doesn't mean God has abandoned us. It simply means we don't understand. Yet. Maybe we never will."

"There's nothing left to understand. They're gone. Period."

"But you're here, Caleb."

"That's pretty obvious."

"And you feel a strong influence urging you to protect others, particularly children?" she asked.

"Yes. So?"

The way she slowly nodded, the way her gaze bathed him in peace, left Caleb wondering if she'd spout stale platitudes. He'd heard enough of them over the years to fill a book and none had helped one iota. He braced himself, ready to fend off sappy feelings and stand strong regardless of what she said. It was bad enough that he'd almost lost it while telling her his story. He was not about to weaken further.

To his astonishment, Vivienne didn't tell him how sorry she was, although he could tell she commiserated. Instead, she gave him a sweet smile. All she said was "Good."

"Good? Of all the…" Caleb never got the chance to finish what he'd started to say because the small package on the floor in front of her apartment door began to smoke.

TEN

Vivienne screamed. Ducked. Gave Caleb a push and dragged Hank after her. The ensuing explosion wasn't big, but it was plenty loud in the enclosed space. She covered her head with her arms as tiny pieces of ceiling plaster rained down on the stairwell. Hank hid behind her legs and Caleb grabbed her in a tight embrace, using his broad shoulders to absorb some of the onslaught.

Boots thundered up the stairs as helmeted officers carrying shields passed them. "Bomb squad is right behind us," one of them yelled. "Evacuate!"

Her ears hurt. The walls seemed to continue vibrating although she knew the puny explosion couldn't be having that much of an effect on the structure. In the grand scope of things, the little bomb had been ineffective. It had, however, proved that someone did know where she lived and was out to terrorize her, whether they caused her harm or not.

That realization hit her hard. She began to tremble.

Caleb tightened an arm around her shoulders. "Come on. We don't need to be breathing this dust. Let's wait in the street and let the pros work."

She complied without thought, glad he was with her,

doubly glad he was guiding her. She'd never admit it but having his physical and moral support was not only wonderful, but it also seemed very necessary. Her head was swimming and her eyes were itching and burning, blurring her vision.

Beside her, Caleb coughed repeatedly. So did Hank, although she knew the air was better closer to the floor. At least at the moment.

Once they were clear of the building, she crouched beside an idling fire truck, pulled Hank closer to check him over, then looked up at Caleb. "See if you can get bottles of water from somebody. Please?"

"Not leaving you. Whoever planted that amateurish explosive device probably meant it to at least make you run, if not do actual bodily harm. They could be waiting out here in ambush."

Chagrined, she had to agree. "Okay. You're right. I guess it rattled me more than I'd thought."

That admission seemed to please him. Not that it should have mattered to her. After all, she was as much law enforcement as Caleb was, although in a different capacity. And yet, for some reason, she cared what he thought—what he thought of *her*.

The arrival of an ambulance completed the traffic jam. Nobody was going anywhere anytime soon. Vivienne was still shaking, and that bothered Hank as much as it bothered her. The intelligent K-9 knew she was scared. Really scared. Events had escalated so rapidly, assuming they were all tied to her rescue of the Potter boy, that she'd been shoved off-center, off-balance. Add a handsome, caring, emotionally wounded kindred spirit to that mix and there were all the necessary elements for a meltdown.

Caleb was standing over her and Hank, keeping himself between them and the gathering crowd. Most of the spectators were behind police lines, but a few had managed to get closer and it looked as if everybody was intent on photographing her and her K-9. Cowering certainly didn't show her unit or the police force in the best light. That wasn't how she normally behaved, and no criminal was going to make her disgrace the badge.

Getting to her feet and dusting off her blue uniform, Vivienne tapped Caleb on the shoulder. "I'm taking Hank with me to the ambulance. You coming?"

"You're staying right here."

She arched an eyebrow. Tilted her head slightly. The shadow of a smile insisted on twitching at the corners of her mouth. "Don't think so."

Pivoting, he grasped her shoulders and stared into her watering eyes. "What do they have to do to make you a believer, Armstrong, level the block?"

"I'm already a believer, only not the way you mean," she snapped back. "My faith isn't built on everything going my way, it's built on trusting the Lord and knowing He will be with me through the good and the bad times. If not for you, and for Hank, of course, I could have walked right up to that package and picked it up. But I didn't do that. Same goes for the times when I was shot at and missed."

"Meaning my wife's murder could have been prevented."

"I didn't say that. I've already told you I don't know why bad things happen to good people. I do know we all have choices and those choices have consequences. But I also know that there are times when we can't win no matter how hard we try. If I were running the universe nobody would ever die. They'd all live happily ever after, like characters in a fairy tale. All pets would live forever, too. But this earth would get awfully crowded awfully fast."

"Is that supposed to be funny?" Caleb was frowning at her.

"Pragmatic," Vivienne said. Sweeping the spectators with a glance, she shouldered past him and started for the ambulance.

Her glance rose to the upper portion of her apartment building, then traveled across the street to a similar structure that shaded and closed in the street as if it were a canyon made of steel and stone.

Sighing, she quoted part of the twenty-third Psalm. "'Yea, though I walk through the valley of the shadow of death…'"

Caleb came up close behind. "What did you say?"

Rather than answer directly Vivienne continued. "'Thy rod and thy staff they comfort me,'" she said, then turned a smile on him and added, "The FBI agent makes a nice addition, too."

Spotting Gavin Sutherland among the responders, Caleb motioned him over while paramedics checked Vivienne. "You're a long way from the K-9 unit. How'd you get here so fast?"

Sutherland nodded. "I was in the area, actually, for a meeting when the call came in. I was definitely right about the safe house."

"About that. I'm not sure the safe-house-sharing business is going to work, Sergeant. Your K-9 officer is too hardheaded."

To Caleb's chagrin, Gavin chuckled. "You don't say."

"I do say. If she hadn't been worried about her dog I suspect she would have grabbed that box before it started smoking and we wouldn't be having this conversation."

"Nonsense. Vivienne Armstrong is one of my most reliable officers."

"Then I take back all the compliments I gave your unit," Caleb said, tamping down his temper. "That woman believes she's invincible."

"I doubt that very much," Gavin replied. "My team knows we're not bulletproof."

"That's not how it looks to me."

Frowning, Gavin asked, "Are you saying *you're* the one in charge of whether somebody lives or dies? That's pretty bold."

Frustrated, Caleb threw up his hands. "If we can't make a difference, why bother coming to work at all?"

"I understand you're speaking from personal experience." Gavin clapped Caleb on the shoulder and leaned in to converse privately. "Look. If I had all the answers I'd be glad to share them. I don't. None of us do. It's not our job to promise a guaranteed outcome. It's our job to do what we've been trained for, to the best of our abilities, and leave the rest to our heavenly Father."

"Even if we don't agree with the end result?"

"Especially if we don't," Gavin said, sighing and nodding. "Especially if we don't."

Vivienne wasn't concerned for herself. It was Hank's health that worried her. She knew that smoke from burning plastic could be lethal—she just wasn't sure whether or not toxic fumes had reached her beloved K-9. She allowed the medics to flush out her eyes only after they had taken care of her four-footed partner. Thankfully he wasn't acting as if he was ill or in pain.

Caleb had paused a short distance away to speak with her boss and she was pretty sure they were discussing her. That was good since she seemed to be under siege. It was much easier to bravely face aggression when it was directed against strangers and all she had to do was intercede on their behalf, which was likely the way the FBI agent felt about her. They really didn't know much about each other besides the intersection of their jobs.

That conclusion brought her up short. She knew far more about what made Caleb Black tick than he did about her. Trauma wasn't a big part of her story. She'd basically had a happy childhood, followed by college courses in law enforcement and specialized training with K-9 units. The moment she'd begun working with Hank she'd known she'd found her calling.

Sooty and looking weary, Caleb joined her. He saluted with a bottle of cold water. "Have you had anything to drink?"

"Not yet."

Presented with the bottle he'd been drinking out of, she didn't hesitate to accept. Normally she didn't share food or beverages, but in his case an exception was easy. "Thanks."

"Welcome. How's the pooch?"

Vivienne smiled. "As you can see, he's fine and raring to go again."

"What do you think about using him to check the hallway by your room? He is the main reason you stopped on the stairs, right?"

"Right. His training is search and rescue, not explosives, so another K-9 might do a better job." She scanned the surroundings, looking for her boss, then pointed. "I need to ask Sarge if he's sending Henry Roarke and his bomb-detection beagle, Cody. That's what I'd do."

It wasn't a surprise to hear Caleb chuckle. "You really like to run things, don't you?"

A smile quirked and her watery eyes focused on him. "I like to see things done properly, that's all."

He returned her grin. "Well, I hate to break this to you but nothing has changed about going to the safe house except what you get to bring. The crime-scene techs will be going over your apartment and that hallway for hours yet. What do you say we go check out our new digs and see what we need?"

With a sign of resignation, Vivienne agreed. "All right. Maybe we'll have to go shopping."

"There's bound to be some extra clothing at the house so don't worry about that."

"Aw. I was looking forward to picking up new outfits."

Judging by the way he rolled his eyes he was expecting a marathon shopping trip. Well, she'd fool him. Generally speaking, she spent more time picking out a dog toy than she did a summer outfit. Shorts and T-shirts were her go-to choices and simple flip-flops would do for shoes. Too bad she hadn't left a jogging outfit at the station.

Vivienne led the way to Gavin and watched Caleb nod when the sergeant told her exactly the same thing. She gave up. "Okay. You win. I'll go to the safe house now. Might as well since I have no home anymore."

A twinge of regret passed quickly as reality became clearer. If there had been any question about what she should do next, circumstances had ended that debate. The safe house awaited. So did her assigned guardian, although she wished she knew whether or not he truly objected to sticking so close to her. Personally, she kind of liked knowing he'd be there if she needed him.

Warmth flooded her cheeks and she bowed her head to hide the telling reaction. Any ideas she'd had about squelching her feelings regarding Caleb Black may as well be discarded. They were going to be forced to share a dwelling in spite of her misgivings and there wasn't a thing she could do to stop it, so she would try to enjoy it…but only a little.

That much mandated togetherness could certainly complicate her life, she concluded, thinking of the way her emotions had so quickly connected her to him.

She sneaked a peek and found him studying her as if she was the face on a Wanted poster. She boldly met and held his gaze. "What?"

His brow furrowed, eyes narrowing. "You like the idea."

"What are you talking about?"

"Me. You. The safe house. You think it's funny that I got stuck with you and your dog."

Well, that hurt! Vivienne managed to laugh. "It's only funny if we look on the bright side, Agent Black. Hank will love having a yard to play in, even if it's a little one. And I won't have to duck every time I step out the door."

"What about my task of babysitting? What's funny about that?"

"Not much. You're a pretty serious guy." She flashed a smile. "Maybe Hank and I can teach you how to loosen up and have a little fun."

"When I'm not busy saving your life, you mean?"

Subdued, Vivienne said, "Yeah. When nobody is trying to shoot me or blow me to bits."

ELEVEN

Brooklyn Heights was fairly quiet as Caleb cruised slowly past the designated safe house and used the electronic opener to raise the garage door. On the second pass he pulled up the narrow drive and into the garage, closing the door as soon as his SUV was clear.

Seated beside him, Vivienne had been silent during the ride. Hank gave a bark that sounded excited. Only then did she stir.

Caleb joined her as she liberated her K-9 from the rear cargo section. "Let me get his food and things for you."

"I want to see the house first," Vivienne said.

"This is the only one in Brooklyn that has any kind of yard," Caleb told her, "just in case you were thinking of rejecting it."

"I never said that."

"You didn't have to." He pulled a tagged key from his pocket and unlocked the door between the garage and house, then stood back.

"Aren't you going to go first and clear it?"

"That was done a few minutes before we arrived. But if you want me to…"

"Of course not. Besides, Hank will tell me if there's a problem."

"I've been meaning to ask you more about that," Caleb said. He followed her into the pristine kitchen. Everything except the beige tiled floor was white, which gave the room a sterile feel. It was, however, nice to be able to tell how spotless the cleaning crew had left it and the light citrus scent was pleasing.

"This, of course, is the kitchen," he said, making conversation because the silence was uncomfortable.

"Could have fooled me. I always keep my stove in the bedroom."

He chose to play along with her sarcasm. "Mine's in the garage. Then if I burn dinner the smoke alarm doesn't go off."

"Very sensible," she said as she made her way across the compact living room. "We may want to throw a sheet or blanket over the sofa. Whoever chose burgundy velour didn't have a dog with white hair."

"Okay. Let's see if we can find a linen closet."

He followed her down the hallway. "There are two bedrooms, two baths and bars on the windows for security."

"Perfect," she said.

Caleb agreed. Vivienne Armstrong was the kind of person who knew how to roll with the punches. Very few of his acquaintances shared her strength of character, let alone her sunny outlook. In a way he envied her the joy she seemed to carry with her and so freely share, yet he knew his heart would never accept such a rosy attitude.

Dark thoughts plagued him daily, so much so that he had become comfortable with them. Was that why he presently felt uneasy? For the first time in seven years, was he starting to question his mode of grieving? Experts taught that there were steps of grief to pass through and deal with. He knew that. He also knew that no two people handled loss the exact same way. Who was to say he was wrong to keep the memory of his family alive as he did? What else did he have?

Ahead of him, Vivienne passed through an open doorway and into the last bedroom. It was decorated very much like an average hotel room, as was the entire house. Heavy brocade drapes covered the single window, there was a television opposite the double bed and a digital clock radio on an end table.

"I'll take this one if you don't mind," she said. "It gives me room for Hank's portable kennel."

"I thought he stayed loose all the time when he was at home."

She smiled. "He does, unless I need him confined for some reason. We try to prepare for all eventualities and sometimes I need a break from all that canine enthusiasm."

"Right. While you look for an extra sheet to protect the couch I'll check the kitchen and see if we have enough food. I assume the crew that prepped the house took care of stocking the refrigerator, but there may be a few things you'd like that we don't have."

"Don't bother. I'm an easy keeper."

"A what?"

"Haven't you ever heard that term? It applies to animals that stay healthy and happy while eating whatever is provided and never demand more. They're easy to keep."

"Okay, then let's go get Hank's gear from my car and set you two up."

Hearing his name, the border collie pranced and circled at the end of his leash. Vivienne laughed. "I'm going to take him out in the fenced yard and make sure it's secure while you do that. He really needs exercise."

"I'll come with you."

She made a grumpy face, then modified it with a lopsided grin before she said, "I wonder if they make a kennel big enough for overly enthusiastic FBI agents."

"You'd never talk me into crawling inside so don't even try," Caleb countered. "I promise I'll stand down as soon as we've both inspected the premises."

"I will believe that when I see it." By this time she was grinning at him. "What happened to trusting the prep crew?"

Staying serious was impossible in the face of her amusement, but he did manage to temper his smile when he said, "One of us has to stay alert twenty-four-seven."

"I'll leave that to Hank." She gently patted his silky fur. "C'mon, guys. Let's see what the grass looks like out back."

He'd made certain they hadn't been followed to the safe house, yet Caleb tensed as he preceded her out the door. There was nothing fancy about the postage-stamp-size yard, but it was neatly mowed and edged against a block wall on one side, with six-foot-high, rough-cut, cedar planks on the other and at the rear. The only exit besides through the house was a narrow metal gate on the east side that was secured with a heavy chain and padlock.

In a defensive mindset, he checked neighboring

houses and noted that none provided a clear view of
the enclosed yard. That was a plus. So was the lack of
easy access from outside.

While Vivienne led Hank along the perimeter on a
leash, presumably to examine the fence, Caleb strode
to the gate and inspected the lock and chain, finding it
more than adequate. All was well.

He paused to watch her and marveled at the way she
took everything in stride. No matter what happened she
seemed to be content—once she'd voiced her opinion, at
least. That thought made him smile. Part of her charm
was the way she stood up for herself and had the courage to question authority. It probably drove her boss
up the wall, but Caleb admired her for it. To a point.

An unexplained shiver shot up his spine despite the
warm evening. Logic contradicted instinct. He chose
to listen to the latter. "Let's go get the dog's stuff. I'm
starving and unless you plan to cook, I'm going to fix
us something."

Vivienne was grinning as she returned to him with
Hank at her heels. "How does peanut butter and jelly
sound?"

"Meager. Why?"

"Because I don't cook much for myself and that's
my favorite recipe. If I want to make a fancy meal I
use jam."

Caleb had to laugh. "That settles it. I'll cook." He
had already shed his suit coat. Now he rolled up the
sleeves of his dress shirt. "The garage is locked so it's
safe for you to bring in the kennel and food. Unless you
want my help."

To his chagrin, she assured him she could manage
alone. It had taken monumental effort to offer to let her

do it without him. He wanted to be there. To guard and guide her despite her off-putting attitude toward accepting help. But *his* attitude made no sense. She was currently armed, as well as accompanied by a trained K-9. She really didn't need him to hover over her so why did he feel such a strong urge to keep doing it?

A sudden realization hit him like a baseball bat to the side of his head. Genuine need was there, of course, but the unquenchable desire to protect came from inside him. When he'd looked at Vivienne in the past he'd seen a shadow of Maggie. Heard gunshots. Felt the bullets pierce his heart.

He was well aware that Vivienne wasn't Maggie; the K-9 officer was very much her own person and he saw her for who she was. Somehow, in an astonishingly brief length of time, he'd managed to let go of his tragic past enough to begin to focus on the present. And perhaps the future, he added to himself. That notion did not sit well. Not well, at all.

Vivienne had felt a shift in the overall atmosphere in the safe house. Any change would have worried her if Hank had acted nervous. Since the K-9 was calm, she was, too. Puzzled, but calm.

Whatever Caleb was cooking smelled heavenly. "How about I set the table?"

"Good idea. I would have asked you to but I figured if I did, you'd argue against it."

She rolled her eyes and struck a theatrical pose. "Oh, please. I am not that bad. I'm just used to handling life by myself and making my own decisions. There's nothing wrong with being independent."

"Not if you add a big dose of logic." He gestured at

the pan sizzling on the stove. "It's like cooking. Leave out a key ingredient and the dish may not be edible."

"You *have* heard about my cooking!"

"Hey, I'm trying to be serious here."

She capitulated as she reached into an upper cupboard for two plates. "Sorry. I get it. I really do. It's just hard for me to admit I need help with anything. I've always taken care of myself."

"Not as a child, I assume."

Heaving a noisy sigh, she shrugged. "Not entirely, no. My parents weren't neglectful the way Penny and Bradley say theirs were. Mine just spent a lot of time working and earning enough to keep us in a nice house and provide all the extras. There were times I did wish they were at home more, particularly my mother."

"You weren't an only child," Caleb remarked without turning to watch her.

"I might as well have been." Another sigh. "My brother was a freshman in college by the time I was born. I decided early that I wanted a big family. Big and noisy like some of my friends' and filling the house with love. Sometimes it was so quiet in my childhood home it was eerie."

She left the plates on the small dinette table and returned for silverware. "How about you? Do you have siblings?"

"Nope. After we lost my dad, I was old enough to be out on my own and my mother was free to go live with her sister in Pennsylvania."

"I'm sorry about your dad," Vivienne said.

Sneaking a peek at his hand as he stirred a pot of spaghetti sauce, she noted that his wedding ring was still in place on his left ring finger. In his heart he was married. Period. Nothing was going to change that.

She couldn't help admiring him for keeping his vows, even now. That kind of love and dedication was rare and precious.

Vivienne almost—*almost*—huffed as her imagination took her deduction one step further. The man was miserable, lonely and wasting God-given years, years that he could be enjoying, at least in some regard, despite his horrific loss. And he thought *she* was the stubborn one? Ha! Caleb Black put her meager resistance to change in the minor leagues. He was by far the champ.

She didn't notice that he had turned until he said, "You look funny."

No doubt. "Funny as in laughable or funny as in strange?"

Shaking his head, he held the long-handled spoon over his cupped hand so it wouldn't drip spaghetti sauce on the floor. "Beats me. I don't know you well enough to judge. You aren't planning on skipping out on me, are you?"

"Not a chance. I've had a long talk with myself and I can see what a big mistake that would be."

"You talk to yourself?"

"Hey, you're the profiler. Doesn't everybody do that?"

"Not and expect a sensible conclusion," Caleb said.

Vivienne smiled over at him. "Not everybody has an invisible target on her back, either. I intend to stay alive to make the best of my life and I don't plan to fight the one person God is apparently using to defend me."

"I told you. I don't call myself a Christian anymore."

Her smile widened. "That's okay. You're still in the game whether you believe it or not."

TWELVE

Caleb barely tasted his meal. Few people had the ability to see past confusing circumstances and pinpoint the crux of a problem the way Vivienne did. When she'd insisted he was still being used for good, he had to agree, at least in principle. That had been his goal from the beginning. And yet, when she'd expressed that same concept he'd seen it from a different angle.

Suppose God hadn't deserted him. Suppose Caleb was the one who had turned his back. All he had to do was… What? Accept the loss of his hopes and dreams? Forgive himself for not saving his wife and their baby? Forgive God for not stepping in and stopping that fatal bullet?

His jaw set as he glanced at Vivienne across the kitchen table. She smiled back at him, then sobered when she saw his expression. "Have you been sucking on a lemon again? You sure look like it."

Caleb didn't want her to know what he was thinking. He refrained, as much to avoid an in-depth conversation as to protect her feelings. "It's been a rough day."

"Um, yeah. I noticed."

She laid her fork on her plate. "Dinner was delicious. Thank you."

"It was nothing, really."

He stood, picked up his half-eaten dinner and reached toward her plate.

She also got to her feet but didn't hand him her dirty dish. "You cooked so I'll clean up."

"Fine."

"No argument? No specific rules for washing the dishes? I'm disappointed."

He managed a smile. "You're the one who keeps trying to run things. So the cleanup is all yours. Have at it."

"What a guy," she said with a smirk. "Just when I thought you weren't going to let me do anything my way you change your tune and turn KP over to me. Thanks, FBI."

He huffed. "Don't celebrate too much. There's a dishwasher next to the sink. All you'll need to do is scrub a couple of pans."

"And feed my dog," Vivienne said. "Hank comes first."

As if to prove the point, the border collie tagged along to the sink and sat obediently next to her. Vivienne smiled at him fondly. "Yes, Hank. Your dinner is coming. I promise."

Watching the officer and her K-9, Caleb had to admit they had an amazing rapport. Her brown eyes sparkled. Her smile telegraphed gentle affection along with command. And Hank's gaze never wavered from hers as long as she was looking at him.

When he saw her lift a long string of pasta and dangle it over the dog's nose, he had to grin. They had apparently played this game before because Hank held his position, quivering and licking his lips but making no effort to lunge for the treat.

She finally said, "Take it," and the pasta disappeared in a blur.

"Finally," Caleb said. "I thought you were going to wait so long your poor dog drooled himself to death."

Vivienne laughed. "I'm not supposed to give him anything but his regulation dog food. I just can't resist adding a special treat once in a while."

"I'm astounded!" Caleb said, with an exaggerated reaction. "You broke a rule?"

"Don't you dare tell," she warned before chuckling again. "I have a reputation for perfection to protect."

He smiled again. "I don't doubt that for a second, as long as everybody else does things your way."

"Now you're catching on," she teased. "I knew you were smart."

"Being sequestered here with you and your K-9 is harder than I thought it would be," he said…very honestly. Suddenly he felt the need to come up with an excuse for what he'd just said. "It's not exactly conducive to working."

"Why not?" She was facing him, hands fisted on her hips. "We won't bother you one bit. Put your computer on the dining table and go at it. Hank and I will finish here and take a stroll around the backyard."

Caleb felt his brow begin to knit. He cast her a glance meant to warn as he said, "Inside the fence. Stay inside the fence, where you can't be seen."

"Now who's giving orders?" she countered, softening the retort with a soft laugh.

His need to protect her was stronger than he was. "I am."

"So you are. And since you happen to be right, I'll gladly promise to keep Hank in the yard."

"Thank you for that," he said.

Caleb was set up on the table as she'd suggested by the time she'd loaded the dishwasher and fed the dog. He'd hung his shoulder holster on the back of his chair and was keeping an eye on her surreptitiously. When she started down the hallway instead of heading for the back door, he asked, "Where are you going?"

"To find the extra clothing you told me about. I'd just as soon not get my uniform dirty until I know I can get a fresh one."

"Always taking chances," Caleb teased. "You just ate spaghetti while wearing your uniform."

"I know. And did dishes." Vivienne rolled her eyes. "I didn't think of changing until dinner was on the table and didn't want to hurt your feelings by being late."

"You actually thought of that? Incredible."

That brought another laugh. "You're just now discovering I'm different? Boy, you must be overtired."

"It's not being tired," Caleb argued. "It's you. You're not the easiest person to figure out." He'd stopped watching her and was focusing on the laptop, where a multitude of case files awaited. "When you get changed and done with the dog, I want to pick your brain about something."

"My brain? Why?"

"Because of the way you described your childhood," Caleb said. "That's been bothering me ever since you told me about it. I'm sure I'm not the first investigator to wonder if that may be part of the reason the McGregor and Emery parents were killed."

"My mom and dad didn't do drugs or neglect me," Vivienne countered. "They loved me. I know they did."

"Inadequate parents can love their kids deeply," Caleb said. "It's more a matter of them not knowing what's right or not being in a position to give their kids what the rest of us consider proper care and guidance."

"I'd never thought of it that way."

"Maybe we could apply that line of thinking to the possible motives that woman had for abducting the Potter boy. It's obvious his mother was taking good care of him. He was clean and healthy and happy."

"Except for his tears when he was snatched," Vivienne added. "I'd also like to figure out how one person could have done all that woman did and still take shots at me after the kidnapping attempt was foiled. I suspect she may have a partner in crime."

"That's definitely possible." He took pains to keep from looking at her because he feared his concern would show. "Go get changed and take care of your K-9. We can talk more about your case later."

"Okay. See ya."

Judging by her lighthearted-sounding reply, she wasn't too worried. That, alone, worried him more than if she had been wringing her hands and trembling with fright—which he couldn't imagine Vivienne Armstrong ever doing.

Before he realized what *he* was doing, Caleb whispered, "Father, protect her."

He stared at the computer screen, seeing nothing but his own reflection. What made him think his prayers would be heard, let alone answered? Nothing did, he realized, reaching out again with his mind. He might not be connected to God, but clearly Vivienne was, so why not pray for her safety? It couldn't hurt and there was the outside possibility it might help.

That alone was enough reason to try.

The clothing Vivienne found in the bedroom closets and dressers was adequate. Size wasn't really a problem, either, since a variety had been provided, so she donned running shorts and a tank top. She thought about laying out something casual for Caleb, then decided against it. He was a big boy. He could take care of himself, at least on a physical plane. Emotionally, not so much.

Suddenly, her alert K-9 stiffened, his hackles raised, and focused on the window. A low growl echoed in the small room.

Vivienne held out a hand to signal *stop* and crept past Hank. Blinds behind heavy drapes covered the inside of the window. She parted the fabric just enough to reach the slats in the white plastic blinds and part them with her fingertips. The trembling of her whole body made peering out more difficult, but she managed to see enough to know the threat was real. A shadowy figure emerged from the bushes and made a dash for the street.

Whirling, Vivienne raced back toward the living room. All she said was "Prowler" as she grabbed for her discarded sidearm.

That was enough to animate Caleb. He beat her to the front door and jerked it open, gun in hand, then took a shooter's stance on the porch, obviously ready to fire if necessary.

The yard was empty when Vivienne joined him seconds later. Cars continued to pass in the street but nobody was close to the house itself. "Left. He ran left," she said, almost shouting.

Caleb stopped her with an extended arm. "Stay here and watch my back."

If the order hadn't been the most sensible choice she might have balked. As things stood, the agent was making more sense than she was, considering her vulnerability standing there on the porch with Hank. She crouched. Kept Caleb in sight until he swung around the corner to where the locked gate was. Her heart was pounding so loud, so rapidly, she was sure her K-9 could hear every beat.

The moment Caleb reappeared, she took a deep breath and blew it out noisily, then asked, "Nothing?"

"Nothing. Are you sure you saw somebody?"

She was miffed and let it show. "Yes, I'm sure. I don't have to imagine threats. There are plenty of real ones around these days."

"Okay. I had to ask, though. Were you able to see a face?"

Vivienne pouted theatrically. "No. But there was a prowler. Right at my window." She edged down the porch steps, staying alert but lowering her gun to her side. "Look at the bushes. You can tell somebody went through them. See?"

"I do. Too bad it isn't safe for Hank to trail the person."

"Who says?"

"I do. Your sergeant agrees, if you'll recall. He's ordered you to stay out of sight. That's what we're doing here."

"And Hank won't work for you," Vivienne added with a frown and a shrug. "Okay. Let's go back inside before we attract too much attention."

"Right. The backyard is safer."

"When you're right, you're right," she said. "Go check it if you want to. I'm going to strap on some of my gear before I join you."

Watching Caleb leave, she couldn't help feeling thankful for his presence. He might be the most cantankerous partner she'd ever had, but he kept his head no matter what was going on around them. That was a virtue she valued beyond words.

Caleb patrolled the perimeter of the rear yard as if he was stalking an armed killer. *Which I might be*, he told himself. He had no doubt that Vivienne had spotted an interloper and under other circumstances he would have chalked it up to curious kids or nosy neighbors. However, given their current dilemma and the fact they knew so little about the threats to her life, he had to assume the worst.

"I hope she does the same," he muttered as he returned to the house. She was waiting in the kitchen with Hank at her side. To Caleb's delight both she and the dog seemed glad to see him.

"All clear," he said, eyeing her filled holster. "I'm glad you've decided to stay armed. Can't be too careful."

"Or too paranoid," she said wryly. "I'm beginning to feel for the partners of the attack and protection K-9s. This is a bit more action than I'm used to."

Caleb opened the door for her, then followed into the yard. "There's usually a lot of paperwork and desk time to my job, too," he said. "With less adrenaline."

That brought a slight smile and she nodded.

"Since the safe house has been compromised—and we have to assume the prowler wasn't random—I'm calling my boss to get us moved." At her nod, he made the call, dismayed to hear there were no other safe houses available tonight. At least a patrol car would be monitoring until morning. It wasn't enough, but he'd take what he could get.

Once they saw a patrol car parking out front Caleb relaxed…just a bit.

"Getting back to what we were talking about," Vivienne said, "boredom can have its upside. Why don't you have a seat on the steps while I exercise Hank. You can keep an eye on us from there and he won't be so distracted."

"You're sure?"

"Positive," she replied. "We all need to dial down the angst or we'll be too exhausted to be at our best."

Caleb nodded, then smiled at her. "There are moments when you actually make sense," he teased.

Vivienne's responding silly face showed that she got the joke. So did saying, "Stick around and I'll show you just how smart I can be, FBI."

After putting Hank through his paces, she let him off his leash to explore at will. The sun was setting. Fireflies blinked near the bushes as they rose in the cooler air. Their season was nearly over yet they continued to flash green, looking for a mate, never giving up as long as they lived.

She would do well to take a lesson from the insects, Vivienne told herself. Even if she got too old to have children of her own she could foster or adopt later in life. It didn't matter whether or not she ever found the perfect husband.

That conclusion took her immediately to thoughts of

Caleb Black and she darted a quick glance his way. *No, no, no! Not him. Anybody but him.* And yet...

Sighing and lifting her eyes and thoughts to heaven, she tried to picture the kind of man she wanted. "Father, you promised to supply all our needs."

Whoa! The difference hit her hard. *Needs, not wants.* So did she truly need an emotionally wounded person like Caleb? Did he need a new life partner despite his resistance to even consider it? In this case, she was delighted to turn the answers over to the Lord and let Him take charge. *Sort of.*

The added disclaimer made her smile and look again to the source of her strength and peace. "Help me do the right thing, please, Father? And not get in Your way too much."

What she yearned for was both understanding and acceptance, no matter what happened. That was a lot to ask for. And it was a lot to expect from herself. The habit of questioning authority in her workplace clearly bled over into her prayer life and that was not good. Human nature, but not good.

A bit disgusted with herself and tired of self-analysis, she opted to go back inside. "Hank. Come," she called, starting for the porch.

He stopped sniffing, raised his head and looked at her.

"Hank?"

The border collie's tail was wagging slowly. She watched his attention go from her to the side gate, then come back. Was their earlier intruder out there again? "Caleb?" she began, expressing her thoughts via a sidelong glance she was hoping he'd understand. Judging by the way he tensed and rose slowly, deliberately, he'd gotten her message.

Caleb crooked a finger at her, his gun in his other hand. "Come here."

She approached. He leaned closer as she passed. "Inside. The dog, too."

"No. I can back you up," she whispered.

The stare he focused on her had her reconsider; he *needed* to protect her, but he had to remember that she was a cop and a good one. Pride insisted that she ignore him and stand her ground. Worried that an argument might interfere with good judgment on both their parts, she chose to open the door. "Hank. Come."

Vivienne was through the doorway in seconds. To her relief, Caleb soon followed. He holstered his weapon. "I didn't see anybody, but that doesn't mean they weren't there and slipped past the patrol. Maybe we should keep trying to find another place to stay."

"There's nowhere else to go that makes sense. A hotel could put others in danger. Besides, there's a cop parked right out front and with both of us armed here inside we have the upper hand. I'm perfectly capable of backing you up, you know."

Caleb retreated. "Don't."

"Don't what?"

"Don't even think of putting yourself in harm's way to protect me."

Of course. Vivienne flashed back to his sad story. His late wife had been trying to outwit a killer and had paid the ultimate price. *Can he be right? Would I do the same?* she asked herself.

To admit it aloud would be unwise. To let herself accept the truth of the premise, however, was just as foolish. Putting her life on the line for strangers had become almost a daily occurrence. That was part of the job. But sticking her neck out beyond her sworn duty was different and that was exactly what Caleb was warning against.

Nevertheless, she knew the answer to her own question. Would she risk everything to help him, to protect him?

In her heart the truth was crystal clear. Not only would she defend him with every ability she possessed, but she was also eager to do so. There might be no such thing as love at first sight, but something had come over her in the short length of time she and Caleb Black had been thrown together. If she ever figured out how she felt and why, she might even tell him.

A heaviness descended over Vivienne. Imagining either of them losing a chance to find out if they belonged together was one of the saddest ideas she'd ever had. She had to take care of him, to see that he came out of this alive and well. Whether he liked it or not.

THIRTEEN

"Ice cream?" Caleb looked up from his computer as Vivienne joined him. "Now?"

"Think of it as medicine. Any woman will tell you it can cure just about anything."

"Even criminals' need to get revenge?" He waited, expecting a contradiction.

"Maybe not that. I still plan to polish off this pint." She frowned. "I am sorry I reminded you of a terrible time in your past."

Before he could come up with a platitude or change the subject, Vivienne licked the spoon and said, "I know it's impossible to stop that from happening, but I promise to do my best to avoid reminding you of your late wife."

Caleb was slowly shaking his head as he leaned back, away from the table holding his laptop. "That's not going to work."

"Why not?" she asked, taking another spoonful of ice cream.

"Because you're a lot like her. It's not your hair or eyes or anything like that. It's what's inside, what makes you tick."

"Is that so bad?"

Watching her for clues to underlying secrets, he shrugged. "So how many times did you run away from home?"

Her jaw dropped. Moments passed.

"Wow. You are a profiler!"

"Told you. You did tell me you weren't neglected but that you had a lonely childhood." He straightened in the chair and turned back to his computer. "I got to thinking about this when I was going over the murder files looking for similarities. Both Penelope McGregor and Lucy Emery were in day-care facilities that had extended hours, most days for fourteen, sixteen hours a day. I'm not saying there's anything wrong with day care—it's a necessity for working parents. But the extended hours struck me. Both sets of parents were barely part of the children's lives. I wonder if the killer—or killers—saw himself as a vigilante who had been similarly treated." He shrugged. "I keep coming back to that. There's not much personal info about Randall Gage in his file. But why would he have targeted the McGregors when there was no other connection between them? Why spare the child? Why give the child a stuffed toy?"

Vivienne nodded. "Talk to my sergeant about your theory in the morning," she said. "And my colleague, K-9 officer Belle Montera's fiancé, Emmett Gage, might be able to offer some insight into his cousin's upbringing. I don't think he and Randall Gage were close, but Emmett could have some information."

He nodded, taking notes as she spoke.

"And by the way, I was never mad at my parents," Vivienne insisted.

"Are you close to them now?"

The lack of a quick answer told him all he needed to know about her thoughts on the subject. "It's not bad to pull away from destructive personality types," Caleb said. "You just don't intend to let anybody else hurt you."

"Nobody wants that."

Caleb could tell she was getting upset so he dialed back his profile of her. "I overheard you telling Penny McGregor that you want a big family, lots of kids. Is that right?"

"Yes. So?"

"So is that really what you want or are you hoping to repair the damage your absent parents did by opening your home and heart to a bunch of kids in need and loving them all?"

Ignoring her gaping mouth and widening eyes, Caleb went on. "This may be why you haven't found a husband."

Her jaw snapped shut, eyebrows arching. "I beg your pardon."

"Being cautious about choosing a mate isn't a fault, Vivienne. It's a virtue. You're brave about everything else. Ask yourself if it's not high time you showed courage about dating."

"Me? What about you?"

He frowned. "We're not talking about me."

"Well, maybe we should be."

Raising both hands, Caleb made the sign of a *T.* "Time-out. I apologize for profiling you when that's not what we're here for."

Flashes of conflicting emotions passed across her face, ending when she took a deep, settling breath and let it out with a whoosh. "Okay. I forgive you. Sort of." She made a face. "So what do you think about the

Potter boy's kidnapper? Having met the mother, Susanna, and Jake, I doubt his abductor did it because she
thought he'd been neglected."

"You're absolutely right. I've been researching local
disappearances of other male toddlers but haven't come
up with any new leads. That's one reason I suspect a
mental illness that may be long-standing. If the woman
who snatched Jake experienced the loss of a child, no
matter when it happened, she may be stuck in a time
warp and be trying to replace a baby she lost years ago.
That gives us far too many possibilities to check out."

"So what else can we do?"

"I think we should start by talking to Mrs. Potter one
more time, the way we'd planned. I have a transcript of
her previous interview from right after the abduction,
but that doesn't show me everything I can deduce in a
face-to-face meeting. Sometimes it's not so much what
a person says as the way they say it."

"My K-9 liked her."

Caleb had to laugh. "That's your criteria?"

"It's a start," Vivienne said. "I'd sooner trust the
opinion of this dog than half the people I know."

"Amen to that," he said without thinking, then sought
to redirect her. "Your ice cream is melting."

"Guess I'll have to hurry and eat the whole carton,
then, huh? What a shame. I was planning on offering
some to you."

"Let me at that ice cream," he said.

She laughed and handed him a spoon. He had to
admit it felt good that they were "okay" again.

If Vivienne hadn't been bone-tired she might have
had more trouble sleeping. The presence of Hank,

curled up at the foot of the bed, did have a calming effect. Yes, he was going to get spoiled and probably need extra refresher training, but that wasn't the end of the world. All the K-9s and handlers went through mandated repetitions, although not necessarily for the same reasons.

She awoke before morning. Hank growled. He was standing at the foot of the mattress, staring at the window, illuminated by light from the motion sensors in the front yard. Someone was outside.

Heart racing, Vivienne reached for her holster and drew her gun. Knowing that nobody could get to her through that barred window wasn't enough. She had to meet possible threats head-on. Police training was useless if she failed to use it.

Hank never moved from the bed, but his focus did shift from the outside to inside. Soon, he was staring at the closed and locked bedroom door. His growling deepened. The doorknob started to move, to turn slightly. Then something rattled at the window and the dog's attention changed.

Vivienne didn't know which threat to respond to first. Hank seemed concerned about both areas, but did either pose danger? She edged toward the window without turning on the lights. The room was small enough to navigate in near darkness and she didn't want to silhouette herself against the blinds. A sharp rap on her door made her jump. Hank barked ferociously.

"Vivienne?" Caleb called, "Are you all right?"

"Yes." Irrational ire rose. "What are you doing wandering around in the middle of the night scaring me to death?" She pulled on a robe over the extralong man's T-shirt she been sleeping in and belted it.

Unlocking the door and jerking it open, she faced Caleb, her gun pointed at the ceiling, the safety on.

"I thought I heard something outside," he said.

Ah, so it was Caleb who'd set off the motion sensors. "Yeah, so did Hank. You. Why did you go outside?"

She saw the muscles in his jaw clenching. His posture gave new meaning to the definition of "tense." When he said, "I haven't been outside," she felt her heart race.

"You haven't?"

"No." Peering past her, Caleb studied the K-9. Hank was still concentrating on the barred window. "Stay here. I'm going to check the yard."

"I'm going with you."

"No. You are not," Caleb said firmly.

She knew where his overprotectiveness was coming from, but he had to get it through his stubborn head that she was a police officer.

"Caleb, I'm a cop. We need to work as a team. The sooner we check to see who or what is bothering Hank, the sooner we can relax."

"I have full respect for your abilities and training, Vivienne. I just—"

He didn't finish his sentence.

She stood firm, shoulders squared. "Let's go, then."

"What about Hank?"

"I want him inside for now so I don't have to worry about him. If we don't find a prowler, I'll harness him to track." Vivienne could tell from the stubborn set of Caleb's jaw that he disagreed once again. Thankfully, he was in too much of a hurry to stop and argue.

The motion-sensor outdoor lights were still activated when Caleb and Vivienne stepped outside. The patrol officer was looking around, shining his flashlight, and let them know he'd hurried over to check front and back when the lights came on, but didn't see anyone. They thanked the officer, who went back to his car.

They searched the yard themselves—no sign of the intruder—and then went back inside.

"Whoever they were, they were scared off," Caleb concluded.

"So now what?"

The tremor in Vivienne's voice touched his heart. Courage was shown by pushing ahead despite normal fear and he had to admire her for it. "Now, I guess we go back to sleep," he said.

"Is that what you plan to do?"

"Probably."

"Meet me in the kitchen instead."

"Why?" Caleb asked. "Is there another pint of ice cream calling your name?"

"Something like that. I may make hot chocolate if we have the ingredients."

He glanced at the clock on the wall. "It's barely five in the morning. We need to sleep more."

"Speak for yourself, FBI. Hank and I are both wide awake and I don't intend to just lie there and stare at the ceiling. I need chocolate. Or maybe just coffee. A lot of coffee."

"And company?" Caleb asked.

"And company," Vivienne admitted. "Know any FBI agents who'd like to join me?"

"I can think of one."

"Good. Give me five minutes. I'm not going to hang around in this ugly robe."

He had to chuckle. He palmed his cell phone and called Gavin Sutherland's private number.

"It's five a.m. This better be important" replaced a standard hello.

"It is," Caleb said. "I can't talk long. Just wanted you to know we've had two more indications that a prowler was outside."

"Are you both all right? The K-9, too?"

"Yes. For a tracking dog he sure has a lot of other useful tricks. He's usually the first one to alert to anything unusual."

"That may be advantageous now, but when he's working he's not supposed to be easily distracted. You're probably ruining a good dog."

"If it keeps Vivienne alive and well, it's worth it," Caleb countered. "Considering all the trouble we've faced since we got here, I suggest you bring her and Hank back into regular service and let them work while I try to come up with a safer place for them to stay."

"Speaking of sticking around, what are your plans? Have you interviewed the Potter woman again? And what about finishing those profiles we need?"

"I'm close to making a report about the murders," Caleb assured him. "In the meantime, I'll stick to Vivienne—I mean Officer Armstrong—like a bulletproof shield."

"You do that," Gavin said. "See you in a few hours."

Caleb was lowering his phone when Vivienne reappeared. His breath caught. Before, she'd been a jogger or a police officer in uniform. Now she looked so feminine he hardly recognized her. She wore a tank top with a ruffle at the neck and a knee-length flippy skirt.

Rather than sound too serious, he quipped, "How do you do, ma'am. I don't believe we've met."

But Vivienne was looking at what he still held—his cell phone. "I didn't hear any phones ring."

"Mine's on silent," Caleb said.

"Care to tell me who you were talking to?"

"I reported to your sergeant about the repeat prowler. There's no point in trying to move safe houses this morning if this one was so easily compromised. I'm sure you'll get word from Gavin shortly. I suggested he put you back to work."

"Hooray!"

"Nice outfit."

She turned in a circle, making the skirt swirl gracefully around her knees. "I don't know what came over me. I was reaching for the clothes I wore last night when I saw this in the closet. Kind of makes me feel like going to church."

"Church?"

"Sure. I felt at home there. Besides, they held a lot of church suppers where a kid like me could get a great meal," she added. "My parents were rarely home so I had to fend for myself."

"You didn't care for the peanut butter sandwiches you told me were your specialty?"

"Not as a steady diet."

He glanced out the window; the sun was just rising. "Now I'm kind of hungry. Bacon and eggs?"

She smiled. "Sounds very good."

He got to work and quickly dished up two plates and put them on the table, then poured coffee for them both and joined her. "Cream or sugar?"

"I'll get it." Jumping up before he could protest, she

scanned the counter for a sugar bowl, then went to the refrigerator for the milk she knew was there, bringing both back with her.

Caleb raised a hand to shield his steaming mug. "None for me."

"I know. I remember. Black to match your name. But I may want a second cup. This is so much better than the coffee at work."

"Anything is better than cop coffee."

"Can't argue with you there." She sipped hers, then started on a crisp strip of bacon. "Just the way I like it. A visit to the Potters is first on our agenda for today, right?"

"Right. It's going to be our job to convince her to leave Brooklyn until the kidnapper is caught."

"I'll take Hank along. The little boy loved him."

"Yeah, he did. I was surprised that a working K-9 was so friendly with civilians."

"It's the breed. And Hank's training. He was never taught to be defensive."

She noted Caleb's scowl before he said, "You're kidding."

"No. Why?"

"He's been looking out for you up until now."

"When he alerts it's instinct, not training. He wouldn't hurt a fly, let alone take down an assailant." She paused for emphasis. "Besides, I don't want to see him hurt."

"Of course not." Caleb peeked beneath the table. "Where is he, anyway?"

"Outside. I took a quick look around. It's still secure and the patrol officer is still here."

"Good." A shadow of doubt seemed to fall on Caleb's

expression. His green eyes darkened. "Maybe it would be best if you let me visit Mrs. Potter and the boy by myself. You could catch up on paperwork and stay at the K-9 unit."

"In your dreams," Vivienne countered.

"No, in *Brooklyn*," Caleb joked.

"That is so not funny. Don't even consider leaving me out of this. I was never a target until I stopped that kidnapping. I deserve to be included."

He was shaking his head. "The kidnapper is after you, Vivienne. You've been shot at multiple times. And she, or an accomplice, may even have found you here. She'll stop at nothing until she has some kind of payback for you foiling the kidnapping. Don't you owe it to your unit and to your K-9 to take all necessary precautions?"

"We'll see," she said. "I'll wait until eight to call the station—that's when Gavin arrives. So for now, I'll clean up since you cooked and then take a hot shower and get ready for work."

She cleared their plates, refusing offers of help. He thanked her and headed to the living room with his laptop. She was both glad to have some distance and kind of missed him at the same time.

It was against Vivienne's nature to waste a minute but this morning was the exception. She took her time getting ready, since they had time to kill. She played with Hank, then prepared for her interview with Mrs. Potter and that sweet little Jake. Finally, she dressed in her uniform and made sure she had everything she needed for work. Then she took a deep breath and headed for the living room...and Caleb Black.

"I'll go take a quick shower myself," he said.

She nodded, then pulled her cell phone out of a pocket and pressed the speed dial for her station. It wasn't exactly 8:00 a.m., when Gavin usually arrived, but it was close enough.

Penny answered. "Brooklyn K-9 Unit. How can I help you?"

"Hi, Penny. It's me, Vivienne. I need to speak with Gavin."

"Sorry. He's not in yet. What's the problem? Is the FBI getting on your nerves?"

Hearing a friendly voice helped immensely. Smiling, Vivienne cradled the phone and spoke quietly, knowing her companion was bound to overhear since he was still in the hallway, but she was unwilling to seek seclusion. Besides, she didn't intend to say anything that needed to be kept from him.

"My last nerve just left," she said. "Gavin told me—us—to interview Susanna Potter today, but a certain FBI agent is trying to keep me out of it."

"I take it he's not succeeding."

"No, he isn't." She raised her glance to meet Caleb's and felt the force of his will zinging up her spine. "I just wanted Gavin to know what was going on in case this agent decides to lock me in a closet or something."

"Is that a possibility?"

She heard Caleb's bedroom door close. "Let's hope not."

Penny chuckled.

"We'll be leaving in around twenty minutes for the Potters'. I'll have my radio, but you can still reach me by phone if you want to keep it private."

"Gotcha." Penelope giggled. "Have a nice day."

Fifteen minutes later, Caleb was back, looking too handsome. "Ready?"

"Ready," she said. "I didn't get to speak to Gavin yet. I'll catch him when I get a chance."

He only nodded at that and they headed out, both of them on red alert. Vivienne didn't see anyone or anything suspicious and Hank was calm. They stopped to let the patrol officer know they were leaving for good and thanked him for helping out.

Vivienne was still wary as she loaded Hank in the back and climbed into the passenger side of the SUV. It didn't help to see Caleb acting as if they were about to pull out into an active war zone instead of a peaceful neighborhood. "We *will* catch the kidnapper-shooter— and her accomplice if she's working with one. I know we will. She'll trip up. She's already taking too many unnecessary risks," Vivienne insisted.

He glanced at her. "I'm the one who's supposed to predict people's behavior," he said. "But I agree. Luckily, Hank's a great judge of danger. That makes me feel better about your safety."

"Hank is good that way—easy to read. If he growls he's upset. If his tail wags, he's happy. I can't tell from minute to minute what's going on in *your* head."

When he stared at her with those piercing eyes, she wondered even harder what he was thinking.

"You're probably better at reading me than you think," he said. "I wish you weren't, actually," he added with a smile.

Vivienne mirrored his grin. "Think about it this way. Suppose you needed to defend me, as you already are, but I needed to come to your aid, too. You'd be glad I could read you enough to know how to help."

"I don't need anybody's help."

She refused to argue. Time would tell. If and when he decided to unburden himself or asked for counsel, she'd be there. If he never did, then so be it, but she was going to be terribly disappointed.

It dawned on Vivienne that if she was having this much trouble letting go of her desire to help Caleb, how much worse must it be for him to feel the weight of how he'd lost his wife and baby every moment of every day. It was a wonder he was functional at all, let alone as good at his job as he was.

She purposely changed the subject. "Have you come to any new conclusions about the Potter kidnapping?"

"Suppositions only," he answered. "We know we're dealing with at least one middle-aged woman. She took a young child for no apparent external reason, so chances are she's looking for a replacement for a child she lost or wanted and never had."

"Okay. If she's open to taking any kid, why is she so mad at me for ruining her plans? Jake Potter must have something special about him or she'd just move on to another target."

She knew she'd impressed him when he said, "I agree. I wish I had more to go on, but that's my guess. A lot of what I do utilizes logic and past experience."

"So a lot of the time you're guessing?"

"I'm not crazy about that term, but yes. Sometimes. It's an educated guess. Just like your conclusion about the kidnapper's motives. The same goes for the profile I've worked out for the McGregor and Emery homicides. Despite the similarities, I think the Emerys were murdered by a copycat—not Randall Gage. Twenty years between the cases? And remember, Gage's DNA wasn't in the system otherwise, so he either hadn't committed other murders or had been careful. He certainly wasn't careful enough at the McGregor house to notice his watch had fallen off."

"Good point," she said, nodding.

"I think he specifically murdered the McGregors, then moved on. And twenty years later, something triggered the copycat, maybe a news report about the decades-old cold case. Of course, I can't be sure, but that's my educated guess."

"Too bad we don't have DNA from the Emery crime scene. A forensic scientist is working on fibers taken from the site, but so far, we don't have anything."

"Well, at least your unit has identified the McGregor murderer. Now all you have to do is catch him. Something tells me he fled upstate, where I'd been looking for him last month, and then came back to where it's easier to hide—New York City."

"Yeah. Maybe," Vivienne said wryly. "New York isn't that big a city. All we'll have to do is eliminate a couple hundred thousand men Randall Gage's age and description and we'll have him. Easy-peasy. Oh, and I *am* coming with you to interview Mrs. Potter, so you may as well head straight over there."

He glanced at her. "Stubborn."

She laughed. "I'm the stubborn one?" She shook her head and even Caleb had to smile.

FOURTEEN

Caleb drove to the Potter apartment and flashed his badge to the patrolman standing guard on the sidewalk. "We'll be inside for about a half hour."

"My relief is due any minute," the young officer said. "I'll wait and tell him you're in there."

Nodding, Caleb shepherded Vivienne and Hank ahead of him. "Potters are on the third floor. Does Hank do elevators?"

"If you mean is he scared of them, no. If you're asking does he push the call button himself, no again."

He smiled. "A lack in his training, obviously. I was expecting him to choose the right floor, too."

"He could if I taught him to. It's scary how intelligent our dogs are, especially my Hank."

"Is he the first K-9 you've worked with?" Caleb asked as they boarded and started up.

"Yes. I'm really going to miss him when he ages out of the program. When he does, I'll adopt him. The majority of police dogs are adopted by their handlers." She smiled at Hank. "Then he can spend his old age napping on a soft blanket and vegging out."

"Sounds good to me."

"Are you planning on that for your retirement?"

The elevator doors slid open. Caleb led the way out so he could check the hallway. "You know how it is in our business. Long-range plans are daydreams."

"Right." She was watching Hank sniff the floor. "They know we're coming, don't they?" she asked as they headed down the hall.

"Your boss spoke with Mrs. Potter yesterday and let her know an FBI agent and the K-9 officer who got Jake back would be by to interview her."

He knocked on the door. Noises from inside were muted, mostly covered by the traffic in the street and sounds from nearby apartments.

"Mrs. Potter," Caleb called. "My name is Caleb Black. I'm with the FBI." He held up his badge wallet in front of the peephole on the door.

"And Vivienne Armstrong with the Brooklyn K-9 Unit," she added. "I have my working dog with me."

Stirring behind the apartment door was followed by a high-pitched order. "Stand in front of the peephole and back up. Never mind the badges. Those can be faked. I want to see your faces and the dog."

Seconds after they complied, locks clicked and the door was opened. "Sorry. I wanted to be sure."

"Perfectly understandable," Caleb said. "I'm Agent Black, FBI. You already know Officer Armstrong and Hank."

Tears filled the mother's eyes. She reached for Vivienne's free hand. "Yes. Thank you again. I owe you so, so much. Please, come in and sit down. Can I get you something to drink? Coffee? Tea?" Her hands were fluttering like a bird with a broken wing.

Vivienne led the way as Caleb assessed the small

apartment. It was neat, though cluttered. A plastic laundry basket filled with child's toys sat in the center of a worn rug.

"Your son isn't here?" Caleb asked.

"He's still asleep. Last night he was so restless since…well, you know, that I let him nap whenever he would. I can wake him if you want."

"Maybe before we leave so he can hug my dog," Vivienne said. "It's you we came to see." She smiled. "Please, sit down."

Caleb had never seen Vivienne working with a victim before. He was impressed. And, since the nervous woman seemed to take to another female better than to him, he backed off and let her continue while he took notes.

"I told the police all I know," Susanna said, perching on the edge of a chair while keeping an eye on the interior hallway.

"We read your statement, Susanna. May I call you Susanna?"

"Of course."

"Good. I'm Vivienne and this is Hank." She smiled and stroked her K-9's head as he lay at her feet. "There have been some new developments since your ordeal on the promenade and we need to ask you a few questions."

The fluttery hands clasped together. "I'll help if I can. I want that awful person behind bars."

"I'm certain the kidnapper was a woman. The police report notes that Jake said 'a lady took him.'"

Susanna nodded. "Right. I never saw her."

Caleb wanted to jump in but refrained, watching Vivienne's composure and marveling at how calm she seemed. If he hadn't known how important this interview was to her he'd have thought she didn't have a worry in the world.

"When I brought him back to you and officers were questioning the two of you, Jake said he didn't recognize her. Has he said otherwise since?"

She shook her head. "No. He kept saying 'Stranger danger' so he made it crystal clear he'd never seen her before."

"How about you?" Vivienne asked, leaning forward slightly, elbows on her knees. "Do you think you may have passed somebody wearing a gray hoodie and walking shorts before you stopped to look at the boats in the river?"

Tears glistened. "I don't know. I've been wracking my brain ever since it happened. So many people dress that way so I'm sure I did, but we hardly ever look at faces, do we? I mean, the city is full of them but they kind of all blur together."

"Unless we have a good reason to notice. Now, you do. How about since? Have you seen anybody like that hanging around?"

"Here?" She jumped to her feet and began to pace. "What's going on? Do you think she'll come back for my baby?"

Caleb thought he was going to have to intervene but Vivienne reached out. "I didn't mean to make you worry. A patrol officer will be stationed outside until she's caught—you already know that, so that has to give you some peace of mind. And we're working very hard to figure out who she is." Susanna seemed to calm and she sat back down. Vivienne smiled gently. "We just have a few more questions. I promise. Agent Black has a sketch for you to look at."

Pulling a piece of white paper from his coat pocket, he unfolded it and passed it to the fearful mother. "How about this? Have you noticed anybody who looks like her?"

Susanna's hands were shaking. She dashed away stray tears then accepted the computer-generated image. Her brow furrowed.

"Does she look familiar?" Caleb prodded.

"I'm not sure. I'd like to say no but there's something about her that *does* seem familiar. A photograph would be better."

Vivienne's raised hand stopped him from commenting. He sat back and waited. It seemed as if the ensuing minute took thirty to pass. Finally, she said, "Why don't you just start talking? Say anything that pops into your head, even if it seems silly."

"Well…while looking at that picture, I keep thinking of shopping. Fresh produce, maybe. It's almost like I smell ripe cantaloupes. That can't be right. There were no fruit stands by the river."

"No, but you may have subconsciously provided a clue."

"How?"

Caleb finally took over. "Because we strongly suspect that the abduction was not spur-of-the-moment. We think it was planned and carried out after observing you and your son for some time, meaning the perpetrator is likely someone from this neighborhood."

"What?" She was on her feet again. "Why?"

"Because of what's been happening to Officer Armstrong, to Vivienne. There have been specific threats." Experience told him to hold back the more violent details. "Whoever was responsible for taking Jake has zeroed in on her and her K-9 for foiling the abduction. If the kidnapping had been random, the perpetrator should have moved on to a different child, maybe even a different borough. Right now we're concentrating our efforts in Brooklyn, specifically near the promenade."

Speechless, Susanna Potter sank into a chair, acting as if her legs would no longer support her.

"In your previous interview you stated that you took Jake there nearly every morning. Is that correct?"

"Yes. It's such a nice place to get some air."

"Have you been there since?" She knew the answer but wanted to make certain.

"I haven't left this apartment. I'm afraid to."

Rising to move closer, Vivienne commanded Hank to stay and crouched in front of the frightened mother, gently touching her forearm. "We want to suggest that you leave the city for a short time. Is there anywhere you can go? A friend you can stay with, maybe?"

"Preferably not close family," Caleb added. "If you've been targeted the kidnapper may have learned a little about your relatives. It's not as likely, but it is possible."

"Jake's godmother lives in Idaho," Susanna said softly. "We went to college together. I can call her and ask."

"We'll supply a new phone in case your old one has been compromised. You'll need to write down any pertinent information so we can get in touch with you once this case is solved."

Vivienne had remained at Susanna's feet. Now, she straightened and pulled up the fearful woman beside her. "I'll help you pack while Agent Black takes care of the details. Give us your friend's name and address so he can book a flight." A hand signal brought Hank to her side. "Let's go surprise Jake with a visit from his favorite K-9 and let them get reacquainted while we pack."

Smooth, Caleb thought. Calmly and successfully done with no hair-pulling or wailing. The K-9 cop was good at her job.

Meaning this was exactly where she belonged, he concluded. There was no way he'd be able to talk her into going into another line of work for her own safety, nor would he try.

For a reason he was nowhere near ready to accept, that conclusion hurt.

Little Jake wasn't asleep. The moment he spotted his furry rescuer he jumped out of bed and threw his arms around the K-9's neck. "I love puppies!"

"Hank loves you, too, honey, but you need to remember that not all dogs are this friendly," Vivienne warned.

Susanna reaffirmed it. "That's right, baby. There are mean doggies, too. You need to ask Mommy before you try to hug them."

His shoulders sagged and he lowered his arms. "Sorry."

Vivienne had one hand on Hank's silky fur to help keep him from getting too excited while he was harnessed to work. "It's okay this time. Just keep him company more quietly. See his vest? That means he's on the job and shouldn't be playing."

Wide, innocent blue eyes looked up at her. "Take it off."

"I can't do that right now," Vivienne said. "You and your mom are going to take a trip. Why don't you go

pick out a couple of toys to take with you? Ones that
will fit into a suitcase, okay?" Seeing him shy away
and retreat to his bed, she smiled. "It's okay. Hank and
I will go with you to the airport. We'll keep you safe.
I promise."

"I don't wanna go."

"You and your mother will get to ride on a big air-
plane. It'll be fun. You'll see."

As he pulled the cover over his head, she heard a
muffled "No."

There were tears in Susanna's eyes. "I can't make
him go out when he's so scared."

"You need to take care of him the best way possible
and if that means leaving the city, you will. You must."

"Why? Just because you say there were threats? Because you and the FBI agent have made up your minds
we're in danger? I don't think so."

Vivienne told Hank to stay. "Let's leave your little
boy where he is and go to your room."

"I'm not packing a bag because I'm not leaving."

"Fine. We still need to talk privately. Please?" Leading the way into the hall, Vivienne eased the door to
the boy's room closed, then did the same to the room
she and Susanna entered.

The slightly younger woman struck a pose, hands
fisted on her hips. "I'm not changing my mind."

"That's your prerogative. I was hoping I wouldn't
have to tell you what's happened to me, but I can see
no alternative."

The tilt of Susanna's head and the dubious-looking
arch of her eyebrows affirmed Vivienne's decision to
speak out. "Since Hank tracked down your son and

his kidnapper from the promenade, I've been shot at. And stalked."

"No!"

"Yes. There has been a threatening phone call made to the station, too." She paused, then added the most frightening event. "A bomb was left outside the door to my apartment. I was staying in an FBI safe house, but it was compromised."

Susanna bit her lip.

"That doesn't matter. What does is that I'm a sworn, armed police officer and I've had to move my residence…temporarily. You're a civilian who has to rely on outside sources of protection that may or may not be available when you need them."

The other woman sank onto the edge of her bed and doubled over, head in her hands. "This is a nightmare."

"I won't argue that. What you need to remember is that your little boy is counting on you to do what's best for him. In my opinion, the best thing is to leave here, where you're known, and go someplace new. If money is a problem there are programs that will help out. You might even qualify for temporary relocation if…" Vivienne had an idea. "I'll be right back."

Caleb rose when she reentered the living room. "Is she ready to go?"

"Not quite." She held out a hand. "Give me that printout of the face."

The instant he produced it she snatched it from him and whirled. Susanna had gone to her son's room and was rocking him while she wept silently.

Vivienne didn't hesitate. "Jake. Remember the bad stranger who grabbed you?"

Susanna pulled him closer, shielding his face. "Get away. You're scaring him."

"No. This is necessary. Please. Let him look at this picture." She crouched next to the bed and drew her K-9 into the group. "My dog isn't scared to look. See?"

One big blue eye peeked from behind Susanna's shoulder.

"It's just a piece of paper with a drawing on it. All you need to do is look at it and tell me if this is the bad lady."

Wiggling, he turned slightly in his mother's arms.

Vivienne smoothed the folds in the paper and held it up for him. One look and terror filled his features. She didn't need verbal confirmation although she got it, anyway, when the boy screeched and threw both arms around his mother's neck.

That poor boy. If leaving filled him with terror, which Vivienne just added to, maybe staying in the apartment would be okay for a little while. She and Caleb would just have to find the kidnapper—and Vivienne's stalker—fast. "Okay. I'm convinced that staying might be in Jake's best interest," Vivienne said. "Stay put. I'll go tell Agent Black."

"Wait!" Susanna said with a shudder. "Tell him to get the tickets. I'll call my boss and ask for some time off. We're leaving."

FIFTEEN

Caleb was still working with law enforcement to arrange a relocation for a safe house for him and Vivienne, using his office as liaison, when they reached the airport. JFK was a main hub so there was plenty of traffic and good opportunities to lose themselves in the crowds, particularly in Terminal 8.

He turned to Vivienne. "You stand out like a beacon. You and the dog should stay with my SUV. We'll use the daily parking to unload baggage and I'll escort our guests to their gate. That way I'll know exactly where you are."

"Excuse me?"

"Sorry. I'll rephrase. Officer Armstrong, since your uniform and K-9 will make you particularly visible to one and all, would you please stay with my car? I would be most grateful and it is best for my other passengers if they don't attract attention while boarding."

"Well, since you put it that way…"

"Good."

Caleb handled Mrs. Potter's wheeled suitcase while she carried her toddler. Traffic was thick. Their only obstacles were taxis that were permitted to unload directly in front of the terminal and were jockeying for curb space.

On full alert, he took Susanna Potter's arm to hurry her safely past. "Once you're through TSA you'll be going on alone," Caleb said.

"No!"

"You'll be fine at that point." He kept walking. "I don't want to call attention to my FBI status by flashing a badge and insisting I wait with you at the gate. My office has stationed extra uniformed transit cops near your departure point so feel free to ask any of them for assistance if you feel you need it."

"What about when we land?"

"You'll be met by local police and escorted to your friend's home. From there on it's up to you to be vigilant. Little Jake can ID his kidnapper so it's really imperative to keep him safe and secluded."

"You don't think that awful woman would try to follow us, do you?"

"No, I really don't. Jake will be safe now." He set her bag on the TSA conveyor belt and handed her the ticket folder. "Boarding pass is in there. Get out your driver's license and you're good to go."

Monitoring her travels through the security system, he stayed on edge until the call for boarding, when she passed through the final checkpoint. Nobody without a valid ticket could catch up to her now, which is why his next stop was the airline ticket counter, where he inquired about available seating, just in case.

"I'm sorry, sir. That flight is fully booked. I can get you a seat for this afternoon."

"Everybody has checked in already?"

"Yes, sir."

"No chance of last-minute openings?"

"Sorry. No."

"Okay. Never mind. I'll pass this time."

Leaving the counter attendant looking puzzled, Caleb turned and strode toward the exit. The sooner he rejoined Vivienne, the happier he'd be.

He was jogging by the time he turned the last corner and spied his vehicle. He'd purposely parked with the hood and front bumper sticking out beyond others in the row, making it easy to spot from a distance.

Arriving at the driver's door, he grabbed the handle and jerked. Locked. Tinted windows kept him from seeing inside clearly. He cupped his hands around his eyes and peered through, expecting either the uniformed officer or the dog or both.

Not only was Vivienne missing, but her K-9 was, too!

Vivienne had meant to keep her promise to Caleb. And she would have if she hadn't thought she'd spotted the very woman who had become her nemesis.

The sun was high, making it hard to see details clearly, so she opted for taking a couple of photos with her phone. Everything about this person was screaming that she was the right one. So now what? If she failed to follow her, to see where she went and who she might be with, she'd be giving up a chance to put an end to the harassment. And to the life-threatening attacks.

The woman didn't come closer, as Vivienne had hoped. Instead, she was wandering around the lot as if she'd forgotten where she'd parked. Maybe she wasn't who Vivienne had thought she was after all. The only way to find out was to follow her.

Slipping from the SUV with Hank leashed at her side, Vivienne had ventured a short way from Caleb's vehicle. Never once did she make eye contact with her quarry, but after a few minutes she did conclude that the woman's movements appeared more furtive than before. Not only that, but she and her dog were also getting farther and farther from the FBI car.

Vivienne was staring at the computer-generated images stored on her cell phone when it vibrated. *Caleb.* If their witness was safely in the air it would be a relief.

The booming voice that answered her pleasant "hello" was so loud she held the phone away.

"Where are you?" he demanded.

"Not far. I think the kidnapper may be here," Vivienne said. "I tried to get a good picture, but she was looking the other way, so I—"

"Tell me you didn't go after her."

"Calm down. I'm an armed law-enforcement officer, remember? I think Hank may be able to track her scent if I can show him which one I want him to follow."

"No!"

"Yes. You're blowing this way out of proportion." Her breathing was rapid as she swiveled to reassess her surroundings. "And now you've made me lose sight of her."

"Direction?"

"Why?"

"North, south, east or west? I'm coming. You need backup."

"Don't." Vivienne huffed, knowing he was right. "Okay, I'll turn back. The heat is starting to bother Hank, and we can cover the parking lot faster in your SUV. Be right there."

Relying on her sense of direction, and on Hank, she ended the phone conversation and made her way toward Caleb as quickly as possible, cutting across lanes and slipping between parked vehicles until she could finally see him. His tie was loosened and hanging lopsided, his face was flushed and his hair looked as if he'd been repeatedly running his fingers through it. Poor guy. He looked nearly frantic. And for no reason. She was fine.

Vivienne stepped into view and waved her arm overhead, intending to put his mind at ease first, then chastise him later when he'd settled down. It was one thing to show concern for a partner in the field and quite another to become unnecessarily distressed.

Caleb turned back to the black SUV without any more acknowledgment of her than a nod, calling over his shoulder.

She started down a row of cars, keeping Hank on a loose lead. Her mind was centered on Caleb, which bothered her because she knew the distraction was counterproductive. What she… What they both should be thinking about was doing their jobs, starting with the possibility that she actually had spotted her elusive stalker.

If she got another opportunity, she'd try to put her K-9 on the trail, as she should have done to start with, she concluded, as upset with herself as she was with Caleb. Even without a scent object Hank might have been able to sort out the right odor and track it, since the sighting of the wandering woman was so fresh.

Caleb paused at the driver's door of his SUV with his hand on the lock, then looked up. Centered on her. His jaw slackened. Eyes widened. "Vivienne! Look out!"

She heard a roar behind her, saw Caleb draw his gun and start to move. Pivoting, she froze for a split second. A speeding car was bearing down on her. Hank! She had to save Hank above all.

Her arms waved, giving the dog direction as she dropped the end of the leash. "Go! Go!"

Spinning on his haunches, the border collie did exactly as ordered. He took off running—away from her.

Had she not taken that precaution she would have had more time to guard her own body. By the time she looked back to see where the speeding car was, it was nearly upon her.

Caleb had stepped dead center into the traffic lane between rows of parked cars and assumed a shooter's stance, feet apart, hands together on his Glock, arms extended. "Stop. FBI!"

The tan car kept coming. Faster and faster. Seconds elapsed in slow motion, giving Vivienne the illusion of having time to seek safety. She actually had no chance to think, let alone plan. If she didn't move she was going to be badly hurt. Or worse. Leaping to the side between a parked car and a cement-filled end post, she smashed into the narrow yellow marker column, bounced off and fell, stunned.

The older model tan car zigzagged past and on down the aisle, avoiding Caleb and taking the turn at the end with a screech of slipping tires. Metal crunched as the car caromed off the rear bumper of a parked pickup truck.

Vivienne briefly assessed her physical condition before moving. Her world was off-kilter. Shimmering. Spinning. But she was alive. And except for a sore knee and a badly bruised ego, she was unhurt. Given the circumstances, that was a win in her book. One that deserved thanks.

Waiting for her equilibrium to return, she closed her eyes and prayed, "Thank You, Lord. Again."

SIXTEEN

Caleb thought his heart had literally stopped beating. Vivienne was down. Had she been hit? Injured? He could see a little movement, but she wasn't getting up.

He was at her side in mere seconds and reached for her past Hank, who had returned and was licking her cheeks. "Are you okay?" Caleb shouted. "Did they get you? Sideswipe you? Talk to me!"

"I'm okay. A little banged up. A concrete post attacked me after the car missed."

Feeling her firm grip on his hands helped. So did pulling her to her feet, so he could look directly into her eyes. "You really are okay?"

"Yes."

Caleb didn't break eye contact and, thankfully, neither did she. There was an unspoken connection between them that reached into his heart. He couldn't keep from gazing into the bottomless depths of her eyes until he saw them begin to grow misty. That was more than enough incentive to pull her fully into an embrace. As he did, he felt her slip her arms around his waist.

He remained vigilant, continuing to watch for threats, while Vivienne leaned against him as if they had always been this close. Although he feared he might be imagining the sincerity of her response to his hug, he chose to prolong it, anyway. It had been a long, long time since he'd felt even a whisper of connection to another person and he was reluctant to let her go.

Vivienne's cheek rested against his chest. He felt her shudder, then finally start to lean away. Instinct urged him to grasp her tightly, but common sense convinced him to relax his hold. When she looked up at him there was something different in her gaze, a quality that surpassed appreciation or mere friendship. Best of all, it bore no resemblance to the pity he had noticed from others. Vivienne wasn't feeling sorry for his loneliness, she was somehow erasing the pain a little at a time.

That thought brought him up short. Having grieved and held on to his anger for seven years, this sense of belonging was frightening.

To Caleb's relief, Vivienne began to smile. "Whew! That was a close one."

"Yeah." He swallowed past a lump in his throat. "Too close."

She glanced down at the K-9 happily spinning in circles at their feet. "At least Hank is okay. Did you get a license number?"

Caleb shook his head. "No, the angle of the sun made it hard to see anything straight on. Did you?"

"Uh-uh. I did see something odd, though." Still holding her hands, he felt her fingers tighten on his as her eyes widened. "It was like I was seeing double."

"Are you now?" He grasped her shoulders and held her still, facing him. "If your vision's been affected, you'll need to go to ER to be checked out."

"No, no. My eyes are fine. It was before the car passed. There were two people in the front seat."

"Men or women?"

"Women. Both of them."

She was beginning to tremble, so he looped one arm around her shoulders to guide her back to his car. "Did you get a good look?"

"Good enough. The passenger was the spitting image of my kidnapper sketch." Caleb started to reach for his phone.

"Wait," she said abruptly, "there's more."

He could tell she'd been shocked and assumed she was reacting to the near miss until she said, "The second person. The driver. She looked enough like our suspect to be her sister or daughter. We were right about there being two of them. Maybe they were both there when I was shot at the first time. It would explain a lot."

That deduction didn't change anything for Caleb other than to increase his vigilance. He beeped his key to unlock the SUV, helped her into the passenger seat and checked her condition once again while Hank hopped the center console and made himself at home in the second seat. "Your pupils are equal and normal."

"That's a plus," she said, still smiling.

Before shutting her door he asked, "Where to? The hospital or our new safe house? My boss arranged it. Not far from the old one but even more private."

"The station. I want to talk to my boss while everything is fresh in my mind."

"You can do that from the house. I'll set up a video-conferencing call." Caleb's jaw clenched. He could tell she was about to shoot down his idea and countermand his orders, such as they were. Insisting he was right was going to get him nowhere. Fast.

After shutting the passenger door, he strode to the other side and slid behind the wheel. Then he used his radio to report the attack at the airport.

"Tan with New York plates," he said. "Two female passengers in the front seats. We'll need to check the video from the parking-lot cameras for thirty minutes on either side of the present time. If we don't see the right car on that footage, pull traffic cams for the off-ramps from Van Wyck and surface roads leading to Terminal Eight."

"What's your twenty?" Dispatch asked.

"We're still at the airport. I'll stop at Security and inform them of the attack, although I doubt they'll be too concerned since nobody was hurt. And I'll leave my card on the parked truck that the fleeing suspects bumped in case they want to report a scratched bumper."

"Will you be requesting a crime scene team?"

Caleb paused then said, "No. I don't think they left anything behind from the collision, but I will go check more closely before we bother to bring in techs."

"Copy. Out."

Backing out, Caleb cruised slowly past the large pickup truck that had been hit, carefully scanning the pavement while Vivienne leaned out her window and did the same. "Do you see anything?" he asked. "Glass or chrome? Paint left behind. Anything?"

"Nope," she replied. "I guess they weren't traveling as fast as it seemed when they almost mowed me down."

"Fast enough to have flattened you," Caleb stressed. "You do know that, don't you?"

"Yes. I guess there's not going to be any place where I'm safe until we catch them."

"I'm relieved to hear you say that."

"I've *always* been cautious," Vivienne argued. "I don't like having to take that to extremes."

"You know what they say." Caleb paused for emphasis. "Tough."

"Yeah. I've been told that before."

He caught a glimpse of her hand reaching toward him then retreating and he wanted desperately to comfort her more. When he'd seen her in mortal danger his whole being had responded. That had been a more emotional response than was called for, he knew, yet if he'd had to do it again he knew he'd embrace her. Gladly.

When he'd seen that near miss he'd aged a hundred years! Caleb swallowed past a cottony throat. Milliseconds had separated Vivienne from grave bodily injury. She could easily have been killed while he stood there, trying to decide if it was safe to discharge his weapon in such a well-used area.

It wasn't safe so he'd let the car pass. Seen Vivienne on the ground. And thought for a heart-wrenching moment that he'd just watched someone else he cared about die.

Processing all that information brought a simple conclusion. Their relationship had crossed the threshold from platonic to something approaching romantic, and he couldn't deny it. Caleb slowed and pulled to the curb, before they reached the security offices. He undid his seat belt so he could swivel to face her.

Although not a word passed between them, she did the same. He once again opened his arms. And Vivi-

enne leaned into his embrace as naturally as if they had
done it hundreds of times before.

The silent kisses he placed on her hair went unno-
ticed, he hoped. It was all he could do to keep from
weeping in gratitude for her survival. He would never
allow himself to show that much emotion, of course.

So he held her. Stroked her back gently and felt her
arms slide around past his shoulder holster. There was
nothing he could say, nothing he could tell her, that
would explain how he felt. Truth to tell, he wasn't all
that sure himself. Sensible thoughts and conclusions
no longer matched his innermost feelings and the conflict was jarring.

His whole world was tilted on its axis. Nothing made
sense anymore, least of all what he was doing in this
very moment. Worse, he yearned to kiss her properly.
What was wrong with him? He'd shunned romance for
seven long years, yet it had taken only two days to
change that comfortable outlook and leave him wondering if he'd lost his mind. This woman craved the one
thing he could never give again. A family. Children.

From his broken heart came a plea that was also new.
He called out to God. *Please, please, help me just walk
away when all this is over.*

Caleb started to lean back, to relax his embrace, and
she did the same. Her expressive eyes glistened. Her soft
lips trembled. She wanted him to kiss her—he knew
she did.

He wasn't going to give in no matter how much he
wanted to.

A wet tongue slurped the side of his face. Rapid
panting sent K-9 breath right after it. The shock was
more than adequate to break Caleb's train of thought.

Apparently, it was enough for Vivienne, too, because she giggled and moved away, blushing. "I forgot to mention," she said between chuckles, "Hank gets jealous sometimes."

Caleb was pretty sure his prayers had just been answered although not in the manner he'd imagined they would be. He still wanted to kiss Vivienne. He still wanted to hug her. But, fortunately, they had a four-legged chaperone along for the ride, one who would be with her 24/7.

Grinning, he reached back to ruffle Hank's ears, grinned and said, "Thanks, buddy. I owe you one."

Vivienne fought to catch her breath. To understand what had just happened and maybe make a little sense of it. She was more than confused. She was astounded. And shocked. And way, way too happy about what Caleb had done.

As he started the engine and pulled back into traffic, she worked to show convincing nonchalance. She needed to pretend that she hugged all her partners the way she'd hugged Caleb.

An amusing thought intruded. She did hug the four-legged ones. That hardly counted, did it? People—men in particular—had always seemed standoffish compared to the way her heart responded to them. And in those cases she'd known better than to be too demonstrative. That was another good thing about little kids. They were almost always ready to accept and return affection without asking questions or overanalyzing.

Say something. Anything, she thought, wishing at first that Caleb could read her mind, then taking it back when she realized what kind of personal thoughts he would be privy to. If she wasn't so rattled this situation would actually be funny. Perhaps the best way to deal with her feelings was to make jokes about them.

"I hope I evaded that speeding car gracefully," she told Caleb. "I wouldn't want to look awkward on the video footage."

"*That's* what you're worried about?"

She raised the hand closest to him. "I was just kidding. I will be interested in seeing if it came as close as it felt."

"It wasn't far off." His hands were fisted on the wheel.

"Sorry if I scared you. I scared myself, too."

"You have to stop acting as though you have a death wish, okay? You're giving me gray hair."

Eyeing his dark blond, short cut, she laughed. "I don't see one gray hair."

"All my hair was brown last week," Caleb teased. "Then I came to Brooklyn and met you."

"Yeah, yeah." Sobering slightly, she continued to smile. "I really do love my job, you know."

"I get it. I wish I'd been on the promenade sooner and could have watched you and your K-9 track the boy."

"He really was something," Vivienne said with tenderness. She turned enough to reach back and pet Hank. He immediately responded, wagging his tail, licking her fingertips and panting gaily. "Yes. Good boy," she cooed.

Acting delighted, the border collie pranced on the leading edge of the seat, then lunged to bestow another kiss on Caleb's right ear and cheek.

"Thanks, Hank. But maybe not when I'm driving."

"What, you don't like kisses on the road?" Vivienne

dissolved into giggles, attributing her reaction to being uptight.

Caleb arched an eyebrow and gave her a sidelong glance. "Not the dog kind."

If she had been braver and hadn't still been trying to figure out how she felt about a man she hardly knew, she might have picked up on his comment and made a witty remark.

Thinking about how close she and Caleb had come to perhaps actually kissing, her mind went blank. If someone had demanded she quote her name and badge number right now, she doubted she could have done it.

Worse, they had arrived at the security booth for that section of the parking lot and he was stopping. Time to stop thinking about kissing.

That conclusion made her blush. It was not going to be easy.

SEVENTEEN

Caleb had been right about the reaction he'd get when he reported the incident, and Vivienne told him so. Cars sped in the airport parking lots and its tiered structure all the time so minor fender-benders were part of a guard's day. Nevertheless, she felt better after they had alerted the security staff.

"We'll make a full report once we get back to your station," Caleb told her. "Brooklyn police can formally request the license number from airport-security cameras, which will probably also give us an ID of the driver. Now that we know there are two women involved it should make the investigation easier. Age won't play as big a part and if we can spot one, she should lead us to the other."

"What do you think? Are they sisters or mother and daughter?"

"Could be either. Without observing the family dynamics between them it's hard to say. If it's mother and daughter, chances are the mother is in charge. With sisters it will depend on birth order and strengths of personality."

"The more I picture their faces, the more I think

they're mother and daughter. But that still doesn't explain why they abducted the Potter boy or why they're so mad at me for stopping them."

"Time will tell. Have patience," Caleb said.

"I'm just nervous. I can't seem to shake the idea that I'm being watched. Know what I mean? It's like, wherever I go, there's somebody out to get me. I can't go home, I can't ride with you to the airport. I can't even safely walk between the station and training facility. How am I going to do my job?"

"Very carefully," he drawled.

Vivienne had to study his face for a second before she was sure he was trying to make a joke to lighten her mood. "Good idea, but it doesn't do much to help my nerves. I feel like I'm climbing the walls."

"Of the Empire State Building?"

"No, smarty. That was too hard to do the first time I tried."

Caleb laughed. "Sounds like something you might do."

She noticed him sobering as he checked traffic behind them on the expressway. "Do you see somebody following us?"

"I don't think so. It's pretty hard to drive and keep a close watch, though."

She looked in her side mirror. No sign of a tan car. Then she turned around as best she could with the seat belt on to check out the back windshield. She didn't see the car.

She saw him cast a quick glance in his side mirror, then jerk his head toward her. "Possible trouble."

"Did you see the tan car that tried to run over me?"

"I think so. There's only one way to tell for sure.

Tell Hank to get down on the floor so he doesn't slide around. We're about to go for a wild ride."

Caleb didn't begin evasive tactics until he was certain his passengers were safe and secure. He pressed on the accelerator and whipped the wheel, passing several cars at once as he changed lanes, then pulled back into the lane he'd been in before.

That kind of abrupt lane change wasn't too rare in city traffic and it gave him the perfect chance to watch the car he suspected. When it followed his pattern he made a second quick maneuver, using a box truck as a foil and darting in front of it. The driver honked and shook his fist.

Vivienne was watching via the side mirror and noticed the angry truck driver. "That guy's upset."

"Can't be helped. Defensive driving is just part of the job. It's other people's reactions I can't control."

"Right. We don't want to scare them enough to cause an accident."

"Exactly." At least she wasn't arguing with him. That was a plus. So was the box truck because it was riding his bumper so closely no other cars could squeeze in.

"Back two car lengths and to my left, in the fast lane," Caleb said, realizing he was nearly shouting. "Can you tell if that's them?"

She swiveled as far as the tight belt would allow, then slipped her right shoulder free to turn farther. "Looks like it. I can't be absolutely positive, but I think so."

"Okay. Call your station and tell them we think we're being followed by the same car that almost ran you down at the airport."

As she made the call, he assessed traffic, hoping to

be able to slip into the far right lane, slow down enough to drop back, then fall in behind the tan car to turn the tables on the occupants. That would help them see the license plate and positively match it when they got the closed-circuit pictures from airport parking.

Traffic was both a help and a hindrance. He didn't dare signal his intent to change lanes when the tan car was close enough to observe him. He also didn't want to cause a wreck or involve innocent civilians.

Several failed attempts made him decide to change tactics. He radioed an updated call for backup on the police frequency and was told response would be delayed so he went to plan B.

"I'm going to try to pull off at an exit while our friends in the other car are still cut off by the truck. Hang on."

"That's too risky," Vivienne countered.

"Only if the drivers I need to pass are daydreaming or talking on cell phones. I'm afraid if we stay here they'll eventually catch up to us and either take a shot at you or try to ram us. Either way they're liable to cause a terrible pileup. We can't take that chance."

"I don't like any of our choices."

"Join the club. Just keep a lookout. You won't be able to see if they're behind us until I hit the off-ramp," Caleb said loudly. "Watch in that outside mirror and hang on. If they try to follow us we'll advise our backup that the situation has worsened."

"I wouldn't dream of letting go," Vivienne yelled back. She cast a brief glance over her left shoulder, apparently checking on her K-9 because she added, "Stay!"

Caleb saw his chance coming up. Almost there. Almost in the clear.

At the last possible second, he veered to the right, tires bumping over a row of raised warning dots on the pavement. "Made it!"

The box truck crossed behind the SUV and blocked his view. Cars ahead were slowing. If he'd been successful in eluding their trackers, he'd bought them time. If not, he'd better be ready for a possible assault on foot.

Beside him, Vivienne was peering into the mirror. "I can't tell!" She swiveled as far as the seat belt would allow. "I don't think they made it off when we did."

"I don't see their car," Caleb said. His palms drummed against the steering wheel as if that would make the cars ahead clear the street. "Come on, come on, come on."

"Push your button to change the signal so we get through the intersections faster," she ordered.

"That's a fire-department, patrol-officer, ambulance gadget," Caleb countered. "I don't have one."

"Super. So drive on the shoulder."

"Only if I have to," he said. "Just keep watching. If you see anybody approaching on foot, let me know."

Her eyes were rolling, her eyebrows arching when she turned to him. "Wow. Like, you think I wouldn't mention it?"

"Okay, okay. I get so focused on keeping you safe that sometimes I forget you're a cop." The moment the words left his mouth he knew he was in trouble.

Vivienne made a face at him. "You sometimes forget I'm a cop? Listen Mr. FBI Agent, having a K-9 partner makes me a bigger and better threat than you and your badge together. And don't you forget it."

"I really didn't mean that the way it came out," Caleb said. "I apologize. I know you're a cop—and a good one."

When she didn't respond he added, "Please? Forgive me?"

"I'll think about it. If the dog says you're still okay I won't hold that part of the ridiculous statement against you."

"Thanks. I think."

Traffic slowly moved ahead and Caleb was able to enter a side street. "Still no signs of our tail," he reported, starting to relax. "You can let Hank up off the floor now."

"You just want to see if he still likes you."

Caleb had to smile in spite of their recent close call and misunderstanding. "Anything that makes you forgive me for coming across like I don't appreciate your skill and training is fine with me," he said. "I do respect you as a fellow officer. It's just…" He'd been going to tell her how attractive she was and just how strongly his instincts insisted he must protect her. That admission would have made things worse, of course, so instead he said, "It's the dog. There's something warm and fuzzy about your working dog that I don't see in German shepherds or Rotties or those other imposing breeds. Hank looks too lovable."

To his relief, Vivienne nodded. "I get it. I do. But don't sell him short. He may be the happiest-looking K-9 in my unit, but he's all business when he's put on a trail. You'll see. I'm really proud of the work he does."

"So I'm forgiven?"

The lopsided smile she gave him was almost convincing. Then she gave Hank a hand signal and he jumped back onto the seat behind them.

Caleb watched in the mirror. The dog never took his eyes off her until she said, "Release," and then he morphed into a friendly backyard pet.

The tongue was quick but Caleb was quicker. His hand blocked the slurp headed for his ear. He chuckled. "Convinced?"

Although Vivienne was laughing, he could tell part of it was due to lingering nervousness. "Yes. You passed the pup test. Anybody who is okayed by my dog is okay in my book."

"And anybody he doesn't like?"

"Deserves watching," she said as her smile grew and evened. "His instincts have never failed me."

"Does he have to pass judgment on the guys you pick from the dating app you were telling Penny about? I can't believe a woman like you needs to find dates that way."

She huffed. "It's the gun and badge. You might sometimes forget I'm a cop, but the rest of the world doesn't."

"Hey, I thought I was forgiven for sounding like a jerk."

"You are."

Despite the thick traffic he kept watching for Vivienne's nemesis. "Keep checking behind us and at cross streets. Even if they didn't get off the expressway when we did they may guess you're headed back to your station and be waiting."

"You really think it was them following us, don't you?"

Caleb nodded. "Yes. I do. And I don't expect them to give up easily, especially now that we know two are working together. One person might get discouraged.

Two can bolster each other and will be far more likely to continue."

"That's what I hate about hanging out with truthful people," Vivienne said, smirking at him. "They tell it like it is and I have to accept it." She snorted derisively. "Thanks."

"You're welcome," Caleb said, meaning every word. If they had to accept a truth they didn't like, why not share the burden with each other?

Sighing, she sank a little lower in her seat. "Sometimes I feel like a lame hamster trying to run on a broken exercise wheel. I make a little progress, then boom."

"Please. I worry enough already. Don't remind me about the bomb."

"Believe it or not, I'd forgotten about that. There's already so much to remember, the threats that didn't part my hair are fading into the background."

"It will be over soon," he promised. "We'll get you out of this mess soon."

She was half-smiling when she glanced over at him and said, "From your lips to God's ears."

Caleb didn't even try to reply.

EIGHTEEN

The following day and night passed in a blur. Vivienne was glad she had a new safe temporary home but regretted the forced closeness to the enigmatic FBI agent. Most of the time they maneuvered around each other as if avoiding inevitable contact. It was the most awkward tango she'd ever tried to dance and the tension of being stuck in the house together was getting to her.

Caleb had made an appointment to interview little Lucy Emery before submitting the profile he'd written of the killer, or killers, of her parents and the McGregor parents. Randall Gage's DNA matched the sample on the watchband found at the McGregor crime scene, but there was no tie to the Emery murders. She wondered if Caleb was right about his theory that the Emery murderer was a copycat. Vivienne was determined to accompany him when he spoke with the child.

"Lucy's only three," Vivienne argued. "You're a big, scary guy. You'll get better results if Hank and I go with you."

"I'll do fine. Penelope McGregor is going to sit in with me because she has such good rapport with the child. That was the only way Detective Nate Slater and his wife, Willow, would permit Lucy to meet with me." Whenever Vivienne thought of how Lucy's aunt and the detective who'd first investigated the Emery murders had fallen in love and become a family with Lucy, her heart warmed.

"I know I'm not assigned to the murder case. I just think having Hank—and me—in the room will be a good addition."

"I already have Slater and his working dog, Willow, Penelope and maybe her brother, Bradley, and his K-9, for backup, plus me. That should be quite a crowd."

"So one more won't matter."

"Two more. You're a duo, in case you've forgotten."

Vivienne reached down to scratch behind Hank's silky ears. "Never. My partner and I are inseparable. Remember last night on the sofa."

She saw Caleb's cheeks flush. Blonds had the kind of complexion that showed the slightest warming and he fit that mold perfectly, even if he had let his chin get scruffy while they were out of the public eye.

"How could I forget?" Caleb asked, deadpan. "He snores. At first I thought it was you making all that racket."

Picturing them both falling asleep sitting up on the sofa with Hank lying upside down between them made Vivienne chuckle. "It was funny. I don't even remember what movie we were watching. I couldn't seem to keep my eyes open and the next thing I knew, all three of us were sawing logs."

"Uh-huh. And your dog was lying between us doing his dead-squirrel-in-the-road impression."

Vivienne smiled. "I know what you mean. When he rolls over with all four paws in the air and lets his head hang off the edge of the cushions that's exactly what he looks like."

"I suspect I may miss him when we're done with this assignment," Caleb admitted, sobering.

Vivienne noted that he had not said he would miss her. Well, so what? Just because he'd hugged her a few times didn't mean he was ready for commitment, let alone the kind of life she'd envisioned for herself, and she'd be wise to keep that in mind, regardless.

Analyzing her recently turbulent emotions, she decided it was time to alter the situation, to ask for relief from the constant togetherness that was obviously counterproductive, particularly with regard to her personal feelings.

She chose to speak her thoughts in a way she hoped he would understand. "It's not your fault but I'm suffocating here at the safe house, Caleb. I need to move, to jog, to exercise my K-9, to go back to work full-time so I can feel useful." She paused for emphasis and pointed to the kitchen. "And I need to stop eating balanced meals instead of easy, uncomplicated PBJs." *Plus, I need an uncomplicated life*, she added silently.

"Not good for you," he argued. "Besides, I thought you liked my cooking."

"That's part of the problem. It's your cooking, not mine. I don't want to be coddled. I want to stand on my own two feet and decide what I do or don't want to eat. Where I want to go. What I want to do all day."

"You're so set in your ways as a single person that you probably scare off any guys who'd give you that big family you say you want."

Thinking he was done, Vivienne opened her mouth to tell him off but he interrupted. "A family isn't a dictatorship, lady, it's a co-op. The best is with two parents who think alike so they present a united front to their kids. They have to support each other, give and take, not decide on a boss and an underling. Not if they want to be happy. And don't get me started on raising kids or we'll be here all morning."

"Are you done?"

"No, but I'll stop."

"Thank you. So since I'm not sitting in on the interview with Lucy Emery, are you going to drive me to the station with you, or do I have to wait until you're gone and then call a cab?"

"Those are my choices?"

She raised her chin and stood tall. "Yes."

"I'm leaving in thirty minutes," he said. "Be ready."

He didn't know her very well if he thought a time limit would deter her, did he? She could be dressed and out the door in half the time he'd allotted. Getting ready was easy. Forgetting what he'd said to her about families wasn't. She'd hated growing up without her much older brother, assuming the main drawback was loneliness. Now, she was beginning to realize that being raised alone may not have equipped her for caring for the big family she craved. Maybe that was why the good Lord hadn't brought her a husband. She'd certainly tried hard enough to find one on her own.

Vivienne brushed her hair and whisked on a light lip gloss, then strapped on her utility belt and holster. Hank was so excited he couldn't stand still. Racing in circles, he passed the window several times before sticking his nose behind the heavy drapes and giving a single, high-pitched woof.

Vivienne joined him, pulled back the drape at one

side and looked out. Nothing seemed amiss. And Hank's bark hadn't been the kind he used for a warning—it was more joyful and excited. Nevertheless, she carefully scanned the residential street.

The weight of her gun and holster were comforting. So was the thought that Caleb would be with her.

That was another problem with being idle in the safe house. Too much time to think, to imagine, to let her mind paint pretty pictures as well as ugly ones.

Reality was what she craved most. Even if it proved dangerous.

Caleb checked his watch when he saw her coming. He should have known she'd be early. There wasn't a lot of mystery left between them…

"Ready?" Vivienne asked without her usual smile.

"Yes. You?"

She turned a full circle. "Of course. To be safe, I want a protective vest, and Hank's, too. The extras you got are out in your car."

"They were. I brought them in." He gestured toward the kitchen table. "Help yourself."

"I'll be glad to get my own vest from headquarters. It fits better."

"You mean, it doesn't say FBI in big white letters, don't you?" he said, getting the smile he was looking for.

"Well, there is that, too."

"Thought so." He, too, donned his own bulletproof vest then started for the side door that led to the garage, expecting her to follow. When she didn't, he looked back. "Coming?"

"Before we go I want to thank you for everything

you've done. I know I haven't been the best housemate and I do apologize. This has been difficult for me." *Difficult? Talk about an understatement.*

Jaw firm, shoulders squared, he nodded as he turned away. "Apology accepted and same here."

She nodded. "Good." Vivienne and Hank breezed past him. She opened the side door and let the K-9 precede her.

As she got Hank settled in the SUV and then fastened her seat belt, Caleb slid behind the wheel and pressed the overhead-door remote. As the heavy mechanized door lifted, he started the engine and backed out.

The neighborhood seemed quiet at this time of day. Residents who went to regular nine-to-five jobs had left, children were back in school and anyone who wanted to putter in the yard had been driven inside by the building heat.

He upped the AC in the car. "Cool enough for you?"

"Yes. Thanks. Wearing this vest is like living in a sauna."

"Yeah."

One of the reasons he'd wanted to conduct his interview of little Lucy at the Brooklyn K-9 Unit was that he wanted to talk to Gavin Sutherland. The sergeant had indicated that they might have been able to capture images from the security cameras at the airport. That would be a big help if those pictures were clear enough. Of course, it would also build a fresh fire under Vivienne. She'd be so ready to hit the streets and begin canvassing businesses around the station and the promenade, it would take him, her boss and half her fellow K-9 officers to hold her back.

What had bothered him most was the way he'd felt

sharing the safe house. It hadn't been nearly as difficult an adjustment as he'd originally assumed. He cooked, she cleaned up after him and the dog provided comic relief. How long this arrangement might have to last troubled him. Wanting to capture her stalker took precedence, yet he knew he would miss their closeness when it ended. He'd almost made the mistake of saying so that morning, but saved himself by switching to saying he'd miss the dog.

Caleb wheeled into an open parking spot along the street that fronted the station. Some kind of a ruckus was occurring directly in front of the entrance.

"I tell you, Rory's my dog," a man shouted.

Caleb circled and joined Vivienne and Hank at the curb. "Do you know who that guy is?"

"Yes." She pulled a face. "His name is Joel Carey. He's been here before, claiming that a stray German shepherd and her puppies we're housing in the kennels belong to him. Belle and Emmett Gage rescued the mama dog from where she was hiding under a porch and brought her here, thinking she'd been abandoned."

"I take it he has no proof of ownership."

"None. No papers, no microchip, nothing. They found her here in Brooklyn so we call her Brooke."

"That guy sounds crooked to me." Giving the argumentative man a wide berth, he led the way inside.

"We thought so, too. That's why we still have possession of the dog and her pups. The plan is to train Brooke as a working dog and hopefully her pups, too. We all adore them."

"Isn't it kind of chancy to bring in a stray? What if she's sick?"

"Our vet examined Brooke and her puppies. And besides, they were kept isolated until we were sure they were healthy," Vivienne assured him. "Caring for our working canines always come first."

Wondering how soon he should mention the video enlargements, Caleb was headed for Sergeant Sutherland's office when Penelope, her brother, Bradley, and a PD officer hailed them. "Over here."

Because Vivienne went, Caleb did, too. She was in her element here, while he felt like an outsider. Being an FBI agent didn't give him special status in the elite K-9 unit. It was comprised of the best of the best and he respected every member. Especially one of them.

Penelope was hugging Vivienne. Bradley was patting her on the back. The detective with the name tag reading "Walker" was grinning as if he knew her well. They were offering moral support for all she'd been through with the kidnapping and attempts on her life. The conversation then turned to another case. As Caleb listened, he learned that the men were part of a contingent that had been scouring Coney Island for a gang of smugglers that apparently had it in for one of the K-9s.

Vivienne spoke aside to include Caleb. "Officer Noelle Orton's K-9, Liberty, broke up an arms-smuggling ring and cost the criminals a lot of money, so they've put a high bounty on Liberty's life." She huffed. "See? I'm not the only member of this unit with enemies."

He nodded, sorry that the brave K-9 and her trainer were under siege. "Yes, but the dogs aren't trained to shoot back," Caleb said soberly."

NINETEEN

The moment Vivienne laid eyes on the printout from the surveillance video, she knew these were the right women. If she hadn't promised to stay in the building while Caleb interviewed Lucy, she'd have taken the telltale images and hit the streets then and there. As it was, Willow was slightly late bringing the sweet three-year-old to her appointment and that wait seemed interminable.

When Willow and Nate arrived, Lucy took one look at the assembled adults and hid behind Willow Slater.

"It's okay, baby," Willow said gently. "When we're done here I'll take you over to play with the puppies. How's that?"

The little blonde girl nodded.

Vivienne felt Hank pull on his leash. He was normally very well-behaved so that drew special attention. Clearly, the sympathetic border collie was concerned for the feelings of the child.

"Can I pet him?" Lucy asked. "I like him."

"Sure," Vivienne said. She let him approach. Lucy had been to the station many times and was familiar with all the K-9s.

The gentle dog pushed his nose against Lucy's hand. Vivienne didn't stop him because she could see a slight change in the child's demeanor. "It's okay to pet him as long as I say you can," Vivienne offered. "He can tell you're a little bit unhappy and he wants to make it all better."

None of the adults interfered. Vivienne wasn't supposed to be part of the interview, but she did seem to be helping. Silence reigned as the three-year-old shyly put out a hand. Hank's lick of her fingers made her giggle. That set off the K-9 and his tail wagged his whole rear half.

"He's happy to see you again. See?"

"Uh-huh."

Vivienne could have cheered to hear Lucy speaking. "Hank likes it when I sit with him." She patted the floor off to the side. "Would you like to join us?"

Without answering verbally, the child plopped down next to Vivienne and was greeted with a swift doggie kiss that made her laugh more. She threw her arms around Hank's ruff, burying her face in the silky fur.

"Can I give him a cookie?" Lucy asked.

"Maybe later. Do you like cookies?"

"Uh-huh. Chocolate chip is my favorite."

"I love chocolate chip, too." At this point, Vivienne looked to Caleb and received a thumbs-up, which she took as an okay to further help prep Lucy for the interview. She smiled at her K-9, who had rolled onto his back, tongue lolling, and was silently begging for a tummy rub. "Here," Vivienne said, demonstrating, "scratch him where the white is. See? He loves that."

Little curled fingers sent loose fur flying. Vivienne laughed softly. "Maybe not quite so hard, okay?"

"Okay."

Planning to set the stage for questions about the stuffed monkey toy that was left at the scene of Lucy's parents' murder, Vivienne brought up a different kind. "I hear you like dolls and teddy bears and stuffed toys like that red fuzzy one that giggles when you tickle him."

"Uh-huh." Her smile was wistful. Leaning over the prostrate border collie and hugging his fur, she said, "I miss Andy."

"Andy?" Vivienne saw Caleb and Nate leaning forward to listen.

Willow approached and squatted down next to the child. "Who's Andy, honey?"

"You know."

Caleb joined them. "No, Lucy, we don't. Tell us about Andy. Where did you meet him? In the park, maybe?"

That was way too much attention for the shy little girl. She pressed her lips together, shook her head vigorously and once again buried her face deep in Hank's silky fur.

Vivienne sent a sour look at the FBI agent, clearly expressing a negative opinion of his pushiness.

Not deterred, Caleb asked, "Do you mean Randy, Lucy?"

By that question, Vivienne understood that Caleb was asking if Lucy meant Randall Gage. She held her breath.

"No!" Lucy started to get teary-eyed. "Andy."

Caleb stood and backed off to speak more privately with Gavin and some of the others. "That's not exactly what I intended to ask but it's enough to confirm my original conclusions. I don't think the two sets of killings are related other than a possible copycat situation. My profiles indicate that Randall Gage is responsible for only the McGregor parents, not the Emerys. Time will tell if I'm right."

Leaving Lucy hugging Hank with Willow sitting close by, Vivienne got to her feet, too. She walked over to where the group was standing, away from Lucy's delicate ears since details needed to be discussed. "So we have neglectful parents in both cases and the possibility that somebody in their lives thought it would help the children to make them orphans?".

"I suspect that contributed," Caleb said. "The killers definitely had a soft spot for little kids. In the McGregor case it's probably a good thing Bradley was at a sleepover and wasn't home that night. He's a lot older than his sister and might have been considered adult enough to be held responsible, too."

"Praise the Lord," Penelope said.

Until now, Bradley McGregor had remained silent. He slipped a supportive arm around his sister. "For us, being taken in by the lead detective on our case and his wife was a lot better than staying at home had been. Our adoptive parents are both gone now but we'll never forget what they did for us. Penny was too young to realize how neglected we were, but I remember sneaking food from my friends' houses and bringing it home to her." He gave his sister an affectionate squeeze and she leaned her head on his shoulder.

Bradley's words got Caleb thinking. "I'd like to see the Emery neighbors interviewed again. We'll be looking for anybody who showed interest in Lucy or sounds critical of her parents."

"I wish I could help more," Willow said as she bent to lift Lucy into her arms.

Lucy immediately hugged Willow's neck and hid her face from the other adults, the same way she had when she'd been on the floor with Hank.

"Willow, when was the last time you saw your brother?" Caleb asked.

"Like I told the investigating detectives on scene that night," Willow said, "it was when I brought the family food. I'd insisted he either cleaned up his act or I'd be forced to call Child Protective Services for my niece's sake instead of enabling him the way I had been."

"Would you have called?" Vivienne asked.

"I never had to decide." Unshed tears glimmered in Willow's eyes. "The last time I stopped by he'd seemed better. When I couldn't reach him by phone a week or so later, I got concerned and swung by his place." She sniffled. "That's when I found them."

Vivienne was sympathetic. "I'm so sorry."

"I'm going to Sergeant Sutherland's office to submit my official profile," Caleb said. "Briefly, I see the perp as being male, in his twenties, involved in other crimes, probably including drugs, and quick to pass judgment. He's likely to be local which is why I want the neighbors canvassed again—and asked about an Andy. One or more of them may also have been friendly with Lucy, so pay special attention to first names or nicknames that sound like Andy, too."

"I'm going with you," Vivienne said, signaling Hank to come to her side. "The sooner I can get Gavin's permission to hit the streets looking for the women in the printout, the sooner I'll be able to get back to living a normal life."

Whether anyone else noticed or not, she saw Caleb flinch. He didn't need to tell her he didn't want her out on the streets. It was evident. She also knew that her boss might side with him, so she began to mentally prepare a rebuttal in the event she was ordered to stand down. That was not going to happen. Not as long as she had one more breath of life in her.

The notion that she might be in mortal danger wasn't new. She'd faced that fact when she'd pinned on her badge. The notable difference now was that she didn't like the idea of not being around Caleb Black anymore.

The portent of *that* thought was anything but welcome.

Caleb figured he knew exactly what was about to happen in Gavin's office. His senses were on high alert. His pulse was beginning to speed up. Like it or not, he was in for a fight, one he felt he had to win.

He presented his printed report, then said, "I've sent you the file electronically, too. If there are any changes in the future I'll notify you by email."

"Fine." Gavin peered past him at Vivienne. "Was there something else?"

"Yes," Caleb said quickly. "I'd appreciate it if you'd keep your gung-ho officer off the streets while we search for the women who are stalking her."

"Do you feel Armstrong is a poor risk? Has she done anything to indicate she's unstable or unsuited to patrol?"

"No, but…"

Gavin smiled at Vivienne. "Then I see no reason to refuse to let her search. If anybody has a stake in this, it's her."

Vivienne stepped forward. "Thank you, Sergeant."

Caleb wasn't through. "Her dog could use backup, too, if Vivienne's out there. Surely you have to agree since Hank's not trained for protection or attack." Gavin looked at Vivienne. At her nod, he turned back to Caleb. "I'll send along others who are," Gavin told him. "I know Belle and Justice are free. And Noelle can take Liberty out as long as she's not working a high-profile case. They can defend Hank or Vivienne if necessary."

"I didn't say I needed that much help," Caleb insisted.

"The more coverage, the better," Gavin said. "You don't all have to stay together. Just keep your radios on and let me know if there's any sign of either of the blonde women in the photo."

"Yes, sir." Caleb didn't try to hide his negative feelings, but agreed because it was his only option. That, or wash his hands of the whole case and head back to Manhattan now that his original assignment was complete. The idea of doing that turned his stomach and he figured it was best to leave the office before Gavin changed his mind about letting him join the search.

Vivienne beat him to the door and left it open as she exited.

"Vest!" he called after her.

"Yeah, yeah. I'll get mine from my locker and meet you and the others in the alley between here and the training building. That way the dogs will have access to grass and we won't have to keep stopping."

Only a handler who thought of the K-9 first would have planned that, Caleb told himself. Vivienne and the others were special. No doubt about that. And he was relieved to have extra K-9s on the hunt with them. It was just as well since most, if not all, of his concentration would be focused on the woman he had come to admire so highly.

Part of him supposed he should say something about it to her while he had the chance. A more sensible part disagreed. One reason for limiting siblings or married couples from working together on the streets or in patrol cars was the tendency to be easily distracted. Nothing could ruin a person's awareness of threats like the presence of a loved one.

That conclusion set him on his heels. Loved one? He didn't have anybody like that in his life anymore. Or did he?

His vest fit snuggly beneath his suit coat and shoulder holster. He pulled on the jacket, wishing the weather was cooler, and headed for the meeting place.

It was unacceptable to think he might have become too fond of Vivienne in the brief time they'd been together. Ridiculous. He was already spoken for. He had a wife. He…

An attempt to bring Maggie's face into focus in his mind failed miserably. Caleb gritted his teeth. He couldn't allow himself to forget her. She'd been too important, too well loved.

Yet what about now? Was it even possible to love twice? As deeply as he had loved once before? He'd believed that impossible until very recently.

Long, purposeful strides carried him out into the alley where the search party was assembling. There were other officers and K-9s there already, but he saw only Vivienne.

When she smiled at him, he knew the truth.

"God help me," he muttered under his breath. "I'm in love with Vivienne Armstrong."

He strode boldly into the center of the grassy strip and raised his hands to claim everyone's attention. "All right. You have your assignments and printouts of the women we're looking for. Video has shown that they frequent this neighborhood and the Brooklyn Heights Promenade, so concentrate your efforts in those areas. Treat the suspects as armed and dangerous whether you see a gun or not. Any questions?"

There weren't any, so he nodded. "Let's go."

Vivienne's presence when she joined him was palpable. The worst thing he could do was reveal his feelings when they were about to search for criminals, so he kept silent. He did, however, meet her gaze, and for an instant he was certain he saw the same emotion reflected there.

Wishful thinking? he wondered. If it was all in his imagination he had to accept that. And if, once he did speak his heart to her, she chose to reject him, he'd have to accept that, too.

Caleb steeled himself against that possibility and headed out onto the street. Right now, they had a job to do and his was to keep the second great love of his life alive.

Failure was not an option.

TWENTY

Vivienne managed to keep her nervousness hidden from the humans, but Hank was aware. That couldn't be helped. She and her K-9 were supposed to be in tune with each other so it wasn't his fault he was behaving oddly.

Unfortunately, Caleb did notice. "What's the matter with your dog?"

"He's okay."

"He is not. I've learned to read him since we've been stuck at the safe house and he's definitely not okay. So what's the deal?"

Vivienne sighed and confessed. "He's picking up vibes from me and they're making him uneasy. That's why his head is down and his tail is tucked."

"Why are you uptight? Do you expect to spot the women we're after or are you just jumpy because Gavin chose to add so many big protection dogs to our party?"

"Hank may not be crazy about that, either, come to think of it," she said, wishing she hadn't already admitted to being ill at ease. "We're usually alone or with other trackers when we're working."

"Well, at least the kid you tracked and rescued before is out of danger. I can see why that's made your enemies mad."

"Yeah." She huffed a chuckle. "Mad enough to shoot at me a few times and then try to run me down at the airport. At least they didn't shoot at me or ram us when we were playing tag on the highway. I don't want them to endanger innocent civilians."

"We will catch them," Caleb said flatly. "Even if they change their hair and clothing, we have that ankle tattoo to look for."

"Right. The orange lotus flower. It's a good thing it's still summer. We'd never spot it in the winter when everybody is wearing boots instead of sandals."

"Another good reason to nab them soon," Caleb said.

She could tell he was scanning faces in the crowd the same way she was. "I'm glad you reminded me of the tattoo. I was forgetting to check feet."

"You do feet and I'll do heads," he said. "We're less likely to miss them if we divide the job."

"I suspect Hank may alert, too," Vivienne offered. "I'll keep one eye on him while I look down." If her dog hadn't veered left at that moment she would have walked into a lamppost. "Oops."

Caleb grabbed her arm, pulled her sideways and steadied her. "Tell you what. You look down and I'll keep you out of trouble."

"I assure you I'm able to walk without assistance."

"Tell that to the post you almost hit. And the cement one at the airport."

"I had help there," she joked back, grinning, before freeing her arm.

His reluctance to let go caused her to glance at him again. The depth of his blue gaze reminded her of the summer sky where it met the ocean and its intensity took her aback. "Caleb?"

"Just watch where you're going," he said gruffly as he dropped his hands to his sides.

She considered asking him for his thoughts, then decided against it. Just because she was smitten with him didn't mean it was wise to share feelings, particularly now.

Sun alternated with shadow as they passed beneath store awnings and between buildings. Caleb had already donned his reflective sunglasses, but she'd left hers behind so she had to rely on the bit of shade provided by the bill of her official baseball cap. The logo in the front identified her as a K-9 officer, as did the patches on her uniform shirt and the lettering on Hank's halter. Because of that, pedestrians tended to give her and Caleb a wider berth than normal.

"See anything yet?" he asked.

"Nope. I can't get a good look at the sides of anybody's ankles. I wish she'd gotten a garland of flowers that went all the way around."

"Picky, picky, picky."

"Yeah, well, you can hardly blame me."

A crackling message came in over her radio. Vivienne cupped the ear containing the receiver and stopped, touching Caleb to get him to halt with her.

"What is it? Did one of the others spot them?"

Vivienne hushed him with the hand holding Hank's leash and listened carefully. Finally, she looked up. "Belle thought she spotted one of the women, but it was an innocent blonde on her way to lunch with a friend."

"There are going to be more sightings like that around noon," he commented. "I never realized how many blondes there were in New York until we started looking for specific ones."

"Yes. Too bad hair coloring is so popular. Genetics like the ones that produced your hair aren't that common."

"Genetics? You mean like what gives Hank his white feet and chest and tail tip?"

"Speaking broadly, yes. It's most confusing when you have one breed of dog that comes in assorted colors, like Labrador retrievers. They're…" The closing of Caleb's hand around her wrist and his tight grip stopped her in midsentence. "What is it? What do you see?"

"Up there. Ahead on the right about half a block. I know that's a long way away but something about one of those women getting out of a cab caught my attention."

"She's looking this way!" Vivienne pivoted to face him so she wouldn't be noticed staring. "Now, look past me. Is she still paying attention to us?"

"I think so." His lips pressed into a thin line and he cupped her shoulders. "Let's step aside and switch positions so you can get a better look."

Vivienne could hardly wait for a second peek. "It's possible. We're too far away to tell. How are we ever going to get closer without scaring her off?"

"Cross the street." He glanced at the last corner they had passed. "The light's green. Come on."

She nearly tripped over Hank's leash as they sprinted for the crosswalk.

Caleb suddenly drew her into a doorway. "Stand back. She's crossing over."

"Which way is she going?"

"Up that next side street," he said. "Come on. If we hurry we can move parallel and overtake her."

"Wait. Running all that way may not help. Suppose she goes into one of those stores before we arrive? Or maybe she has a car waiting for her. We'll lose her."

"What do you want to do?"

"Circle the block with Hank while you trail her that way." Vivienne pointed. "Belle is only two blocks over and coming this direction fast so Hank and I will have backup if I need it before I meet up with you again."

"No way."

Vivienne was so frustrated she was angry. "Okay. Stand here wasting time while my stalker gets away if that's what you want. There's an alley halfway up the block. I'll cut through there and try to get ahead of her. If you were behind her..."

She evaded Caleb's hands as he made a grab for her and took off at a fast jog, Hank falling in at her side and keeping pace. She didn't have to look back to know that Caleb had not followed. The sense of his presence wasn't with her.

All she could hope at this point was that he had heeded her sensible instructions and would be in place to provide backup by the time she ambushed the suspect. This was it. She could feel it. They'd be one giant step closer to catching a kidnapper and stalker within the next few minutes.

Breathing hard, Vivienne nevertheless managed a smile and a wordless prayer of thanks.

Caleb was dumbfounded when she took off like a world-class runner leaving the starting blocks.

Some battles were worth fighting. This one was not. He spun on his heel and started for the corner where they'd seen the blonde woman get out of the taxi.

Despite the rapid walking habits typical of many New Yorkers, he had to dodge and weave between pedestrians in order to have any hope of reaching the corner before Vivienne emerged from the alley. Sergeant Sutherland hadn't issued him a radio and since it wasn't a part of his normal gear he hadn't considered a need until now. He and Vivienne were expected to stay together and use hers. *Yeah, right.*

Perspiration dotted his forehead and trickled down his temples. Between the oppressive heat and the bulletproof vest he was wearing, he was baking alive. But he pressed on. How much longer would it be before Vivienne confronted the blonde woman and ascertained whether she was their quarry?

Sure, it had occurred to him they might be wrong. That was possible. Anything was, unfortunately. As much as Caleb wanted to capture the criminal duo and remove the ongoing threat, he hoped they were pursuing the wrong person this time because Vivienne was temporarily on her own. He needed to be there, to be with her, to protect her if it became necessary.

Skidding around the corner, he touched the sidewalk briefly with one hand, pushed himself back up and regained speed. Shops passed in a blur.

He peered into the distance. "Where are you?" Not only did he not see Vivienne, but he also didn't see any blonde women the right height and age, either.

His cell phone vibrated in his pocket. Slowing to a fast walk, he answered. "Black."

"I lost her," Vivienne said. "Where are you? Do you see her?"

"No. Never mind where I am. Where are you?"

"I stepped back into the alley out of sight when she

wasn't visible on the street. We'll need to check each store she passed."

"Maybe she got by you. Stay there and wait for me. I'll look in stores as I pass but we don't have time to do a thorough search. Not if she's ahead. It'll take too long."

"You're right. I'll have Belle Montera and her K-9, Justice, check businesses as they work their way toward us."

Caleb wanted to cheer. "Once in a while I actually am right," he said.

"Well, don't take too much time to celebrate. I'm not quitting."

"I never imagined you would." He was already on the move again, this time walking rapidly. "I don't have a radio. Did you notify the other K-9 pairs of our possible sighting?"

"Yes. Open channel on the radio. 'Bye."

"Wait. Stay on the phone with me." He waited for affirmation. "Vivienne?"

She was already gone. He thumbed redial. The call went to voice mail. The short hair on the back of his neck prickled. His heart was already racing from his run. Now, it sped even more.

Caleb rose on tiptoe to look for her. If she'd left the alley by now he'd be able to spot her with Hank. But, no. A nearby light standard provided a slight elevation at its base. By leaning out and bracing one shoe against it, he was able to gain another eight or ten inches.

There! There she was. Someone—a woman with long, dark hair—had stopped her midblock and engaged her in conversation. That scenario was all wrong. It didn't fit Vivienne's insistence on continuing the search or mesh with what she'd told him moments before.

He saw her glance his way, so he waved his free arm, hoping, praying she'd spot him. It was impossible to tell if she had.

Caleb jumped down and hit the sidewalk running. At least he knew where she was and that she was still okay. All he had to do was reach her and everything would be fine.

Closer. Closer. Dodging, pushing people aside when he had to, he tried to act polite when he wanted to shout at them all to get out of his way.

A clearer view was short-lived. Caleb gasped. Vivienne had left Hank sitting obediently on the sidewalk and was approaching the street where a black car idled. The rear door was open.

"Vivienne!" he yelled. "Stop!"

Passersby closed in. Blocked his view. Stole the sight of her and left him so bereft he stumbled. "Vivienne!"

TWENTY-ONE

Vivienne had seen the frantic-looking, dark-haired woman leave an idling car in the right-hand traffic lane and jump out. She wore dark glasses but her panic was still evident.

"You're a cop," the woman had said. "You have to help me! My son…"

Immediate concern had taken precedence and Vivienne halted. "What's wrong, ma'am?"

"He's—he's choking. I was driving him to the hospital but he's turning blue." The woman's long, thin fingers tightened around Vivienne's arm. "Please! I don't know how to do CPR."

Forgetting everything else, Vivienne had headed toward the car with the mother. At the curb she'd put Hank on a sit-stay and dropped his leash.

"Have you checked the boy's airway?" Vivienne asked.

"No."

Reaching for the mic to her radio, Vivienne wasn't too surprised when the woman tried to stop her by making a grab for it. "Calm down, ma'am. I'm going to request an ambulance. It'll only take a second."

"My son!" It was a wail. "He's dying and you're wasting time talking."

"All right." She continued to request medical assistance as she moved toward the car. "Is he in the back seat?"

"Yes. On the floor."

"What?"

She bent to look inside, seeing a pile of blankets that she assumed covered the child. Of all the ridiculous things to do. In this high August temperature the poor kid was probably having a heat stroke instead of choking.

"Don't crowd me," Vivienne ordered. "Please." She'd placed her left hand on the seat and was reaching for the blankets with her other while the woman pressed in behind and bumped her. "You need to give us breathing room."

Then she felt pain in her head and a hard push, lost her balance and tumbled headfirst into the car. Half on the seat, half on the floor, she reached for her gun by instinct.

The holster was empty!

Vivienne tried to turn, to regain her balance, but she was too dizzy. Someone slammed the car door into her ankles, making her double up and pull her feet inside. The door banged shut. She reached for her phone—that was gone, too.

She heard Hank barking viciously outside the vehicle and managed to thank God that she hadn't brought him closer.

Horns were honking. The car lurched into traffic. Vivienne's stomach roiled and she tasted blood from biting her tongue.

The woman who had tricked her was sitting in the

front passenger seat while someone else drove. Both people were laughing. "See how easy that was?" one of them said. "I told you it would be. She's so softhearted she had to come help my *son*."

"What're we gonna do with her, Mama?"

"Shut up. I don't know. But you can be sure it's not gonna be pretty." She whipped off her long brown wig and tossed it aside, revealing the blond hair everyone had been looking for.

"It won't help you find that little boy again, you know."

"I told you. His name is Tommy. He's my baby brother. I was supposed to be watching him and he wandered off. I've been looking for him all my life. I could hardly believe my eyes when I spotted him right here in Brooklyn."

Listening, Vivienne could tell that one of her abductors was mentally unbalanced and was also in charge. The mother ran the operation, as Caleb had predicted, so things were definitely not in her favor. Still, when it came to plotting assault or even murder, maybe she could convince the daughter to defy her vindictive parent. If the younger woman refused to listen to reason, she didn't know what else she could do.

The holdout gun strapped to her ankle fit her hand perfectly as she slid it free of its holster. Rising slowly, she kept waiting for her vision to clear and her head to stop spinning. Whatever her captors had hit her with had obviously done some damage. She could only hope it wasn't long-lasting because she needed to get control of this situation ASAP.

Blinking rapidly and praying she'd be able to function efficiently, Vivienne pushed herself into a sitting position, extended her arm and pressed the muzzle of the gun to the back of the older woman's head, then ordered, "Stop this car."

The passenger merely cackled. The car's driver screamed, "Mama!"

"She ain't gonna shoot me in the back," the older woman said, still clearly amused.

"I said, pull over," Vivienne insisted.

"Should I?" the driver asked.

"What do you think? Listen to how scared she sounds." The mother was grinning as she turned to face Vivienne and said, "Drop your gun."

Vivienne was not about to comply. She gritted her teeth against the pain in her head and the throbbing in her ankles where the woman had slammed them in the car door. "Not a chance."

"Then I'll have to shoot you," the old woman said, producing a black automatic weapon and swinging it to bear on the back seat.

"You'll be dead as fast as I am," Vivienne said bravely. "I can't miss at this distance." Although her insides were trembling, she managed to keep her voice steady.

"No, you probably would kill me if you shot," her nemesis said. "Tell you what. Instead of me shooting you, suppose I kill this other gal? Does that change your mind?"

Vivienne was stymied. She might choose to risk her own life to end this standoff, but she would not risk the life of a civilian. For all she knew, the younger woman was innocent of wrongdoing, just as she was. There was only one proven criminal in the car and she was now aiming at her own daughter. What kind of person even considers doing that? she wondered.

"All right. Lower your weapon and I'll lower mine," Vivienne said, waiting for the woman in the front seat to make the first move. She had no intention of relinquishing her gun.

Instead, her older captor reached over and jerked the wheel. The car swerved wildly. A wave of dizziness washed over Vivienne and by the time she'd regained her balance the woman had closed her hand over the top of Vivienne's smaller pistol and twisted it out of her hand.

The speed of the car and the danger to innocent bystanders would have kept the K-9 officer from pulling the trigger even if she hadn't been so dizzy, as the captor had undoubtedly assumed.

Everything was over in seconds. Vivienne sat back, temporarily defeated by her spinning head and her strong moral code.

In the front seat, the older woman was chuckling while her younger look-alike wept as if she was barely able to see to drive.

"Stop sniveling and find a place to pull over. We need to tie up this cop so she behaves herself."

If ever there was a right time to pray for deliverance, this was it, Vivienne thought, but all she could come up with was a heartfelt "Father, help."

If she could have gone back in time and made a different decision she would have listened to Caleb and stayed with him. Now that it was too late, she wished mightily for the chance to tell him he was right. In person. And hopefully not with her final breath.

Caleb used his phone to notify the K-9 unit's headquarters and was patched through to Gavin in his patrol car.

"That's right," Caleb nearly shouted. "I saw them take her. Black sedan. New York plates." He recited the letters and numbers he'd seen.

"I'm close to your location. Which way were they headed?"

"Up 65th toward the Gowanus Expressway, unless they turn."

"Okay. Stay put. I'm almost there."

The rise and fall of one cycle of his siren was all Gavin used when he swung to the curb. Caleb was waiting with Hank. The dog jumped into the car first, then bounded over the center console into the back seat as if he'd done it a hundred times.

Caleb pointed. "That way!"

"Code three?"

"No. I wouldn't use lights and sirens. If they think they've gotten away they'll be less likely to speed or drive evasively."

"Good point. Officer Armstrong did manage to request an ambulance before you saw her shoved into the car. Are you sure it's them? I thought the vehicle we were looking for was tan."

"It's them. It has to be. Either they had two cars or stole one that Vivienne wouldn't recognize."

Gavin immediately radioed Dispatch, giving his other officers the car's full description. "And tell Eden Chang I want a trace on that license. Agent Black thinks it's probably recently stolen so have her start there."

Hearing "affirmative" didn't calm Caleb's nerves one bit. "I told Vivienne to stay with me but she was determined to do this her way. We'd almost joined forces again when she was shoved into that car."

"Why would she allow herself to be drawn that close?" Gavin asked.

"Good question." Caleb continued to scan the thick traffic ahead, hoping against hope to spot the right car. "I have to assume she thought there was a strong need to deviate from her original task." He felt Hank's hot breath on his neck. "I can't understand why she left the K-9 behind, though."

"Because she didn't feel he was going to be a help in her current situation?"

"Possibly. Probably. I'm glad she did. If they leave the car he'll be able to track her."

"Only if we find it," Gavin reminded him. He pushed a button on his dash and the red traffic light ahead of them switched to green, allowing them to pass.

Caleb nodded. The chances of finding the right car in a busy place like Brooklyn were slim and none. Yet they had to try. *He* had to try. And keep trying no matter what. It seemed impossible that they would simply stumble on Vivienne as they randomly drove. The futility of that option settled over him like a lead weight and blotted out the sunny day as if a dark cloud covered the city.

In retrospect he wished he'd given in to the urge to follow her instead of taking orders. That had been a tactical as well as an emotional error. He'd wanted so badly to increase their opportunities to capture her stalker that he'd temporarily lost sight of the possibility that danger could come from another source. That, and she'd upset him when she'd insisted on getting her way.

"It's my fault," Caleb said. "I should have stuck closer."

"That was a judgment call," the sergeant said. "Any

of us might have done the same thing. Don't second-guess yourself."

"I thought…" Caleb stopped before expressing his negative opinion of something he already knew was important to Gavin Sutherland.

"What? What did you think? Anything might help us. You know that. So talk."

"It's not a clue," Caleb admitted ruefully. "It's personal."

"Such as?"

The guy wasn't going to quit, was he? Well, it wouldn't make any difference if he aired his grievances. "I told Vivienne I'd given up on praying, and on God, but when all this started with her, the safe house and all, I started to pray again."

"And?"

"And, look what good it did me. Vivienne's been kidnapped, we don't know the names of the women who took her or where they were going. Does that sound like answered prayer to you?"

"Hmm." Continuing to weave in and out of traffic and change lights to green as needed, Gavin finally spoke. "Were you a committed believer once?"

"Yes. I'd dedicated my life to Christ."

"And something, probably your losses, turned you away?"

"I was mad at everybody and everything, even God."

"That's understandable. Do you think God gave up on you just because you gave up on Him?"

Caleb frowned at him. "I'd never thought of it quite that way."

"Well, do. And be ready for answers to your prayers. You may not like what those answers are, but they will come. Eventually."

"Soon would be nice."

Gavin chuckled. "Yeah. Soon would be very nice."

The radio had been providing brief bulletins as they drove. Gavin handed the mic to Caleb. "Keep them posted. I'm going to stay on 65th until we see something or another unit spots them."

"Copy." Being careful not to grasp the mic so tightly that he keyed it and broadcast before he was ready, Caleb peered out to get his bearings.

"Sutherland and Black passing Sixth on 65th," he told Dispatch.

"Brooklyn K-9 copies." There was a brief pause. "Be advised, a black car matching the description of your kidnappers' has been spotted stopping under the Gowanus Expressway at Fifth."

"Almost on scene," Caleb replied. He leaned forward as far as his seat belt would allow and stared into the shadows beneath the elevated highway overpass.

His racing, pounding heart made him momentarily light-headed. "There!" He pointed with his whole arm. "Over there! That's the car."

As she was lying on the rear seat, Vivienne had slipped one hand up and tried to open the door. It was locked. That wasn't a big surprise, but it was disappointing because it limited her escape options. If they decided to get on the expressway they'd be traveling so fast she wouldn't dare jump out even if she could get the door open later.

From the front seat she'd heard a harsh "Over there. Park over there," and had realized her only chance might be coming.

The driver had sniffled. "Right on the shoulder? In front of everybody?"

"We're not staying. I want to get into the back seat with our guest and have a little chat while you take us out into the country, like we planned."

"Mama, really… I think you should let her go. I mean, she was just doing her job."

"Ha! If the cops had done their jobs when Tommy disappeared I wouldn't have had to keep searching for him all these years. My mama and daddy are gonna be so surprised when I finally bring him home."

At this point, Vivienne was fairly sure she understood the delusion that drove the older woman. She was reliving her childhood and the traumatic loss of her little brother, thinking she had seen him again and that he'd been taken from her by the police.

By me, Vivienne added. *She blames me for something that probably happened before I was born.*

The engine noise echoed louder. Movement ceased. Vivienne peeked out and saw that they had stopped beneath a cement overpass. She only had a rough idea where they were and had lost her earbud when she was shoved into the car so she'd been unable to listen to radio chatter. She figured if she could key her mic, even though she wouldn't hear responses, it might help the department track her.

That meant moving and possibly tipping off her captors. Given the fact that one of them was getting into the back seat with her, she decided to hold off.

The moment she saw the round, dark hole at the end of the gun barrel that was pointing at her again she wished she'd loosened the mic when she'd first thought of it.

"I'm sorry about Tommy. About your little brother,"

Vivienne said when the older woman shoved aside her legs and forced her to move over.

Her aim never wavered. "Get back here with those zip ties and fasten her wrists together. Now!"

Another door clicked open. Vivienne felt hot air. Smelled gasoline fumes. No cars stopped, so clearly the women were being surreptitious and not looking like they needed assistance.

Gesturing with the gun, the mother ordered her to turn and present her hands to the daughter. As she complied, Vivienne mouthed, *Please?* It brought a corresponding look of chagrin but no change in the circumstances.

"Sorry," the younger woman said, sniffling more. "Mama knows best."

"You know she's sick, right?" Vivienne was whispering.

"She's my mother. I love her."

"Then help her by doing the right thing. She needs to see a doctor."

"I'm sorry," the woman said, tightening the plastic tie so it held fast.

Vivienne's heart dropped along with her spirits. This was not looking good. Now that she was partially immobilized, her situation was even worse than before.

Several ideas occurred simultaneously. All involved getting herself out of the car before it moved again. The armed woman was less likely to fire at her own daughter despite the earlier threat, so getting a hold on her was probably the best choice. Plus, the daughter was markedly less antagonistic so she'd probably give way more easily.

But that gun. It was a smaller caliber than Vivienne's duty weapon but still potentially lethal, particularly at such close range. Therefore, that had to be her first target.

She prayed wordlessly for support and discernment. The younger woman was turning to get back out. Her mother also retreated slightly. It was now or never.

Vivienne swung her right foot toward the gun. She gave a mighty lunge, kicked the revolver loose while ducking, then pushed off against the floorboard and hurled her body out the opposite door, taking the younger woman with her.

They landed in a heap as a gun went off under the overpass, sounding louder than usual because of the echo.

Vivienne rolled off her younger captor and scrambled to her feet, still battling recurring waves of dizziness.

On the opposite side of the car her assailant had apparently dropped the gun when it had fired and was down on her hands and knees, searching for it beneath the sedan.

Knowing that running would make her a perfect target, Vivienne dragged the adult daughter to her feet and looped her bound wrists over the woman's head like a noose. It wasn't perfect but it couldn't hurt. Hopefully, her assailant wouldn't realize that a bullet, fired at close range, could pass through one person and also wound the second.

Just the way it did with Caleb's former family, Vivienne added. Was this shooter mentally unbalanced enough to shoot her own daughter in order to get revenge on a police officer?

Maybe. She didn't want to find out.

TWENTY-TWO

Caleb bailed out of the patrol car before it came to a complete halt, drew his gun and raced toward the scene of mayhem. So did Hank.

Barking and growling, the usually placid K-9 was a blur as he made a beeline for the crouching older woman, hit her like a football linebacker and knocked her over. Then he stood, growling, with his bared teeth right next to her cheek, as if daring her to move.

Knowing Gavin was right behind him, Caleb left one kidnapper to the dog and the sergeant while he went straight for Vivienne. To say he was glad to see her was the biggest understatement of his life.

"It's okay, honey. I've got you," he said as he holstered his gun, lifted her joined wrists over her prisoner's head, then got out his pocket knife to cut the zip tie.

Tears were streaking Vivienne's cheeks. "She tricked me. She said her little boy was choking and when I went to help…"

"I saw her push you into the car but I was too far away to stop her."

"My fault," Vivienne said. "All my fault. I should have listened to you." The moment her hands were unbound she wrapped both arms around him and held tight.

That was more than fine with Caleb since Gavin's requested backup had arrived from the opposite direction and those officers were taking charge of the prisoners and evidence while Gavin led Hank away to the safety of his patrol car.

Caleb began to rub Vivienne's back as he held her. There was no way he could even begin to express the love he was feeling. It encompassed him, went so deep into his heart he thought it might burst. This woman, this stubborn, determined, wonderfully dedicated woman, had to become his wife. She just had to. The only thing holding him back was the fear that she wasn't ready to hear all that yet.

Shuddering signaled the end of her weeping. Caleb laid his cheek against her hair and waited. He started to silently pray—*Please, God*—then realized he should offer thanks instead. Thanks that she had survived. Thanks that he and Gavin had arrived in time. Thanks that the kidnappers had decided to pull over and were seen. Thanks for each detail that had led to this extraordinary moment.

When he whispered, "Thank You, Jesus," Vivienne raised her glistening brown eyes to meet his. He'd never seen a lovelier, more amazing sight.

"You're back," she whispered. It wasn't a question, it was a celebration.

Caleb nodded. "Yes. And I'm never abandoning my faith again. It's a miserable way to live."

She smiled slightly and whisked away remaining tears. "I wish I were a part of that vow," she said.

"You were. You are. Meeting you helped bring me back."

Lowering her lashes, she spoke quietly, just for him, as the noisy world rushed by all around them. "I don't mean believing in God, I mean the part about never leaving."

His hands cupped her cheeks and lifted her face to his. Was she saying what he thought she was saying? If he let this moment pass he feared he might never get another chance when she'd be this open to his confession, so he sighed and began to speak. "I don't intend to disappear from your life. Ever. And I want you in mine for as long as the Lord gives us."

When her trembling lips parted, he shushed her with a tender kiss. "Hear me out. I know this is way too soon to be admitting I love you, but I don't want anything to interfere with what we have together. Someday, I'd like to ask you to marry me. I know you said you wanted a lot of kids and I thought I'd never be ready for a family again, but everything has changed. Everything."

She was blinking away fresh tears. "How can you be sure?"

"I don't know. Don't have a clue. Some of the alterations in my mindset were so slight I almost missed them. I know we'll need to sit down and talk all this out before you're certain about a future with me but I'm willing to wait as long as it takes."

"That long, huh?"

Caleb studied her expression. Could she be teasing him? At a time like this, when she'd almost died and he'd poured out his heart to her, was she making a joke?

He released her and started to step back. "You think I'm kidding."

Her soft hand reached out and caressed his cheek. "No, no. It just struck me funny that I've been hiding how much I loved you so it wouldn't scare you away, and now I see we we've both been acting nonchalant for nothing."

"You love me? You're sure?"

Vivienne nodded. "Yes. I love you just as you are... or were. Without reservations. Until a few minutes ago I thought you'd go back to your job and forget all about me once this case was solved. That made me so sad I could hardly think straight."

"Never," Caleb vowed, embracing her again.

A grin lit her face despite her damp cheeks. "I get that now. That's why I was teasing you. It's made me so happy I'm giddy. Acting silly. Feeling so much joy I could dance." She sobered slightly. "If I wasn't so sore from being pushed around I might do it."

Caleb looped one arm over her shoulders and started to guide her toward a waiting ambulance. "Come on, then. Let's get you checked out."

"Not yet."

"Haven't you learned that I don't take orders well?"

"Haven't you learned that I'm going to keep giving them?" She chuckled. "I didn't mean I wouldn't let the medics look over my injuries. I meant, I want at least one real, genuine, Caleb Black kiss first."

"Here and now? In front of your boss?"

"Oh, yes. The best you've got, Mr. FBI Agent. Go ahead. Sarge is busy and not even looking our way."

"Well," he drawled, grinning. "If you're sure."

"I am so sure it's mean to make me wait." She pointed to her lips. "Lay one on me."

"That's not the most romantic invitation I've ever

gotten," he said. Then he leaned closer and tried to give her more than she had asked for.

When she opened her eyes again and looked at him he had to laugh. "Good enough?"

"Uh-huh. Whew!"

Caleb was equally impressed. As he lifted her in his arms and carried her to the ambulance, he mentally thanked God for answers to his prayers. They weren't exactly made to his order, were they? That thought was oddly comforting because the results were far better than anything he'd imagined.

Life was going to be different going forward because he was different. In a good way. He worked his old wedding ring off his finger and slipped it into his pocket. After seven lonely years he was going to have a family again.

EPILOGUE

Vivienne had been more than ready to admit her feelings for Caleb. What she hadn't thought through was how they could make a marriage work when they were both in law enforcement and both knew the daily risks and dangers. Would he be able to accept that she was a cop and a dedicated member of the K-9 unit without panicking every time he knew she was working?

Conversely, she thought she'd be okay with his future FBI assignments, but what if they sent him out of New York? What then? Would she go crazy with worry?

By the following day, when he was helping her move back into her Brooklyn apartment, her fertile imagination had come up with dozens of obstacles to their mutual happiness. She knew her nervousness was evident, she just didn't know how best to bring up the subject.

Caleb solved the problem for her when he asked, "Are you sorry already?"

"What? No!" She slipped her arms around his waist. "Are you?"

"If I was, I'd say so. I expect the same honesty out of you."

Standing her ground, she prayed he'd understand

what she was trying to say without getting upset. "I think too much. I keep coming up with reasons why we can't be happy together and it's killing me."

"I know what you mean."

"You do?" Her spirits began to lift.

"Sure. How do you think I went from being a miserable widower to being ready for a new life as a husband and maybe even a father? As I fell in love with you, I kept thinking up reasons why we couldn't be happy or why I wasn't the right man to make you happy."

"Happiness is an inside job, not a feeling dependent upon circumstances," Vivienne said. "You can't make me *be* anything, any more than I can do things that guarantee you're always going to be delighted with me. That would be a terrible burden to have to bear."

"I'm not sure I understand."

"When you accepted a terrible event as something that could not be changed, you were able to anticipate a better future. Nobody could force you to let go, it had to come from inside you. You chose joy over grieving."

Laying her cheek on his chest, she listened to the steady beat of his beloved heart as she went on. "Joy can bring happiness, sure, but it's so much deeper. I believe it comes from knowing God cares and from trusting Him. We all fall short at times. That's human nature. But beneath all the sorrow and angst and beyond all the terrible things we have to deal with on the job, there is a divine peace that's beyond explanation. I think you'll be able to accept that I'm a cop now."

Caleb pulled her closer. "I can, Vivienne. You did a great job of explaining."

"Did I? Well, don't expect deep spiritual discussions from me on a regular basis. It's taken me a long time to get this far and I know there's a lot more I have yet to figure out."

She felt laughter rumbling in his chest as he said, "I have no doubt you will tell me all about it. So when are we getting married?"

"Are you proposing, Agent Black?"

"You could say that."

"Well, okay, as long as Hank approves," Vivienne said sweetly.

Hearing his name, the border collie jumped to his feet and began to spin in circles, clearly anticipating something exciting, like a long walk.

Vivienne laughed and clapped her hands. "Good boy! Shall we all go to the *park*?"

Since Caleb had dressed more casually on his day off she didn't hesitate to take his hand and pull him toward the door. "Come on, handsome, our furry family member wants to go out." She slowed and sobered slightly so he would know she was taking his marriage proposal seriously. "We can go to the promenade and people watch while we plan our future. We'll need a home with a yard like the FBI safe house, for starters. We'll support each other in our jobs. We were both meant to be out there helping people."

His nod and wide grin warmed her heart. "Is that all?"

So filled with joy and anticipation she could hardly stay quiet, she chuckled and gave him a look that she hoped conveyed even a tiny bit of her elation. "Oh, no," she drawled. "I'm just getting started."

When Caleb made a face and said, "That's what I was afraid of," she erupted into laughter that echoed down the corridor of the apartment building.

"Will you settle down and get serious for a second," he asked.

"Why?"

The moment he pulled her back into his arms and gave her another kiss, she had her answer. No words were necessary.

* * * * *

Ever since she found the Nancy Drew books with the pink covers in her country school library, **Sharon Dunn** has loved mystery and suspense. Most of her books take place in Montana, where she lives with three nearly grown children and a hyper border collie. She lost her beloved husband of twenty-seven years to cancer in 2014. When she isn't writing, she loves to hike surrounded by God's beauty.

Books by Sharon Dunn

Love Inspired Suspense

Visit the Author Profile page at LoveInspired.com for more titles.

SCENE OF THE CRIME

Sharon Dunn

Thou art my hiding place; thou shalt preserve me
from trouble; thou shalt compass me
about with songs of deliverance.
—*Psalm* 32:7

For my counselor and king,
comforter and friend, Jesus.

ONE

Brooklyn K-9 Unit officer Jackson Davison opened the back of his SUV where his partner, Smokey, was crated. Eager to work, the chocolate Lab wagged his tail and jumped down at Jackson's command.

Jackson studied the arch of Grand Army Plaza and, beyond that, Prospect Park.

"Let's go find a body," he said. Trained as a cadaver dog, Smokey was part of the Emergency Services Division for the recently formed Brooklyn K-9 Unit.

Jackson clicked Smokey into his leash and took off at a jog toward the memorial. The vendors around the arch were still selling food, though the crowds were smaller than earlier in the day.

A call had come into Dispatch that someone had seen a body in a cluster of trees not too far from the arch. The caller had not identified him or herself and had hung up before giving any details.

Jackson and Smokey ran toward the trees that bordered the entrance to the park. The botanic garden was closed for the day but plenty of people rested on the lawn and utilized the paths as the sky turned gray on this cool September evening.

The leash remained slack. Smokey hadn't alerted to anything, though he kept his nose to the ground. The call could be a total hoax, Jackson knew, but the K-9 Unit would of course respond. The nature of the call bothered him. From the information the dispatcher had given him, the caller had not stayed on the line or provided any information other than a vague location. If the call was genuine, why not identify yourself and why hang up?

Smokey kept his nose on the path as they passed joggers, bicyclists, couples pushing baby strollers. With a jerk on the leash, Smokey veered off deeper into the trees. Jackson's heartbeat revved up a notch. Smokey had picked up on something.

Jackson commanded Smokey to sit so he could unclick his leash. He patted the Lab on the chest, the signal that he could let his nose do its thing. "Find."

Smokey took off into the deep brush and through more trees. The Lab could find remains that were years old and buried. Most civilians didn't want to think about the five stages of smells of a body after death or the different types of odors Smokey was trained to detect. Tonight would be easy for the Lab, given it was a body above ground. Jackson had no idea how long it had been in the park or the state of decomposition. Or even if there was a body.

Jackson focused on how finding bodies often gave loved ones closure in tragic situations. It wasn't a job for the fainthearted, but it was meaningful. And working with Smokey had brought a renewed sense of purpose into Jackson's life after his breakup with his fiancée.

Smokey disappeared into some bushes where an abundance of gold and red leaves hung on the foliage.

Jackson pushed branches out of the way, searching for his partner in the waning light. He could hear the dog moving through the undergrowth, yipping excitedly. They were close.

Jackson caught movement out of the corner of his eye: a face in the trees fading out of view. His heart beat a little faster. Was someone watching him? He could hear people on the paths some distance away, but this part of the park in the deep brush was not where most people wanted to be unless they were up to something. The hairs on the back of Jackson's neck stood at attention as a light breeze brushed his face. Even as he studied the foliage, he felt the weight of a gaze on him. The sound of Smokey's barking brought his mission back into focus.

When he caught up with his partner, the dog was sitting. The signal that he'd found something. "Good boy." Jackson tossed out the toy he carried on his belt for Smokey to play with, his reward for doing his job. The dog whipped the toy back and forth in his mouth.

"Drop," Jackson said. He picked up the toy and patted Smokey on the head. "Sit. Stay."

The body, partially covered by branches, was clothed in neutral colors and would not be easy to spot unless you were looking for it. Plus, it was getting dark. Another hour or so and someone wouldn't see it unless they stumbled over it, which made Jackson wonder how the caller had known it was there.

He keyed his radio. "Officer Davison here. I've got a body in Prospect Park. Male Caucasian under the age of forty, about two hundred yards in, just southwest of the Brooklyn Botanic Garden." He stepped closer to the body and shone his flashlight on it. "Looks like a bullet wound to the chest. We're going to need a forensics team here." It was too much to hope that someone had died of natural causes. Every death was hard for him.

Dispatch responded, "Ten-Four. Help is on the way."

Jackson clicked off his radio. He studied the trees just in time to catch the face again, barely visible, like a fading mist. He was being watched. The person wore a hood that covered part of his or her face. "Did you see something?" Jackson shouted. "Did you call this in?"

The person turned and ran, disappearing into the thick brush.

Jackson took off in the direction the runner had gone. Radioing for backup would slow him down. As his feet pounded the hard earth, another thought occurred to him. Was this the person who had shot the man in the chest? Sometimes criminals hung around to witness the police response to their handiwork. The caller and the killer could be one in the same.

Pulling his weapon, he hurried in the direction the hooded figure had gone, knowing that Smokey would stay with the body.

He came out into an open area where a dozen or so people were having a barbecue and playing guitar and bongos. The revelers stopped their activity and stared at him: a normal reaction to seeing a cop with a gun. Jackson caught a flash of motion in his peripheral vision and resumed his pursuit. He could hear the watcher in the bushes up ahead though he did not catch a glimpse of him. He came out on a path that was mostly deserted. Several runners disappeared over a hill and then he was by himself.

Jackson tuned his ears to the sounds around him. The wind rustling the dried leaves on the trees, music and voices in the distance. He studied the trees in sectors, not seeing any movement. His attention was drawn to a garbage can just as an object hit the back of his head with intense force. He swayed and blinked. Pain radiated from the base of his skull. He heard metal tinging as something was thrown into the garbage can and then the pounding of retreating footsteps. He crumpled to the ground and his world went black.

Minutes or hours later, he didn't know which, his eyes fluttered open and he winced at the bright light shining in his face.

"Hey, there," said a singsongy female voice.

Jackson shaded his eyes. "Get that thing out of my face."

The flashlight was clicked off. "Sorry, I was checking your pupils to see if they were dilated."

He kind of liked the voice. It reminded him of the nonjudgmental woman who gave directions in his truck GPS. When he'd first moved to New York two years ago, from Texas, that voice had been a comfort as he'd tried to navigate a new city.

He looked up into her face with his eyes still half closed, fearing another dose of blinding light. Soft eyes, blond curls and dimples. Only the forensic suit and booties gave her away. She looked more like a kindergarten teacher than a tech. He'd seen Darcy Fields, the forensics specialist, at a distance when she came into K-9 headquarters or to work a crime scene, but he'd never talked to her.

She leaned back, resting on her knees. "You're the officer who called in the body, right?"

"How did you find me?"

"It took some coaxing—he didn't want to leave the

body—but your dog led me to you, and the gathering crowd was a good hint." She turned slightly so he had view of Smokey. Sitting obediently, his tail did a little thump on the ground when Jackson looked at him. And then Jackson saw the gathering crowd around him.

His cheeks grew warm and he stood. Now he felt stupid. How had he managed to let himself get knocked unconscious? He'd never hear the end it from the rest of the K-9 team.

She held out hand for him to help him up. "I'm Darcy Fields, Forensics."

"I know who you are." He pointed to her paper bodysuit. "The outfit gives it away."

She laughed. "Believe it or not, I was at a very fancy shindig when I got the call." She unzipped her suit slightly to reveal a sequined dress. "Normally my hair is pulled back when I work, not curly." She had a sort of bouncy bright quality that didn't fit with being a crime tech. "So why were you all the way over here playing Rip Van Winkle?"

"There was someone hiding in the foliage where I found the body. The person took off running and I chased. I think he or she wanted to make sure I found the dead man, but didn't want to get caught. I think that's why I was hit in the head."

Darcy narrowed her eyes. "But you don't know for sure if the same person you saw in the trees hit you in the head?"

"No, I didn't see who hit me and I never got a good look at the person who was watching me." He knew Darcy must see everything in terms of how it would play in court. She wasn't wrong. His theory was only speculation at this point. "I know we can't draw conclusions until the evidence is examined."

"Right. I don't know anything until the evidence speaks to me," she said. "Could be the person you saw in the trees was the concerned citizen who called it in, could be connected to the crime, could be something else entirely."

Concerned citizen, he doubted it. "I didn't get a good look, couldn't tell you if it was a man or a woman. But I think he or she dropped something in that trash can."

Darcy pushed through the crowd of onlookers and moved toward the garbage can, pulling gloves out of a back pocket. She sorted through a pile of plastic cups and fast-food wrappers before pulling out a small gun. "Okay, now things are getting weird."

Some of the crowd dispersed, having lost interest, while others watched Darcy bag the gun.

"I don't think the person I chased was a concerned citizen. I think he or she was a witness to, or a part of, the crime that led to that man being shot," said Jackson.

"That doesn't make sense. Why leave evidence behind? Are we dealing with the world's dumbest criminal?" Darcy held up the bagged gun.

"Believe me, I've encountered some pretty dumb criminals."

Darcy pursed and released her lips as though she were thinking. "Did you actually see him or her drop the gun in the trash can?"

"No. I thought I heard it as I was losing consciousness." Now he realized how flimsy his story sounded from a legal standpoint. "I know it won't stand up in court. Just because events happened close together doesn't mean they're related."

"This could be from a different crime. We won't know until we get it to the lab." Darcy turned to face him.

Even though his gut told him this was all connected, he saw now how he didn't have any solid evidence to link anything together. All he had was what lawyers would call "circumstantial."

"I have to get back to work." She took several steps and then looked over her shoulder. He liked her smile. "I'm glad we found you. I didn't need another mystery on my hands."

He followed her back to the body, where other techs had already cordoned off an area with crime scene tape. A van belonging to the coroner had driven onto the grass. The coroner and his assistant stood by the vehicle, waiting to approach the body.

Several uniformed officers stood around, as well. Jackson approached one of them and gave his statement about the watcher in the woods and being hit in the back of the head. "I'm not the detective on this case, but I think my being hit is somehow connected to that man's death."

The uniformed officer nodded. "I'll make sure the detective assigned to the case gets your statement."

"I'll file a report about being assaulted." Jackson turned his attention back to the crime scene.

Once the coroner examined the body, the forensic team went to work. After pulling her hair up in one of those hair ties women wore like bracelets, Darcy examined the body while the other two techs combed the area around the deceased man.

Jackson clicked Smokey back into his leash. Still stirred up by the face in the woods and what it meant,

Jackson hung back to watch Darcy and the others work, curious as to what they might find.

Darcy took notes and performed a cursory study of the body. The autopsy would reveal more. The victim was dressed in casual clothes appropriate for the time of year. Flannel shirt in grays and browns, tan denim jacket, boots and jeans.

As she stared into the victim's lifeless face, Darcy said a prayer for him and for the family members who would soon be getting the news of the man's death. "Shot at close range. I'd say maybe a .38," she said aloud.

About a month ago, she'd been in the same park dealing with another person shot at point-blank range. The perpetrator of that crime, Reuben Bray, was now in jail awaiting trial.

Jackson Davison and his cute dog were still hanging around. She felt a little distracted by the K-9 officer's presence. He had a faint accent that suggested he wasn't from New York. Somewhere from the South maybe. Every time their eyes locked, her heart fluttered a little. He was probably just hanging around in a professional capacity anyway. What did it matter if she found him attractive? She had a rule about not dating cops. The last time she'd opened her heart to an officer, he'd only been using her to expedite evidence. As nice as Jackson seemed, she'd vowed to never again fall for a police officer.

She looked at the other tech. Harlan Germaine was an older man with gray hair and a beard, and glasses much too big for his thin face. "Did the coroner pull ID on him?" she asked.

"Man's name is Griffin Martel," Harlan said. "Sorry about you having to leave your night out for this."

"Actually, I was grateful. It was kind of not going anywhere." Her church had decided to have a fancy dress-up night followed by a catered meal for all the young singles in the congregation. "Most men's eyes glaze over when I talk about my work. Guess I should get an interesting hobby, so I have something else to talk about. Don't know why I get my hopes up." She spoke under her breath more to herself than to Harlan. "No one wants to the date the nerdy science girl."

Harlan shook his head. "Don't give up so easily, Darcy." Harlan walked away from the body, eyes studying the ground. "I still don't see any shell casings."

"Even if we don't find any, I say the guy was shot here. Plenty of people in the park. Someone would have noticed a body being dragged or hauled here. There is no way to get a vehicle to this area without raising alarm bells. If he was shot here, the killer must have used a sound suppressor," she noted. "Otherwise someone would have heard the shots and phoned it in much sooner. I can see the early stages of rigor in the face and neck muscles, I would put the TOD at less than three hours ago."

"You know this is about the same area that Reuben Bray shot that guy. Same MO, too, shot at point-blank range," Harlan said.

Darcy had thought of that, too. "Reuben is sitting in a jail cell in Rikers. I'm set to testify at his trial soon." She looked back at the dead man. "I hope we don't have a copycat on our hands."

She tilted her head. The overcast sky hinted of rain.

"We better hurry or a bunch of evidence is going to be washed away."

Jackson Davison came to the edge of the crime scene. "Smokey's getting restless. I'm going to take him for a run. I'd be curious to know about that gun."

Focused on her work, Darcy barely looked up. "Sure, I'll let you know once we get the lab results. Fingerprints. How recently it was fired. Who it's registered to…blah, blah, blah. You know the drill."

Jackson laughed.

She liked that he seemed to get her sense of humor.

The team worked on, taking photographs and collecting any possible evidence just as rain started to sprinkle from the sky. The coroner moved in to load the body to be taken in for an autopsy.

She unzipped her suit and took off her booties, handing them over to Harlan to dispose of.

"Need a ride?" Harlan shouted over his shoulder.

"Thanks, I took the subway here. I can take it home if you can pack my gear out." The gear would stay in the forensics van for the next time she got called to the scene of a crime on her day off.

She walked the crime scene one final time, taking mental photographs and making sure she hadn't missed anything that might be important later. It was a practice she'd learned early in her career. Though the team was meticulous in photographing everything, she needed to keep a picture in her head, as well.

"Satisfied?" Harlan asked as he loaded the last piece of equipment into the van.

Darcy nodded. She just wanted to get home and soak in a hot tub. Not so much because of work—she loved her job—but because the church event had been such a disaster. "See you bright and early in the morning."

Harlan gave her a salute before walking away.

The crime scene tape remained in place. Darcy picked up her coat and purse from where she'd set them next to an officer guarding the scene when she'd arrived. She stared at the empty space now that everyone had left. Already her mind was trying to picture the scenario that had brought the dead man here. She looked at these cases as a puzzle to be solved. Right now, she only had a few pieces to work with. "How and why did you end up here, Griffin Martel? What is your story?"

Rain started showering from the sky. It was dark. She shone the flashlight where the body had been one more time, searching for a shell casing. She looked up, aware that she was alone. It was so late that she couldn't even hear people in the park. Most everyone had gone home.

A branch cracked in the trees that surrounded the crime scene. Jackson's story of someone watching the body became foremost in her mind. "Hello, is someone out there?"

She shook off her paranoia. All the same, she turned and walked through the trees at a brisk pace, heading for a more open area. When she got to the path that led to the park entrance, she didn't see anyone.

Darcy stepped toward the crosswalk to cross Flatbush Avenue. Halfway across, bright lights shone in her eyes as the roar of an engine surrounded her. A car was coming straight for her. She ran to get to the other side of the street. The car followed her up on the grass just as a body slammed against hers, taking her to the ground. The car sped past and then peeled out of view.

Off to her side, a dog barked.

"What was that about?" The voice was Jackson Davison's. He rolled away from her.

Her heart was still racing. "I have no idea."

He stood and reached out a hand to help her up. His hand was strong and callused. She stood on wobbly knees, resting her palm against her raging heart.

"Some crazy freak, huh?"

"Yeah, I guess," she said.

"I didn't get a look at the make or model of the car or we could call it in."

Her mind tried to rationalize why someone would try to run over her. "Maybe just a guy who had one too many. I'm glad you were here. That car might have mowed me down." Her hands were still shaking.

"After I took Smokey for a run, I was hoping to catch you or one of the other techs," he said. "See what you figured out."

"Any information we have is preliminary. We'll release official statements when we know more and next of kin has been notified. Your department will get a briefing if it's pertinent." Her voice sounded cold. This wasn't about Jackson. She was being defensive because of what had happened with the officer who had only dated her to move his case along. "I'm sorry. It's just that I need to follow proper protocol."

"I understand," Jackson said. "Guess I'm embarrassed that I let myself get hit on the noggin like that. Just wanted to know if it was connected to finding that body."

"Like I said, we've just started to connect the dots." Darcy studied him for a long moment.

The rain intensified and the few remaining people in

the area scattered. He touched her arm above the elbow. "Let's get out of this."

They found shelter underneath a gazebo.

Smokey nestled between them on the bench as they took seats to watch the rain. "Sorry about that," said Jackson. "He gets kind of jealous."

Smokey licked his face and then turned his head and groaned at Darcy.

Darcy laughed.

They stared out at the rain and listened to its symphony on the roof of the gazebo.

"You look nice, by the way," he said. "Sorry you got pulled away from your shindig."

"Thank you."

Jackson seemed like a nice guy, but he was a cop, and that made him off-limits to her. Darcy stared down at the dress she'd paid way too much money for and would probably not ever wear again. The disappointment of the party at church, the crime scene and nearly being mowed down by that car—it all hit her at once. She thought she might cry. "I need to get to the subway. I want to go home."

"You seem kind of shook up. A car coming at you like that can take its toll. How about I drive you home?"

"I don't mind the subway."

"Okay, let us at least walk you to the entrance." His voice was filled with compassion. He clicked the leash on Smokey. "I won't take no for an answer."

As they walked through the rain to the subway entrance, she found herself grateful that Jackson and Smokey were with her. The whole evening had left her out of sorts.

At the top of the stairs that led to the subway, Darcy

turned to face Jackson. "Thank you. I will let you know if we find anything once we start combing through the evidence."

Jackson gave her a nod. She watched as he turned with his dog and disappeared into the crowd. As she made her way down the subway stairs, she had the oddest feeling that she was being watched.

She stared around at the sea of faces on the platform. Her heart beat a little faster. The crowd compressed, preparing to board the train. Someone bumped her from behind, setting her off balance. She recovered before she fell. She craned her neck to see who had pushed her. All eyes were looking elsewhere.

The doors slid open. Even as she stepped inside the train, she sensed the weight of a gaze on her.

TWO

Jackson watched from the sidelines as Darcy moved toward a throng of reporters outside the building that housed the forensics lab. Cameras flashed and news reporters pressed in close with microphones. Darcy had texted him that she'd be making a statement about the Griffin Martel murder. He'd appreciated the heads-up.

She was dressed in a navy blue suit, but he noticed that her shoes were pink and red, with colorful leather flowers, and she wore a hot-pink scarf.

Thanks to his ex-fiancée, Jackson noticed things like that. Two years ago, Amelia had wanted to make it as a fashion stylist in New York. Wanting to be supportive of her and her dreams, Jackson had put in for a transfer from Dallas. While they'd lived in separate apartments, they had continued to plan their wedding. The idea had been to stay in New York for a few years and then return to Texas. Five months after the move, she'd informed him she was in love with the photographer she worked with on the fashion shoots. Jackson and Amelia had been high school sweethearts. They'd planned a life together from the time they were sixteen. Even a year and half after their breakup, he didn't think the hole inside would ever heal.

From what Amelia had taught him, Darcy was breaking all kinds of fashion rules. He kind of liked that about her. Though he didn't know the reason why, it was common knowledge that Darcy Fields didn't date cops. That suited him just fine. He was not in the market to get involved with anybody. A friendship with someone who understood the nature of his work would be nice, though.

Darcy pulled a typed statement out of her pocket. She gave Jackson a quick smile that showed her dimples then focused her attention on the waiting reporters.

"The body found in Prospect Park on Monday night was identified as Griffin Martel from Trenton, New Jersey. We still do not know why Mr. Martel was here in Brooklyn. We believe he was lured or lead to the secluded spot in the park and shot at point-blank range. No motive has yet been determined, though Martel did have a record for selling prescription drugs. Detectives are currently interviewing his known associates. Police are following all possible leads. We believe at this point that this is an isolated incident and that there is no reason for people visiting or living in New York to be afraid."

A female reporter pushed her way to the front. "Isn't this murder similar to the murder Reuben Bray allegedly committed? Same part of the park? Same method of death?"

Darcy remained poised despite the reporters moving in tightly around her. "Yes, there are similarities. But Reuben Bray was in a jail cell at the time of Mr. Martel's murder."

A male reporter asked, "Is it possible you put the wrong man in jail and that a killer is still on the streets?"

Another reporter piped up. "Are we looking at a serial killer?"

Jackson clenched his jaw. He hated the fear mongering the press tended to elicit. And he didn't like the way they were treating Darcy.

"No, the evidence on Reuben Bray was solid," she said.

The reporters began peppering her with questions. Because of his movie-star good looks, Reuben Bray had become a sort of media darling.

"Aren't you scheduled to give expert testimony in his trial soon?"

"Isn't it true that there was some controversy around charging Reuben with murder?"

"He was low-level criminal who stole cell phones and purses and then he moved on to murder. Isn't it rare for criminals to change the type of crime they commit?"

From his vantage point, Jackson could see that Darcy was gripping the podium. But her voice remained calm. "Yes, but Mr. Bray's psychological profile showed he was a man who couldn't bear to be humiliated. And the man he killed had done that by chasing him down to get his cell phone back. Please, we are here to talk about the murder of Griffin Martel."

The reporters began to crowd Darcy. She took a step back as they surrounded her, essentially blocking the door to the building.

Jackson couldn't stand it anymore. He swooped in and gathered Darcy in the crook of his arm. "I think Ms. Fields has answered enough of your questions today."

"Are you her protection?" a reporter asked.

"I'm her police escort."

"Why does she need to be protected?" The female

reporter trailed behind Jackson and Darcy as he led to her toward his K-9 patrol vehicle. "Ms. Fields, do you know how to do your job?"

Darcy planted her feet, her lips drawn into a straight line.

Jackson whispered in her ear, keeping his arm around her. "Don't react. Just keep walking."

As the reporters crowded toward the K-9 patrol SUV, Jackson led Darcy to the front passenger side. Smokey perched in the back seat in his crate, chin in the air. Smart dog, he knew better than to bark or to get excited by the people surrounding the vehicle.

"Excuse me," said Jackson, pushing past a reporter to open the driver's-side door once he'd settled Darcy inside.

A female reporter with a ponytail and penciled-in eyebrows stepped up to him. "Why is the K-9 Unit involved in protecting a forensics tech?" The reporter leaned a little closer to him. "Aren't you the officer who was hit on the head the night Griffin Martel's body was found?"

The assault had made the news. Jackson was standing so the car door acted as shield between him and the reporters. "I'm not protecting her in an official capacity. I'm doing this as a friend. It's clear to me you guys are looking for a controversy where there is none."

The reporter leaned over the open car door and looked straight at Darcy. "Two men are dead. Killed in a similar way and place. How do we know it won't happen again?"

Jackson shook his head and got into the SUV. He gripped the steering wheel and let out a heavy breath.

"Thank you for getting me out of there. The evidence

in the Reuben Bray case was solid. I don't know why they have to stir things up like this."

"'Cause they're reporters," Jackson said.

She glanced over at the journalists mingling outside the building. "I need to get back to the lab."

"It's Friday night and you're going back to work?"

"What can I say? I live on the wild side. Stuff is piled up—I want to deal with it. It's not like I have any place to go."

"What are you working on that is so important that you have to give up your Friday night?"

"That home invasion—double homicide, husband and wife, little girl left alive. Lucy Emery?" Darcy said.

Jackson nodded. "I know the case well. Trust me, those unsolved homicides are of foremost importance to the entire K-9 Unit. One of our officers, Nate Slater, married Lucy's aunt. They've filed papers to adopt her."

The case hit very close to home for the entire unit. The Emerys had been murdered on the twentieth anniversary of another set of parents' double homicide. Same MO, down to the description of the killer, and a young child left unharmed at the scene. That child Penelope McGregor, and her older brother Bradley, who hadn't been home during the murders, now worked for the Brooklyn K-9 Unit. The team believed they knew who killed the McGregors' parents twenty years ago, but he'd eluded capture so far. They were also pretty sure the recent murders had been committed by a copycat.

"I'd like to close that case, too," Darcy said. "There were fibers left on the doorknob at the Emery house that might contain the killer's DNA—if I can just isolate and extract them."

"You're not going to get back into the lab without being swarmed. You can take a break for dinner, can't you? They should be gone by then." Jackson stuck the key in the ignition.

"Sure. I can phone Harlan and let him know." She pulled her phone from her pants' pocket.

He started the SUV and pulled away from the curb. "I know just the place."

While she phoned the lab to let her tech partner know where she was, Jackson wove through traffic to a great pizza place close to the lab. It wasn't Sal's Pizza, his favorite pizzeria, which was down the street from K-9 headquarters in Bay Ridge, but it came a close second. After looking for a parking spot for ten minutes, he finally found one.

Darcy pressed her phone against her chest. "I hope we're going to Park Pizza. It's my favorite."

"You've gotta try Sal's sometime. But yes. And we can eat in the car since getting a table is rough."

Jackson's dinner choice was purposely informal; he didn't want her thinking this was a date. They walked to Park Pizza, which was brimming, as usual, and stood in line.

They each ordered two slices to go and drinks. Once they were settled back in the SUV, Smokey rested his nose on the back seat making sniffing noises when Jackson opened the crate door so the dog could stretch and be with them while they were parked.

"He looks like he wants a bite of pizza," Darcy said.

"He loves the smell of people food, but he'll only eat out of my hand," Jackson told her. "People food isn't good for him anyway."

With her to-go container resting on her lap, Darcy

reached back and brushed the top of Smokey's head. "He's pretty charming, looking at me with those big brown eyes."

She laughed and took a bite of her pepperoni pizza. Smokey moved so his nose was still resting on the back of the seat, but he was closer to Darcy.

"I can feel his breath on my neck." She seemed mildly amused. "He really likes the smell of this pizza."

Jackson petted Smokey's head and then under his chin when the dog came closer to him. "What a good boy!" Smokey licked Jackson's face.

Her phone rang. She stared at it. "It's Harlan." She pressed her talk button and listened. "Okay, have a good time with your wife." Darcy ended the call and stared at her phone before putting it away.

"Sounds like everyone else is calling it a night. Are you sure you want to get back to the lab?" he asked.

She looked at him after taking a sip of her drink. "Jackson, thanks. This was a nice break, but I do want to get back to work. The colder the Emery case gets, the less chance we have of solving it."

When they finished their pizza, Jackson commanded Smokey to get back in his crate. After latching the door to the crate, Jackson started the SUV. Heading back toward the lab, he noted that the traffic was lighter. It was dark already when he pulled into the empty lot. "Where's your car?"

"I use public transit except when in a professional capacity—less expensive."

"Are you all right with working in the lab alone?"

"I do it all the time." She pushed the SUV door open. "Thanks again, Jackson, for the rescue from the reporters." Darcy seemed lost in thought.

"No problem."

He watched her walk to the outside entrance to the lab and swipe her badge across the sensor by the door so it clicked open. Darcy disappeared inside. It seemed sad to him that such a cute and smart woman was working on a Friday night. But then again, what was he doing on a Friday night? "Streaming a movie with my best friend, right Smokey?"

The dog let out a yip.

He was about to pull back onto the street when he saw shadows and movement. Someone disappeared around the side of the building.

Great. A reporter had waited around and was now looking for a way into the lab to bother Darcy some more.

Darcy hurried down the hall. Her footsteps echoed on the hard floor. After donning her lab coat, she walked over to the microscope that contained a slide with one of the fibers from the Emery case. The fiber was natural, cotton, probably from a piece of clothing. There had been DNA on the fiber, but it was a minute specimen. To make the sample usable, she'd had to grow it using polymerase chain reaction to make the DNA replicate itself.

She let out a breath. She'd actually explained that process to a man at the church dinner she'd gotten dressed up for and watched his eyes glaze over.

She peered at the lens, feeling a heaviness. This was her life, working alone on a Friday night. Dinner with Jackson Davison had been a brief reprieve even if it had been very informal. Though he seemed a bit guarded, she felt drawn to Jackson's quiet nature. He wasn't a man who talked just to hear the sound of his voice. He chose his words carefully. Maybe this would be the start of a friendship for both of them.

She looked through the lens of the microscope just as an odd pounding noise caused her to lift her head. Was Jackson at the door? The sound was coming from somewhere else. Above her, maybe? The lab was on the ground floor of a three-story building. As far as she knew, the offices above her were a nine-to-five operation. Was someone working late?

She shook her head. Her first thought had been that Jackson had come back to tell her something. Funny how thoughts of him lingered in her mind. He'd have to knock on the main door to get in, though. It locked from the inside.

Darcy walked over to a shelf of textbooks and pulled one down. She suspected the DNA on the fiber was skin flakes. The challenge was that it was such a small sample.

She leaned on the counter and flipped through the book, hoping for clarity on how to proceed. Anything that fell outside of standard lab procedure might be called into question in court. Her mind was always on the little girl who had been in the home at the time of the murders. She was in a secure, loving home now. And if they could catch the man who had killed her mom and dad, she would grow up with a sense of closure and that justice did prevail.

Darcy closed the textbook. The lights in the lab flickered off. Darcy stepped toward the switch, toggling it. But the room remained dark. A breaker must have blown. Holding her hands out in front of her so she wouldn't bump into anything, she moved to the drawer where a flashlight was kept.

A hand went over her mouth. Another wrapped around her waist, holding her arms in place.

Terror raged through her. She twisted to get away, thrashing with all the strength she had. She freed herself and whirled around. This time her assailant attacked her from the front, reaching for her throat. In the process, she was backed into a counter. Her assailant's hold on her remained strong. As they struggled, pieces of evidence and equipment fell to the floor. She tried to pull away from the counters before more work could be destroyed.

She moved with such force that though she broke free from the grip of her assailant, she fell on the floor. She crawled on all fours toward where she thought the door might be. The assailant pushed more things off the counter. Items crashed against the floor. Glass shattered.

Gasping for air, Darcy reached out for a wall and pulled herself to her feet.

A body slammed against hers and she was facedown on the floor again. She flipped over onto her back. Hands wrapped around her neck and squeezed. She clawed at the hands trying to choke her.

"Darcy." A voice sounded in the distance and then she heard footsteps up the hall. The same direction the assailant had come from. The voice was Jackson's.

The hands let go of her. Her assailant crashed toward the door and then retreating footfalls echoed up the hallway. Choking and coughing, she wheezed in air. Another set of footsteps hurried past her in the hallway. That must be Jackson going after her attacker.

She sat up, still in shock from the assault. She reached out for a wall to steady herself, her heart pounding wildly. Her legs felt like cooked noodles, but she pulled herself to her feet. She glanced over her shoulder. Because it was so dark, she was unable to fully assess the damage to the lab.

She made her way to the door.

When she peered down the hallway where the two sets of footsteps had passed, a flashlight shone in her face, coming toward her.

"Jackson?" Her voice was hoarse.

He ran to her. "I tried to catch him. He got away through the main door of the lab on this floor."

"Yes, you can open it from the inside, but it locks behind you."

His hand reached out for her in the dark. "You okay?"

She was still shaking. "What happened? How did that guy get in?" More than the attack, she was upset about the work that had been destroyed by her struggle with the assailant.

"He got down to this floor through the ductwork on the floor above you. I followed him. He accesed the second floor through an unlatched window by the fire escape. I was just getting ready to pull out of the lot when I saw someone sneaking around outside. I thought it was some reporter looking for a scoop."

"No." Tears warmed the corners of her eyes. "Oh, Jackson. He broke things in the lab and then tried to strangle me." Her voice faltered.

He took her in his arms. "Hey, it's okay."

She rested her face against his chest. "I don't mean to be such a basket case."

"You've had quite a shake-up." He held her until she pulled way.

Darcy wiped at her eyes. "I'm going to go look at the breaker box to see if I can get the electricity back on. I have to know how much damage was done. Can I borrow your flashlight?"

"I'll go with you."

She was grateful for his offer. Though it appeared that the attacker had escaped, she was still not calmed down. She moved down the hallway to the breaker box. Jackson shone the light for her while she pushed the breakers back on. Light filled the hallway and spilled out of the main lab.

"Darcy, I have to call this in."

"I know. The attacker might have touched stuff, maybe there are fingerprints." She thought for a moment, trying to remember. "I think he was wearing gloves."

"You can't do the dusting. You're the crime victim."

She let go a nervous laugh. "Yes, of course, that would represent a conflict of interest. Me investigating my own crime."

"Look, the detectives will be here shortly. You can make a statement and then I'll take you home. No way am I letting you ride the subway."

"Jackson, thank you so much. I just need to get my jacket."

She stepped back into the brightly lit lab. The sight of the smashed glass on the floor made her feel like she'd been punched in the stomach. "Oh, no." She moved to pick up an evidence bag with shell casings.

Jackson grabbed her at the elbow. "Don't touch anything."

"Of course. What was I thinking?" She stared at the mess. The attack had thrown her so far off-kilter, she'd almost contaminated the crime scene. A total rookie move. As she stared at the disarray, she still couldn't absorb what had happened. "The stuff on the counter that got pushed off was mostly from some cold cases we're working on. Nothing current. But all the same, it's messed-up evidence."

"It does seem kind of random and angry."

She shook her head. "Who would do such a thing? A reporter just would have tried to corner me and ask me questions."

"Yeah, maybe we can rule them out," Jackson said.

"The list is a mile long of people who don't like the results the lab produces for trials," said Darcy. "Do you think this attack was about revenge or anger?"

"It's clear that someone doesn't want you or the other techs to be able to do your work. But if they wanted to destroy evidence for a specific case, this wouldn't be the way to do it."

"Or they don't want us working on a current case. If you destroy the lab, it slows down our ability to move cases toward trial." She touched her neck where the assailant had tried to choke her. "It would take time for someone to find evidence connected to a specific case. Maybe they thought they were going to have time to look around and didn't count on me being here."

Jackson shook his head. "Hard to say."

A chill ran up her spine. She leaned a little closer to Jackson, relishing the sense of safety she felt when she was close to him but unable to shake the fear that invaded her thoughts.

THREE

Once detectives arrived and took Darcy's statement, Jackson ushered her up the hallway and out the door. She seemed to have regained her composure and now was focused her concern on the lab being processed properly. Maybe thinking about gathering evidence had distracted her from the trauma of the attack. Jackson knew from experience that there could be a delayed effect where Darcy's emotional response was concerned. He wanted to stay with her until he was sure she was going to be okay.

A forensics van from Manhattan pulled up outside. Two techs, a man and a woman, got out.

Darcy watched them enter the building. "Guess that is the outside team who will process the evidence. I know one of them. I would really like to talk to him."

Jackson cleared his throat.

"I know. I know. It's not my case. It can't be. I just hope I can go back to work tomorrow," Darcy said.

"Where do you live?"

"Williamsburg."

"Me, too. Come on, Smokey and I will take you

home." Jackson held the SUV door for her and then got in behind the wheel. She gave him the address.

He drove through the city streets, past neighborhoods that were quiet and others where the night had clearly just begun. He circled the block several times before he found a parking space not too far from her apartment building.

"Do you live alone?"

"My sister lives with me, but she is away on an overnight field trip. She's a choir teacher at a private high school."

"How about I walk you to your door?"

Her wrinkled forehead suggested she wasn't crazy about the idea.

"I know you can take care of yourself, Darcy. This is for my peace of mind and, besides, Smokey needs to stretch his legs. There was no time to get him out of the crate when I was chasing the intruder. He would have gotten some exercise then."

"Well, I can't deny Smokey some exercise."

They got out of the SUV and headed up the block toward her place.

Smokey emitted a low-level growl.

"What is that about?"

"I'm not sure," Jackson said. "Something's bothering him."

She placed the key in building's entrance lock but didn't turn it.

Darcy took her hand away from the door, leaving the key in the lock. The hesitation suggested she was concerned about entering her building. Smokey's agitation had given them both pause.

"Why don't you let Smokey and I go inside and clear your place?"

She nodded.

He was glad she wasn't brushing off safety concerns. "You stand back. Let me open the door."

Darcy stepped to one side while Jackson turned the key in the lock and opened the door. Her apartment was on the ground floor. As he opened the door to her place with her key, she said, "The light switch is just on the inside of the wall."

He felt along the wall, flipped on the light and then commanded Smokey to enter and search. "Stay in the hallway for now," he told Darcy.

Smokey circled the room, sniffing the couch and the overstuffed chair. The dog padded into the kitchenette but never alerted.

Darcy's apartment was done up with furniture that looked like it had come from thrift and antique stores, albeit repainted in bright colors. She had a lot of antique-looking, floral-printed curtains and pillows, and he noted a tablecloth and doilies. The whole room looked like a place his grandmother would like, only more vibrant.

Smokey came and sat at Jackson's feet. "Looks like it's all clear."

"I suppose that's good news." Darcy untied her scarf, tossed it over the back of a chair, kicked off her shoes and flopped onto the couch. "At least I can catch my breath."

Maybe, Jackson thought, Darcy had been at the wrong place at the wrong time and the attack was about revenge against someone else or destroying evidence. But then he thought about the car that had tried to run her over near Grand Army Plaza. He was concerned about her safety. He really didn't feel comfortable leaving her. Darcy struck him as being a very independent woman. She probably would rebuff his offer to protect her.

He sat on the opposite end of the couch. Maybe he could keep the conversation going. "So why do you think that person was in the lab tonight?"

She closed her eyes and thought for a moment. "It has to be the attack was about something the lab did, not me personally. Somebody didn't like results that sent someone to prison." She put her hand on her hip. "We've already talked about this, Jackson."

Maybe she'd figured out he was trying to delay leaving her. "True. I'm just trying to figure it out."

"The destruction of the evidence seemed kind of random," she said. "I think it is someone mad because our work sent a loved one to jail. That would be my guess."

A scratching noise made both him and Smokey jump. Jackson stood.

"That's just Mr. Tubbs, my cat. He wants out. He must have been hiding when you cleared the room." She disappeared down the hall.

"Sorry about that. I must have shut the door after I cleared the room. He was well hidden for Smokey not to alert to his prescence." Jackson hadn't realized how on edge he was until the noise of a cat put him on high alert. Smokey picked up on his nervousness and paced. As partners, they were tuned in to each other just as he would be if with a human officer.

Darcy emerged from the hallway, a fat gray cat plodding behind her. "Don't worry, Mr. Tubbs likes dogs."

Jackson moved toward the Lab and commanded him

to sit. "Smokey has been trained to deal with all kinds of animals." Homing in on the cat, the dog thumped his tail on the hardwood floor and emitted a whine.

Mr. Tubbs, acting as though he had not even seen Smokey, jumped up on the couch. The feline did not so much as rest on the arm of the couch as he draped himself. His round body made his legs appear stubby.

"So do you want a cup of tea or something?" Darcy asked.

"That would be nice," Jackson said. She must have sensed his reluctance to go but wasn't going to push him out the door.

"Go ahead and sit down." Darcy busied herself in the kitchenette, pulling things out of cupboards and putting the kettle on.

Jackson again settled on the couch, away from Mr. Tubbs. Still sitting, Smokey watched the cat intently. The cat flicked his tail and narrowed his eyes.

Darcy took her seat on the couch, saying, "It will take a minute for the kettle to boil." She turned to face him. Her light brown eyes were full of life. "I appreciate you being worried about me, but I'm okay here. I'll lock my door and windows. I always do."

Jackson rose to his feet and shoved his hands in his pockets. He wandered across the room where one wall was a floor-to-ceiling bookshelf. In addition to the science, chemistry and crime detection books, Darcy also had books on art and some classic literature. "I've read a lot of these books. Grew up in the country with no television."

"Jackson, you're avoiding what I just said."

He ran his fingers though his hair. "Look, Darcy, I know you can take care of yourself, but I think maybe

Smokey and I should at least do a quick search around the building."

"Then will you feel comfortable going home?"

The answer to that question was no, but he nodded all the same.

"Do the search. The tea will be ready by then."

"Lock the door behind me. I'll knock three times when I come back." He wasn't sure why he felt protective of her. It certainly wasn't because she acted like some kind of damsel in distress. Maybe he was starting to have big brother feelings toward her. He missed his siblings in Texas. Since his breakup with Amelia, he hadn't gotten out much to meet new people. His idea of a social outing was basketball with the other K-9 officers. Maybe it was time to change that.

Darcy rose. "Okay, I'll wait for your knock."

Jackson clicked the leash on Smokey and headed for the door.

Once outside the apartment, Jackson waited for the sound of the dead bolt clicking into place. He then left the building, searched the side streets, circled the building and then took Smokey up the stairwell. Smokey didn't growl. The September night was dark and crisp. Several streets away, he heard the thrum of Friday-night traffic but the streets around Darcy's place were pretty quiet.

Satisfied, Jackson returned to Darcy's door and knocked three times.

Darcy slid back dead bolt and undid the locks.

"All clear," he told her as she opened the door.

She seemed mildly amused by his protective nature. He nodded.

"Tea's hot."

"Great, I'll have some and then Smokey and I will be out of your hair."

She handed him a steaming mug. "You haven't been bad company." He liked her smile. Those dimples really got to him. "It's not like I had a crazy night planned. Just hanging with Mr. Tubbs and a good book."

"Yeah, it's pretty much the same for me and Smokey."

"Well, we should do something about that." She took a sip of her tea. "As friends, I mean. I don't date cops."

"Yeah, I heard." He turned toward the window by the door that looked out on the street where the residents of the building probably parked.

She stood beside him. "You asked around about me?"

"It's sort of common knowledge." He shrugged, feeling his cheeks grow warm. "That policy is all right by me."

He took another sip of tea. Behind him, Smokey became suddenly agitated. He emitted a high-pitched bark. Jackson turned to look at the dog as a percussive boom hit his eardrums. Glass shattered all around him. Taking Darcy down with him, he dove for the cover of the coffee table.

The last thing he heard was Darcy's scream.

Long, straight shards of glass came at Darcy. Fueled by some primitive survival instinct, she'd taken a step back right before the booming sound vibrated through her chest. Glass rained down on her. Smokey's barking surrounded her. The dog was frantically bouncing around Jackson, who lay on top of her behind the coffee table. He rolled off of her but remained close to the floor.

"Stay down. That was most likely a rifle shot from

a distance. The shooter might still be in place, ready to fire again."

She lay on her stomach and peered into his face. Tense seconds ticked by.

She noticed that her hand was bleeding. The sight of the blood did not bother her, but she was suddenly aware of the pain of the cuts.

Jackson reached out, touching his hand to her cheek. "You all right?"

She nodded, unable to form words.

A voice came at her from the side. "What happened to break your window like that? I was up the block when I heard it. I phoned it in, Darcy."

It took her a moment to realize the man staring at her through her shattered window was her upstairs neighbor, Mr. Blake. He was an older, hunched-over man who wore a wide-brimmed hat all the time.

"Thank you." Her voice sounded like a child's voice.

Jackson said from beside her, "Sir, get down and out of the way. We think someone shot the window out from across the street."

Mr. Blake's eyes grew wide with fear and he stepped out of view.

Jackson lifted his head and peered through the shattered window at the high-rise building across the street. "The shooter must have scouted the area, got into place and waited for you to stand in front of the window."

The high-rise was mostly offices with some eateries on the ground floor. All the windows were dark. "Long-range rifle. Maybe four or five stories up," Darcy said. "I wonder what caliber bullet the shooter used."

Jackson's forehead furrowed.

"Thinking about the tech part of a crime calms me

down." She looked around, taking in her surroundings. The damage was largely to the window. Mr. Tubbs, she noted, had disappeared like the smart cat he was.

She heard sirens in the distance.

"Smokey and I are going to search that building across the street. Maybe the shooter is still around. You stay back and down low."

Jackson and Smokey headed out the door and across the street.

Within minutes, the flashing lights of the police, fire department and ambulance filled the street.

Jackson returned, shaking his head. Whoever had shot at her had gotten away. He came to stand facing her.

He reached up to touch her forehead. "You have a cut there."

His touch was warm on her skin. For some reason, she wanted him to hold her. Silly. She shook her head and took a step back. Maybe it was just because the shooting had frightened her. "I'm sure the EMTs can fix me up."

They were ushered out to the ambulance. Smokey trailed behind them. Harlan and the other members of the forensics team arrived. Darcy knew it would not be appropriate for her to work the scene. But that didn't mean she couldn't ask questions. Harlan approached her. "I heard about the lab break-in. We might not be able to work tomorrow."

She nodded and Harlan jogged away to join the rest of the team.

A patrol officer wandered over to ask them questions about what had happened as an EMT cleaned and bandaged her cuts. They were sitting inside an ambulance, the warmth of the blanket the EMT had offered her giving Darcy some comfort. Still, she felt like she was shaking from the inside.

Jackson got to his feet, throwing off his blanket. "I see glass in Smokey's fur." He combed his fingers through the dog's coat. "I'll need to brush him when I get home." Smokey remained still.

"I'm so sorry that happened. He's such a good dog."

"It's not your fault, Darcy," he said. "All of it's just another day at work for him."

Jackson ran his hand over Smokey's sleek, dark head and then under his chin.

Mr. Blake walked over to her. "I talked to the super. He can order replacement glass in the morning and they can start the install, but you'll have to find someplace to stay for tonight."

"Thanks, Mr. Blake, for doing all that." She watched as the old man wandered back toward the growing crowd of onlookers.

"Do you have a place to go?"

"No place close," she said. "I have relatives in Connecticut. I don't feel comfortable calling a friend at this late hour. I suppose I could get a hotel room."

"Given the nature of this attack, I don't think you should be alone." Jackson turned back toward the broken window. "You can stay with me. I have a roommate, but we could set up an air mattress on the floor. The couch isn't too bad to sleep on, either."

Darcy clutched the blanket at her neck. She didn't have a lot of options here. "I'm not sure what to do."

"Between me and Smokey, you'd be safe for the night. Maybe we can talk the department into providing you with some protection." Jackson took a few steps away from the ambulance and then ran his fingers through his hair. He seemed hesitant to say what he wanted to say. "It's clear now that this isn't directed at the whole lab. Someone is upset about something you've done, probably connected to your work."

Jackson had vocalized the thought that had been spinning through her mind. The attacks were personal. There was nothing in her private life that warranted this level of violence. She barely had a private life. It had to be over a case she'd worked or was working. As the spokesperson for the Brooklyn forensics unit, she'd gotten used to dealing with attacks and accusation from the press, but this was a whole new ballgame. "This is getting serious, isn't it?" She took in a deep breath to summon up some courage.

A Bible verse came to mind.

I can do all things through Christ who strengthens me.

"If it helps with your decision, no expectations are placed on my offer other than friendship and keeping a colleague safe."

"Give me a minute to make sure Mr. Tubbs has water and food for the night. He's used to being shut in the back room, so he won't be able to jump out the broken window. I'll throw some things in an overnight bag and text my sister to let her know what's going on." She studied Jackson for a long moment. His features softened as he met her gaze. "Then we can head over to your place."

A few minutes later, Darcy was buckled into the passenger seat as Jackson drove through the mostly dark residential streets. She rested her head against the seatback, feeling the fatigue in her body. "Do you think whoever attacked me meant to kill me or is it just anger that is boiling over?"

Jackson kept his hands on the wheel as he looked straight ahead.

As she thought about the nature of the attacks, his silence told her everything she needed to know.

Someone wanted her dead.

FOUR

Even though it was his day off, Jackson awoke early to let Smokey out into the fenced yard and put the coffee on. Darcy slept on the couch, partially covered by the quilt one of his sisters had made. One of her legs stuck out as she slept on her side, turned away from the back of the couch. Blond hair fell over her face.

His roommate, who worked in finance, had gotten up even earlier than he had and left for the day. Jackson tossed a load of laundry in, let Smokey back inside and started to break some eggs for breakfast before Darcy stirred. Smokey munched his food in his bowl.

There was no wall between the kitchen and the living room. Darcy sat up, stretching her arms and yawning.

"Hey, you want some coffee?"

"Sure."

"We're not in a hurry this morning," he said, reaching for the coffeepot. "It's my day off and I doubt the lab is going to be accessible just yet."

"Harlan texted me. They are taking the most pressing evidence over to the Manhattan lab, but they're backed up, too. Everything is at a standstill for now. It will be at least a day before they will let any of the techs in to fully assess how much damage was done to the cases we were working on." The tone of her voice suggested frustration.

He poured her coffee and brought it to her. She took the mug, wrapping her hands around it while the steam swirled up.

Jackson beat the eggs he'd broken in the bowl and poured them into the sizzling frying pan. "Hope you like scrambled eggs with green peppers and onions."

"That sounds delicious." Clutching her coffee, she rose and wandered toward the living room window.

Jackson spoke in a calm but intense voice. "Darcy, get away from the window please."

Her face blanched as fear clouded her features. "Sorry, I forgot." She stepped back and wandered into the kitchen, which had only one small window above the sink.

"Didn't mean to upset you. We just can't take any chances."

"No, I get it." Her voice was somber.

If the memory of last night was enough to make his chest feel like it was in a vise, he couldn't imagine how it had affected Darcy emotionally. Though he was impressed with how well she held herself together.

He tossed the veggies into the frying pan and moved the eggs around with a spatula. Offering to set the table while he cooked, she searched cupboards for plates and pulled silverware from the drawer.

They sat across from each other. Darcy took several bites of the scrambled eggs. "This is really good. Thank you."

"You're welcome." Jackson liked that she enjoyed eating his cooking. She didn't seem like the kind of woman who would order a salad if they went to a steak house together. Now why had he thought of that? Amelia had always eaten like a bird.

Smokey wandered over to the table and rested his chin on Jackson's leg.

"He really wishes he could have some eggs." Amusement danced through her words.

Smokey wagged his tail.

Jackson leaned closer to his partner. "You need to stick to your dog food, buddy."

"He is charming," said Darcy.

Smokey turned his head toward Darcy and wagged his tail.

"He likes you. He doesn't respond to everyone that way," Jackson said.

She reached out and stroked Smokey's head. "That means I've made two friends."

They ate for several minutes without talking.

Darcy took the last few bites of her eggs. "I feel a little lost today. I can't go to work. And I doubt I can go home. Even if they've cleared the scene, it will take time to replace that window in my apartment."

He met her gaze across the table. That sweet, welcoming face with the light brown eyes just never seemed to fit with the level of scientific knowledge she displayed. He liked the contrast. Darcy was a person with depth and interest. "It's my day off. Smokey and I were headed over to Dog Beach in Prospect Park. But I don't feel comfortable leaving you here alone."

"That makes us both prisoners," she said. Her full mouth curved up into a soft smile. "I appreciate you wanting to make sure I'm not attacked again."

"You got me figured out, don't you?"

"I don't mind. Yesterday was a bit much. And I am concerned." Her shoulders jerked up to her ears and then she leaned toward him. "I can call Mr. Blake to see if they have pulled the crime scene tape away. If they have, I'd like to get my laptop. I would be able to access some of the current files so I can start narrowing the list of people who might have something against me."

"Sure, we can do that."

Light danced through her eyes. "Your accent comes out just a little bit. Texas, I'm guessing."

"Good guess. Been here two years, you'd think I'd manage to sound a little less like a country boy."

"I kind of like it." She took a sip of coffee.

They finished breakfast and washed the dishes together.

Darcy made her phone call. "Mr. Blake said the window installer has been delayed, but the crime scene tape is gone. So I can at least check on my cat and grab my laptop."

"Okay, I'll take you over there."

While Darcy was in the bathroom, Jackson made a call to ask about permanent protection for Darcy. As expected, he got the usual story about how stretched thin the regular police units were, and that the amount of paperwork involved and level of bureaucratic hoops he'd have to jump through made him wonder if it would just be easier for the K-9 Unit to informally protect her.

Darcy emerged from the bathroom with her blond hair pulled back in a ponytail. She wore capris, a blouse and jacket and canvas shoes imprinted with cats.

Jackson loaded Smokey into the back of his crew cab truck and Darcy got into the passenger seat.

They drove through Williamsburg, Darcy seemingly lost in thought.

"I wonder…" she said. "That night you and Smokey found the body in the park…and that car that came after me. Maybe it wasn't random."

A chill skittered across his spine. "I suppose the list of relatives who vowed revenge over the years for your testimony putting one of their relatives in prison is pretty long. Someone could have seen the forensic van and looked for you."

"I've gotten my share of hate mail. It doesn't help that I'm the spokesperson for Brooklyn forensics. We shouldn't assume it's a case from the past. It might be a current case, maybe someone is afraid of what I will find, or it could be a case that is about to go to trial."

Traffic slowed and then stopped all together. Jackson looked in his rearview mirror. Though he did not want to alarm Darcy, a compact car seemed to be following them.

As traffic came to a standstill, Jackson seemed to tense up. Darcy's stomach tightened in response to his change of mood.

They were on a street that had lots of coffee shops and places to eat. She watched the people on the street, focusing in on a woman who looked to be about her age. The woman was with a man who had a baby in a backpack-style baby carrier while she pushed a stroller with a second child.

"I used to think that was going to be me by now."

Jackson followed her line of sight. "They look like a happy family. Why can't it be you?"

"I'm twenty-nine." She shrugged. "It's hard to meet

people when all you do is work." She shook her head. "My sister is two years younger than me and she's engaged."

"You never know. Everyone operates on a different timeline."

"How about you?" Darcy asked. "Have you met anyone?"

He tapped his hands on the steering wheel. "I was engaged when I transferred up here. We moved so she could get ahead in her job. We found separate places to live and were making wedding plans. We talked about going back to Texas once she got some experience." His words seemed tainted with intense emotion. Hurt or maybe even anger? Jackson looked through the windshield, focusing on some far-away object.

Smokey emitted a small whine from the back seat.

Dogs, she knew, tended to pick up on the emotions of their owners, so she reached out to pet him. "My question upset him, didn't it?" She spoke in a whisper.

Smokey licked her face.

Jackson glanced over at her. "Look, there is just no point in bringing up the past. It's all behind me. I've come to love this city. I found a great church. I love my dog. I have a good life."

So he wasn't going to tell her any more about what sounded like a past-tense relationship and some deep hurt. That was okay. As a friend, Darcy knew enough not to push. "I hope the window installer shows up soon at my apartment. I appreciate your hospitality, but Mr. Tubbs shouldn't spend too much time alone, and I miss my little place, my kitchen, my bed, my reading chair."

"Do me a favor when you do get to go back to your

apartment. Stay inside and keep the doors locked until we can get a handle on who did this and why."

Her stomach twisted into a knot. She knew Jackson was making the suggestion because he wanted her to be safe, but being a prisoner in her own home would only prolong the ordeal. "I'll stay away from the windows and keep the curtains drawn, but I'm not going to hide. The sooner I can figure out who is behind the attacks, the sooner this will be over. I am aware of the danger, but I intend to be proactive about this."

He stared at her. A faint smile made his eyes light up. "Well then, I reserve the right to check in on you... as your friend."

She studied him for a long moment. The sun shining on his brown hair brought out the coppery strands. His eyes were a light green. She hadn't noticed that before. "You may do that...as a friend."

Traffic started to inch along again.

After they'd driven for several blocks, he checked the rearview mirror and then the side one. In the back seat of the crew cab, Smokey stood.

Darcy tensed. "Something's up."

"Just paying attention." He turned to her and winked. "It's my job, remember."

She craned her neck. Smokey licked her face, blocking her view in the process. The dog seemed nervous. Even if Jackson was good at hiding his emotion, his partner gave everything away.

"Smokey is not so sure about that."

Jackson released a single chuckle. "Okay, I give up. There's a dark-colored compact car behind us. Sorta blue, sorta black. It has been behind us almost from the time we left my house. I've noticed it twice when I checked my mirrors. A couple of cars back, same lane. Don't look behind you, use your mirror."

Darcy tilted her head to look into the side mirror. She had a view of just part of the car.

The light turned green, but traffic was still moving very slowly. Jackson switched lanes without signaling and then made a tight turn down a side street. She waited a moment before checking to see if the car had followed. "I don't see it."

Jackson took several more turns.

"Could be nothing," he said after a long silence. "Traffic is really slow. I'm wondering if there wasn't an accident or a construction job that went sideways. Now that I have taken all these detours, I'm thinking it might just be faster to get on the expressway."

"I'm with you," she said.

He inched forward until he could turn onto a street that led to the expressway. Traffic whizzed around them as they merged into the flow. A florist delivery van erratically changed lanes several times. At one point, she had a view of the driver as he pulled into the lane next to them. He was clearly talking on his phone.

"That guy makes me nervous."

"Me, too," Jackson admitted.

The van slowed until his front end lined up with the bumper of Jackson's truck, then pulled in behind them. All around them cars changed lanes or surged ahead. She glanced through Jackson's side window. The small car off to the side looked like the one they'd seen earlier. She zeroed in on it, trying to get a look at the driver.

Metal crunched against metal. The florist's van hit them from behind. Before she could recover, there was another bump, this one more intense. Her body swung forward and then slammed back against the seat. The truck jerked and the scenery whirled around her in flashes of color as Jackson's truck seemed to be flying and twisting through space. Her only clear view was of the guardrail looming large in Jackson's window.

Jackson gripped the wheel, his jaw like granite, eyes focused straight ahead. The truck vibrated and skidded at the same time. Brakes squealed. More metal bent, crunched, scraped against something. Her view was of the van, then a red car, then Smokey slamming against the seat.

The crew cab stopped moving. Other vehicles gave them wide berth as they sped around the truck, which was braced against the bent guardrail. Another vehicle, a delivery truck, faced them, its front bumper lying on the pavement. Darcy had no memory of having hit the delivery truck. It must have spun around in the process.

Her body felt like it had been jarred and shaken.

Jackson had already clicked out of his seat belt and was crawling in the back to check on Smokey.

A moment later, she heard sirens in the distance. She looked around, not seeing the florist's van or the little compact car anywhere.

FIVE

Jackson's heart was still racing as he reached over and touched Darcy's shoulder. Her face had drained of color and her gaze was unfocused. "Are you okay?"

She nodded. "I'm still breathing, and I don't think anything is broken…if that's what you mean."

He gave her shoulder a squeeze before turning his attention back to his dog.

Jackson made soothing sound as he ran his hands over Smokey's fur. The dog seemed okay physically but was extremely agitated.

The flashing lights of police cars and other first responders surrounded them. A man approached the truck and knocked on Jackson's window.

It took Jackson a moment to realize it was Tyler Walker, a detective with the Brooklyn K-9 Unit. If his cognitive processes were that messed up, there was no denying that the collision had affected him. Jackson was a strong man mentally and physically. The thing that had him the most shaken was how the accident had endangered Smokey and Darcy.

Jackson rolled down the window.

"You three okay? I happened to be in the area

running down a lead and recognized your truck," Tyler said.

Jackson nodded. "I don't think anyone has any broken bones."

"Why don't we get the EMTs to check you out, and I'll give you a ride. Looks like your truck is going to need to be towed."

As Tyler yanked open the driver's-side door, Jackson said a quick thank-you prayer that another member of the team had been so close by.

Both Darcy and he had to crawl out the driver's side of the truck because the passenger door was pressed against the bent guardrail.

As he exited, Jackson assured Smokey that he would return. The dog offered him a halfhearted tail wag. "We got to get him to the vet," Jackson told Tyler, "just to make sure there is no internal damage."

"No problem. He can ride with Dusty." Dusty was Tyler's K-9, a golden retriever who specialized in tracking. "Why don't you guys go get checked out? Smokey should calm down once he's in the SUV with me and Dusty."

Uniformed police were already taking measurements of skid marks and photographs. Another officer was talking to the driver of the delivery truck.

Darcy walked beside Jackson as they made their way to the ambulance.

"It was a florist's van that caused the accident," she said. "Both the woman in the compact car and the van driver were on the phone. What if they were talking to each other?"

Once again, Jackson was impressed by Darcy's keen powers of observation. "We can't prove that until we track down one of the drivers and can get a warrant to get a look at their phone." He hadn't been able to get a read on the dirty license plate; most of it was obscured. The compact car was a popular make and model all over Brooklyn and would be impossible to track down by description. "Do you remember what florist it was?"

"No, but I would recognize the logo if I saw it."

The EMT, a slender man probably in his early twenties, stepped toward them. "You folks were in the accident?"

Jackson turned his attention to the EMT. "I think we're both okay, but we can't take chances."

The EMT eyed Darcy and then Jackson. "Did either of you hit your head?"

Both shook their head.

"And neither of you is in any pain?"

"Just kind of shaky," Darcy said.

"I'll look at you first," the EMT said.

Darcy sat inside the open ambulance. Jackson pulled his phone out and searched for "Florist Brooklyn." As each businesses came up on the screen, he showed it to Darcy until they found one with a logo that matched the van she'd seen.

Once Jackson was checked out and declared okay, they got into the SUV with Tyler. Dusty was in her crate in the back with Smokey.

Tyler dropped them off at headquarters, which was right next to the K-9 training center and veterinarian. On the way over, Jackson had called Gina Mazelli, the resident vet, to let her know they were bringing Smokey over.

With Smokey in tow, they entered the veterinary clinic and were led into an examination room. An exam table was situated in the center of the room. Counter space containing equipment and medical supplies took up most of three walls. The fourth wall had a small desk with a computer and a file cabinet.

Gina called out from an adjoining room where the yipping and yapping of puppies could be heard. "Be with you in just a second."

Darcy bent over to pet Smokey's back.

"Gina's living in the training center temporarily as a sort of foster mom," Jackson told her. "One of the other officers found a German shepherd a few months back who'd just given birth," said Jackson.

"I heard about Brooke. She had five pups, right?"

"Yeah, how did you know?"

"Officers talk when they bring in evidence for me. Brooke caused quite a stir when they were finally able to bring her in. Officer Lani Jameson told me."

Gina poked her head through the door. Her red hair was pulled back in a ponytail. She held a puppy in one arm. With her free hand she pushed her silver-framed glasses back on her nose. Gina always reminded Jackson of his older sister. Melody was a champion barrel racer and a cowgirl to the core, but what always got Jackson was her big heart. She would take in any kind of stray from a houseplant to a horse with a bum leg. Gina Mazelli was the same way.

"Let's get Smokey on the exam table," Gina said.

The veterinarian's wrinkled forehead told Jackson that something was stressing her out. The puppy in her arms, he noted, seemed listless and looked to be half asleep. The puppy licked Gina's forearm.

"Everything okay?" he asked.

"It's Maverick. She's having digestive issues again," Gina said.

Darcy stepped forward. "I can hold her while you examine Smokey, so you don't have to put her down. I'm sure that is scary for a puppy who is not feeling very good."

Gina's expression brightened. "Thank you." She handed the puppy over to Darcy who put Maverick's belly against her chest while she stroked her back.

Jackson lifted Smokey onto the exam table.

"So you said he was in a car wreck?" Gina stroked Smokey's ears.

"Yes," Jackson said. "I'm sure he got slammed around on impact."

Gina pressed her hands on Smokey's belly, watching his reaction. "We should probably do an X-ray just to make sure no bones are fractured. He wouldn't necessary be yelping in pain over that." She probed each of his legs then glanced over at Darcy.

Maverick was wagging her tiny tail and licking the underside of Darcy's chin.

"Looks like somebody made a new friend," Jackson quipped.

"She's sweet," Darcy said.

"I don't suppose you'd be interested in babysitting tonight?" Gina asked. "I have to be with my grandmother through some surgery she needs. I don't have anyone to cover the night shift with Brooke and her pups for me. With Maverick still kind of touch and go, I don't feel right leaving them alone."

"Well, I'd like to, but I'm not an expert on dogs or anything," Darcy replied.

"I can stay with them, too," Jackson said. Given the

accident, he didn't want to leave Darcy alone and, even if her window was fixed, he didn't think it was a good idea for her to go back to her apartment.

Gina glanced at Darcy and then at Jackson. "Between the two of you, you should be able to handle it just fine."

Maverick grunted.

"I'll go get Smokey x-rayed. If you want to, see if you can get Maverick to eat something and keep it down. Her food is in the next room, the soft stuff. She's used to being hand fed." Gina disappeared into an adjoining room with Smokey.

Darcy and Jackson took Maverick into the room where Mama Brooke was settled with her four other puppies. They all appeared healthy and energetic as they crawled on mom and played with each other in the pen.

Jackson found the shelf that contained soft puppy food. Darcy sat in a chair that was covered in dog hair, though she didn't seem to mind. Her focus was on Maverick.

Jackson handed her the dish. She dipped her fingers into the food and placed them close to Maverick's mouth. "Come on, sweetie, you've got to eat."

Jackson stroked Maverick's head with a single finger. "Come on, girl."

The dog nestled against Darcy but didn't take the food. "I'll just hold her for a minute and then we'll try again. Poor little thing. I hope she makes it. I always root for the underdog."

"Me, too," Jackson said.

A glow had come into Darcy's cheeks as she'd looked down at the puppy. Jackson felt himself drawn to her in a deeper way. The level of compassion she showed for the little fighter of a puppy moved him. He liked the size of Darcy's heart, too. "You'll be a good mom someday."

"Puppies and babies are two different things. Besides, I just don't see any sign of a husband anywhere."

"You never know," Jackson said.

She shrugged. "My sister will probably make me an auntie in a couple of years after she gets married." Darcy drew the puppy even closer to her. "Maybe that is supposed to be my role in life." She lifted her gaze to look at him. "I'm glad you're my friend, Jackson."

He felt a surge close to his heart. There was a part of him that wanted to be more than friends with Darcy. He let go of the thought almost as quickly as it had entered his head. He reached out to pet the puppy. His fingers brushed over her hand. "Yes, it's been good for both of us."

Maverick licked her fingers where there was still food residue.

"Let's try one more time." Jackson dipped his fingers into the food dish and placed his hand close to Maverick's nose so she could sniff first. Then he brushed her mouth with the food. This time the dog licked it up.

"There you go, little one." Darcy's voice was filled with joy.

"You two make a good team." Gina stood in the doorway, Smokey beside her.

They both turned to look at Gina.

From where she lay inside the pen, surrounded by puppies, Brooke thumped her tail and whined. Smokey trotted over to the pen.

"Smokey checks out. No fractures or anything," Gina told Jackson. "He's good to go."

"Great then," he said. "We've got some police work to do."

"I'll see you guys tonight then. I'm sure Maverick will be glad to see you, too," Gina said as she reached her arms out to take the little dog.

Darcy gave Maverick a kiss on the head before handing her over.

As they stepped back into the reception area, Jackson phoned Gavin Sutherland, the sergeant of the Brooklyn K-9 Unit. He explained the situation about the accident and Darcy maybe being able to identify the driver of the florist's van. "I'm without a personal vehicle right now and I would like to treat this as official police business."

"No problem," Gavin said. "You can use your K-9 vehicle. Also, I'll ask around—one of the other K-9 officers probably has a beater car you can borrow until your truck is out of the shop."

"Thanks for doing that," Jackson said.

"Bear in mind that Darcy is technically a civilian. Keep her safe."

Jackson glanced at Darcy, who was twirling a strand of her blond hair and studying a piece of lab equipment on the counter. "No problem."

"Let's send another unit with you just to be on the safe side. I'll find out who's available," said Gavin.

Jackson, Darcy and Smokey left the veterinarian's and headed over to the parking area where a few of the K-9 vehicles were kept. After securing Smokey in his crate in the back of an SUV, Jackson got behind the wheel.

He offered Darcy a smile and a pat on the shoulder as she got in on the passenger side and buckled up. "Let's get this done."

"Yes," Darcy said, letting out a heavy breath. "So I can get on with my life and work."

Jackson hoped that would be the case.

Darcy could feel her stomach twist into knots so tight it almost hurt. She pressed her hand against her belly. It was scary to think she might soon be looking at the man who had attacked her and then run her off the road and maybe even had gone after her in the park when she left the crime scene. She said a prayer of thanks that Jackson and Smokey were with her. She wasn't sure what the woman in the compact car had to do with anything.

"So where exactly are we going?" Jackson asked. "I need to GPS the address."

Darcy paged through the information about the florists on her phone. "It looks like they have several storefronts throughout Brooklyn, but they get their flowers from the greenhouses at Brooklyn Nurseries." She came to pictures of the interior and exterior of several greenhouses. Vans like the one that had caused Jackson to wreck his truck were parked in a gravel lot by one of the greenhouses. "I think our best hope would be to go to the greenhouse. The delivery vans must do their pick-ups there, and it looks like they are parked there at the end of the day." She recited the address to him.

"Sounds good. I know where that is." Jackson keyed the radio to talk to Dispatch. "We're headed to the greenhouses off New York Avenue. Sergeant Sutherland said he'd send another unit."

"Detective Walker is back in that area now. I'll have him meet you there," the dispatcher said.

"Ten-Four," Jackson responded. He stared through the windshield of the SUV and sped up.

"Wow this is pretty big," Jackson said as they neared the entrance to the nursery.

"The ad said 20,000 square feet." It looked like there were enclosed greenhouses as well as some outdoor plant areas. The delivery vans were parked in the lot in front of the third greenhouse, just like the picture had shown.

They pulled into the gravel lot where Tyler Walker was already parked. He stood outside his vehicle, Dusty on a leash.

The knot in Darcy's stomach grew even tighter as she pushed open the passenger's-side door and stepped down.

Jackson and Smokey came to stand beside her as she stared at the delivery vans. There were no people inside the vans or around them. "He might be out on deliveries."

"Maybe, but we've got to start somewhere," Jackson said.

Tyler stepped over to them. "Dusty and I will go have a look at those vans. There might be paint residue from your truck. Do you remember what part of the van hit your truck?"

Both of them shook their heads.

"We were hit from behind," Jackson said.

Tyler trotted off with Dusty in tow. Every time Darcy saw Tyler and Dusty together, she thought about that saying that owners looked like their dogs. Tyler's blond hair was the same color as the golden retriever's fur.

Jackson peered inside the greenhouse. "Looks like there is someone in there watering plants. Let's go describe the guy to her to see if she knows who we're talking about."

"Okay, but the description will be kind of basic. Like I said, if I saw the guy, I would know that it was him."

The greenhouse worker looked to be a woman of about forty. She wore a straw hat and baggy coveralls and a checked shirt. She filled a water can up from a spigot, smiling when Jackson and Darcy came toward her. Her gaze rested on Smokey for a moment. "Can I help you?"

"I'm Officer Davison from the Brooklyn K-9 Unit. Are you in charge around here?"

The woman nodded and held out her hand to Jackson. "I'm Lynn Costello, the owner."

"We're looking for one of your delivery drivers who may have been involved in an accident earlier today."

The woman put down her watering can. "Are you saying one of my drivers left the scene of an accident?"

"We don't know anything for sure. We just need to question the man." Jackson turned to Darcy. "This woman was involved in the accident. She saw one of your delivery trucks and the driver."

Jackson was doing what police officers did best, trying not to raise alarm bells so the suspect wouldn't be warned and have a chance to bolt.

Darcy stepped forward. "He had short dark hair, sort of shiny. Medium build. He had on a blue shirt."

The woman straightened and wiped her forehead with the back of her hand. "All the drivers wear the blue shirts. And you are describing at least three of the guys who do deliveries for us."

As Darcy had feared, finding the driver would not be straightforward.

"Are any of the men who fit that description here right now or due to return anytime soon?" Jackson asked.

Darcy appreciated that he wasn't going to give up easily.

"The drivers pick their stuff up early in the morning and then are out for most of the day. Unless, for some reason, we don't have the usual number of orders. I'd have to check, but think all the trucks went out full this morning."

"But there are trucks sitting over by that other greenhouse," Jackson noted.

"You know, I'd have to check the log to find out if someone came back early. Don't recall any of the trucks looking like they'd been in a crash. I don't pay that much attention to the delivery trucks coming and going. I'm in the greenhouse some of the time and in office the rest of the time." The woman picked up her watering can with a jerky motion, indicating that she was becoming a little irritated with Jackson's questions. "Some of those trucks need repairs and others are for overflow days."

Jackson pulled a business card out of his shirt pocket. "We'd like to question the three men who might match this woman's description." He pointed at Darcy.

The woman took the card and put it in her shirt pocket. "If one of my drivers left the scene of an accident, that is a serious offense. I just can't believe one of them would do that."

Jackson pulled out a notebook and pen. "Could you give me the names of the three who fit the description we gave you?"

"Joe Donnelly, Angus Graft and Spencer Fisher."

"Thank you so much for your time," Jackson said.

"If you will excuse me, I have a great deal of work

to do." After grabbing her watering can, she turned and walked down one of the aisles that contained rows of pink carnations.

Darcy and Jackson turned toward the entrance of the greenhouse. A single pink carnation lay on the dirt floor of the greenhouse. Jackson reached down and picked it up. He handed it to Darcy. "It's your color."

Her cheeks warmed. "Thank you." It was such an impulsive thing to do but, for some reason, receiving a flower from Jackson, even one that had probably fallen out of a bouquet, made her heart flutter. If only he wasn't a police officer, she could see herself wanting for them to be more than just friends.

They stepped outside. Detective Walker and Dusty stood some distance away by their vehicle. He shook his head, meaning he hadn't found anything.

Jackson shook his head, as well. Both officers loaded their dogs into the K-9 vehicles before getting in behind the wheel.

Jackson turned to face Darcy. "That wasn't a dead end. We've got some names to go on."

She still held the carnation. "I know. I'm not giving up."

Jackson turned the key in the ignition and looked over his shoulder to check behind him.

Darcy looked through the windshield. Detective Walker had already pulled out onto the street when a delivery van pulled into the parking lot with the other vans. She could just make out the man behind the wheel as he reached to open the door and get out. He had black hair.

"That's him," she said. "That's the man who caused the accident."

SIX

Jackson snapped his head around in time to see the driver, who had just arrived, slam his door shut and hit the gas. The van's tires spat up gravel as he peeled toward the street, swerving around Tyler's vehicle and almost hitting an oncoming car.

Jackson turned and headed out after the speeding florist's van. Tyler must have deduced that something was up because he sped up, as well.

Tyler slipped in front of the van and Jackson pulled up to its side in an effort to box him in and force him to stop. The driver of the van did a sharp turn off the street. Jackson noted the sign that said Wingate Park was within blocks, cranked his steering wheel and followed, pressing the gas. The van headed toward the park but veered off the street and drove over the grass past a racquetball court. Alarmed park-goers scrambled to get out of the path of the van as Jackson followed it onto the grass.

Staying on the street, Tyler did a wide arc with his vehicle, trying to head the van off once it got on the other side of the park. The van dipped down into a culvert but didn't come up the other side. Either the guy had stalled out his motor or he was stuck.

Jackson stopped his vehicle. Having seen from the street what happened, Tyler moved in closer still in his SUV.

The van driver spun his tires for only a few more seconds before the door popped open and he stumbled out. He took off running across the park toward a cluster of trees where a car could not go.

"Looks like the chase is on." Jackson pushed open his door. "Stay here, Darcy, lock the doors. He might be armed."

Smokey barked from the back.

Tyler drove across the grass toward the stalled-out van then stopped and unloaded Dusty from the K-9 SUV. Because Dusty was a tracking dog, she would pick up the scent that the panicked suspect left in the air. Though Smokey wasn't trained to track, he'd still be able to follow Dusty's lead. He would be a help apprehending the suspect. The sound of a barking dog was often terrifying enough to make a suspect give up rather than be taken down by a K-9.

When the two officers with their K-9 partners made an appearance, the people close by scattered to other parts of the park.

Jackson and Tyler headed for the trees where the driver had disappeared. Dusty put her nose to the ground and picked up the suspect's scent almost right away. Because he was in a heighted state of fear from being chased, the delivery driver emanated an odor in the air that was like a map to a dog trained to track. With the dogs leading the way, they hurried through the trees and brush.

As they ran, Jackson caught flashes of blue in the trees. The noises of the delivery driver hurrying through the foliage reached Jackson's ears from time to time. Smokey ran ahead of him as Tyler and Dusty drew farther away, still on the same parallel path. He lost sight of the fugitive, but the wavering tree branches told him they were still headed in the right direction.

He could hear the rush of traffic as it sped by on the street. A reminder that the city still surrounded this oasis of greenery.

"Let's split up," Jackson shouted. "Smokey and I will try to flank him to make sure he doesn't get over to that street to flag down a ride." Or worse, hold someone at gunpoint. Because they still didn't know if the suspect was armed or not, they had to assume he was.

Tyler and Dusty veered in the direction that led straight through the trees.

Jackson commanded Smokey to come back to him then the two of them took off running. He saw the driver pass by the concert grandstand before he ran back into a cluster of trees. Jackson radioed Tyler about the location. His feet pounded the hard ground as Smokey kept pace with him. The dog was used to running. He frequently heeled at Jackson's side when he jogged.

Off to his side, Dusty's barking grew fainter and then louder.

Jackson scanned the trees, not seeing any blue or hearing any movement that was human. He kept running toward the edge of the trees as the sound of traffic droned in his ears. They were getting close to the street. His goal was to get to the street before the fugitive did. Dusty would be coming at him from the other side.

Smokey emitted an intense bark, indicating he'd seen

something. Jackson heart pounded as he came to a stop. His K-9 stood beside him but did not sit. He barked three more times. Jackson followed the direction that Smokey indicated. Though it was nearly drowned out by the sounds of the busy street and surrounding city, he could hear but not see someone moving through the brush.

Unsure of Dusty and Tyler's location, he commanded Smokey to "Find" and they took off at a sprint.

Up ahead, Jackson could see the driver running toward the street. The suspect had shed his blue shirt, apparently thinking the brown shirt underneath would not contrast as much with the foliage.

The man was only feet away from the street.

Once he was clear of the trees, Jackson pulled his weapon. "Police! Hold it right there."

Smokey stood his ground, but the twitching of his body indicated he was ready to take the man down if commanded.

The man's eyes grew wide. He moved as though he was going to surrender but then dropped to the ground and rolled back toward the trees.

That was unexpected.

"Get him," Jackson commanded and Smokey surged ahead. Jackson returned his weapon to his holster and sprinted after the dog.

Dusty's barking had faded. Jackson wondered if the K-9 had lost the scent. The loss would be temporary. Dusty was among the best tracking dogs he'd worked with. The suspect had likely doubled back and was headed toward the racquetball courts. He and Tyler should be able to flank him and take him down before he had a chance to get away.

Jackson's heart pounded as he hurried through the brush, trying to put a visual on Smokey.

He didn't see Smokey. Fear that something had happened to his partner or a civilian made him run even faster. He pumped his legs as his strides ate up the ground.

He saw movement in the trees and pulled his weapon. Dusty and Tyler emerged.

The detective shook his head. Dusty put her nose to the ground. Once she recovered the scent, both officer and partner headed along a park trail.

Jackson shouted a command for Smokey to return to him. The dog didn't show up. He stood, listening, hoping. His heart squeezed tight.

Come on, Smokey, where are you?

A surge of adrenaline flooded his body and he ran even faster, hoping to spot Smokey.

The foliage at his side rustled. He turned and raised his gun. Smokey emerged, wagging his tail and hanging his head.

Relief flooded Jackson. "So glad to see you, buddy." Another stronger scent must have crossed Smokey's path to cause him to go off track. "Let's get back to work." He tried to sound stern, but gratitude laced his words.

"We've got a job to do, come on," Jackson said. Still not sure which direction to head, he turned in a half circle.

Smokey growled. The dog had either smelled or heard something.

"Lead the way. Let's go."

Smokey hightailed it through the brush, back toward the stalled van.

Jackson heard Dusty barking and then an enraged voice. "Call the dog off right now or she gets it!"

Jackson's heart squeezed tight as he sprinted even faster. Did the delivery driver have Darcy?

Tyler said something in a low voice and the barking stopped. With Smokey by his side, Jackson hurried to the edge of the trees and peered out. Fear seized his heart. The driver must have tried to jack the K-9 vehicle where Darcy had been waiting. The driver's-side window was broken. He must have smashed it to get access, then grabbed Darcy as a hostage. As he stood beside the SUV, the driver had one arm wrapped around Darcy and held a knife to her neck.

Jackson glanced from side to side. Some people were off in the distance, but there were no other civilians in harm's way.

Tyler held his weapon on the driver but spoke in a calming voice. Dusty had come to his side when she'd been called off. The dog's body language, though, suggested a high level of agitation and a readiness to take the suspect down on command.

Jackson couldn't hear the words. Darcy's face was pale, and her expression was strained, but she seemed to be holding it together. She, too, spoke to the driver, her tone suggesting she was trying to convince him to let her go.

"Shut up! Shut up both of you," shouted the driver. "I'm taking the car and I'm taking her with me as an insurance policy. Gimme the keys or she's dead."

Jackson pushed past the rising panic and guilt over Darcy being dragged into this. There was no cover that would allow him to move toward the driver without being noticed. He couldn't risk Darcy's life by commanding Smokey to go after the suspect. Smokey would have a stretch of ground to cover before he could get close enough, allowing too much time for the driver to use the knife.

Faced with nothing but bad options, he raised his gun and stepped out into the open. "You heard the lady, drop your weapon and back off."

Darcy could feel the pressure of the knife against her neck. Her heart pounded and she struggled to take a deep breath. The delivery driver's other arm dug into her stomach where he held her, so she couldn't get away. With a knife pressed against her skin, she dared not even try.

All the same, a sense of calm washed over Darcy when Jackson and Smokey stepped out of the trees and he pointed his gun at the driver. Her body was tensed up. She was still afraid for her life, but seeing Jackson renewed her hope that this wasn't the end for her.

"Both of you back off. I'm getting in that police car and she's coming with me."

The driver's tone had switched from rage to fear. That wasn't necessarily good news. A fearful man was just as likely to kill as an angry man.

"Look, we know you caused the accident with my truck earlier." With his weapon still aimed at the man, Jackson took a step toward him.

"You don't want additional charges against you, do you?" Tyler added.

"You got two officers with guns trained on you," Jackson pointed out. "What do you think your chances are of getting out of here alive?"

The man let up some of the pressure of the knife.

His resolve was weakening. "It wasn't me. She offered me money," he said.

Darcy wondered if he was referencing the woman in the compact car, the one that had been following them right before the accident.

"We can talk about this," Jackson said. "Just toss the knife and let the woman go."

She could hear the man take in a breath. He must still be considering his options. The moment filled with tension.

She said a quick prayer. *God, please help all of us to stay alive. Including this man.*

"Please, let me go," Darcy whispered.

The driver tightened his grip around her stomach. Both Smokey and Dusty looked ready to jump the man and take him down if commanded to do so. The guy must realize the possibility for escape was not good. He might be able to use the threat of hurting her to prevent the officers from coming close to the police vehicle before he drove away. But he must know he wouldn't get far even if he did escape.

Darcy had to prevent him from taking her in that car. If he was backed into a corner and saw no escape, he might just stab her. There was no way she could free herself from his grip and get to safety before he used the knife.

Darcy looked to Jackson, hoping her expression communicated that she was wondering what to do.

"Stay right where you are, Darcy. He knows he's out of options." Jackson softened the tone of his voice as he told the guy, "You said yourself this wasn't all you. Let the woman go."

"Drop the gun and back away," Tyler said.

The seconds stretched out. Darcy could hear her own heartbeat thrumming in her ears. The driver was breathing so heavily that his exhale was like puffs of wind against her cheek.

The man let go of Darcy and pushed her forward. She heard the thud of the knife falling on the ground. She rushed toward Jackson as relief flooded through her body. Knowing that Jackson had to focus on the suspect, she stepped out of the way.

As he and Tyler moved in, Jackson winked at her.

Her heart was still pounding as she watched Jackson cuff the man.

"So somebody put you up to this?" Tyler asked.

"A woman called me when I was on the expressway and offered me money to ram a truck. I don't know how she got my cell number."

"Did she pay up?" The man had been bent over the hood of the SUV while Jackson cuffed him. Gripping the cuffs, Jackson pulled him upright, so he had to straighten.

"Yes, but I didn't see her. She asked me where my next delivery stop was. The money was waiting for me in an envelope," the driver said.

Interesting. So it was confirmed—whoever was behind the attacks was a woman. The attempt to run her over, the shooting at her apartment, the attack in the lab. Her attacker had been very strong, but it had happened so fast. Then again, if the woman was willing to let this driver do her dirty work, maybe someone else had been hired to attack her in the lab.

Tyler stepped up to the suspect. "I can take him in my car since you need to transport Darcy," he said to Jackson.

"Sounds good." Jackson patted Tyler on the shoulder and then turned his attention to Darcy. "You all right?"

She nodded but then tears streamed down her face. "I guess I was pretty scared." She felt a torrential flow of emotion that had been at bay while her life was under threat. She wiped the tears away.

"Anyone would be," he said. "You handled yourself just fine."

She knew she needed to process what had happened to her by talking about it. "At first, when he held the knife on me, he just wanted me out of the car so he could take it, but then when Dusty came toward him, he grabbed me."

"Let's take you back to the station. You can file a report."

"We need to make sure we get that guy's phone," Darcy said as Jackson opened the passenger door for her. "We might be able to trace the woman who put him up to this through the call she made." The phone had probably already been ditched or was a throwaway in the first place, but every avenue of investigation needed to be explored. "And we'll find out where he picked up his payment. The woman might have been caught on camera." She was talking a mile a minute because she was still worked up from having been held at knifepoint.

While Jackson loaded Smokey into his crate, she closed her eyes and rested the back of her head against the seat.

Jackson got behind the wheel and buckled his seat belt. He placed his hands on the steering wheel but didn't turn the key in the ignition. "It was scary for me, too. I know you were the one with a knife to your throat, but I don't know what I would have done if I'd lost you. I shouldn't have put you in that kind of danger."

"Don't feel bad. You left me in the safest place possible. You had no way of knowing that guy was going to double back like that."

He smiled at her. "All the same, I like being your friend. I don't want to lose you." He turned the key. "Let's go get your statement and then I'll take you back to your place. I'm sure there is stuff you want to get for tonight when we watch the pups."

"Yes, I need to pick up some things, including that laptop I never got." She rested her palm against her chest. Her heart still hadn't slowed down. "I miss my apartment and my cat, but I don't want to put my sister in danger. I wish this was over with."

"Me, too." Jackson put the SUV in gear. "We'll see if the detectives can get any more information out of that driver."

"You think he was telling the truth, that he never saw the woman who paid him to cause the wreck?"

"I do, actually," Jackson admitted. "The guy was really scared." He turned to look at the broken driver's-side window. "Looks like my K-9 vehicle is going into the shop, too."

"At least now we know that it is a woman who is behind the attempts on my life. That narrows down the possibilities," Darcy said. "Once I have my laptop, I'll be able to access some of my cases."

Jackson headed toward K-9 headquarters.

There was no safer place for her than to be with Jackson and Smokey, but Darcy knew until she figured out which case had caused someone to desire her dead, it was just a matter of time before there would be another attempt on her life.

SEVEN

After they dropped the K-9 patrol vehicle with the broken window off at a shop that serviced all the vehicles, they waited for a replacement car. Gavin Sutherland and Lani Jameson showed up in separate K-9 cars, leaving one for Jackson to use. They drove to Darcy's place to get the laptop.

As they pulled into Darcy's neighborhood, Jackson tensed. If the woman in the compact car was lying in wait anywhere, it would be at Darcy's apartment. He circled the block several times, finding a space that required them to walk several blocks out in the open and cross the street. Smokey walked between him and Darcy.

He stared up at the building where the shooter had probably been watching Darcy's place, waiting for a chance to shoot at her when she stood in front of the window. Had their suspect done the shooting herself or had she hired that out, too?

They crossed the street. The window had been replaced in Darcy's ground-floor apartment and the curtains were drawn. Darcy slowed, her features growing taut.

Jackson placed a supportive hand on her back. "Smokey and I are right here with you."

Darcy twisted the necklace she wore, clearly nervous. "I texted my sister that I'd be by. She's not home right now, but she said Mr. Tubbs was fine." She pulled her keys from her purse.

"We should maybe call your neighbor to see if he noticed anyone suspicious hanging around here today. What was his name, Mr. Blake?"

She nodded. "That would be a good idea. I don't want to spend too much time here."

The little waver in her voice revealed how afraid she was. She might be reliving the shooting, as well. He knew from experience that it took a long time to heal from a trauma like being shot at. As a police officer, getting shot at was just part of the job. But Darcy was used to being tucked away with her samples and microscopes.

She turned the key in the door lock and gripped the knob. He touched her arm. "Why don't we let Smokey go in first? You stand at the apartment door and I'll stand behind you while Smokey has a sniff around."

"Good idea." She pushed the door open and stepped inside. Jackson closed the door behind them. His hand wavered over his gun.

They walked the short distance to her apartment door. Jackson commanded Smokey to go inside. Mr. Tubbs, who was lying on the couch, jumped down and sought the safety of a window ledge. Smokey moved through each of the rooms and then returned to sit at Jackson's feet.

"If you want to give me Mr. Blake's number, I'll call him while you get your laptop. Smokey has given us the thumbs-up that no one is in here, but I'll be right behind you all the same."

"My laptop is in the bedroom," Darcy said then recited Mr. Blake's number.

"Let me make the call first."

Once Mr. Blake picked up, Jackson identified himself. "Have you noticed anyone or anything strange since Darcy's window was shot out?"

Mr. Blake cleared his throat. "A woman who said she was a friend of Darcy's stopped me on the street this afternoon. She asked if I knew when Darcy would be back."

Jackson's heart skipped a beat. "And she wasn't someone you had seen around here before?"

"No."

"Can you describe her for me?"

"Shoulder-length brown hair. Kind of a muscular gal. Not old, probably thirty or so."

That could be a third of the women in New York City. "Nothing distinct about her?" Jackson asked.

"No, not really. Can't say as if I would recognize her if I saw her again. Just talked to her for a couple of seconds."

"Thank you, Mr. Blake." Jackson ended the call.

Darcy twisted the pendant on her necklace. Something Jackson realized she did when she was nervous. "So she was here asking around about me, huh?"

Tension wove through his chest. None of this made him feel any better about Darcy staying here. Even if her sister was around. At least she'd be safe tonight. "Let's go get your laptop."

Darcy headed down a hallway toward her bedroom. Jackson and Smokey followed her.

She picked her laptop up off the quilt on her bed. She hesitated for just a moment, glancing out her bedroom window. The curtains had not been drawn.

He caught movement outside the window. "Darcy, get down." Something thudded against the wall outside her bedroom.

Still holding the laptop, she fell to the floor by her bed.

Smokey barked.

Jackson drew his weapon and pressed his back against the wall by the window. He angled his head so he had a view of the sidewalk and the apartment building across the street. The only people on the sidewalk close to Darcy's place were two kids kicking a soccer ball. That must have been what had made the thudding noise.

"All clear," he said. "Guess we are both just a little on edge."

She rose to her feet. "That's an understatement."

They returned to the living room and Darcy grabbed a book and some snacks, placing them in a bag along with her laptop. She petted Mr. Tubbs. "I'll be home soon, big guy."

They stepped outside. While Darcy double-checked to make sure the door was locked, Jackson and Smokey headed outside to watch the street and surrounding buildings.

The street by Darcy's bedroom was a quiet one, but the one her living room faced was a busy thoroughfare at this hour. Though it had been quiet the night Darcy had been shot at, it was bustling with activity now. People were coming home from work and headed out to dinner.

Staying on high alert, he walked close to Darcy as people brushed past them on the sidewalk. He watched Smokey's reaction, knowing that his hackles would go up at anyone he perceived to be a threat. He opened the car door for her and waited before loading Smokey

in the back. He continued to watch the traffic behind
and around him as he headed to Bay Ridge and the K-9
Unit training center, where he and Darcy would babysit
Brooke and her pups for the night.

He didn't relax until he and Darcy were inside the
training center with the doors locked. In the veterinary
clinic, Gina had left a note explaining about giving medication to Maverick and the feeding and care for the other
puppies and Brooke. Gina instructed them to check on
Maverick through the night and to call her if the condition
worsened. The dogs were in a pen in the training center.

Darcy found a fold-out chair in one of the storage
closets. "Did Mr. Blake say anything helpful in narrowing down who might be behind the attacks?" There was
also a rocking chair in the corner of the training center
that was likely used when holding the puppies. It looked
like the one that had been in the veterinarian's area.

"Not in appearance. Mr. Blake's description was
kind of generic. Brown hair and in good shape. He did
say he thought the woman was probably around thirty
years old."

"That is helpful. I can eliminate any of the older
women connected to cases I worked." She got her laptop out and flipped it open. She clicked several keys. "I
need to call Harlan to jog his memory at some point. It
occurs to me that someone I put away and who's now
out might want revenge. My work hasn't sent that many
thirty-something women to prison. We can check my
list against recent parolees."

Darcy seemed less afraid when she could focus on
catching the woman who was after her.

While Darcy worked on her laptop, Jackson played
with the other puppies and then held Maverick. The

training center had both an indoor and small outdoor area for the dogs. He took Smokey and the puppies outside while Brooke remained close to Maverick. When he returned with the puppies trailing behind him, Darcy was still busy on her laptop.

"Find anything?"

She leaned back in the chair and rubbed her eyes. "I've come up with five possibilities. Once I have access to the files on the computer at work, the list will get longer." She glanced down at Maverick as the other puppies raced toward their mom. The pup still looked kind of listless. She closed her laptop. "Maybe I should hold Maverick for a while if you like. I don't think she's up for any rough puppy play."

"Sure, why don't I order some takeout?" He reached down to pick up the puppy and hand her to Darcy.

"Chinese sounds good. Anything from the Dumpling House would be great," she said.

Jackson dialed the number and wandered away from the noise of the puppies so he could place their order.

He walked the floor, coming to stand at a window. While he spoke on the phone, he separated the blinds just a tiny bit to peer out. It was dark outside though the streetlights did provide a level of illumination. A person in a hoodie leaned against a pole. Jackson could only see the individual from the side. He couldn't even tell if it was a male or female. A chill skipped up his spine as he was reminded of the watcher in the woods the night he and Smokey had found Griffin Martel's body.

He knew Brooke would need to go for a long walk later since she needed more exercise than her puppies. That would give him an opportunity to make sure no one suspicious was hanging around the training center.

After placing his order, he clicked his phone off and turned around. Darcy was sitting in the rocking chair, holding Maverick. "When the take-out comes, it might be a good idea for you to stay out of sight and let me get the door," he told her.

She nodded, drawing the puppy closer to her chest. "I get why I have to do that. It doesn't mean I have to like it." Maverick let out a whimper. "She doesn't like it, either."

"I'm glad you have a sense of humor about this." Jackson walked over to her and stroked the puppy's head.

They sat and visited until there was a knock on the outside door.

Darcy got up and retreated to a back room. Jackson called Smokey, who walked beside him as he moved to answer the outside door. A police officer in uniform with a K-9 would probably be enough to intimidate anyone who had violence on her mind.

Knowing he had to be ready for anything, Jackson had not removed his shoulder holster with his police-issue Glock. He knew the woman behind the attacks wasn't above hiring muscle to help her and every attempt on Darcy's life had, up to this point, come out of nowhere.

Jackson took in a breath and reached for the doorknob.

Darcy sat on the floor, holding Maverick while she listened to Jackson interact with the delivery person. The other puppies played at her feet. All of them had followed her.

Though she understood Jackson's reasons for making her hide, it felt like the very thing she was trying to prevent was happening. The attacker was calling the shots on her life. She would be a virtual captive until this woman was caught and put behind bars. Darcy had never been one to back down from a challenge, but she was battling a sense of defeat over the whole thing. She had to do something.

With Maverick still resting in her lap, she pulled her phone out and texted Harlan.

Any chance we will be able to go back to work tomorrow?

She heard the outside door close and Jackson's footsteps, along with the patter of Smokey's paws, coming toward her. Jackson appeared, holding a brown paper bag. His smile lifted her spirits.

"Not sure where the most sanitary place is to eat, considering the whole place is dog central," he said.

Darcy stood, still holding Maverick. "Probably Gina's desk in the clinic. We can wipe it down." She lay Maverick in her little separate bed carefully. The puppy licked her hands as she drew back.

It took only a few minutes to find some disinfecting wipes and another chair for their makeshift dinner table. Jackson sat kitty-corner to her as they both pulled containers from the bag. Darcy checked the contents of several boxes before choosing the sweet-and-sour chicken.

"I hope you like what I got." Jackson spooned some rice onto his paper plate.

"Looks like you got the special sampler of a bunch of different things on the menu. It's what I always order from that great place near the lab." After spooning out half the chicken, she handed him the take-out box.

"Do you order from them a lot?"

She nodded. "They're our go-to place for not only lunch but late nights at the lab. My sister and I order from them quite a bit, too, since my apartment isn't far from the lab." She opened several more boxes and put the food on her plate before settling in to enjoy her meal after they said grace.

Something about sharing a meal with him felt very comfortable. Smokey lay down at Jackson's feet.

When she smiled at the dog, he thudded his tail against the floor. "He doesn't act very hungry."

Jackson looked at his dog and smiled. He scooped up a big bite of steak and broccoli stir-fry. "I think he helped himself to Brooke's food."

Darcy took a bite of her chicken. "Tastes a lot like the place I get takeout. Glad I didn't have to be at home alone. I don't think I can handle that just yet."

"I'm glad I can be here with you. I have to work a long shift tomorrow," Jackson said. "I can see if one of the other K-9 officers has the day off." As a colleague, Darcy and her safety were important to the entire team.

"I'm hoping the lab will be open." She pulled her phone out. Harlan had left her a happy face emoticon. "Looks we're cleared to go back to work." A look of concern clouded Jackson's features. "I should be safe in the lab. I won't stay late or work alone."

"We can arrange for a police escort for you to and from work. At the very least, we'll have a patrol car go past your place and an officer go through the lab. Make sure there is no one suspicious hanging around."

A knot formed at the back of Darcy's neck. This was her reality; she had to accept it. It occurred to her that the officer she most wanted to escort her was sitting at the table with her. "Thanks for doing that. Maybe it will work out with the hours of your shift that you could escort me at least one way."

"I hope it works out that way, too. Smokey and I start at seven and get off at five."

The glow of affection she saw in Jackson's eyes made her heart flutter. "I can go early to the lab. We can just leave from here in the morning."

They finished their meal and cleaned up.

"I'm going to have to walk Brooke," Jackson said. "I'll leave Smokey here for protection and walk him separate."

"I know the drill. I'll lock the door behind you and not open it until I hear your knock."

"I'll knock five times. Three fast and two slow." He cupped his hand on her shoulder as he faced her. "That way you'll know it's me." He winked at her, which seemed to be his signature move and a way of telling her not to worry. "I'll press the entry code, but the knock will confirm that it's me. This woman is clever. We shouldn't assume she wouldn't be able to figure out the entry code or know how to bypass it."

Jackson called Brooke and hooked the leash on her. Darcy followed them out to the entryway. Once the door closed behind Jackson, she locked it electronically.

She stepped away from the door and returned to the room with the puppies. Her stomach clenched as she collapsed into the rocking chair. She knew the fear would not go away until Jackson returned.

EIGHT

Jackson walked Brooke around the neighborhood. The person he'd seen in the hoodie leaning against the pole was no longer around. He circled the entire block, looking for anyone suspicious. There was a car parked at the curb with a woman sitting behind the wheel looking at her phone. She was wearing a hat, so he couldn't see her hair color. Nothing alarming about someone parked looking at their phone, but he couldn't take any chances. He made a mental note to come back this way to see if she was still around.

He and Brooke headed toward a pocket park. Though he was anxious to get back to Darcy, time with Brooke was always pleasant. She had potential as a K-9. It had taken some doing for the K-9 team to rescue her and the puppies, and the entire team was rallying for Brooke to become part of the unit. Her pups, too, upon time and assessment.

Brooke sniffed around some plants.

A man sitting on a bench, who was probably homeless, judging from his appearance, lifted his head and smiled when he saw Brooke.

"Hey, Rory. How you been girl?"

Brooke wagged her tail and pulled on the leash to get closer to the man, who reached out to pet her.

Jackson froze, feeling a tightening around his middle. "You know this dog?"

The man rubbed Brooke's head. "Sure, I seen this dog before. A while back, a tall guy with reddish hair kept trying to lure her out from where she was hiding. The dog got scared and ran away. He called her name over and over—Rory." The man leaned closer to the dog's head. "Good to see you again, girl."

A month ago, a man named Joel Carey had come into headquarters claiming that Brooke was named Rory and that the dog and pups were his. The man had seemed cagey and the team had brushed his claim off, gathering that he only wanted to sell Brooke and her pups. Brooke's rescue had been in the news. If Joel had been looking for Brooke, why hadn't there been posters put up? He hadn't come back, either, to demand the return of his dog, but maybe he was waiting for the unit to get back to him about the claim.

But now, seeing that Brooke was responsive to the name the man had used, caused Jackson to wonder if Joel, as unlikable as he was, had been telling the truth. Jackson walked back to the training center with a heavy heart. He didn't like the idea of having to give Brooke and her pups up.

The woman who had been sitting in her car looking at her phone was no longer around. A good sign, he supposed. He was still trying to process what the news that Brooke was Rory meant. He'd grown attached to the dog. He'd have to tell Gavin when he got on shift tomorrow. He turned the corner and knocked on the door of the training center.

He was glad to see Darcy's bright expression when she opened the door. He explained to her why he was upset.

"That would be a blow to the whole team if they had to turn Brooke and her brood over to that man," she said. "Especially Maverick. It sounds like this guy Joel is kind of a jerk."

They sat together and talked for a while longer before Jackson took Smokey out for his last walk of the night. The rest of the night was uneventful with each of them taking shifts to check on Maverick and to sleep. Gina had set up a cot in a back room since she was living full-time at the training center for the time being.

They arose early in the morning and cleaned up. Once Gina arrived, Jackson drove Darcy across Brooklyn to the lab. A lightness had come into her demeanor that he hadn't seen since the first attack at the lab. "I'm so glad to be getting back to work. I'm really far behind, and I have to do some prep for Reuben Bray's trial."

He pulled into the parking lot adjacent to the lab and pressed the brakes. "I'm sure it does feel good to get back to doing what you love." Already, Jackson felt a tight knot form in his stomach. He didn't want to leave her. "I'll wait until you are inside before I pull out of the lot."

She unclicked her seat belt and then looked at him. "Thank you, Jackson, for everything. I know it wasn't the best of circumstances, but last night, taking care of Maverick and everything... I enjoyed our time together."

"Me, too." He felt his cheeks heating up like he was some junior high kid and a girl had just told him she liked him. "I'll see you when I get off shift. If I get caught up with some investigation, just call headquarters. One of the K-9 team will be able to give you a ride home if I can't."

"Got it." She pushed open the door and hopped out of the SUV.

Warmth spread through his chest as he watched her cross the parking lot. Smokey made a yipping sound from the back seat. "I know she's all right, isn't she? She's a good friend."

Smokey whined.

Darcy swiped her card on sensor to open the door. She waved at Jackson before disappearing inside.

"Okay, maybe I think sometimes I would like for her to be more than a friend."

With Darcy still on his mind, Jackson shifted into Reverse. He wasn't even out of the parking lot when the first call came in for a cadaver dog.

He and Smokey stayed busy throughout the day. The second he had some downtime, he drove past the lab and Darcy's apartment building, checking for anything suspicious.

It wasn't until late in the afternoon that he was able to get back to headquarters. He entered the reception area, sending a smile to Penelope McGregor as he walked past the front desk. He was never able to pass Penny—or her brother, Detective Bradley McGregor—without thinking of the two cases the unit was working on. How hard it must be for the siblings to know their parents' killer had finally been identified but had eluded law enforcement, who were searching for him. He thought of Penny as a young child, her parents murdered while she was left unharmed—just like little Lucy Emery in the copycat murder several months ago. He knew there would be justice for both families. The team was getting closer to that every day.

As he stepped toward the offices, Noelle Orton, a rookie K-9 officer who used be a trainer, emerged looking distressed and holding an evidence bag filled with dog food. Her K-9 partner, Liberty, a yellow Lab with the distinctive black mark on her ear, walked beside her.

"Something wrong?" he asked, Smokey standing at attention beside him. He sure hoped not. For months now, an elusive drug smuggler they only knew as "Gunther" had put a bounty on Liberty's head because the K-9 was too good at her job and had foiled shipments in Atlantic Terminal. Attempts had made on Liberty's life, and Noelle kept her partner as safe as possible.

"I'm pretty sure someone tried to poison Liberty's food. Not sure how they got into the police vehicle. I keep some in there for when the shift gets long. Of course, she's smart enough not to eat it. She must have picked up on a scent on the food that wasn't mine or the poison has a distinct smell." Noelle lifted the bag. "I need to take this over to the lab to be tested."

"I can do that for you," Jackson said.

"This wouldn't have anything to do with a cute blond forensic scientist, would it? I hear the two of you have been spending lots of time together."

"We're just friends and, I'm sure you've heard, she needs some protection."

"I know. I feel awful about that. I was just teasing you." She smiled and handed him the bag.

Jackson looked at the bag of dog food. "This has to be connected to the bounty on Liberty's head from the gunrunner." Jackson had heard in the morning briefing that a raid had been set up on the gun smuggler's "office" in Coney Island today, but he hadn't heard the outcome. Gavin had previously made contact with an informant who'd given up Gunther's real name—Ivan Holland—and the location he was using on Coney Island.

"Anytime someone goes after Liberty, we have to assume Ivan is behind it. I'm sure the raid got him riled. Police showed up in riot gear. Ivan is still operating one step ahead of us—the place was empty." Noelle cast her gaze to the ground. "Unfortunately, the informant was swinging from the rafters."

It took a second for Jackson to process the gravity of what had taken place. A man trying to do the right thing had died. "I'm sorry to hear that." Jackson petted Liberty's head. "We'll catch him. We don't want anything happening to our girl, Liberty."

"Thanks, Jackson," Noelle said.

"Well, I'm headed over to the lab."

Jackson and Smokey left headquarters. As he drove the K-9 vehicle toward the forensics lab, he called Darcy, explaining that he had dog food sample she needed to test.

Darcy's voice came across the line sweet and clear. "A dog food sample, huh?"

"Yeah, someone may have tried to poison one of the K-9s," Jackson said. "Depending on traffic, I'm about twenty or so minutes from the lab."

"You don't have to text me when you get here. They installed an extra security measure. There is an outside camera and we have a monitor we can watch in the lab, so I'll see you pull into the parking lot and I'll come out and grab the bag from you. I love technology. I don't know why we didn't do it sooner."

Darcy sounded upbeat. She probably was feeling a lot better now that she was back at work.

"Got it. See you soon."

Traffic wasn't too congested and within twenty minutes, he pulled into the lot. He got out of his SUV and reached across the seat to grab the evidence bag. He stared through the windshield. Darcy stood with the door partially open, waiting for him.

An ultrasonic sound pummeled past his ear. It took only a nanosecond for him to register that it was likely a rifle shot aimed at Darcy. He crawled back into the vehicle and stayed low, noting that Darcy had shut the door and disappeared. He lifted his head up to peer though the back window. The shot had probably come from a tall building across the street. He stared back at the door of the lab. Had Darcy closed it in time, or had she been hit and was laying just inside?

The next shot pinged off his police vehicle. So, he was the target now. He was sure the shooter saw him as an obstacle in being able to get to Darcy. Not only was Jackson concerned that Darcy might have been hit, he was worried that a bullet would find Smokey, who was confined in his crate.

After calling for backup, Jackson slipped out of his vehicle. He crouched, using the door as a shield. Maybe he could get to the shooter before she got away—assuming it was the woman who had been after Darcy, which was his best guess.

He studied the windows of the building across the street, not seeing any movement. The shooter may have taken the shots and run, realizing that she would be caught if she stayed around.

His phone rang. It was Darcy.

He breathed a sigh of relief. "Are you okay?"

"Yes, got back inside in time and ran back to the lab. The bullet is probably stuck in the door. I think I might be able to extract it later. I saw on the monitor that she's taking shots at you now."

Jackson glanced across the street. No one entered or exited the building but that didn't mean there wasn't a back way out. "I'm just in the way. I'm sure she doesn't like that I can protect you. She's trying to get at you and figures part of that is taking me out of the equation."

"You're a sitting duck out there. I don't want you to be hurt."

"Darcy, I have a job to do. Backup is on the way," he said. "You stay inside where it's safe. I'm going to see if we can catch her and end this thing." He hung up before she could protest. Smokey would be less of an easy target if he wasn't secured in the crate. Jackson knew he didn't have time to wait for backup if he was going to get this woman. He and Smokey had to act now.

Darcy watched on the monitor as Jackson unloaded Smokey and then drew his weapon. He crouched low, using the cars as cover as he moved toward the street and the building opposite. Her lungs felt like an elephant was sitting on them. "Why doesn't he wait for the other cops?"

"He probably figures he doesn't have that kind of time." Harlan stood beside her, staring at the monitor, as well. "He'll be all right, Darcy. He's a good cop with a great partner."

Her gaze shot upward as she heard the pounding of footsteps above her. There were occupied offices up there, but the noise was always at a minimum. Could the shooter have snuck out the back of the building and made her way across the street?

The last time she was attacked in the lab, the perp had crawled through the ductwork to get to this floor. "Maybe we should lock the door to the lab too not just the outside door." She hurried across the floor and pressed in the code that would lock the door. When she checked the monitor, Jackson had made it across the street, but had made an about-face with Smokey and was headed back toward the lab. He'd seen something on this side of the street.

Harlan closed his laptop.

More footsteps echoed above them. Then the world fell silent.

A moment later, the door to the lab rattled. Someone was trying to get in.

Whoever was shaking the door stopped. Several more tense seconds passed. Darcy stood paralyzed as a rifle shot blasted a hole through the door. Followed immediately by another. Darcy jumped back. The shooter was going to blast her way in.

Both Darcy and Harlan dropped to the floor and crawled toward the far side of the lab, seeking cover behind a desk. There was only one way in and out of the lab. Darcy braced for another rifle shot, but then heard retreating footsteps. Something had scared the shooter off. The hallway where the shooter had been had a window that looked out onto the parking lot. Maybe she'd seen Jackson headed back this way.

"There, in the parking lot." Harlan peered around the desk and pointed at the monitor.

Darcy ran over to it just in time to see a person, probably a woman, running. She had a rifle slung over her shoulder. She was on-screen for just a second. A moment later, Darcy saw Jackson and Smokey in hot pursuit.

Two patrol cars pulled into the lot and uniformed officers got out. She could not see Jackson or the woman anymore.

The two officers ran off-screen in the same direction Jackson had gone.

Darcy heard gunshots. She closed her eyes and said a prayer for their safety.

She stared at the screen, which only showed the parking lot and the unoccupied police cars. The sound of her breathing seemed to intensify as she waited.

"Hope they're okay," Harlan said. He patted her shoulder, but she picked up on the fear in his voice.

The moment seemed to last forever before the two officers ran back on-screen. She let out a heavy sigh. "They're okay." The officers returned to their patrol cars and sped out of the lot.

Jackson and Smokey finally came on-screen, running toward the building. "Jackson is coming to the lab. I'll go let him in."

After unlocking the door to the lab, she ran down the hallway and held open the main door. Jackson and Smokey stood outside and she resisted the urge to fall into his arms. She was so relieved neither he nor Smokey had been hurt. "I'm so glad you're okay."

"Suspect got away. She had a car with a driver waiting. Patrol cars are going to try to catch her." Jackson glanced around nervously. "I don't think it's good for me to stand outside like this—now that she's decided to come after me. A drive-by is still a possibility."

She stepped to one side. "Oh, sorry."

Jackson and Smokey came inside, allowing the door to lock behind him. "And it wasn't good for you to be out in the open like that, either." He reached up, brushing his hand over her cheek with a feather-light touch. "You should not have stood in the doorway like that."

"I know. I have to keep reminding myself," Darcy said. His touch, though brief, had made her heart beat faster for a whole different reason. "I was scared for you and Smokey. I heard the gunshots and I thought maybe one of you had been hit. When I saw you were okay, I just wasn't thinking for a moment."

"You don't need to worry about me. Being in danger is just the nature of my work, Darcy. Good thing you don't date cops."

"That doesn't matter," she said. "Even as a friend, I was worried for you." Her hand brushed his sleeve.

"I appreciate that." He looked down at her and, for a moment, a charge of electricity seemed to pass between them. The thought zinged through her mind that if Jackson wasn't a police officer, she could so fall for him.

She took a step back. "So that woman must have been shooting from across the street and then snuck over her to try to get at me."

"It looks that way," Jackson said. "Another lab is going to have to come in and process all this. I'd say you and Harlan are done working for the day."

Darcy clenched her jaw. More delays in getting her work done. "You can at least bring me that dog food sample, and I will catalog it. Hopefully processing this scene won't take long and I can get back to work."

After commanding Smokey to stay, Jackson swung the door open and disappeared outside. Darcy stepped out of view as the door eased shut. She could see the holes in the metal doors where the bullets had gone through. Though the chances of the shooter coming back were slim, she knew she needed to make a habit of being hypervigilant. She kneeled down to pet Smokey. The dog licked her face as if to comfort her. He must have picked up on her agitation. She was still stirred up from having been shot at through the locked door.

Jackson knocked on the outside door. She rose and pushed it open, careful not to stand in the open doorway. He handed her the dog food sample. "When you do get a chance to process it, you can phone headquarters to let Noelle and Gavin know."

"We're so backed up," Darcy said. "I wish I could get my work done."

The evidence for the Emery case had been put on the back burner for now. Thankfully, it hadn't been destroyed in the previous attack. Once she isolated the DNA, Darcy; hoped she would at least be able to rule out one suspect. Randall Gage, who was still at large, was a DNA match for the double homicide twenty years ago that was so close to home for the K-9 Unit. Gage had murdered Eddie and Anna McGregor, the parents of Bradley and Penelope McGregor. Either Randall had committed the Emery murder, too, or they were looking at a copycat. She knew the unit was thinking copycat, which meant there was another killer out there—and this time, they didn't know his identity.

"You and Harlan should probably go home. I can drive you. I'll talk to Gavin to see if we can have a patrol car put outside your place."

The last thing she wanted to do was to sit at home like some kind of a prisoner. "Look, I did have time to put together a list of potential females who might have a grudge against me. Can you go with me to question them?" At least that way she would be doing something to end this nightmare.

"Sure," he said. "If I can clear it with Gavin."

Once they had access to the lab again, the next thing on her list to process was the gun found close to where Griffin Martel had been killed. Maybe she could at least make some headway on that case.

NINE

By the time Jackson had gotten the okay from Gavin to start working through Darcy's list of suspects, the parking lot and the lab were swarming with law enforcement and forensic staff from the Manhattan unit.

Darcy and Jackson waited in the hallway while the techs moved in and out, processing both the outside door and the door that led to the lab. They had also gone across the street to see if they could find where the shooter had lain in wait.

Harlan had already left.

It was unlikely that the woman would come back, but Jackson knew he had to heed his own advice and exercise caution at all times. He looked at Darcy. "You ready to go?" He'd snagged an extra bulletproof vest for her given they were going to be out in the open questioning suspects. He and Smokey already had theirs on.

She nodded and they stepped outside.

Jackson took up a position on one side of Darcy and Smokey walked on the other as they approached his vehicle. He did a visual of the area and across the street once Darcy was safely inside the SUV.

Jackson loaded Smokey back up and got in behind the wheel. "Who's our first suspect?"

"A woman named Lydia Harmon. My work helped put her brother away for robbery. She claimed her brother was innocent. She sent several threatening emails after the trial. She's ex-military. I know that this woman who is after me hires goons, but she's the one doing the shooting at me and now at you. Lydia probably has some marksman skills because of her background."

"Sounds like a smart place to start," Jackson said. "Are you hungry? We can grab a quick bite somewhere first."

"Starved," she said.

"The safest place would be where cops hang out. I know a good diner near a police precinct nearby. They have a little of everything. And always a lot of cops at the counter and tables."

"Sounds good to me," Darcy said.

"We can get it to go, so we're not inside long."

Jackson drove through downtown Brooklyn. He waited for a spot by the diner to open up and pulled in. They got out of the SUV together.

The noise of people chatting and eating greeted them when Jackson opened the door. The air smelled of grease and salt.

Jackson pointed up at a whiteboard. "Any of the specials look good to you? They bring those out real fast."

They took seats at the counter. Though this was probably the safest place for him to take Darcy if she had to be out in the open, Jackson's nerves were still on edge.

"The fried chicken special sounds great to me," she said.

"Same here. You can put in the order. I'm going to watch the room." He swung around on his stool.

Fear flashed through her eyes and then she turned to get the waiter's attention. Jackson studied the people at the tables, giving a nod toward the officers he recognized from working across Brooklyn. He was aware that even the off-duty officers were probably armed. He felt himself relax a little. Only a fool would try something in a place that was so packed with cops.

Once they had their food, they walked back to the SUV and got inside, the delicious smell of their takeout making his stomach growl.

Darcy opened her to-go box and took a bite of her chicken. "This is really good."

He smiled. "Another fine dining experience brought to you by Jackson and Smokey."

"No. I mean it, this is really tasty," she said.

He found himself wishing that he could take her out to a nice restaurant. What a difference from a few days ago when he'd taken her to the pizza joint so she wouldn't think they were on a date. As much as he had dug his heels in, he had to admit his heart was opening up to the possibility of something more than friendship with her. Too bad she didn't date cops.

"Why are you looking at me like that?" Darcy munched on a French fry.

He shook his head. "Nothing. Just thinking." He had no idea if her feelings had shifted. He kind of doubted it. A woman who draws a line in the sand about not dating cops probably wouldn't change her mind.

"Darcy, that rule that you have about not dating cops, is there a reason behind it?"

Darcy took a nibble on her French fry and chewed for a moment. "If I let the personal get mixed up with the professional, it can cause trouble for cases. In my job, integrity is everything, and it can be the differ-

ence between a guilty man going to jail or walking."
An intensity he hadn't heard from her before colored
her words. "I just figured if I couldn't separate my romantic feelings for someone from my work, the safest
thing to do was to not ever let the personal and professional get tangled together."

That settled that. He sat staring out of the window
for a moment, not sure what to say. "I get it." He turned
the key in the ignition. "Where are we going to talk to
Lydia Harmon?"

Darcy crushed the cardboard container her meal had
been in. "She's works security at the Brooklyn Navy
Yard. She's on duty now. I got the information from her
roommate by pretending to be an old friend. She doesn't
know we're going to interview her. I think the element
of surprise comes in handy when you're trying to get
the truth out of someone."

"You managed to do that?" He continued to be impressed at how smart and clever Darcy was. "You may
have missed your calling as a detective."

She smiled. "No, my calling is as a forensics expert.
I'm sure of it. But thanks for the compliment."

He shifted into Reverse. "Let's go check it out."

As they drew closer to the Brooklyn Navy Yard,
they had a view of lower Manhattan across the water.
Though the over two hundred acres of buildings, cranes
and dry docks was still called the "Navy Yard," it hadn't
been used for building and repairing ships for years. It
had been turned into an industrial park. A museum,
businesses and eateries now occupied the multiple
buildings on the site.

Darcy checked her phone again. "The security office is in Building 77, first floor. If Lydia's not there, they will know where to find her."

Jackson wondered if it would be best for Darcy to stay in the SUV with Smokey with the doors locked.

His thoughts must have been evident in his expression. "I'm going with you," she said. "The last time I stayed in a locked car, it didn't make a bit of difference in keeping me safe."

Jackson opened his mouth to protest.

"If we have learned anything, it's that I'm in danger no matter what," she said. "Besides, I'm the one with the detective skills, remember."

Jackson shook his head and chuckled. "Okay. Stay close to Smokey and me."

As they walked up Flushing Avenue toward Vanderbilt, Jackson went on high alert. He paid attention to the people around him, but the thing that concerned him the most were the location possibilities that someone might take up a position to fire a rifle. There was no way the suspect could know ahead of time that Jackson and Darcy were going here, but they might have been followed.

He had to assume that they were still on the attacker's radar. History had proven that anytime he let his guard down, bad things happened. Though it would take a moment for someone with a rifle to get into position, there were numerous possibilities in the multistoried buildings around them, some of which were only partially occupied. If the female attacker had a goon helping her out, there was no telling what could happen.

Once they were inside Building 77, Jackson relaxed a little. They were most vulnerable out on the street. A placard inside the lobby showed that there were plenty of businesses inside the building. They walked across the lobby to the security office. The woman behind the desk informed them that Lydia was probably at the museum.

A knot of tension formed at the back of Jackson's neck. That meant going back outside on the street. Once they were outside, Jackson stayed close to Darcy while Darcy held Smokey's leash so he could walk on the other side of her.

"Pay attention to Smokey," Jackson advised. "He's a good barometer for threats and danger. His hackles will go up, or he'll stutter or stop in his step. He might lift his nose."

He allowed Darcy and Smokey to enter the museum first so he could give the street one final survey. People bustled by without glancing in his direction.

The entrance to the museum had a huge metal anchor the size of a whale. A docent stood by it, explaining to a small cluster of people how much it weighed.

Darcy pointed across the room. "There, I just saw a woman in uniform disappear around that corner. That's probably Lydia."

They hurried across the crowded floor, pressing through a group of people. Darcy glanced over her shoulder and then Smokey stopped.

Jackson pressed closer to her, touching her arm just above the elbow. "What?"

She shook her head. "Just a feeling."

Whatever had caused Darcy to slow down had also set off an alarm bell for Smokey.

The woman in uniform returned to the open area.

"That's Lydia Harmon," Darcy said.

The security guard made eye contact with them and stepped in their direction.

Smoky jerked on the leash and faced the entrance to the building. He emitted a sharp, intense bark. Darcy whirled around, as well.

Her voice slipped into monotone and grew as cold as ice. "It's her. She's here."

Jackson stared at the crowd, not seeing anyone that resembled the woman he only gotten a glimpse of at the lab. "Are you sure?"

Lydia Harmon had stepped close enough to talk to them. "You look like you need something. Can I help you folks?"

The crowd cleared. A woman dressed in running clothes, a jacket and a baseball hat, locked in to Jackson's gaze for less than a second before whirling around and leaving the museum. She wasn't running, but she was walking at a brisk pace so as not to call attention to herself.

It was the expression—that intense look of fear on her face—that tipped Jackson off. That had to be her. Jackson sprinted across the museum floor.

He hurried outside, scanning the sidewalk filled with people, not seeing the woman. The baseball hat had been an indistinct color.

The crowds cleared on part of the sidewalk. He saw a pale baseball hat tossed on the path that led to the shipyard. She'd been smart enough to toss the one thing that might allow him to pick her out of a crowd. But dumb enough to leave something behind that a forensic scientist could test for DNA to ID her. He wished he had Smokey with him; even though the

K-9 was trained to find human remains, not track suspects on the run, Smokey had helped with the watcher in the park.

After pulling the evidence bag from the cargo pocket of his uniform, Jackson bagged the hat, scanned the faces on the street, and kept walking at a brisk pace. Most likely the suspect would try to blend in with the rest of the crowd.

He keyed his radio and requested backup while he sped up his pace. He gave a description of the woman to Dispatch. "We need to cover as many streets as possible. I don't want her getting away."

"Ten-Four," said the dispatcher. "Looks like three units are in the area. We can't cover all the streets leading into the Navy Yard, but they can run a patrol for several blocks each. They should be in place in less than ten minutes."

Ten minutes was a long time where a search was concerned. And if she had parked close by, she would be able to get to her car and escape.

Still watching the sidewalks filled with people, he backtracked to get his K-9, noting that Darcy and Smokey had emerged from the museum. Smokey might be able to pick up on a scent while they waited for the tracking dogs to arrive.

Before he could get back to Darcy, Smokey jerked on the leash and took off running along the street, dragging Darcy with him. The dog had noticed or smelled something.

Jackson sprinted to catch up with them. He couldn't leave Darcy exposed. There was a chance the woman would turn on her and take her.

Or worse, if she was armed with a handgun, she might be able to shoot Darcy and disappear into the crowd.

Darcy ran hard to keep up with Smokey. The K-9 must have seen or smelled something. He seemed intent on crossing the street. She trusted the dog's training over anything her senses might tell her. The woman at the entrance to the museum had acted very suspiciously. Though Darcy had never gotten a clear look at the woman's face, there was something about the way she'd moved that was distinct. She ran like an athlete.

Darcy picked up her pace. Off to the side, she saw Jackson coming toward her.

He caught up with her just as Smokey stopped outside a shop that sold imported home goods. The dog paced back and forth.

"Do you think she went in there?"

"It's worth a shot." Jackson reached for Smokey's leash.

They stepped inside. The place was more like a warehouse than a shop, with its high ceilings, and shelving and displays that were almost as high.

"There is no safe place for you right now," Jackson said, "so just stay close to me and Smokey."

"Two sets of eyes are better than one," she said.

"Actually, we have three sets of eyes and one good nose."

They worked their way up one aisle and down another. The final aisle was much more crowded. Darcy pressed close to Jackson as they squeezed through the shoppers. A woman bumped shoulders with Darcy, setting off her personal alarm bells.

"Oh, sorry," she said.

Darcy looked at the woman. Not their suspect. "No problem."

Smokey jerked on the leash, indicating the entrance to the shop. "Let's get back outside," Jackson said.

As they stepped out onto the sidewalk, Jackson's radio blared. Something about units being in place.

A popping sound reverberated in Darcy's ear, followed quickly by another gunshot. Jackson pushed her to the wall, dropping Smokey's leash. The dog paced and barked but remained close.

The crowd dispersed, running in all directions.

Jackson pressed his face very close to Darcy's. "She's shooting at us from the second floor. Probably with a handgun. She didn't have a rifle with her, and no way could she have had time to stash it. She must have followed us here. But how could she have made it across the street and upstairs to shoot at us as we were leaving? That makes no sense." He shook his head. "Get back in the shop. You'll be safe where there are lots of people. Take Smokey, just to be sure."

Jackson took off before she could respond. He spoke frantically into his radio.

Darcy flattened against the wall and worked her way toward the shop entrance. There was no one else on the sidewalk. She slipped into the shop, which was still crowded, though everyone had moved toward the rear of the shop. Some people were talking on their phones in urgent voices. Others were just pressed against the wall, staring at nothing. No one was shopping. She stood off to the side at the back of the store, as well, separated from the cluster of people.

Her heart squeezed tight with fear for Jackson's safety. Smokey sat at her feet, moving his head back and forth, watching the other people.

Something hard pressed against her back and a male voice spoke into her ear. "Drop the dog leash and come with me. You make a fuss and I'll shoot you and the dog on the spot. You understand?"

Darcy shook her head. When she dropped the leash, Smokey turned to face her. His face filled with expectation, awaiting a command.

"Tell him to stay," the man whispered in her ear.

"Sit. Stay, Smokey." Her voice quivered with fear.

The dog did as he was told.

"Now let's you and me head out the back door."

Darcy glanced around at the crowd, wondering if she could get someone's attention before a bullet entered her back. Not likely, as the man sounded serious. Would he risk being caught? The ideal plan was probably to take her someplace more secluded. Either way, it was clear his intent was to kill her.

TEN

Jackson hurried up the stairs. He was greeted by a long hallway with doors indicating various offices, lawyers and accountants mostly. He could only guess at where the shots had come from. Judging from the sound, they had not been from a rifle but a handgun. He wondered if the woman intended to get them into a vulnerable place and then take her shot at Darcy. A handgun didn't have the long-distant accuracy of a rifle, so chances were she'd been firing from the second floor. But still, how had she so quickly gotten from the shop to here and in place to shoot at them?

There were three possibilities for where the shots had originated. The first door indicated the office of a financial planner. Jackson knocked on the door.

"Yes, come in." The voice sounded frightened.

Jackson opened the door and stuck his head in. The first thing he saw was a desk with two computer monitors and a headset that had been tossed on the floor. A man in a suit was pressed against a far wall. He looked at Jackson's uniform. The man's stiff shoulders relaxed a little. "I heard the shots. What's going on?"

Off to his side, Jackson heard banging and shuffling.

He poked his head out of the office just in time to see a woman running toward the stairwell.

Jackson sprinted after her. By the time he flung the door open and glanced up the twisting stairwell, the woman was not in sight, though he heard the tap, tap, tap of footsteps above him. She had to be in good shape to have run that quickly, but why not run down to the street?

Jackson raced up the stairs until he reached the rooftop where there was a garden and several storage sheds. No one was currently working in the garden. He scanned side to side. The rooftops were connected well enough that you could run from one to the other. There was a small group of people several rooftops over. They were sitting at tables and had a barbecue going. He didn't see the woman anywhere. That meant she must be hiding behind or in one of the storage sheds.

Pulling his weapon, he checked around the first storage shed. When he tried to open it, he found it was locked. He moved to the second shed, making a sweeping pattern with his gun. He moved toward the next shed.

A bullet whizzed by him, so close that his skin tingled and his eardrum felt like it been hit with a tiny hammer. He fell to the ground and then peered up. The shot had come from the garden of corn and sunflowers, which were high and thick enough to hide someone. The foliage rustled and a woman half rose then took off in the direction of the next rooftop. Would she risk trying to jump across? She sought shelter behind the final shed just as Jackson rose and aimed his weapon. He didn't want to kill her, only wound her.

"Police!" he said. "Come out with your hands up!"

He stepped steadily toward the shed. In the distance, he heard sirens. Once the shooting had happened, NYPD sent all kinds of backup, not just the units that were in the area. Judging from the sound of the sirens, some were probably still five minutes away.

"Give yourself up," he said. "This place is going to be surrounded in just minutes." He kept his weapon aimed at the shed as he moved in.

A strange noise not too far from the shed caught his attention. It sort of sounded like metal creaking or something that needed to be greased. Still on high alert, he raced to the edge of the building. Using the shed to shield her from view, the woman had climbed down a fire escape as far as it would take her. She was now hanging from a windowsill. He watched as she dropped the ten feet to the ground and raced up a back alley. She ran like lightning. No way could he make that climb and catch up with her.

He clicked on his radio. "Suspect is on the run. Looks like she's headed up an alley toward Flushing. Suspect is considered armed and dangerous."

He hurried back to the stairwell and sprinted down, taking the stairs two at a time. Though he headed up the alley, running as fast as he could, he knew that his efforts were probably futile. The woman had some athletic chops; he had to hand it to her.

He ran all the way out to Flushing Avenue, searching everywhere while he caught his breath. The crowds were just too abundant. It would be too easy for her to blend in. The rest of the NYPD would put an all points out for her, and the search would continue in a five-block radius around the Navy Yard.

He pulled out the bagged hat he'd picked up. One of

the tracker dogs might be able to find her. He hurried back to the building where he'd left Darcy and Smokey. Outside the building, Tyler Walker was waiting with Dusty, along with dozens of other police units, both K-9 and patrol. Tyler must have been one of the units that was close by to get here so fast.

Jackson handed Tyler the hat. Dusty picked up on a scent right away. After Jackson briefed the other officers on all that happened, he headed into the imported home goods store. At least Darcy had been kept safe.

He hurried inside. Most of the people were still gathered at the back of the store. Their expressions communicated fear and alarm.

He moved up one aisle and down the other, not seeing Darcy or Smokey. He stepped into the third aisle. When Smokey came running toward him, dragging the leash, Jackson knew something was terribly wrong.

Still pressing the gun in her back, the man led her onto a back street. At least ten people stood in the street, which was normally not that busy as it was the backside of businesses where the Dumpsters were kept.

He spoke through gritted teeth. "Where are all these people coming from?"

She'd heard the sirens. NYPD had probably sent many units to deal with the active shooter. These people probably had taken shelter in the back alleys thinking it was safer from potential violence.

"Once your friend shot at me, I'm sure the NYPD pulled out all the stops."

"Shut up," he said. "Do what I say." He poked her with the barrel of the gun. His free hand was wrapped around her forearm. To the world, they probably looked like a couple out for a stroll. Though Darcy thought the expression on her face might indicate they were a couple who had just had a fight.

She scanned the faces around her. No one was even looking in their direction.

Yelling for help or that she was being kidnapped might mean he would just shoot her on the spot and run, aiming the gun at anyone who tried to take him down. The police were close by…if she could just get on a street where they were. If Jackson had figured out what happened to her, he might have given the other officers a description of her.

"This place is crawling with police." She still felt the pressure of the gun against her back. "Even if you shoot me, you won't get away."

"I'm Brooklyn born and raised. I know every back alley and shortcut." The man sounded nervous to her.

He pushed her forward around a corner and onto another street. Two blocks up, she saw the flashing lights of a police vehicle. He yanked her back around the corner. He must have seen it, too.

"Like I said. You're surrounded. Why don't you let me go? You can get away."

He pushed on her back. "Let's just keep going down this street."

Darcy walked, moving her eyes while her head remained still. She had to find the opportunity for escape. "You're not even doing this for yourself, are you? It's that woman who is behind it all." Maybe she could get some information out of him. Maybe she could break his resolve. "What is she to you, your girlfriend?"

"Shut up, I said." His voice broke. "I should just shoot you now. Take my chances."

Of course, if she ended up dead, any information Darcy gathered would not help anyone. She could tell the man was growing more frustrated. He could be pushed toward giving up as fast as he could be pushed toward just shooting her.

They walked by a building where Darcy noticed a homeless man was passed out. He wouldn't have slept through all the sirens. He must been unconscious from some kind of drug or too much alcohol. The shooter stopped and stared at the prone man. "It would be nothing to shoot you and leave you to look like you were sleeping just like him."

Fear charged through her like a raging bull. There would be no time to scream even at this close range. "There would be blood. People would see."

Still gripping her upper arm, he pushed the gun barrel into her back again. "Up there, that street."

The street he was pointing to looked like more of an alley or side street. Chances were, it would be deserted. She had to get away before they turned the corner.

Sirens sounded in the distance, but some were growing louder, maybe two blocks away. The man hesitated in his step. His grip on her arm loosened. This was her opportunity.

She wrenched her body, wrestling free of his grip. His gun was visible. She shouted, "Help! Help me!"

Several people looked in her direction.

The man pointed his gun at them. "You come at me and I'll shoot."

The few people who had looked her way took a step back, fear clouding their expressions just as a patrol car rounded the corner.

The man shoved her forward and ran down the alley just as the patrol officer got out of his car.

Darcy fell, putting her hands out in front of her to brace for impact with the concrete. The patrol officer assessed the situation. One of the onlookers pointed up the alley. The officer sprinted toward the street where the armed man had gone.

An older woman came up to Darcy and held out her hand to her. Darcy could barely stand. She felt like every bone in her body was vibrating. She'd managed to stay levelheaded through the whole ordeal. Now that she was safe, all the fear and panic she'd held at bay flooded through her like a tsunami.

The older woman didn't say anything, only patted her shoulder. The rest of the people watched Darcy as she brushed off her pant legs. Her heart was still racing.

Jackson and Smokey came around the corner. She stumbled toward them and fell into his arms.

He held her and whispered in her ear. "It's all right now. You're safe." He drew her closer. "I was so worried about you, Darcy."

"He could have killed me." The realization made her weak-kneed all over again. But it was different now with Jackson so close. As she reveled in the safety she felt in Jackson's arms, a sense of calm returned.

Smokey whined at his feet. He wagged his tail when Darcy lifted her head to look in his direction. "You were worried, too, weren't you?"

Jackson tightened his embrace and drew her closer. She had the sense that he wanted the moment to last as much as she did.

He pulled free of the hug and looked into her eyes. "Let's get you home. There are plenty of officers here to continue searching," he said. "You have been through enough for one day. I think my priority needs to be with getting you home safe."

She so appreciated his sensitivity to how shredded she felt right now. They waited around for a while longer. After giving their statements, they returned to his SUV and loaded up.

He talked as they drove through traffic. "Considering everything that has happened, I think I can get a patrol car to park outside your house for the whole night."

"That would be great." She was still trying to calm down. Part of her wished that it would be Jackson parked outside her place. She only truly felt safe when she was with him.

He made the call to Gavin while they were en route. Jackson explained the situation and added, "She needs a higher level of security than I alone can manage in my off-duty hours." He glanced over at her and gave her his trademark wink.

"Let me put you on hold one minute," Gavin said. "I'll see what I can authorize."

Jackson turned to Darcy. "I'm sure they will put someone in place. If not, I'll park outside your building."

His offer touched her heart. "But you have to go on shift in the morning. You'd be exhausted."

"I'd do it for you, Darcy."

Jackson had the phone on speaker and Gavin's voice came back across the line. "We can have a car outside her building within half an hour."

"Ten-Four," Jackson responded.

They fell into a comfortable silence. It was still early in the evening, the sky had just started to turn gray.

Though her heartbeat had returned to normal, Darcy was stirred up from the trauma of having had a gun held on her again. She thanked God that she was alive. That she had such a good friend like Jackson. And then she tried to focus on something positive. "It will be good to see my sister and my cat again."

Jackson found a parking space a few blocks from her building. "I'll walk you to your door and then I'm going to stay parked outside until a patrol car shows up."

"You can come inside, if you like."

"Your sister's been home for most of the day, right?"

"Yes," she said. "So what you're saying is that there is no chance of anyone waiting to jump me inside." She was a little disappointed to not be able to spend even a few more minutes in Jackson's company.

Leaving Smokey in the car, they made their way up the sidewalk. "I'll watch the street, and I'll text you when the patrol unit shows. He or she will stay here all night until I can come to get you in the morning."

They stood outside her apartment building door, facing each other. "Thank you for everything, Jackson."

A moment passed as they gazed at each other.

Darcy fell into his arms again, seeking the comfort of his strength and steady nature. She pulled back and looked into his eyes. "Could you call me instead of texting when the patrol officer shows up? I'd love to hear the sound of your voice. I don't know… It gives me a sense of peace."

"Sure." He seemed amused by her request. "You have a good rest of your night."

"Okay." She fumbled in her purse for the key, grateful that there was a streetlamp to illuminate the entranceway so she could see to shove it into the lock.

Opening the door, she turned back to look at Jackson. "See you in the morning."

"Remember not to stand in front of the windows," he said.

"I know," she said.

"Sorry to sound like a broken record. I just want to make sure I see your smiling face and dimples in the morning."

His remark softened the blow of having to live with the reality of her life being under constant threat. They both seemed to be prolonging the goodbye. Jackson's company and protection felt so natural, like breathing. Darcy found herself not wanting to be away from him.

She stepped inside, closing the door behind her, then headed to her apartment.

Her sister was sitting at the table working on a laptop. She smiled up at her. Mr. Tubbs rested on the couch. This was home.

Darcy collapsed on the couch and petted the cat. "I've had quite the day."

She stared at the ceiling thinking about her growing attachment to Jackson and how hopeless she felt about it.

ELEVEN

The next morning, Jackson got a call from Darcy saying she was free to go back to work, so he picked her up. After dropping her at the lab, he found himself distracted at the morning briefing for the Brooklyn K-9 Unit. His mind was on Darcy and her safety. And if he was honest with himself, he would rather be with her than anywhere else, not just to protect her but because he genuinely liked being around her.

From the front of the room, Gavin briefed them on what had happened to Darcy yesterday, advising that any unit that was in the area of the lab or her home should be on the lookout for anything suspicious and report it in right away.

"We have the man in custody who held her at gunpoint. He's not talking. We believe he is just hired muscle and a woman is behind the attacks on Darcy Fields. Now, Detective Walker will brief us on the Emery double homicide and the progress made in locating the person little Lucy had said she missed during a recent interview." *I miss Andy* was all Lucy had said on the subject, and her aunt and uncle had confirmed that there was no one named Andy in her life. "We believe,"

Gavin continued, "that finding this person of interest might help us make a break in the murder of her parents. Tyler?"

Tyler rose from his chair and walked to the front of the room. He had told Jackson that he felt like the Emery case was deeply personal, not just because Lucy's aunt had married one of their own—Detective Nate Slater—but because every time he looked at Lucy, he thought about his own eighteen-month-old little girl who was also growing up without her mother. But they were both grateful that Lucy had a loving mother figure in her aunt and that Willow and Nate were in the process of adopting her.

Tyler ran his hand, through his blond hair and cleared his throat. "As you know, several times I have been out to where the Emerys lived, trying to track down this 'Andy' that Lucy refers to. We've found several people who go by that name or a similar-sounding name, but when we show Lucy a photograph, she shakes her head."

Jackson picked up on the frustration in Tyler's voice. "What about a kid who goes by that name? Maybe from the playground or day care in that neighborhood," suggested Jackson.

"Covered those bases," Tyler said. "Also looked into the possibility that it was a senior citizen she might have had contact within the neighborhood." Tyler shook his head. "I feel like I'm at a dead end."

Detective Nate Slater spoke up. "We really need a break in this case for Lucy's sake. I need to know my little girl is safe." His voice filled with intense emotion.

Jackson clenched his teeth. When was this case going to break? "I agree. This thing needs to move forward. If we can't track down this Andy guy, maybe Darcy can get something usable off the fiber from the crime scene."

Gavin thanked Tyler and excused everyone from the briefing, reminding them to stay safe. Officers with K-9 partners dispersed in different directions. Jackson was walking past the front desk counter, where Penny Mac-Gregor typed on a computer keyboard, when his phone rang. He recognized the number as Darcy's.

He pressed the connect button. "Darcy, how are you?"

"So, I thought you might want to know that the gun you found in the trash can in Prospect Park is a ballistics match for the one that killed Griffin Martel."

"That's good news, right? It's a step forward in that case." He'd detected a slight lilt in Darcy's voice that he had not heard before.

"That's not what has me bent out of shape, though. I also got a print match off the gun." She hesitated for a moment. It sounded like she had taken in a sharp, quick breath. "You're not going to believe who it belongs to."

Even through the phone, he detected a level of tension. "Try me?"

"Reuben Bray."

It took Jackson a moment to process what she'd said. When the information sunk in, it was like a slap across his jaw. "You mean the guy who is sitting in jail right now and has been for months?"

"The press is going to have a field day with this," Darcy said. "But I can't avoid it. I have to hold a press conference. They already think I didn't do my job with Reuben's case." Her voice filled with tension. "I can't prove it, but my gut tells me the evidence was planted to make me look bad. Griffin Martel's death somehow connects back to Reuben Bray—and not because Reuben killed him. That would be impossible. Someone is trying to set me up to look incompetent. It's the only thing that makes sense."

"The trial is soon, right? There's a potential that the whole thing could be thrown out because of this," Jackson noted.

"Exactly, maybe someone is trying to bungle the trial so Reuben walks," she said. "The one bit of forensic evidence that supports my theory is that the fingerprints were a match, but they were partials. There was some smudging and smearing, which makes me think that someone wearing gloves could have fired the gun after Reuben held it."

"Is that something that could be brought up in court for Griffin Martel's case?"

"It's a stretch. We really need more to go on," she said. "Plus, it's not the Griffin Martel case I'm worried about. It's Reuben Bray's that this taints."

"When is your press conference?"

"Toward the end of my day. We've already sent out notice to the news outlets. We're holding it inside the lab so there is no chance of that woman shooting at me from far away. There's a small conference room at the end of the hallway."

Although he was sure security measures were in place, the press conference meant lots of strange people milling around the lab. A fake press pass could be used easily enough if it wasn't examined closely. Darcy would still be in danger. "I'll still be on shift, but I'm sure Gavin will let me be there for protection as long as Smokey and I are not out on a call."

"That makes me feel a little better," she said. "This is going to be a long day."

"If you are feeling up to it… Maybe when you're done with the reporters, we can go out to Rikers and talk to Reuben. He could have set this whole thing up from his jail cell."

"Oh, I'm more than feeling up to it. I want this resolved. There is no way I will let Reuben Bray walk out of that jail a free man. See you later today."

"If I can't be there for the press conference, I'll make sure someone from the unit is, Darcy. We have your back."

"You have no idea how good it is to hear that."

He clicked off the phone. Stirred up by the news that Darcy had given him, he and Smokey headed out to the patrol SUV. He made the decision that when he went over to provide protection for Darcy, he would try to commandeer the help of at least one other K-9 officer.

Darcy's stomach did flip-flops as she watched the security screen in the lab that provided a view of the parking lot. Several press vans had already pulled in. "They're early."

Harlan cupped a hand on her shoulder. "I'll point them toward the conference room. You don't have to make an appearance until your protection shows up."

"Thanks, Harlan."

Harlan stepped toward the door. "Lock the door behind me."

Her throat tightened a little. They both were acutely aware of the danger she faced 24/7. After Harlan left, she returned her attention to the security screen. Two more cars with news logos on the side pulled into the lot. She watched the screen, hoping, praying, that it would be Jackson and Smokey standing by the podium with her.

A dog and his handler came on-screen—Vivienne Armstrong and her border collie, Hank. Then a second K-9 pair, Detective Bradley McGregor and his Malinois, King, came into view. They were followed by Belle Montera and her German shepherd, Justice. Finally, Jackson and Smokey appeared on-screen, as well. Darcy thought she might cry. They really did have her back.

She watched as the two female officers stopped the first reporters before they could enter the building. Vivienne, Hank heeled at her side, checked their credentials and did a pat-down for weapons before the reporters were allowed to enter. Belle and Justice stood by. Darcy knew from having interacted with the K-9 Unit that Justice was trained for protection.

A few minutes later, there were five knocks on the lab door, three fast and two slow. Jackson's code. She pressed the security code to unlock the door.

Jackson, dressed in full uniform, stood there with Smokey. "I'm here to escort you to the conference room," he said, adding, "One officer and his K-9 are in place in the room already. King, Detective McGregor's Malinois, is trained in protection, so you are in good hands. Officer Vivienne Armstrong and Hank, along with Belle Montera and Justice, will guard the outside door, controlling who gets in."

Her heart swelled with gratitude. "I saw how many officers showed up to help. Thanks, Jackson."

She stepped out, making sure the lab was locked behind her. Jackson had thought of everything to keep her safe.

She smoothed over the front of her tan blazer and then glanced down at her polka-dotted pumps. The shoes made her smile.

They walked together down the hall. All eyes were on her as she entered the room and took her place behind the podium. Jackson and Smokey stood to one side, while Bradley and King were positioned by the door.

Darcy laced her hands together and rested them on the podium. She looked out at the eager faces waiting for her to speak and took in a breath that she hoped would quiet her turbulent stomach.

"As you know, the killer of Griffin Martel is still at large. We had a breakthrough in the case today. On the night the body was located, Officer Davison of the Brooklyn K-9 Unit found a gun in a nearby trash can, after chasing an unknown person who'd been hiding in the foliage near the victim. We don't know if that person was involved in the homicide of Mr. Martel or who the gun belonged to, but we do know it was the murder weapon." She turned her head slightly toward Jackson and Smokey.

Ever the professionals, they both stood at attention, focusing on the crowd of gathered reporters.

She looked out at the journalists while cameras flashed. "The bullet that killed Griffin Martel is a match for the gun we found. The gun was not registered, which means it was probably obtained illegally." She stared down at the podium for a moment before taking a breath and looking up. "There was a set of prints found on the gun. Those prints belong to Reuben Bray."

She braced for the barrage of questions and accusations.

"Aren't you set to testify in his trial this week?"

"Yes," she said. Her heart raced and her stomach felt like it had rock in it.

"How can a man sitting in a prison cell commit a murder?"

"He can't." Darcy knew she wasn't allowed to offer her theory that she was being set up to look like she couldn't do her job. She had to deal in the facts. She reiterated the evidence that had initially led to Reuben's indictment for murder.

"Do you think you might have made in a mistake analyzing the evidence that sent Reuben Bray to jail for murder in the first place?"

"No, I do not."

A female reporter, who Darcy recognized from a regional television station, took two steps toward her. "Miss Fields, since the Brooklyn K-9 Unit was involved in Reuben Bray's initial capture, maybe you were feeling some pressure from them to bring forth some evidence to put him away."

"That is not the case." Her voice rose half an octave. She swallowed and gripped the sides of the podium to try to regain control of her emotions. Out of the corner of her eye, she saw Jackson twitch. The accusation bothered him, too. "I assure you that Forensics works with all of the units in the NYPD with the utmost integrity."

A male reporter interjected, "So the trial of Reuben Bray will go forward?"

Motion at the back of the room by the door caught Darcy's attention. A blonde stepped out from behind a camera being operated by a man. She looked right at Darcy and then stepped through the door. A chill ran down Darcy's spine.

"Miss Fields? Are you going to answer the question?" another reporter called out.

The blond woman had been dressed in a suit and had a press pass around her neck. The look she had given Darcy had been filled with malice. Darcy's heart raged in her chest.

Jackson must have picked up on her alarm. He and Smokey moved toward her and, wrapping his arm across her back, Jackson led her away from the podium. "I think Miss Fields has answered enough questions today."

"You're from the Brooklyn K-9 Unit, aren't you? You and Miss Fields seem very cozy," a female reporter, who Darcy knew to be from a local newspaper, quipped.

Jackson's jaw turned to granite. "Miss Fields has had threats against her life. She requires protection."

One of the reporters spoke under his breath. "This whole thing stinks of collusion."

More than anything, Darcy wanted to respond to the accusation, but she knew silence was the more professional choice.

Jackson led her through the crowded room toward the conference room door as the peppering of questions continued. Smokey remained close. Once they were in the hallway, the reporters followed them to the lab.

Harlan was waiting for them, holding the lab door open. They slipped inside while the lab tech stood in the hallway to answer the reporters' questions.

Darcy turned to face him. "Jackson, I saw her. She was at the news conference at the back of the room. I know it was her." It had been at least five minutes since the woman had left the room. There had been no opportunity to tell him earlier with the reporters crowding them.

Jackson's eyes grew wide. He pressed the call button on his radio. "Suspect on the run just outside the forensics lab." He clicked off the radio. "What did she look like?"

"Blond, dressed in a navy suit. Press pass."

Jackson relayed the information.

She could still hear the commotion of the reporters on the other side of the door though it sounded like it was dying down a little.

Darcy glanced at the surveillance screen. Some of the news vans were pulling out of the parking lot. She watched as Vivienne ran across the lot with Hank and disappeared.

A moment later, her voice came across Jackson's radio. "I found a blond wig and a press pass in the garbage."

"She's probably long gone." Darcy sighed, trying not to give in to despair. She had a feeling the woman had also been wearing a wig when she'd thrown off the baseball cap after fleeing the museum. The Manhattan forensics lab was testing it for DNA, but Darcy didn't hold out too much hope that the perp would be ID'd that way.

"We're not giving up that easily," Jackson said. "At least we can use the wig to put the tracking dog onto her. If she's close by and hasn't gotten into a car, we might still have a chance at catching her. She might be hiding somewhere close waiting for her chance to get at you."

Darcy allowed a realization to sink in. "I think all of this is connected to Reuben Bray and his trial. The gun was planted to make me look incompetent. And that woman…" She shook her head. "I think she's trying to stop the trial either by getting it thrown out or by killing me."

"You might be right," Jackson conceded. "One thing is for sure. We have to get out to Rikers and talk to Reuben Bray. We need to find out who she is and if she has a connection to Reuben."

"Let's go," Darcy said.

They passed through the door as Harlan entered the lab. A trickle of reporters remained in the hallway and in the parking lot. As they hurried to Jackson's SUV, some continued to snap pictures of Jackson and Darcy together. Darcy knew she couldn't control the press's fixated narrative, though it bothered her that a cloud had shadowed her work and that of the Brooklyn K-9 Unit for unfair reasons.

TWELVE

After informing Dispatch where he was going and why, Jackson focused on driving to the prison. The report came across his radio that the search for the woman Darcy had seen at the press conference had yielded nothing.

That meant she was still at large. The tracking dogs would have located her if she had remained anywhere close. As long as she was out there, he had to assume that they both were still under threat.

Darcy's phone rang. She clicked it on and gave short one-word answers to whomever she was talking to on the other end of the line. "Thanks, Harlan." She ended the call and told Jackson, "So the judge was informed about the fingerprints on the gun before I held the press conference. He just sent us a response. He wants to go forward with Reuben's trial. He regards the Griffin Martel murder as a separate case." He picked up on the distress in Darcy's voice. She turned and stared out the window.

"Legally, that's true, but the press won't treat it that way."

Once they arrived at Rikers, they left Smokey in the

SUV with the air-conditioning on and the doors locked, a feature he appreciated, and walked across the parking lot to the entrance of the prison.

Jackson explained to the desk clerk that they needed to speak to Reuben Bray. They were searched and led through a series of security gates into a room where they were instructed to sit at a desk separated by a wall of glass with another desk on the other side. Reuben was only allowed non-contact visits. Less violent prisoners could sit at a table with their loved ones and lawyers. There were at least ten visitor stations in this room. Only one station on the far side was occupied by a gray-haired woman who clutched her purse and spoke to a twentysomething man on the other side of the glass.

Jackson retrieved a second chair. He patted Darcy's hand where it rested on the desk. She glanced at him, smiling. A door at the end of the room opened and Reuben Bray was escorted by a guard. He took his seat at the desk opposite them. The guard stood behind him.

"Darcy, how good to see you. And I see you brought a friend." Reuben offered her a hundred-watt smile.

The press might be taken in by his good looks and charm, but Jackson could barely contain his irritation. The guy was a slimy manipulator.

Darcy's stern expression suggested she wasn't fooled by his act, either.

"I'm sure you heard—or maybe you already knew— that we found your prints on the gun that killed Griffin Martel."

Again, Reuben grinned. "Wow, that's interesting." He sat back in his chair, crossed his arms over his chest and leered at her. "How could that happen? I've been in this jail cell the whole time." His tone became sarcastic. "Are you sure you did the fingerprint test right, Darcy?"

Jackson leaned forward, his hand balled into a fist. "Her name is Miss Fields."

"Look, Reuben," Darcy said, "the judge made the decision to move forward with your trial."

A curtain seemed to drop over Reuben's features and he pressed his lips together. The change was subtle, but Jackson was good at reading body language. Darcy's news about the trial going forward had upset him.

"Whatever you and your female accomplice were hoping to sabotage by planting that gun didn't work," Jackson said.

Reuben's brows knit together. "I don't know what you're talking about." He burst to his feet. "I'm done here. I want to go back to my cell."

They waited until Reuben and the guard disappeared behind the door.

"He tried to hide it, but I think we're onto something," Jackson said. "Let's go check the visitor logs to find out who's been to see him."

They left the visitation room and returned to the front desk where they had signed in before seeing Reuben. "We need to know who has been coming to see Reuben Bray," Jackson told the clerk.

The clerk pulled out a computer notebook and typed something before sliding the notebook across the counter.

Jackson looked at the names and dates.

Darcy stared over his shoulder.

Several of the names also had the last name "Bray."

"Maybe it's not a girlfriend. Maybe it's a sister who's

been doing his dirty work or some other relative," Darcy suggested.

"Could be," Jackson said.

Darcy pointed to some of the names on the list. "That one is a reporter and so is that one."

Both the names were female.

"You said the perp wore a press pass at the lab—it could have been a fake or maybe she's one of these reporters. Do you think she might be involved with him?"

"Maybe." Darcy pointed to one of the names and shook her head. "This woman is like fifty and she's a really good journalist. The other one is Reuben's age." Darcy flipped the page and scanned it. "Looks like she's been here only three times in the last month, though. But she is a possibility. The press pass was probably a fake."

Darcy pulled out her phone and recorded the name on her virtual notebook.

Jackson continued to look for any repeat names. "What about this one? Chloe Cleaves?"

"It's not a name I recognize. Looks like she visits at least once a week."

"Let's start with her," Jackson said. "I'll phone into headquarters. Eden Chang, our tech expert, can input her name to see if she has a record."

"We can find out if the guard who usually is on duty during visiting hours is here. They watch the interaction between prisoners and visitors. He might have some insight into the nature of their relationship and could tell us what she looks like."

Jackson shook his head. "Your mind really does work like a detective's."

Darcy's face brightened at the compliment. "I'll stick to the lab."

It took them only a few minutes to track down a guard who had watched most of Reuben's interactions with his visitors. He met them at the entrance to the prison. They asked about family members and then the reporters.

The guard rubbed his bald spot. "He has had his share of reporters show up, but I wouldn't say they were here for anything but a story or a statement from him."

"And what about Chloe Cleaves?" Darcy asked.

The guard let out a heavy breath and nodded. "She's here a lot. Even though the visits are 'no contact,' everything about her body language says they're involved."

Jackson leaned a little closer to the prison guard. He felt a sense of excitement. They were on the right track. "What does she look like?"

"Dark brown hair. Slender. Not a lot of makeup. Usually has her hair braided. You know, that fancy way," said the guard.

"You mean a French braid," Darcy said.

The guard nodded. "I guess."

They thanked the man and returned to the K-9 vehicle. Jackson opened the back door. "I need to take Smokey for a quick walk. Why don't you get in and lock the doors? I won't go far."

He walked Smokey to the edge of the parking lot. When he looked over his shoulder, Darcy was sitting in the passenger seat staring in his direction.

There was something in her expression that suggested a deep level of trust. These small moments—a look on her face or her hand brushing over his—brought light into his day. Somehow she'd managed to chip away at the stone around his heart. Not what he had counted on at all.

After a few minutes, Jackson returned to the SUV and loaded his partner in the back. Before he got in himself, he had a look around. After seeing Reuben, they had spent at least another half hour in the prison getting information. He didn't know what kind of communication privileges Reuben had, but a half hour would have been plenty of time for him to alert whoever was doing his bidding on the outside that they were at Rikers.

Jackson got into his vehicle and pulled out of the lot just as Eden Chang's voice came on the radio.

"Hey, Jackson. I pulled up the sheet on Chloe Cleaves."

"So, she has a record?"

"A recent arrest for prescription drug abuse. But wait, there's more!" Eden's bright voice came across the line.

"What else did you find out?"

"I did a quick search of her name. It's unusual enough, I thought something might come up."

"And you found something interesting, right?" Jackson prompted. "We wouldn't be talking if you hadn't."

"She hasn't posted on her Facebook for well over a year, but Chloe used to be in training for the biathlon."

"Really, a biathlon?"

Darcy sat up in her seat and looked at Jackson.

Eden continued. "And guess who one of her assistant coaches used to be?"

"Not Reuben Bray?" Jackson couldn't picture Reuben as the athletic type. He was mostly an unemployed hustler and purse snatcher.

"No, but one of her coaches was Griffin Martel. He

looked familiar in the group photo she posted, so I ran it through some facial recognition software. He lost his job as a coach when he was arrested for selling prescription drugs to the athletes."

"You have no idea how much that helps us."

"I don't know why she would have killed Martel. Surely not just to plant a gun with Reuben's prints on it to discredit Darcy," the tech guru said. "And I can't find how she knows Reuben. He's not anywhere on her Facebook page."

"Reuben was in constant trouble with the law. If she was in trouble, too, they might have crossed paths in a courthouse or some other place connected with being arrested," Jackson said.

"That would be my theory, too."

"Good work. Thanks, Eden. I'm assuming it was easy to pull a current address on her?"

"Yes. I had Dispatch send a patrol car over there to bring her in for questioning."

He doubted that Chloe would be home, but it was a place to start. Because of her connection to Reuben, she was a person of interest. At the very least they needed to talk to her.

He clicked off his radio. He relayed the information Eden had given him to Darcy.

"I finally feel like we're getting somewhere," said Darcy. "A biathlete shoots a rifle and then skis. That could explain our shooter's marksmanship skills and why she's so athletic."

"Chloe's looking pretty good for our suspect."

He turned up the street that led to the long bridge connecting Rikers Island to Queens. Only buses and authorized vehicles could travel on the girded structure. He could see LaGuardia Airport through his side window.

Dispatch came over the radio. "Chloe Cleaves is not at her apartment, but we have a patrol officer parked outside in case she does show."

"Not surprised," Jackson said to Darcy.

They were almost to the end of the bridge when the windshield of the SUV turned into a thousand tiny pieces. On reflex, he lifted his hand to protect his eyes from possible flying shards.

They'd been shot at.

"Get down!" he shouted at Darcy.

A horn honked as Jackson inadvertently swerved into oncoming traffic. He overcorrected. The SUV hit the guardrail, slid for several feet, then broke through and fell into the East River.

Darcy's vision blurred. The impact of hitting the water had left her disoriented. Her whole body seemed to be shaking. Jackson's voice brought her back to reality. The SUV was sinking.

"Get out," Jackson said.

The passenger's-side window was nearly submerged. It was too late to try to get out that way. She unfastened her seat belt, knowing not to try to escape through the door until the car was covered in water so there would be equal pressure inside and out.

Jackson had already released of his seat belt and had turned to reach for the latch on Smokey's crate to free him.

Heart racing, blood pumping, she fumbled for her door handle. Once the latch released, Darcy turned and pushed with her feet, knowing it would take effort to open the door. She squeezed through and swam upward. The cold water of the East River presented a challenge as she stroked her arms and kicked her legs. She bobbed to the surface, gasping for air, and turning her head one way and then the other. She didn't see Jackson or Smokey.

People had begun to gather on shore. She heard sirens in the distance.

The waters were turbulent and she had to work hard to keep her head above the waves. She could feel the cold seeping in. A boat with the Coast Guard insignia was moving at a steady pace toward her.

She turned her head, searching for Jackson and Smokey, and feeling a rising panic.

Dear God, please say they made it.

Suddenly she caught sight of an object so dark, it was almost the same color as the water. Smokey swam toward her.

Fear gripped her heart.

What if Jackson had drowned?

All she could see was the black churning water all around. Then some distance away from where she and Smokey had come up, she saw Jackson's head.

She breathed a sigh of relief as he swam toward her. His muscular arms cut through the roiling water as if it were nothing.

"We made it," he said as he reached her and Smokey. "All three of us."

As the Coast Guard boat drew near, Darcy swam the short distance to it and waited to be towed in while she clutched the life preserver. Once on board, a blanket was thrown over her and a Coast Guard ensign tossed the life ring out again. Jackson wrapped an arm around Smokey so they could be towed in together.

Jackson climbed on board. He addressed one of the Coast Guard members who threw a blanket over Smokey and offered him one. "I need to use your radio. We were shot at. Mostly likely from those trees that surround the Little League park. We need to do a search and get a lockdown in the area as quickly as possible before the shooter disappears into the city."

Still clutching her own blanket, Darcy rubbed Smokey with his to dry him off. The dog turned and licked her face. She was shivering and so was Smokey. Jackson seemed unfazed by the accident and submersion into cold water.

"We can do that," said the young Coast Guard ensign. He touched Jackson's arm. "Sir, you may have suffered a degree of hypothermia. You need to focus on warming your core temperature. There are places belowdecks for the two of you to change into dry clothes."

Jackson paced as water dripped off his uniform and hair. His radio was most likely too waterlogged to work. "We need a thorough search of the entire area. We have wasted precious minutes."

"Yes, sir," said the ensign. "We'll radio that message to the shore right away if you will focus on getting warm and dry."

Jackson seemed to be still running on adrenaline. Darcy shivered as she stepped up to him and took his hand. "He's right, Jackson. We need to take care of ourselves. Our bodies have had a terrible shock."

Jackson turned and looked at her.

"They'll take care of the search. You're not good to anyone like this."

He shook his head. "You're right. I just don't want her to get away."

They were escorted belowdecks by a female member of the Coast Guard who showed them where to change. Before she headed back toward the ladder that led topside, she pointed to a narrow counter space that held a coffeemaker and microwave. "You can make yourself a cup of tea or coffee once you get out of those wet clothes."

Darcy changed into the sweats the Coast Guard provided. Once she stepped out, Smokey was waiting for her. "Jackson?" He must have gone above deck. His focus was on catching the woman who had almost killed all three of them.

"Come here, Smokey." The K-9 wagged his tail and stepped over to her. She wrapped her arms around the chocolate Lab, glad his shivering had stopped. "I'm so glad we all made it." She held the dog close.

Chloe Cleaves had to be the one behind the attacks. She had a motive for wanting Darcy dead. She didn't want her to testify at Reuben's trial. Who else would have known they would be on that bridge at that time? Reuben must have contacted her so she could get into place and wait. Every call from jail would be traced. Maybe Reuben had phoned someone who'd then contacted Chloe. She could only guess at how the message had been transmitted.

Unless the police caught Chloe today, it was just a matter of time before she came after Darcy again.

Darcy held Smokey close, fighting off the fear that threatened to overwhelm her.

THIRTEEN

Jackson paced the deck of the Coast Guard boat as they drew near to shore. He saw at least five police cars, thinking they must be from the Queens precinct to have gotten there so quickly. Unless Chloe'd had a car waiting for her, she was probably still close by. Darcy had only seen her a few hours ago at the press conference. She probably hadn't had time to make arrangements for a getaway car and driver. The boat drew close to the dock.

Darcy and Smokey came up on deck. Her hair was still wet, but the color had come back into her cheeks. Smokey had mostly dried off.

Jackson stepped toward her. "When we get to shore, I need you to stay in one of the police cars until Smokey and I come for you. Chloe is probably still around here. She might decide to take another shot at you. I'll make sure there is an officer close by to watch over you. Do you understand?"

She nodded and looked up at him. The affection that radiated from her expression moved him deeply.

"Smokey and I are going to find her." He rested his hand on her cheek. "I want this to be over for you."

"And for you, too," she said.

The boat jerked slightly as it slipped into the dock. He fell toward her, catching himself in her arms. His lips found hers and he kissed her. As she wrapped her arms around his neck, he deepened the kiss. All the uncertainty seemed to fall away when he held her. She remained close and he kissed her head.

"It's going to be okay," he said. "I promise."

She rested her forehead against his and gripped his collar. "I know it will be, Jackson."

With the electric energy of the kiss still making his head buzz, they disembarked and Jackson escorted her to a police car in the parking lot by the dock.

Jackson opened the back door of the patrol car for Darcy. She got in and gazed up at him.

Resting his arm on the door, he leaned in a little closer to her. "This is the safest place for you." He reached over and brushed her chin with his knuckles.

She smiled up at him before closing the door.

With Smokey heeled beside him—Smokey's leash had been lost in the sunken police vehicle—Jackson made his way over to a patrol officer. "I'm here to help with the search," he told him, taking his badge out of the pocket of his sweats to show it to the officer. Though his radio was no good, he had put his utility belt with his firearm back on.

"We need all the help we can get," said the officer.

Jackson pointed to the police car where Darcy waited. "Can you keep an eye on her?"

"Sure, no problem," said the officer. "I'm watching the parking lot and the area around it in case the shooter comes this way. Two of our guys went through the trees toward the Little League field, one went up toward 19th Avenue, and the other is searching the parking lot through the trees on the other side of the street."

Because Jackson was without a radio, he wouldn't be able to communicate with the other officers, which would hinder him. "If the shooter makes it to 19th Avenue, we have a strong indication the shooter is female with an athletic build. If we don't catch her, she could disappear into the crowded neighborhood of Astoria even if she was still on foot. Are K-9 officers on the way so we can search the city streets, as well?"

"Officers are getting here as fast as they can. Some are even heading over from the Brooklyn unit. Right now, we have patrol officers on the ground."

It made sense to search the immediate area first. "Thanks. Can you please radio the patrol officers headed toward the baseball field that I'm joining the search with my dog, so they don't hear me coming and think I'm the fugitive?"

The other officer nodded.

Jackson took off at a dead run toward where he thought the shots had come from.

He sprinted through the band of trees that bordered the baseball fields. Smokey ran close to him.

Noises to the side caused him to stop. Another officer emerged through the trees.

Jackson held up his badge. "I'm Officer Davison."

The officer, a forty-something man built like a football player, nodded. "I heard over the radio you were helping out. We need all the manpower we can get. Some other officers are working 80th Street by the water. A few of us have the trees on this side covered. If you want to head through the Little League field toward Bowery Bay, we will have this area covered. If we don't locate the shooter, we'll push the search into Manhattan. Patrol cars are on their way to help with that."

Jackson nodded. "Once I get to the edge of the field, I'm going to cut toward 19th. My guess is she's going to try to get to where people are as fast as she can."

"Or she'll find a hiding place close to the water. She'd have to be running pretty fast to get to 19th Avenue."

"Don't underestimate her. She's very athletic," Jackson said.

The Queens' officer disappeared into the trees while Jackson ran the other way. Within minutes, the K-9 team was clear of the trees. Jackson's feet pounded across the baseball diamonds as he looked side to side. Up ahead was another cluster of trees where 80th Street and 19th Avenue intersected.

Sirens wailed in the distance. More help was on the way. Smokey picked up the pace as they got closer to the trees. He must have detected something.

They entered the treed area. Jackson could hear the hum of traffic on 19th Avenue not far away. A closer noise drew his attention back to the trees. He and Smokey headed in that direction.

He stopped when something shiny on the ground caught his attention. The rifle. Chloe must have ditched it because she'd be too easy to spot hauling it on the street. That meant she was panicked and close by.

With Smokey's help, he did a quick search for her in the area where the rifle had been dropped then raced toward the street. Once clear of the trees, his view was of cars, streets, people and buildings. He scanned everywhere, locking on to the face of every pedestrian. All she had to do was blend in and not call attention to herself. He tried to get a look at the people in the cars, as well.

Not wanting to be slowed down by carrying the rifle, Jackson continued his search, running for several blocks before giving up. The smart thing to do would be to get the rifle before someone snatched it, so it could be taken into evidence. He also needed to find a cop with a radio so the other officers could shift their search parameters, though now that Chloe was in the city, the chances of catching her were substantially reduced.

He went back to where the rifle was, conducting an even deeper search of the area on the outside chance Chloe had returned. He found nothing.

As he carried the rifle, Jackson gritted his teeth. A sense of frustration overtook him. At least Chloe couldn't shoot from a distance anymore. That just meant she would find some other way to get to Darcy.

Darcy sat in the back of the patrol car wishing she could be helping in some way. Several calls came over the radio, indicating that the police had completed searches of different areas without finding Chloe and that more officers were arriving.

The patrol officer paced through the parking lot and searched the edges of it. He looked in Darcy's direction every five minutes. She waited, staring at the ceiling.

Another call came over the police radio. A rifle had been found, but still no shooter.

Darcy tapped her fingers on the seat.

Her phone rang. Good, it still worked. She was glad she'd sprung for the waterproof model. The number was Harlan's, not Jackson's. She quelled her disappointment.

"Hey, Harlan. What's up?"

"Darcy, have you been watching the news?"

"No, I've been a bit preoccupied."

"Maybe it's better that way." Harlan sounded distressed.

"What's going on?"

"Look, this was not my decision. But I asked to be the one to break the news to you even though I'm not your boss."

Darcy felt that familiar twisting knot in her stomach. "Don't drag it out. Just tell me."

"This whole thing with Reuben and the gun found at the Martel crime scene... The press won't let go of the idea that the K-9 Unit put pressure on Forensics to come up with evidence that linked the first murder to Reuben Bray."

This was not news to her. "Harlan, tell me something I don't already know." She knew Harlan was probably taking a long time to get to the point because he cared about her feelings.

"The higher-ups think it would be good if you went on paid leave until the air clears over this. They will make a statement and there will be an investigation into the allegations. I know that you are good at your job. They think once Reuben's trial takes place, and the details get out to the press, this will blow over. You're always amazing on the stand, Darcy," he said. "The trial will be televised. People will know you would never be sloppy in your work or cave to pressure from anyone."

Her throat went tight. "Okay, I guess if that's how it has to be."

"Darcy, I'm really sorry about this."

"It's not your fault. The trial will go forward, and people will see the truth." She ended the call, determined not to give in to negative thoughts. The thing that bothered her the most was that her work on the Emery case would be put on the back burner again.

Someone tapped on her window.

She started, not realizing how deep in thought she'd been. It was Jackson, Smokey heeled at his side.

She rolled down the window, noting Jackson's grim expression. "I heard on the radio what happened. At least she doesn't have a rifle anymore."

He nodded. "Since it is only a strong theory that Chloe is behind all this... If the rifle can be linked to her, it won't be just a theory anymore."

"That's how cases get solved. One piece of evidence at a time." She tried to sound hopeful.

Jackson shook his head. "Look, I'm going to see if I can get a patrol car to take us back to your apartment. I'll clear the place and stay with you until an officer is parked outside. I'm kind of useless without a radio anyway. I do need to swing by somewhere and get a temp phone. Too dangerous to be without one."

She heard the despair in his voice. She felt it, too. When would this be over?

FOURTEEN

Jackson awoke in Darcy's dark living room to Smokey's low-level growl.

He'd fallen asleep on her couch. When it looked like the department couldn't spare a patrol car to sit outside for several hours, he'd opted to stay with her, especially because her sister was away on another school trip and Darcy would be alone. The plunge into the river had caught up with both of them. Darcy had gone to sleep in her room, and he had conked out, as well, falling into a deep sleep.

Jackson reached out to touch Smokey where he lay on the floor by the couch. "What is it, boy?" It could just be a loud noise on the street that had alarmed Smokey.

All the same, Jackson needed to check it out. Except for a light from the kitchen, which was bright enough to see by, the room was dark.

He sat up. The shades on Darcy's repaired window had been drawn. Feeling rested, he rose and walked across the room, pulling the curtain back so he had a view of the street. Though it was past ten, the neighborhood was still very much alive at this time of night.

Traffic, though sparse, clipped by on the street. Behind him, Smokey was still agitated.

Jackson moved down the hallway, padding softly. He eased Darcy's door open just a crack to make sure she was okay. The night-light illuminated her sleeping form, Mr. Tubbs next to her.

It was still at least an hour before the patrol division would have an officer available to protect Darcy. He stepped back down the hall and returned to the living room/kitchen area. He stopped by the couch. Though he could not say why, something had shifted since he'd left the room. The hairs on the back of his neck stood at attention. His heartbeat thrummed in his ears. He couldn't see or hear Smokey.

He stepped closer to the kitchen. His dog lay on his side, motionless.

He barely had time to register the blow to the back of his head before he crumpled to the ground unconscious.

Darcy awoke with as start in total darkness. Her night-light had stopped working. Mr. Tubbs leaped off the bed, making a yowling noise that indicated distress.

Darcy sat up, waiting for her eyes to adjust to the darkness and for the fog of sleep to lift. As she rose from the bed, her heart beat a little faster. Maybe it was just the darkness that was making her so afraid.

Now that she was more awake, she could find her way to the light switch in the dark. She took several steps on the carpet, holding her hand out in front of her. She stepped carefully over the objects on the floor. Her hand found the wall and then the light switch.

Just as the room lit up, she saw that her night-light had been pulled out of the outlet. Before what that meant could even register in her brain, a hand went over her mouth.

The person who had grabbed her was a woman. A very strong woman. Darcy felt herself being dragged backward. She twisted to try to free herself. She struggled with such force that she got away but fell on the floor on her stomach.

She crawled on all fours to escape. Then flipped over. The woman stepped toward Darcy, her face red, teeth showing. Chloe.

Chloe pulled a Taser out of her pocket.

Darcy yelled out Jackson's name twice. Chloe stalked toward her, weapon in hand.

Darcy reached for the first object her hand could find—a boot, which she threw at the other woman. She hit her mark, smacking Chloe in the head, causing her to drop the Taser.

Frantic, Darcy glanced around for another object to throw. She turned over and crawled toward the other boot, which she threw, hitting Chloe in the stomach. The distraction gave Darcy time to stand. She grabbed everything she could, hurling it all at her attacker: a curling iron, a hairbrush, makeup. Chloe held her hands up in a defensive posture. Darcy's caught sight of the Taser on the floor, but there was no way she could get to it in time.

Chloe's eyes were filled with murderous rage as she lunged toward Darcy.

Darcy jumped on the bed, thinking something must have happened to Jackson or he would have come by now. There was now only one way out of the bedroom. Chloe was closer to the door than Darcy was. She couldn't get out that way without being caught.

Maybe she could fling the window open and yell for help at least. She wouldn't be able to get out because of the bars. She slid off the bed and reached for the latch.

Chloe grabbed her from behind, yanking her pajama shirt back so hard that the collar dug into her neck. Darcy twisted, trying to break free. She kicked wildly, not making impact with anything.

Chloe spun her around and grabbed her neck under the chin with one hand.

Darcy choked and gasped for air as Chloe pressed on her windpipe. Black dots filled Darcy's field of vision. Chloe used her free hand to pull a sheathed knife from her back pocket.

Air. Darcy needed air. It would be easier for Chloe to kill her with the knife if she was unconscious and couldn't fight back. Chloe's original intent must have been to disable her with the Taser and then stab her.

Chloe let go of Darcy to pull the sheath off the knife. Darcy gasped and sputtered. She bent over, wheezing in air. When she looked up, the knife blade caught the light.

Fear enveloped her at the same time an instinct to survive kicked into high gear. She had to get away.

Darcy took a step toward Chloe, intending to push her out of the way so she could get to the bedroom door. Chloe pointed the knife at her, causing her to freeze. Darcy reached for the hand that held the knife, but Chloe was faster and stronger.

She knocked Darcy's hand away and grabbed her throat again, squeezing as she backed her up to a wall. Though she could get some breath, Darcy was growing light-headed.

Chloe raised the knife.

Darcy clawed at the hand that held her neck at the same time that she angled her body with all the force she could muster.

She felt a slice of pain on her upper arm and then the warm ooze of blood. She reached a hand out to push Chloe out of the way. The blade went into her stomach.

This is not happening.

The sound of Smokey's barking seemed to come from very far away.

A look of shock clouded Chloe's expression. She turned and ran out of the room.

Darcy looked down at the red drops of blood on her floor. She turned away, seeking to protect herself, pressing her hand against the expanding red circle on her stomach as she doubled over.

Her vision narrowed to a pinpoint. She was losing consciousness.

She was going down.

Her head hit the corner of the dresser.

As her world went black, a thought cascaded through her mind.

I'm going to die here.

FIFTEEN

As Jackson regained consciousness, the first thing to register was that Smokey was barking and pacing around him, clearly upset that Jackson was lying on the floor, not moving. Fear seized his heart. Chloe must have knocked him unconscious to get to Darcy. He could only guess at what she had used to disable Smokey. He pushed himself to his feet, swaying as his head throbbed with pain. He hurried through the living room. He heard banging noises. And then silence. He pulled his weapon and stepped down the hallway seeing a very scared cat seek refuge in the other bedroom.

A breeze from the open bathroom door caused him to peer inside. A window had been left open. The only window that didn't have bars across it. That must have been how Chloe had gotten in, despite the lock.

His primary concern was for Darcy. He ran to her bedroom, pulling his phone out. He dialed headquarters and advised Gavin of Chloe's possible location.

He pushed the door open. Darcy lay facedown on the floor, not moving. His breathing became shallow as he ran over to her. Kneeling, he turned her over. She was unresponsive. She had a bleeding gash on her forehead and her upper arm had been cut, but it was the stain of blood on her pajama shirt that made him gasp. The side of her neck pulsed. She was alive but unconscious and losing a lot of blood. He still had Gavin on the line. "Get an ambulance to Darcy's address."

Smokey's barking must have caused Chloe to flee before she'd had a chance to stab Darcy with the fatal blow. She must have been concerned about getting in and out quickly or she would have taken the time to kill him and Smokey, too. He saw the Taser on the floor— no doubt that had disabled Smokey long enough for Chloe to have hit Jackson on the back of the head.

There were bruises on Darcy's neck, consistent with someone trying to strangle her. The gash on her forehead suggested she had been hit by an object. The blow was probably what had knocked her out.

"Come on, Darcy," he said. He drew her closer to his chest and whispered in her ear. "Come back to me. I don't want to lose you."

He heard the paramedics knocking on the locked front door. He ran to let them in.

Within minutes, they had taken Darcy's vitals and loaded her on a stretcher. She had not regained consciousness. Jackson stood back, feeling helpless as they wheeled her outside. He didn't want to leave Smokey behind and the K-9 couldn't ride in the ambulance. "I'll catch a ride and follow you guys."

Several police units were now in the area searching for Chloe. Jackson chased down one of the officers and asked to use the patrol car. He secured Smokey in the passenger seat. Smokey whined and licked Jackson's cheeks.

"She's in a real tough spot, Smokey."

Jackson pulled out onto the street. Focusing in on the flashing lights of the ambulance, he sped up. The ambulance remained several blocks ahead of him all the way to the emergency room. By the time he found a parking space, Darcy had been unloaded and was being transported into the ER. He got behind the stretcher and followed it into the exam area.

A curtain was pulled around her. He watched as doctors and other medical staff entered her cubicle. He could hear their chatter and medical jargon.

His heart squeezed tight. He stepped toward where the curtain was open a sliver.

A nurse stepped up to him from inside the cubicle. "Sir, are you family?"

"No, I'm a friend. A good friend."

"Why don't you take a chair and we'll let you know as soon as we can what the prognosis is for her. We need to stabilize her and get that cut in abdomen stitched up."

"I can't sit still. I'll check back in a few minutes." He stepped outside into the chill September night. Jackson walked over to his loaner patrol car, opened the door and commanded Smokey to jump down.

He couldn't shake off his nerves and worry over what was going to happen with Darcy. Seeing her so lifeless in that unconscious state had really shaken him. With Smokey next to him, he did a brisk walk that turned into a run. As his steps ate up distance over both sidewalk and grass, he prayed for Darcy's recovery.

She was part of his life now. A big part.

In addition to how fun she was, the nice thing about Darcy was that she understood what it meant to be a police officer. The kiss they'd shared had been a little impulsive, but that didn't mean he hadn't liked kissing her. His feelings for her were such a tangled mess. In his heart, he knew that friendship was the kindest thing he could offer Darcy. If he was still on guard from the wounds of his last relationship, he wouldn't be any good to her as a boyfriend. If there was to be anything between them, he had to know that he could give 100 percent. What did it matter anyway? She didn't date cops.

His run slowed to a walk. He'd gone completely around the hospital and his car was now in sight. He loaded Smokey back into the vehicle, put the air-conditioning on low and locked the car, again grateful for that feature because he didn't know how long he'd be inside. He was just turning back toward the ER entrance when he noticed a hunched-over figure in baggy clothes disappear inside.

Would Chloe be so bold as to show up here? It would be easy enough to conclude that Darcy had ended up in the hospital even if Chloe hadn't hidden somewhere to watch what had happened.

His heart beat a little faster and he sprinted across the parking lot to the ER entrance. When he stepped inside the brightly lit room, he saw no one in the waiting area who resembled the hooded figure.

Jackson walked the aisles of the ER, past pulled curtains, a closed door where a man groaned in agony, and past another partially open door where he heard a child crying. He widened his search, stepping toward the elevators. He had nothing to go on but his gut instinct. The hooded figure reminded him of the watcher in the woods when he and Smokey had found Griffin Martel's body.

She's here.

Jackson headed for the ER as he pulled his phone out and pressed Gavin's number which he had memorized.

Gavin picked up right away. "Jackson. How is she?"

"I don't know. The doctors haven't said anything. The cut in her stomach looked pretty bad and she suffered a blow to the head. I'm sure she'll be admitted. We need to get her some protection. I'll stay with her until an officer can be put outside her hospital door."

"Give me a couple of hours. I'm pretty sure we can put something like that in place given the level of threat against her," Gavin said.

"It wouldn't hurt to do a search of the hospital," Jackson suggested.

"You have some evidence that Chloe may be hiding in the hospital?"

"Just a hunch based on her past behavior."

"Jackson, I understand your concern, but I can't send officers over on a hunch. We're stretched thin as it is combing the city for her. Because of the past attacks and Chloe being at large again, I acknowledge that Darcy is in significant danger. It makes sense to have some protection for her. That is the best that I can do right now."

"I understand," Jackson said.

"We're looking into all her known associates besides Reuben Bray," Gavin told him. "She may be staying with one of them. She's from upstate and has no relatives in the area. We believe that as long as Darcy is alive and Reuben Bray's trial goes forward, she will stay in the city. I'll let you know if we get any leads. Also, we got a warrant to search her place. We recovered a handgun."

No wonder Chloe had used a knife and Taser. "What else can we do, right? Thanks, Sarge." Jackson shut off his phone and wandered back to the ER. Darcy wasn't there anymore. He double-checked with a nurse that she'd been taken into surgery.

Jackson found a seat and rested his head in his hands. He straightened and watched the people milling through the ER. Mostly doctors and nurses. He looked at each one a little closer, remembering that Chloe had worn a disguise to the press conference, so she wouldn't be above dressing like a medical professional to gain access to Darcy.

He settled deeper into his chair once he was confident none of the medical staff was Chloe. Gavin was right. Jackson had no solid evidence that Chloe was in the hospital. He knew, though, that letting his guard down was not an option.

He waited.

Twenty minutes later, the nurse he had talked to earlier came toward him. He burst to his feet. "How is she?"

"In addition to the cut to her stomach, the blow to her head was pretty severe. The doctors want to see if she wakes up on her own. We'll need to do a scan of her brain to assess if there is any permanent damage. The cut on her arm was superficial."

"I need to be with her. I'm a police officer and she's in a degree of danger of being attacked again."

The nurse's eyes grew wide, but she seemed to regain her composure. "I'll make sure the staff who will be taking care of her on the third floor knows that."

"Good, we're working on getting an officer posted outside her door. Until then, I'll stay in the room with her," Jackson said. "What room is she being taken to?"

"Three thirteen," the nurse replied.

Jackson jogged toward the elevators. He pushed the button to call the elevator and waited for the car to arrive. Growing impatient and not wanting Darcy to be alone for even a few minutes, he glanced around for the stairs. The run would get rid of some of his nervous energy.

He sprinted up the stairs to the third floor. A nurse was just stepping out of Darcy's room when he arrived. Jackson explained the situation.

"I just took her vitals. Everything seems stable," the nurse said. "Does Miss Fields have any relatives?"

"Her sister, who's on an overnight field trip."

"You might want to give her a call just to let her know."

"I don't know the number and I think Darcy's phone is still back at the house."

"Maybe later then. In these kinds of situations, it's good to have family around." The nurse headed down the hall toward the nurses' station.

Jackson entered the room and scooted a chair closer to Darcy's bed. The nurse mentioning about family made Jackson remember that he hadn't locked up Darcy's apartment in his haste to follow the ambulance. He didn't know when her sister was due back.

He made a call into headquarters to request an officer go to the apartment, search it, get Darcy's phone and make sure the place was locked up.

Jackson pushed up from his chair and leaned over Darcy. Even in the dim light, she looked cute. Her cheeks had a pink tinge to them. "Come back to me, Darcy." He brushed his thumb over her chin. "I miss you already."

Jackson sat back down in the silent dark room. His

eyelids grew heavy with fatigue. At some point, he knew he'd have to go out to check on Smokey and let him out of the car for a while. He napped in short spurts, waking when a nurse came in to check on Darcy and when he heard hushed voices in the hallway.

His phone buzzed with a text from Lani Jameson that Darcy's apartment was locked up tight and that she'd arrange for the phone to be dropped off. He drifted off again and then woke some time later. The sound of Darcy's breathing was a comfort to him.

He checked to see if an officer was posted outside her room. Glad to see one there, Jackson left to check on Smokey. Even though she had protection, he didn't want to leave her at all.

Darcy awoke in total darkness. Fear gripped her heart. She had no idea where she was. She waited for her eyes to adjust to the light and to absorb the sensory information around her.

She had a moment of thinking Chloe had kidnapped her and was holding her hostage. The last thing she remembered was breaking free of Chloe's grasp. Even the memory of the attack caused her to take in an intense breath.

Her hand touched the cool metal of the railing that surrounded her bed. She could just discern the outline of an IV stand with a bag hanging from it. She was in a hospital. She turned her head one way and then the other.

An empty chair had been pushed very close to her bed. Someone had been in the room with her. Her sister? Or maybe Jackson?

Feet padded in the hallway then stopped. It sounded

like someone was standing right outside her open door. A new wave of fear gripped her. When she turned her head to look, there was no one standing on the threshold. Her mind was playing tricks on her.

She listened to her heartbeat drumming in her ears. The window curtains were drawn. She had no idea what time it was or how long she'd been out. It must be late at night.

She heard more voices outside her door. One of them sounded familiar. Jackson was here in the hospital. She released a breath and rested her palm on her chest. Everything was going to be okay.

Jackson stood in the doorway. Light coming from the hallway revealed that his expression and even his posture changed when he saw her. He rushed over to her and gripped her hand. "Hey, you're awake."

"Barely," she said. "Did Chloe get away again?"

Jackson nodded. "Every officer is on high alert at this point. They don't think she'll leave the city with the trial so close and you still able to testify."

She touched her forehead where there was a bandage. "What happened?"

"You had a pretty big gash. The doctor will do a scan and wants to keep you until he's sure you are out of the woods. The cut into your stomach was pretty deep."

"Right now, I have a pounding headache." She rested her head on the pillow and touched her stomach. "And I think the pain pills are wearing off."

Jackson leaned over her, gazing into her eyes. Even in the dim light, he beamed affection and connection. "Sorry I wasn't here when you came to. I had to go out and walk Smokey."

"Thank you for staying with me."

"There's an officer posted outside your door. Unfortunately, I have to start my shift any minute."

She felt a tightening in her chest.

"Sarge extended me some grace because I wanted to make sure you were going to be okay." He reached for her hand and squeezed.

Releasing her hand, he sat in the chair that had been scooted close to her bed.

She stared at the ceiling. "What time is it?"

"Just a little past 2:00 a.m."

"I'm starving. Do you think they would bring me some food?"

He laughed. "It never hurts to try." He pushed the call button toward her hand.

She fumbled with the device, which was the size of a TV remote control, until it made a binging noise.

A woman in her early twenties stuck her head inside the room. "Hey, you're awake."

"Awake and starving. Is there any way I could get something to eat?" Darcy asked.

"The cafeteria is closed, but they might be able to bring up a sandwich."

"Anything would be fine with me," she said.

A few minutes later, a tray with two sandwiches and two juice boxes was brought in by a different woman. "The nurse suggested putting an extra serving on there in case your friend was hungry. Both of you have had quite a long night."

"Thanks," Jackson said, standing. He unwrapped the first sandwich while Darcy struggled into a sitting position. "Here, let me help you with that." He readjusted her pillow and then pushed the button that raised the top end of the bed.

His attentiveness touched her heart.

He grabbed the second sandwich and unwrapped it, handing it to Darcy.

She bit into the sandwich. Cold ham and cheese never tasted so good.

Jackson spoke between bites. "I got in touch with your sister. She'll come by as soon as she gets home from the field trip, and your phone is here."

"You took care of a lot while I was out of it."

While they ate, a uniformed officer stuck his head inside. "Just saying hi now that you're awake. I'm here to guard you, Miss Fields."

She smiled at him.

Jackson took the last bites of his sandwich in a hurry. He must be anxious to get to work, Darcy thought as she sipped at her orange juice.

Jackson answered his ringing phone. "I'm ready to go to work... Really... You think it might be her... Yes, count me in. I want to be there for the takedown... I can meet you there in twenty. Bring a uniform for me," he said, turning off his phone and rising from his chair.

"There's an athletic facility where the biathlon team trains," he told Darcy. "Someone who lives near the facility phoned in and said they thought they saw a person wandering around like they were looking for a way in. It could be Chloe. Three other K-9 officers are meeting me there." He touched her shoulder and then pointed to the door where the guard was partially visible. "You're in good hands."

He leaned over and kissed the uninjured side of her forehead. "Hopefully, the next time you see me, I'll have good news about Chloe's capture."

He stepped out of her room.

She felt like a balloon losing air when he was no longer close to her. The care he'd showed her made her want to be with him always. When he wasn't close, she could feel the chasm of loss. What was this feeling blossoming inside her? Maybe it was just because he had been so kind and attentive. She shook her head softly. There was something deeper going on.

Darcy lay back and closed her eyes. She prayed for Jackson's safety and for the rest of the team.

SIXTEEN

In the predawn hours, Jackson and the rest of the assigned team assembled near the athletic facility. Gavin, who was there to coordinate the search, had obtained a blueprint of the layout, which included a pool, weight room and running track, along with a rifle range. The team—Belle Montera, Tyler Walker, Jackson and their K-9 partners—had positioned itself a few blocks from the facility so the lights of their vehicles wouldn't draw attention if Chloe was hiding there.

They each agreed to search a separate quadrant and look for a point of entry where the "suspicious person," whom they believed to be Chloe Cleaves, might have broken in. Since the call had come in that the facility might have an intruder, a patrol officer had been dispatched to circle the facility. He had reported no sign of someone trying to enter or leave.

Gavin rolled up the blueprint. "Keep radio communication to a minimum. Use flashlights only as necessary. If she is in there, we don't want to alert her to our presence. The tracker dog will work off the scent from the wig she left behind. Be safe. Let's go."

After putting on their night-vision goggles, they separated and hurried up the street. The buildings they ran past were all dark. The athletic facility was a two-story brick structure with an adjacent parking lot. The only car in the lot was the patrol officer's and he was still watching the place. That didn't mean Chloe hadn't found a way of escape out of view of the officer—if it was even her who had been spotted—or that she wasn't hiding somewhere inside just waiting for the officer to leave.

Heart pounding, Jackson circled the building with Smokey, moving slowly in the dark. He had a view of the pool through several large windows. From what he could see, everything looked quiet inside.

His radio beeped and Belle came on the line, speaking in a whisper. "I think we found the point of entry. Southside door is open. Looks like the lock has been jiggered."

Jackson circled the facility again, looking for signs of movement inside and outside. The windows on the part of the structure he had just passed were small and high up, likely the dressing rooms.

He found the open door that Belle had mentioned. Procedure dictated that they search their assigned quadrant even if it meant filtering through the open door. Once he entered, he didn't see any other member of the team.

"I'm in," he said into his radio.

As he moved through the facility to where he was supposed to search, he heard the other officers whisper a quiet "I'm in" over their radios, as well.

Jackson circled the swimming pool. The smell of chlorine was heady in the air. Above the pool, on the

second floor, there was a viewing area with a railing—
a sort of balcony that looked down on the pool.

He and Smokey cleared several of the rooms adjacent to pool, an equipment storage room and an office.

With Smokey taking the lead, Jackson returned to
the main pool area. The night-vision goggles revealed
other doors on the other side of the pool that he needed
to check out. He looked once again at the viewing area
above the pool.

His heart skipped a beat. A shadow danced on the
back wall. Something or someone was moving around
up there. He advised the team of where he was headed
and circled the pool until he found the narrow stairway
that led up to the viewing area.

Jackson took the stairs slowly, trying to be as quiet
as possible. If Chloe was there, she would have seen
him enter the pool area. He came to a door that was
slightly ajar and pulled his weapon, Smokey perched
beside him.

Easing the door open, he stepped inside and turned
in a half circle to clear all four corners of the viewing
area. The room contained some folding chairs positioned close to the railing that looked down on the pool.
A couch and beanbag chair were positioned by the far
wall. Some children's books and toys were stored in a
box by the couch. There was a second door that led to
a hallway.

He let out a heavy breath. Maybe he'd been wrong.
He stepped toward the railing and gazed at the pool.

Static came across his radio and then he heard Tyler's voice. "I'm in the area where the rifles and ammunition are stored. The scent was really strong through
here." There was a pause on the other end. "Looks like

someone broke the glass and took a rifle. The lock on the ammunition drawer is disabled, as well."

Jackson froze in his tracks. Chloe was armed again. His first thought was that she wasn't even there anymore. She'd broken in to get the gun and ammo and could be across town by now, trying to get access to Darcy. Before they could draw that kind of a conclusion, they needed to clear the entire facility. He moved back down the stairs and worked his way over to the doors on the other side of the pool. He and Smokey entered the first locker room and checked the larger lockers, bathrooms and shower stalls. He stepped back out into the main area and hurried to the second locker room.

Smokey stiffened when they stood on the threshold. With his weapon drawn, Jackson entered slowly, working in his way past the benches and pulling back shower curtains. These lockers were too small for a person to hide in. Smokey still seemed agitated. The place was empty but maybe Chloe had been in there at some point.

The rest of the team had grown quiet. No mention of even having cleared a section of the facility. The silence was eerie. The thrumming of his heart in his ears augmented as he returned to the pool area.

Once again, he stared up at the observation balcony. If he was Chloe, he would hide there. It provided a view of much of the facility and of the people coming and going. The pool was at the center of the building. Most of the doors to other parts of facility connected to the pool, with the exception of the rifle range, which was separated by a long corridor.

Jackson circled the pool deck again, wondering if there was a second way to access the observation area, which would mean a way to escape. He remembered the second door. He returned to the balcony, stepped through the second door and out into the hallway. He followed it all the way to the end. There was another stairway down.

A door slammed somewhere not too far from his and Smokey's position. He hurried down the stairs, where he found Belle with her German shepherd, Justice. She looked not quite human in her goggles.

"Sorry," she whispered. "I was trying to shut the door quietly."

"Find anything?"

"Justice picked up a hint of a scent, nothing strong. Honestly, I think she came and got the gun and left. That's where the scent was a for-sure thing."

"With that patrol officer circling the facility, escape would be tricky. He would have seen her if she went out the door she broke in through. We know she was here at some point. I'm not convinced she was able to leave. I'm doing one more sweep," Jackson said.

"Sarge hasn't called us off yet. I'm going to take Justice down that hall and up to those second-floor offices. Leave no stone unturned, right?"

"Lots of places a person could hide in here. Might as well check every nook and cranny." Jackson headed back up the stairs to the observation deck that provided him with a bird's-eye view of much of the facility. He stared out the window, taking in each segment of the area around the pool.

He caught a flash of movement out of the corner of his eye. For a moment, he thought it was an officer who had traveled outside an assigned area because the K-9 had picked up on a scent. Whoever it was had slipped out of view through an open door.

If something had been found, why wasn't anyone on the radio?

"Davison, here. Has another officer slipped into my quadrant?"

Gavin answered back immediately. "Negative."

Another door, ten feet from the open one where he had seen movement, popped open. Jackson barely had time to register that he was seeing a rifle barrel aimed at him before the shot reverberated through the whole facility.

Pain sliced into his shoulder, causing his entire body to shudder. He leaned over the railing with a view of the water below. He reached for his radio.

The intensity of having been shot was like nothing he'd ever experienced. His vision blurred as he fumbled to make his fingers work the radio. He felt like he couldn't breathe, as though the air was being suctioned out of his lungs.

He clicked on his radio. His voice was whispy-weak. All he could manage to say was, "She's here. I'm shot."

Sarge's voice came across the line. "On my way."

Jackson looked up. Everything in front of him was wavy and out of focus. He thought he saw Chloe step out from behind the door and raise her rifle to take another shot at him. He doubled over in pain. He was a sitting duck up here.

The rest of the team had to be headed toward his quadrant. He was half hung over the railing, trying to move, to at least find the strength to lay flat on the floor and crawl backward. He could not will his body into motion.

His world started to go black. He had the sensation of whirling through space. Had he been hit again? Was he losing consciousness? His vision narrowed right before he felt his body falling. He hit the water. Then he was gasping for air and flaying his arms and legs.

Dark brown sticks moved through the water toward him. They weren't sticks. It was his dog. Smokey had jumped in after him.

Jackson felt a tug on his back of his neck. Smokey was trying to pull him to the surface. It was a struggle to make his arm with the bullet wound work, but he kicked his legs. He felt himself being dragged. His head popped up above the surface. Gavin had jumped into the pool and was swimming toward him. He saw two other sets of legs—one K-9 and one human—at the edge of the pool.

He felt himself being half carried, half dragged and then being stretched out on the tile surrounding the pool.

Smokey licked his forehead.

"Did you get her?" he asked.

Gavin put his face very close to Jackson's, water dripping off his hair onto Jackson's face. "Tyler and Dusty are after her."

"You have to get her." Pain surged through Jackson's body. He groaned.

Gavin's expression changed and he spoke to Belle. "That ambulance is on its way, right?" He sounded upset.

"Yes, sir."

Jackson could barely get the words out. "The bullet wound. How bad?"

Gavin stared at his shoulder for a second. "No major organs. Tore through quite a bit of flesh."

Jackson put his head down on the cold tile. Everything seemed to be whirling around him. The only thing that was real was his dog lying beside him and licking his cheek.

"You have to catch Chloe. For Darcy's sake." Jackson wasn't sure if he had spoken the words or just thought them.

The pain was unbearable.

Darcy was sitting up in bed when a nurse pushing a wheelchair and wearing a very serious expression came into the room. The police officer who had been standing outside Darcy's door was right behind her.

"What's going on?"

"A decision has been made to move you to a room with no windows," the nurse said.

The officer stepped forward. "I'll be escorting you."

"What's happened? What's going on?" Her mind reeled. Jackson and the other officers must not have been able to catch Chloe. "Let me guess. Chloe is out there and she's armed. They think she might try to shoot me through the window."

The patrol officer looked at the nurse and then at Darcy. "It's just a precaution."

"They wouldn't be moving me unless they thought I was in even more danger."

The nurse pushed the wheelchair toward her. "You haven't been out of that bed since you were brought in. If you feel at all dizzy, we can move you in the chair."

"I'd like to try to walk."

The nurse pushed the bedside rail down out of the way. "Take it slow. Swing your legs off the side of the bed first."

As she sat with her legs dangling, Darcy still felt light-headed. The nurse held out a hand for support.

"Walking will be good for you at this point, but if you feel at all unstable, let me know."

Dragging her IV with her, Darcy took a few hesitant steps. "I walk like an old lady." They worked their way slowly out into the hall. Fear overtook her as she stared at all the people bustling around.

Chloe was still out there. Chloe wanted her dead. If she couldn't shoot Darcy from a distance, she'd find another way. Darcy hadn't been willing to admit it until now, but the attack in her apartment had traumatized her in a deep way, more so than the others. She had seen the intensity of Chloe's rage up close.

The nurse held Darcy's arm while the officer walked on the other side of her, pushing the wheelchair. She was in good hands, but that didn't mean Chloe wouldn't make an appearance.

The officer cleared his throat. "You should probably know that your friend who sat with you, Officer Davison, was brought in a few hours ago."

Darcy stopped and stared up at the police officer. "What happened?"

"A gunshot wound," the nurse said.

"Some of Chloe Cleaves' handiwork, unfortunately," the officer admitted. "He's in surgery right now. The bullet didn't hit any vital organs, but it tore his shoulder up."

Maybe it was just panic over what might happen to Jackson, but the news gave her strength and energy. "I don't want to go to my room. I want to sit with the K-9 officers. I'm sure some of them are standing by."

"You're still very weak." The nurse looked up at the officer.

"I insist," Darcy said. "I'm not going to lie in a bed alone when Jackson might be fighting for his life. He has been there for me through everything."

The officer shrugged. "No safer place for her to be than surrounded by police officers. I'll stay with her, no matter what."

"I suppose it would be better for you to be sitting up and maybe moving around a little. I'll have to clear it with the doctor. I'll come to get you if he doesn't give the okay."

They led Darcy to the waiting room outside the surgery wing. Officers Belle Montera and Lani Jameson were there. Belle stood when Darcy came into the room. She walked over to Darcy and grasped her hands. "Good to see you. Jackson has been in surgery for about an hour now. Gavin had to get back to headquarters, so Lani came over." Belle nodded at the tall blonde.

"Chloe is still on the run. The whole K-9 Unit has been praying for a good outcome for Jackson and getting Chloe back into custody," Lani told her.

Belle led her to a seat and Darcy lowered herself slowly into the chair. Feeling a sharp pain through her stomach where she'd been stabbed, a light patina of sweat appeared on her forehead from the effort of moving around. The news that Chloe had not been captured didn't sit well with her.

Belle patted her hand. "I know it will mean so much to Jackson that you came here to support him. His family in Texas has been notified. He doesn't have any family close by, except for Smokey, and they won't allow him into the waiting room."

"I think you guys are his family."

"And you, too. He talks about you a lot," Lani said.

"He and Smokey are a big part of my life, too," Darcy said. *I'm starting to wish he could be an even bigger part*, she thought. "Is one of the other officers looking out for Smokey?"

"Yes, Tyler will watch him until Jackson is strong enough to care for him."

Darcy felt herself growing weak as they waited for close to three quarters of an hour. Belle got her some hot coffee and a bag of chips from the vending machine. Moving around had taken a lot out of her. She probably should be lying down in her bed, but she didn't want to miss any news about Jackson or lose out on an opportunity to see him once he was out of surgery. He had been strong for her, so she would be strong for him.

Darcy sipped her coffee and waited with Belle, Lani and her personal protection officer.

A man dressed in surgical scrubs emerged from a hallway and walked toward them. They all stood.

"He's been out of surgery for about half an hour and he's awake. I didn't want to alert you until he was stabilized. He can have one visitor at a time. If he starts to fatigue, we need to leave him so he can fully recover." The surgeon turned toward Darcy. "Are you Darcy?"

She nodded.

"He's been asking for you," he said.

"You should go see him first then," Belle said as she cupped a hand on Darcy's shoulder.

The surgeon left and the officer escorted Darcy down the hall to the recovery room. It made her feel good to know that with no family close by, she was the first person Jackson had wanted to see.

"I'll just be right outside the door," the officer said.

"Thanks."

Darcy stepped into the room. The paleness of Jackson's expression and the way his skin seemed to hang on his face sent a shockwave through her.

"Hey, don't look so glum." Jackson gave her his trademark wink.

"She got to you." Darcy moved to the side of his bed and leaned in close to him. Even his eyes had lost their brightness.

Jackson grabbed her hand. "It's going to be okay."

Tears flowed as she squeezed his hand tighter. "I hate seeing you like this."

"Just part of the job," he said.

She wiped at her eyes. "I'm sorry. I think I have finally reached my breaking point."

"Don't worry about the tears. You're a strong lady, Darcy. Anyone else would have fallen apart way sooner."

She met his eyes, seeing deep affection in his gaze. "So what did the doctors say about your injury?"

"The bullet tore up a lot of tissue. The damaged shoulder is not connected to my shooting hand, but I will probably be out of commission for a while. If I can work at all, I'll probably be on light duty or behind a desk."

The news upset her. Jackson was in his element when he was working with Smokey and the other K-9 officers. "I'm sure that won't be easy. We have both been forced to take a vacation neither of us wanted."

His expression grew serious. "Did you hear from anyone? Did they get Chloe?"

Darcy hated giving him the news that his valiant effort had all been for nothing. She shook her head. "I'm so sorry," she said.

The disappointment in his features was intense.

She took a seat in the bedside chair, and they visited a while longer until Jackson started to nod off. She felt quite fatigued herself. She pushed herself to her feet but held on to the back of the chair for support. "I'll come by later in the day, after you've had a good sleep."

Though she could tell he was struggling to keep his eyes open, he managed another wink. "Or maybe I'll come by and see you since I'm in the neighborhood."

"I'm sure we'll work something out."

She made her way out of his room. The officer was waiting for her in the hallway. All the movement had made her rather achy and she was now kind of wishing for the wheelchair…

She was escorted to her new windowless room and, with some help from the nurse, got into her bed. She winced, the pain from her stomach wound intensifying.

"Still feeling some pain?" the nurse asked.

She nodded. "I think I overdid it."

"We can get you some more pain medication."

Darcy nodded again, struggling to stay awake. "I'm glad I got up and moved around."

The nurse left and returned with pain medication and a pill to help her sleep.

Darcy slept, barely waking when the nurses came in to check her vitals, after which she fell into an even deeper sleep.

The next time she stirred, the room was dark, as was the hallway. A different officer was probably on duty outside her door by now. Someone was moving around in her room. She recognized a nurse's uniform, though she wasn't sure what the nurse was doing on the other side of the room so close to the bathroom.

Her eyelids were heavy as the nurse fussed around her bedside and then switched out the IV bag. Darcy was having a hard time putting her thoughts together. The sleep medication hadn't worn off yet. She had no idea how long she'd been sleeping, and she didn't have the strength to turn to check the clock on her bedside table.

She closed her eyes as the fog of fatigue overtook her.

She heard the nurse's shoes pad softly out the door. She listened to the drip of the IV, feeling a stinging sensation at the point where the fluid entered her body.

Darcy's eyes shot open. She grabbed the IV tube and squeezed it so no more of the fluid could reach her body. It had taken her a second to process what had been off about the nurse who had been in her room. The IV bag she had discarded had still been full.

Maybe it was just her imagination, but Darcy thought she could feel the little bit of poison that had gotten into her burning her veins. A sweat broke out on her forehead. Her heart raced.

She couldn't reach her call button without letting go of the IV.

She cried out. "Somebody, help me! Please!" Though she feared that it would be Chloe who would return to her room.

A female officer stuck her head inside the room. "Is everything okay?"

"Use my call button to get medical staff in here. I'm pretty sure there's poison in this IV." Darcy fought off the dizziness. "I think some of it got into me. Chloe

Cleaves was in my room. You need to find her before she gets away."

"My instructions are to stay with you at all times."

"Make an exception and see if you can get a search for her started. I don't know if there are other officers in the building or what."

"I'll go as soon as the medical staff gets here," the policewoman told her.

That seemed like the wisest thing in case Chloe was waiting around to make sure her handiwork had been successful.

The officer said "Did you see her? Do you know for sure it was Chloe?"

Darcy had no idea what Chloe had put in the IV, but her heart was beating erratically. Was that just panic or was the poison something that would make her heart explode? Talking cohesively took some effort. "I never saw her face. I was half asleep. But she was acting weird. She didn't take my vitals. She was standing over by the bathroom. The IV bag she discarded was still full."

"That does sound suspicious," the policewoman agreed.

The officer waited until a nurse and then a doctor entered, which took less than a minute.

The doctor looked at Darcy. "What's going on here?"

Darcy let out a breath but could not form the words. She felt like she was shutting down. Her fear escalated. How much poison had gotten into her?

The female officer answered for her. "She thinks she might have been poisoned through that IV."

Darcy had a hard time focusing as the doctor leaned in and disconnected the IV.

"I don't want to take any chances. Let's flush her system," the doctor said to the nurse. "Take a blood sample to find out what's in that IV. See if we can figure out what is going on. Let's get this done. Stat."

Still feeling like her brain was in ether, Darcy turned her head to where the woman she was pretty sure was Chloe had been. A chair with a plastic bag containing Darcy's personal items had been pushed close to the bathroom. Her thoughts became foggy as she wondered if Chloe had taken something out of her bag.

SEVENTEEN

Jackson sat up in the hospital bed. He was bored out of his mind. Through the window, he saw that it was dark outside. He had slept through most of the day and into the night. Sitting still didn't agree with him, let alone just lying in bed. He wanted to be moving, to be doing something, and he missed Smokey. He swung his legs over the side of the bed and stepped onto the floor with care. The painkillers were still working. His shoulder felt stiff and sore, but it wasn't screaming with pain.

He walked over to the bag containing his personal items and pulled out his phone.

The only people he knew who would be up at this hour would be on-duty K-9 officers and he didn't want to distract them while they were on the job.

There was a text message from Darcy. Just the sight of her name and number made him smile.

When you feel up to it, can we meet to talk? There is a place on the fourth floor that is super quiet.

He typed in his reply.

Hi, Darcy. I'm up and could use some company.

Her reply was almost immediate. She must be as bored as he was.

Great. Fourth floor lounge, west wing. See you in ten minutes.

He had no idea where the west wing was, but it would be easy enough to find out. Taking his phone with him, he walked out into the hallway, which was quiet. He saw no sign of a nurses' or administrative station, but he did find an unoccupied waiting area that had a map of the hospital. The west wing was down a floor from where he was on the fifth floor.

As he made his way to the elevator, he passed a janitor mopping the floor, a woman in hospital gown sitting by a window, and a woman carrying a clipboard, whom he presumed to be a doctor. Other than that, he didn't see any other people.

He pressed the elevator button and stepped inside when the car arrived, getting off on the floor below his. Darcy, he recalled, was on the third floor; she must have figured this would be a good in-between place to meet.

Once he was on the fourth floor, he encountered a nurses' station with only one nurse bent over a keyboard and focused on her work. As he walked past, she didn't even look up to acknowledge him.

The earbuds she wore probably shut out most of the sound or maybe she was transcribing something. She had a sort of dashboard in front of her where, he assumed, lights would flash when a patient pressed a call button. He ambled past numerous rooms where the people inside, hooked to machines, lay nearly lifeless in their beds. This must be an ICU floor, he thought to himself.

He kept walking until he found a sign that informed him he was in the west wing. He entered a large lounge area, noting the circular setup of three different couch arrangements. Large floor-to-ceiling windows looked out on both sides of the city. The place was completely empty.

The hall beyond the lounge was completely dark. It must be a part of the hospital that wasn't used.

He turned a half circle and pulled out his phone.

Where are you?

On my way. I move slow.

The walk had tired him out. He sat in a lounge chair and stared out the large window at the city lights. Just across the street was another high-rise building that was part of the hospital.

He stared down at his phone as his heartbeat kicked up a notch.

This was a setup. Darcy was not on her way.

He dove to the ground just as glass shattered around him. Pain shot through his wounded shoulder as he tried to drag himself across the floor to seek cover behind a couch, an almost impossible task with his bad shoulder. Another shot was fired. He pressed even lower into the floor.

He doubted the nurse who was way down the hall and wearing earbuds would respond. As far as he knew, no one on the floor could get out of bed.

He wasn't going to get anywhere trying to drag himself soldier-style. Instead he rolled toward a chair that would provide some cover. Though he tried to protect his shoulder, the move caused pain that radiated through his whole body. With some effort, he tucked himself up behind the chair, realizing he'd dropped his phone in the effort to save himself. To try to retrieve it would make him an easy target. It was a long stretch where he'd be out in the open before he could get to the safety of the hallway. Because of his injury, crawling was out of the question. He'd have to stand and run.

Jackson angled his body and craned his neck so he had a view of the building not more than the width of a street away. The building where Chloe was probably lying on her stomach, looking through the scope of her rifle, and waiting for the chance to take him out.

She must have gotten Darcy's phone.

That realization sent a new wave of fear through him. What if Chloe had done Darcy in and now was coming back to finish him off? He had to get to that nurses' station. He bolted to his feet and ran at an angle toward the hallway. Gripping his shoulder where the pain had intensified, he bent forward and kept running. He sprinted past the hospital rooms where people lay unconscious.

He was doubled over by the time he made it to the nurses' station. The nurse stood and pulled out her earbuds, running to him just as he collapsed on the floor.

Darcy pulled the covers up to her neck and stared at the ceiling. It had been hours since the medical staff had flushed the poison from her body and still she couldn't sleep. All the trauma to her body had made her sleep through most of the day and there'd been no word on whether they had tracked down Chloe.

The female officer was still outside her door, so Darcy took in several deep breaths and prayed, trying to calm down.

A nurse entered her room. "Still awake, huh?"

Darcy nodded her head.

"The doctor had a preliminary test done on the IV solution. It seemed it contained a lethal amount of digitalis."

"Heart medication," Darcy said.

"So, you were right."

The nurse took Darcy's vitals and had just turned to leave when Darcy called out to her. "Can you get me my phone? It's over in that plastic bag."

"Sure, no problem."

Darcy doubted anyone would be up at this hour, but she could send some texts to her sister, to Harlan and, of course, to Jackson if he hadn't heard the news already.

The nurse pulled out the watch Darcy had been wearing when she was admitted to the hospital. She searched the bag. "Mind if I dump this out? I can't seem to find your phone."

"Go ahead," Darcy said. "I know it was in there. Jackson had it delivered from my apartment."

The nurse spilled the contents of the bag onto the rolling table by Darcy's bed. No phone.

Fear gripped her.

"Chloe must have taken it." Why? Chloe must of have left the room assuming that the poison would kill Darcy. Her stomach tightened. Chloe had made it clear she wanted Jackson dead, too. "I have a friend staying in the hospital. Jackson Davison. Could you check on his status for me?"

The nurse, who had been picking up Darcy's personal items, slowed in her action. "We didn't want to worry you. There was another attempt on his life a short time ago. He was on the fourth floor. Someone shot at him through the window."

"Is he okay?"

"Relatively. He never should have been out of bed in his condition so soon after being shot in the first place. He wore himself out."

"Did they catch the person who shot at him?" She knew it had to have been Chloe and that Chloe must have somehow lured Jackson to the fourth floor with her phone.

"I don't know. If I hear any news, I will let you know."

"Look, I can't sleep. Can the officer on duty wheel me down to his room? Even if he's still sleeping. Can I just hang out until he wakes up?"

"I'll see what I can do," the nurse said. "I was on duty earlier when he asked to see you. You two seem very close. It must be true love."

"We're friends. Good friends. That's all." Even as she spoke, Darcy knew that wasn't true anymore. What was between them ran way deeper than that.

The nurse left the room.

Darcy rested her head on the pillow and waited for the nurse to return.

Within minutes, the female police officer entered her room, pushing a wheelchair. "Heard you wanted to go for a ride."

The officer helped her out of bed and wheeled her down the hall and into the elevator.

When they entered Jackson's room, he was wide awake and sitting up.

"Guess we both had a little excitement." Darcy said as the policewoman left to wait outside the door.

"Yeah, I heard. I'm glad you're here." He lifted his hand, showing that he was holding his phone. "They recovered my phone, but not yours. They thought they might be able to track Chloe by your phone. She may have ditched it. The doctors won't let me do anything but rest, which is making me nuts."

"Sometimes, doctors have good advice." Darcy pushed the wheelchair closer to his bed. "You look more worn out than me."

"I have been on the phone. NYPD has a ton of officers combing the building where Chloe probably set up shop to take aim at me."

"But they haven't found her yet?"

He shook his head.

"She might be dressed as a nurse."

"When they told me what had happened to you, I thought that might be the case. How else could she have gotten past that officer?" Jackson placed his head back on the pillow. "I know they didn't tell me sooner about you being poisoned because I needed to rest, but I wish I had known."

"Maybe you should try to get some sleep."

He smiled. "You're not sleeping, either."

A silence fell between them and Darcy remembered what the nurse had said. *It must be true love.* What she realized was that if she had used discernment about the character of the detective who had only showed her affection to move his case along, she would not have been hurt. It wasn't about not dating cops. It was about seeing the heart of the person in front of her. Darcy knew now that Jackson had shown over and over that he was a man of integrity. The right time to talk about how her feelings for him had changed never seemed to happen. If she was honest with herself, bringing up the subject made her afraid. Everything he'd said in the past indicated he wasn't over his last breakup. Her affection for him ran so deep, she wasn't sure if their friendship could survive a rebuff from him. She didn't want to risk the friendship by asking for something more.

When Jackson was ready, he would have to be the one to open that door. She couldn't bear the thought of his rejection.

"Some deep thoughts going on in that genius brain of yours," he said.

She shook her head. "Just pondering."

In the hallway, a familiar tune started to play. All the air left her lungs. She knew that melody. It was the ringtone for her phone.

She stood, still feeling a little wobbly.

Jackson sat straighter in his bed. "Darcy, what is it?"

The phone stopped ringing.

When she stepped out into the hall, the female officer assigned to protect her was standing by a medical cart, holding a phone.

"Someone left their phone on the cart."

"That's my ringtone. May I see it?" She held out her hand. There were probably other people in the world who chose old hymns as ringtones. Even before the officer handed it over, Darcy knew it was her phone. The glittery cover was hers.

"Did you see anyone by that cart who might have left it?"

"There was a lot of traffic through here a minute ago," the officer said. "Some kind of emergency up the hall. The cart has been there for at least twenty minutes."

Jackson stood in the doorway. "Darcy, what is it?"

"I think Chloe was here either twenty minutes ago and she left my phone on the cart or she swept through with a crowd of people a minute ago and left it."

Jackson still held his phone. "I'll let the other officers know. Some of them are still searching the hospital. If it was a few minutes ago, she might still be in the area."

"She's probably dressed as a nurse." Darcy stared down at the phone. She had five new texts. She clicked on the message icon. All five texts were from the same number and they all said the same thing.

You will not live to testify at Reuben's trial.

EIGHTEEN

Jackson paced the floor of the house where he and Darcy had stayed under protective custody since being released from the hospital three days ago. The trial was in two hours.

The house belonged to a retired police chief and his wife who'd gone south for the winter. A rotation of patrol and K-9 officers had been assigned to watch over him and Darcy.

As he paced, Smokey thudded his tail and licked his jaw. His way of asking if everything was okay.

"I'm just real nervous," said Jackson. He glanced at his police utility belt resting on the table. He was dressed in full uniform. Still not cleared for field duty, he had talked Gavin into letting him be one of the officers that escorted Darcy to and from the trial. Though he had healed a great deal, his shoulder still hurt when he tried to raise his arm up high.

Darcy entered the room. She wore jeans and a baggy sweater. "Aren't you getting ready a little early?" she asked.

"I just feel like I need to do something."

She stared down at her clothes. "I guess I have the

opposite response. I want to pretend like is not happening until the last minute."

He walked over to her and took her hands in his. "All of the NYPD has taken every measure to ensure your safety. Since Chloe's favorite thing is to shoot from a distance, officers are watching the tall buildings surrounding the courthouse. And no one will get into or out of those buildings without having to go past at least three officers and a metal detector."

She looked up into his eyes. "I know that they will do everything to keep me safe. And I know that once I testify, the question about me being able to do my job will go away." She glanced to the side at a window with its curtains drawn, as it had been since they'd both been brought here. Her lip quivered. "But it doesn't mean Chloe will leave me alone. I'm sure she will want revenge for Reuben being put away for good."

Jackson cupped her arm just below the shoulder. "If Chloe shows up for that trial, which we believe she will, we have taken every measure to ensure her capture."

He did not want to tell Darcy that they couldn't guard every inch of the route that led to the courthouse. They had chosen a route that was not predictable, but there were only so many ways to get to the courthouse. If Chloe had figured out where they were hiding, she would have attacked by now. They both had received threatening texts. Always from a throwaway phone. The texts made it clear that Chloe wanted both of them dead.

"I can put some coffee on for us if you like," Darcy offered. "And I think there are still some leftovers of that casserole Lani brought when she came on duty."

"Food sounds good. I don't think coffee would help me calm down."

She laughed and retreated into the kitchen. He followed her. Smokey waited until he was given the command to follow, as well.

He watched as Darcy pulled down, plated and heated up the casserole in the microwave. Even under these trying circumstances, he had enjoyed his time with Darcy. The curtains had remained drawn and neither of them had stepped outside since they had taken up residence.

The officer standing guard was also the one to stay with Smokey when he went out in the yard.

The days had been spent praying together, playing board games or sitting together on the couch, each of them reading their respective books. Even with the shadow of danger that had hung over each day, Jackson relished their time together. These days had made him realize that he could picture them having a life together of being more than just friends.

She set a steaming plate of lasagna on the table where he was seated. "Why are you looking at me like that?"

He shook his head. "Just thinking."

She dished up some of the leftovers for herself and sat opposite him. "Just thinking about what?"

He shrugged. Now was not the time to broach the subject. They needed to get through the trial and the K-9 Unit needed to make sure Chloe was brought into custody.

He knew that one way or another, Chloe would make a last-ditch effort to get at Darcy before the trial. The text had made it clear that Chloe was out for revenge. After the trial, she might become a lot dodgier, laying low for months and then going after Darcy or him.

They had to catch her today.

* * *

Darcy finished her meal and went upstairs to shower and dress. The plan was to arrive an hour before the trial and enter the courthouse by a back door, though the amount of police they had surrounding her would call attention to her if anybody was watching.

Half an hour later, she met Jackson and Smokey downstairs. Belle Montera was waiting outside in the yard with Justice, who was trained for protection. Darcy pulled back the living-room curtain a few inches for a limited view of the street. There was a dark-colored SUV parked at the curb.

Jackson stepped toward her. "We'll be traveling in an umarked police car."

"That must be it out there right now." Her chest squeezed a little tighter.

He held out his arms and she fell into his embrace.

"I want to say that it's going to be okay. But I know that's not true. Not until we catch her," Jackson said.

Closing her eyes, Darcy relished the safety of his arms around her. "Thank you for being honest. You know I would have seen past you trying to paint a rosy picture."

He drew her closer, hugging her tight and then letting her go. "Let's do this. I'll go let Belle know we're ready. We'll walk out together. She and Justice will be behind us in a different car, also unmarked. We don't want to call attention in any way." Jackson left the room and opened the front door to call out to Belle.

Darcy took a deep breath, as though she were about to dive under water. Jackson returned, Belle and Justice right behind him. He commanded Smokey to fall in. "Let Smokey and I take the front." He looked over at Belle. "You and Justice can be behind Darcy until you have to get in your own car."

"Ready when you are," Belle said.

They walked out to the black SUV where a driver, another police officer, sat behind the wheel.

"I'll be up front. Smokey will ride in the back with you," Jackson told Darcy.

There was a comfort in knowing that the dog would be so close. He was a true protector.

Jackson opened the back door.

She caught a glimpse of Belle loading Justice into the vehicle that was parked about a block away before she got into the SUV. The windows of the SUV were tinted so no one could see her sitting inside.

Every precaution had been taken to ensure her safety. Why, then, did she still feel so afraid?

Jackson waited for Darcy to settle in the back seat and for Smokey to jump in beside her. He did a quick survey of his surroundings, glancing in his side mirror at Belle, who had her motor running and was waiting to pull away from the curb and slip in behind them.

There was no reason to think that Chloe knew where they'd been staying. Yet she'd been so clever about getting to both him and Darcy in the past, he knew he couldn't let his guard down.

He got in on the passenger side of the front seat.

"We're ready," he said.

Jackson had a feeling the drive through the city to the courthouse was going to be one of the longest of his life. The driver turned his wheel and pressed the gas, pulling out onto the street.

As the city whizzed by, Jackson found himself scanning the bridges and buildings and other high places a shooter might be waiting.

Traffic intensified around the courthouse. They took a side street that would lead to the back entrance. He noted that the number of news vans was triple what it usually was for a trial.

Darcy leaned toward Jackson, gripping the back of his seat. "That's her. I saw her."

Jackson scanned where Darcy had just pointed, seeing only an ocean of faces. It might be that Darcy was just on edge, but they couldn't take any chances. Jackson radioed to the K-9 officers who were standing by outside the courthouse, giving the street name and approximate location Darcy had said she'd seen Chloe.

Darcy looked down at the floor of the car. "She was there and then she faded back into the crowd. I know she can't see me in here...but still."

They were forced to double park in the parking lot behind the courthouse. Belle radioed that she had gotten stuck behind a truck in traffic that was at a standstill. Their driver couldn't leave the vehicle. Jackson and Smokey would be escorting Darcy into the courthouse alone.

"Stay in the vehicle until I am out and can open the door for you," Jackson said. He pushed open his door, glancing in every direction. There were several news vans parked a block away.

He opened the back door. Smokey jumped down on command. "We better hurry," he said, reaching in for Darcy. When he glanced over his shoulder, he saw one of the news crews racing toward them, followed by another two.

He wrapped his arms around Darcy. Smokey took up

a position on the other side of her. The reporters clamored behind them, getting closer as they hurried to the courthouse rear entrance. Jackson reached out for the door and Darcy stepped inside. Jackson stayed between her and the approaching reporters until the door closed.

They stood in a long silent corridor.

"I have no idea how to get to the courtroom from here. I always go in the front or side entrance," said Darcy.

Jackson looked one way and then the other. "It can't be that hard. Let's go this way. I'm sure we'll see some signs or something familiar soon enough."

He pressed the button on his radio. They had positioned two other officers and their K-9s inside the courthouse. "Tyler, we've entered the back of the courthouse. I'm alone with Darcy. Can you tell me your position?"

"Waiting for you in the hallway just outside courtroom 203. There is a room off to the side of the courtroom where Darcy can wait until it's her turn to testify. We've made sure it's secure."

"We're on our way." Jackson signed off.

They worked their way through the labyrinth of the courthouse hallways, going up a set of stairs and following the signs that directed them down lengthy corridors. They encountered more people the closer they got to courtroom 203.

Jackson read numbers on the doors once they were in the right hallway. It wasn't hard to guess where Reuben's trial was to be held. At the end of the hall there was a cluster of police, reporters and curious citizens.

Darcy stopped when she saw the crowd. Several reporters spotted them and began to move in their direction. Tyler Walker stepped into their path along with

Dusty. The intimidation factor of the K-9 was effective in stopping the reporters.

Tyler hurried over to Jackson and Darcy. "This way." He pointed down a hallway and led them into a room with no windows. Two couches faced each other on opposite walls. Darcy took a seat on one and Jackson sat beside her. Smokey rested at Jackson's feet.

"We'll be right outside this door." Tyler pointed to the door that led to the hallway they had just exited.

Darcy knew from having testified before that the door on the opposite side of the room lead to the courtroom.

She tilted her head toward the ceiling. "I wonder how long it's going to be."

Jackson rested his hand on hers. "Not sure."

"They must not have caught or even seen Chloe. It would have come across your radio, right?"

"Probably, yes."

She stood and paced. "I know I saw her in that crowd. I'm not making it up."

"I believe you."

"What if she's in the courtroom?"

"The dogs will alert to her scent. Everyone watching the trial was screened before they were seated." Though she was putting up a good front, Jackson could tell she was afraid. He held out his arms. "You want a hug?"

She fell into his embrace. He held her tight.

A moment later, there was a knock on the door and the bailiff stuck his head inside the room. "Miss Fields, they are ready for you now."

Darcy glanced at Jackson and then petted Smokey. Jackson could not go with her into the courtroom.

"I'll see you in there in just a few minutes. And then I'll come back here when you're done."

She nodded. The bailiff opened the door and waited.

Once the door closed, Jackson commanded Smokey to fall in and they headed down into the courtroom where the public was allowed to enter. Jackson had to show his badge and squeeze through a substantial crowd outside the courtroom. By the time he was at the back of the room, Darcy had taken the stand and been sworn in. Jackson could only see the back of Reuben Bray's head. He didn't have to see the guy's face to know that he was probably smirking.

Darcy glanced at Reuben. Though she was trying not to show emotion, Jackson could tell that seeing him had shaken her.

Be strong, Darcy.

The prosecutor stepped toward her. "Miss Fields, would you please explain your qualifications as an expert witness?"

Darcy recited her qualifications and then answered a set of questions specific to the evidence that had led to Reuben's arrest and incarceration. Her answers were precise and to the point. Her voice exuded a natural confidence when she spoke about her work.

Jackson glanced over at one of the reporters. The woman, who had been so accusatory at a previous press conference, now wore an expression that suggested she was in a state of shock. As they had hoped, Darcy's professionalism would put an end to all the lies leveled at her and the Brooklyn K-9 Unit.

It was pretty clear to Jackson that Reuben was going to jail for a long time based on Darcy's expert testimony.

He took in a deep breath for the first time in a long time.

A boom and a rush of wind surrounded Jackson. He felt his body being lifted up and thrown back down. Plaster and rubble rained down on top of him. Shoes scrambled all around him as chaos in the wake of the bomb blast broke out.

He could see people screaming but not hear them. The blast had caused temporary deafness. He stumbled to his feet. Smokey licked his hand. The dog was covered in dust and plaster, but appeared okay. He saw only one fellow officer hunched over but conscious. Jackson's attention was drawn to the front of the room. Darcy was no longer on the witness stand.

The panicked crowd was working its way out into the hallway. When he turned to look in that direction, a portion of the wall by the door was missing. The bomb may have just been placed outside the door. Maybe Chloe had gotten a grunt to do it for her. The explosion hadn't been strong enough to destroy the entire courtroom, just to create a distraction. Maybe so Chloe could get access to Darcy. In the confusion, she would have been able to sneak in.

The bomb had to have been dropped outside the door only minutes before it went off. The K-9 team had taken every precaution. So he had to assume that Cody, the bomb detection beagle, and his partner Detective Henry Roarke had been through the courtroom and surrounding area before the trial began.

Working his way toward the witness stand was like swimming upstream through the escaping crowd. He didn't see Reuben or his attorney. Maybe they had fled for the doors, as well.

Jackson didn't see Darcy anywhere. The bailiff was gone, as well. Maybe he had escorted her back to the waiting room. He found the door where witnesses entered.

A lady in a suit grabbed his arm. Her lips were moving but he couldn't hear her. He shook his head and pointed to his ears.

He opened the door and headed down the hallway. There were several doors where witnesses must wait to take the stand. When he checked the rooms, only one was occupied with an older man in a suit, probably someone who had been a victim of Reuben's theft. The man rose, indicating that he thought Jackson must have come to take him to testify. Jackson shook his head and gave a hand signal that the man should remain where he was.

With his hearing out of order, Jackson couldn't use his radio. He stepped out into the hallway, searching every face. People were crouched over and covered in dust and plaster. He feared the worst for Darcy.

He pushed through the crowd. Smokey remained close to him. The back of a blond woman's head caught his attention. The hair looked too shiny and perfect to be real. Chloe had brown hair, but she'd worn a disguise before at the press conference.

The woman was swallowed up by the crowd of panicked people. Jackson pressed forward. He spotted the back of the blond head again only farther away. This time he saw that the woman had her arm around another much shorter blonde. His heart skipped a beat. Darcy.

He lost sight of them again. He searched the faces of the people around him, hoping to enlist a fellow officer to help him capture Chloe and ensure Darcy was kept alive. He saw no other officers close by. True to their sense of duty, they must have all rushed toward where the bomb had gone off to help.

Jackson squeezed past people, praying that he would get to Darcy on time.

NINETEEN

Chloe held Darcy tightly around the waist. As the taller woman dragged her through the crowd, Darcy feared her stomach would end up bruised. Chloe seemed to know where her knife wound had been. She pressed her fingers against it, causing pain any time Darcy tried to twist free of her intense grip. Chloe was very strong. Any attempt to get away from her would be thwarted. The people around them were in such a panic over the bomb blast that there was no way she could get their attention. She didn't see any police officers close by.

Chloe guided her through the side door of the building. Darcy had a momentary view of the pandemonium on the wide front steps of the courthouse, but they were too far away for her to attract anyone's attention. Reporters, who had been watching the trial from news vans, were trying to get inside while people affected by the bomb blast pushed to get down the stairs.

Darcy tried to look over her shoulder. Again, Chloe pressed into her stomach. Pain shot through Darcy's body. She'd seen Jackson and Smokey at the back of the courtroom when she'd begun her testimony. Where were they now?

Outside at the front of the courthouse even more police officers and other first responders were arriving. The area surrounding the building was a sea of flashing lights.

Darcy had no doubt that Chloe's intention was to kill her, but knew she wasn't about to do it within the sight of law enforcement and risk getting caught. Chloe pulled her away from the crowd and down a side street, probably dragging her to a secluded spot so she could kill her and escape.

Darcy knew that. The crowd thinned. She had to get away. Chloe pushed her down an alley. Though she could still hear the panic of the crowd, there was no one in the alley. Chloe dragged her toward a Dumpster. She swept her hand over the top of the closed container, grabbing a knife she must have stashed there earlier. In the three days they'd waited for the trial, Chloe had had time to scout the area around the courthouse and carefully plan.

Behind her, a dog barked. Chloe whirled her around as she pressed the knife into Darcy's throat. The dog was Smokey—but where was Jackson? The K-9 drew closer, continuing to bark in a threatening manner. When he was within a few feet of them, he stopped moving but kept barking.

"Get away!" Chloe shouted, clearly rattled by the dog.

Jackson came around the corner. He seemed almost surprised at seeing Chloe and Darcy. He must have been following Smokey's lead. He drew his weapon and said something, but his words were unintelligible.

Darcy could guess at why his speech sounded so messed up. He'd likely suffered temporary deafness from the bomb blast. By her estimation, the bomb had been placed in the hallway and blown away part of the courtroom wall. Jackson had been standing very close to where the bomb had gone off.

Chloe laughed and dug the knife deeper into Darcy's throat. "Back off or she gets it." Chloe tilted her head toward Smokey. "And call your dog off."

Darcy tasted bile in her throat. The coppery scent of blood reached her nose and pain seized her neck. Chloe had made a cut in her neck deep enough to cause bleeding.

Jackson's expression changed. All the color left his face. His gaze fell on Darcy and then went to Chloe, who was now using Darcy as a full body shield. For Jackson to take Chloe out without risking Darcy's life, it would be an almost impossible shot.

The knife dug once again into Darcy's skin. The cut, however small, still stung. Based on everything she knew about the woman who held her at knifepoint, Darcy's best guess was that Chloe would slash her throat and then make a run for it, assuming that Jackson's focus would be on trying to save Darcy's life.

Would this be the last time she'd see Jackson? She mouthed the words *I love you*. It didn't matter if he felt the same way or not. She wanted him to know.

His expression showed that he'd understood though he did not say the words back to her.

Still holding the gun on Chloe, Jackson took a step forward, so that he was parallel with Smokey.

Chloe tightened her grip at Darcy's waist. "I said back off!"

Smokey watched Jackson, waiting for a command.

Jackson adjusted his grip on the gun. He tilted his

head to the side, which must have been a command to Smokey because the dog started to bark aggressively as he advanced on Chloe. Definitely not something that was in the K-9 training manual.

"Call the dog off." Chloe took a step back, pulling Darcy with her, though the knife was no longer resting against Darcy's skin.

Darcy stepped on Chloe's toe and then elbowed her in the stomach. The move was enough that she could get away. Chloe turned and ran. Smokey was right on her heels.

Jackson returned his gun to its holster and took off after her. Darcy fell into a run behind them. When she looked up the street, she could no longer see Chloe or Smokey, and Jackson had disappeared down a side street.

The smart thing for Darcy to do would be to find help. Jackson probably couldn't use his radio because his voice was so hard to understand. She ran back toward the front of the courthouse, where she was likely to find another police officer.

As she ran, she caught a flash of movement one street over. Chloe running. Chloe must have made an about-face and was heading back to hide in the crowds of people affected by the chaos.

Darcy bolted up one block, thinking she might be able to cut Chloe off, but that plan would only work if Jackson came up on Chloe from the other side. Darcy had no weapon and Chloe had a knife and was stronger than she was. Maybe that wasn't such a good idea.

Darcy sprinted toward where she'd seen Chloe and pressed against the side of the building before peering out. She caught just a glimpse of Chloe as she turned another corner. Darcy looked the other way as Jackson and Smokey approached.

"She's going to try to hide in the crowd again." Darcy looked right at Jackson so he could read her lips. She wasn't sure if he understood her or not.

Jackson pulled his radio off his shoulder and touched his ears indicating he still couldn't hear very well. Darcy clicked the radio on and spoke into it.

"Attention all Brooklyn K-9 Units and patrol officers in the area. I'm Darcy Fields, speaking for Officer Jackson Davison. Chloe Cleaves is in the area surrounding the front of the courthouse. She is wearing a blond wig, but she might ditch that, and has on workout clothes— all dark colors."

Tyler came on the radio. "Darcy, what's going on with Jackson?"

"He has temporary deafness."

"We'll be on the lookout for Chloe, but we are sort of all-hands-on-deck at this point dealing with injured people."

Several other officers also responded that they had gotten the message and would search as much as they could.

Jackson reattached his radio to his shoulder and they both ran back toward the crowd. They slowed as they drew closer.

She could be anywhere.

"Maybe we should split up," Darcy said.

Jackson shook his head and then tugged on her sleeve. His gaze went to the outer circle of the crowd first. Chloe would probably try to escape before the mayhem died down.

All the faces were starting to look alike…

Please, God, don't let her get away again.

They drew a little closer to the crowd outside the courthouse. Darcy was losing hope.

Smokey took off running even though Jackson hadn't commanded him to do anything. The dog raced toward an EMT and tackled her. The woman was wearing a baseball hat and a vest that identified her as an EMT.

Jackson ran after Smokey. Darcy followed.

The EMT was Chloe.

She scrambled to her feet and turned to run.

Smokey lunged at her again, this time hanging on to the hem of her vest.

Jackson aimed his gun.

"Hands up! You're under arrest!" Darcy shouted.

Jackson gave her a raised-eyebrow look.

Darcy shrugged. "You can't talk very well, and I've always wanted to say that."

Chloe broke free of the vest. She whirled around, slicing the knife through the air at the K-9. Smokey backed up but started in again with his aggressive barking.

Jackson bellowed something that sounded a little bit like *"Back off"* as he ran toward Chloe, firing a warning shot into the air. Chloe put her hands up.

Knowing that Jackson's words weren't going to make a lot of sense, Darcy moved in. "Drop the knife, Chloe. It's over."

Chloe let the knife fall to the ground.

Jackson used a hand motion to direct Smokey to sit and stop barking.

"At least the trial got interrupted," Chloe said.

"I'm sure they will reschedule," Darcy returned. "Due to extenuating circumstances."

Within minutes, they were able to lead Chloe to a patrol car.

As the car drove away, Darcy felt like she could finally take in a deep breath and relax. It was over.

She grabbed Jackson's sleeve and looked into his eyes. "Jackson, I meant it when I mouthed the words 'I love you.' It wasn't just because I thought Chloe was going to kill me."

He nodded in understanding and then mouthed the words *I love you, too.*

He gathered Darcy into his arms, kissed her and then held her. She rested her face against his chest, breathing in the scent of his skin as her heart filled with joy.

Smokey whined at their feet. They both laughed and knelt to pet the Lab.

EPILOGUE

The next day, Jackson waited at headquarters for Darcy to come by. As soon as Chloe had been taken into custody, Reuben had pled guilty and turned on her. Numerous charges, including attempted murder, had been filed against the woman. Both offenders were going to be locked up for a long time.

Jackson felt both tense and excited for what he had planned when Darcy arrived in about an hour. He was still on duty, so she'd agreed to meet him, thinking they were going to walk to Sal's for lunch. He had something much bigger planned. He'd bought a scarf for Darcy that looked like something she would wear, all bright and colorful. He looked down to where his K-9 sat at his feet. The scarf looked good tied around Smokey's neck.

Penny McGregor sat behind the front desk, tapping away on her keyboard.

She lifted her hands from the keyboard. Jackson looked over at her. Her face had drained of color. On a pale-skinned redhead, it made her look almost like she was coming down with the flu.

Jackson sensed the shift in mood. "Everything okay?" He stepped toward her.

She rested her hand on her chest. "I just got a threatening email. The source is anonymous, but since we know Randall Gage killed my parents, it must be from him."

Jackson knew some of the K-9 Unit was actively searching for Gage, whose DNA had been found at the crime scene. It had taken twenty years to get that DNA, but now that they knew the killer's identity, he was still eluding justice. They had to find Randall Gage.

Several other members of the team, including Bradley, Penelope's brother, had just entered the reception area.

"What is it, Penny?" Bradley asked. "What does it say?"

She read from the screen. "'It was a mistake to let you live…you first, then your brother.'"

A tense silence invaded the room.

Gavin, who had been among the team members to enter the reception area, spoke up. "I don't want either of you to worry. We're going to catch Randall Gage."

"I know you will," Penny said. She glanced nervously over at her brother before returning to work.

"Forward that email to me," Gavin said. "We might be able to figure out where it originated from."

"I'll do that." Penny's jaw tightened. She was still clearly upset.

Bradley walked over to her and patted her shoulder. "We will catch him." Jackson caught the promise in the detective's expression before he disappeared down a hallway along with the other officers.

Jackson offered her a reassuring nod. "We'll make sure he is put behind bars."

"I know everybody has my back and Bradley's,"

Penny said. "That doesn't mean messages like this don't make me afraid."

"Understood," Jackson said.

The unit got back to work. Threats, even those that hit very close to home, were unfortunately a routine part of their day as law-enforcement officers. They would get Randall Gage—and the killer of Lucy Emery's parents. Jackson had no doubt.

His phone dinged. Finally. It was a text from Darcy saying she was two minutes away. Jackson thought it best to meet her outside. He wanted the moment to be somewhat private.

He stepped outside with Smokey just as Darcy got out of a taxi. She waved at him.

"This is it, buddy," Jackson said.

Smokey wagged his tail.

Darcy came toward him. Her eyes were bright and clear. "It's good to be back at work."

"Yeah, now life can get back to normal for both of us." Though he managed to look and sound calm, Jackson's heart was pounding.

Darcy looked over at Smokey. "Nice scarf."

"Actually, it's for you. Smokey just wanted to try it on."

She laughed.

"Go ahead. Let's see how it looks on you."

She knelt to untie the scarf.

Jackson had twisted it to hide the surprise inside. He waited in anticipation as Darcy flattened the scarf. A ring fell on the concrete.

Darcy stared at it for a long moment before picking it up. "What's this?"

Jackson got down on his knee, took the ring and held

it up. "Darcy, I love being your friend, but I would like to be your best friend for the rest of your life. Will you marry me?"

Darcy let out a light breath. "Oh, Jackson. Yes, I will marry you."

He placed the engagement ring on her finger as she looked into his eyes.

Smokey licked her cheek and they both laughed.

Jackson rose and held his hands out to her. She stood. The look of love in her eyes warmed his heart. He leaned in and kissed her.

Behind him, the entire K-9 Unit broke into applause.

Penny smiled. "I saw what was going on out the window and called the team over. When it was clear she said yes, we came outside. I'm glad something good like this happened today."

Considering the threatening email Penelope had received an hour ago, the gesture of support touched his heart.

Jackson spoke to Darcy. "Sorry, I wanted it to be a little more private."

"It's okay. They are sort like family anyway," Darcy said.

He gathered her into his arms and joy filled his heart. Smokey let out a little bark of approval and sat at their feet looking up at them.

* * * * *